THE
UNKILLABLE
KITTY
O'KANE

THE UNKILLABLE KITTY O'KANE

COLIN FALCONER

Published by Lake Union Publishing, Seattle

www.apub.com

Amazon, the Amazon logo, and Lake Union Publishing are trademarks of Amazon.com, Inc., or its affiliates.

ISBN-13: 9781542048972
ISBN-10: 1542048974

Cover design by Shasti O'Leary Soudant

Printed in the United States of America

For Lise. Who made me take all the boring bits out of "Kitty." You took all the boring bits out of my life as well. Thank you, sweetheart. This book is for you.

AUTHOR'S NOTE

The Unkillable Kitty O'Kane is inspired by true events. However, in my telling of the story, certain factual elements and timing of events have often been altered for the sake of the narrative.

CHAPTER 1

The Liberties, Dublin, 1905

Kitty O'Kane dreamed of a kind husband and a just life; what she had was haddock water for supper and a dribble of her own blood, seen at close quarters, on the toe of her father's scuffed boot.

Big boots he had, sturdy. Good kicking boots. She tried to raise her head from the straw, but it was too much effort. She turned her head sideways; her ma stood in the doorway, she had her apron bunched in her fist, Mary in her arms, Liam and Ann peering from behind her skirts. Sean sat in the corner, a moldy blanket over his head, sobbing. No help for her there.

It'd been a good hard punch that took her down, and she hadn't seen it coming. Already she couldn't see a thing out of her left eye, but if she squinted with her other, she could see Liam shouting something at her daddy. Strange how she couldn't hear anything. Perhaps he'd sent her deaf.

She looked up at the wall, the little pictures of Jesus with his Sacred Heart and Mother Mary beside him, a little red lamp lighting them up. *Pray for us sinners now and in the hour of our death. Or maybe save me from death at all, if it's not too much trouble.*

Now her daddy was taking off his belt; Liam tried to hold on to his arm, and got a backhander for it. No point arguing with him when he was filthy drunk like this. She saw his lips moving, his face red and twisted like it got sometimes, she still couldn't hear what he was saying, but she could smell him, smell the drink, a sour smell, and bitter like hate.

She tried to wriggle into the corner. Couldn't move her arms much, but her legs worked well enough, and she reckoned if she could get into the corner, she'd make a smaller target for him. The strap was all right. She'd had the strap enough times; if he didn't beat her with the buckle end, there'd be no harm done.

Just bear it, Kit. Think of something else and it will be over.

The walls were a brick color—pink distemper her ma called it, some kind of powder they'd mix in water. There was a great smell off it. The wood was buggy, and up close she could see the little brown bugs that were getting through the walls. She wondered where they came from.

The strap of the belt slashed across her hip. Her body jerked a bit; there was no controlling it. He was too drunk to aim properly, so that was a blessing then. *Just stay away from my face,* she thought. *It'll be bad enough having to explain away this black eye at school tomorrow.*

She got tired of crawling, so she lay there and waited for the next stripe. She could hear things again now, the horn from an ocean steamer leaving the docks. Wouldn't she love to be away on that one right now. *If I ever leave the Liberties,* she promised herself, *I'm never coming back.*

Liam and her mother were screaming now. Her daddy was yelling something too, but she couldn't make out what it was he was saying, something about her answering back. Was that what she did? She couldn't remember anything before he started banging on her, but answering back, that sounded like the kind of thing that she'd do.

She could smell beer and blood, that sour, copper stink of the two together. She heard the slap of the belt, realized he must still be hitting her. It didn't hurt like it should. If he stopped now, as beatings go, well it wouldn't be too bad.

So that was hope then. She started crawling again, inched herself further into the corner, curled up like a bug tossed in a fire. *Don't look up at him, don't yell out, don't provoke him. Pretend it's not happening, pretend you're on that ship, the sea wind is in your hair, salt and cold, and you're headed out to the white waves and only the gulls are screaming.*

"You'd be a fookin' little devil," he yelled at her. "Now that'll be teaching ya some respect!"

She watched his big boots stamp away, he shoved her ma aside, little Liam was still screaming at him. *Be careful, Liam, you're not too little to get hit, boy, not in this family.* She felt the sea move beneath her, not got her sea legs yet, maybe going to be sick. And there was new straw on the floor today; Ma would be cross.

"Oh God in heaven, what's he done to you, Kitty?" her ma said and squatted down beside her.

Done what he always does, she thought. *What all daddies do.* And she closed her eyes and let the great sea take her, away from Dublin, away from the Liberties, and away from her daddy's raw, red fists.

A long line outside the pawn, as there was every morning when she went to school. She knew most of them: Mrs. O'Mara with some bed-clothes, Jack Donnelly with a suit—what good was a suit? And some old dear with a brick, God love her. Would the pawn give her something for a brick? They was good in the pawn, they made allowance.

The national school was on the Coombe, at the back of the private school. As she turned the corner on Cork Street, there appeared a group of boys in their fancy uniforms, and when they saw her, they started laughing and shouting things. Well she never minded them, but that Tom Doyle was with them, and so she tried walking faster, so he couldn't see her face.

But Tom was Tom, and he started saying things to the other boys and shoving them, and then a couple of them shoved back, and she could see he was going to get into a fight over her, and Tom was never a fighter, no matter that he tried. There was nothing for it. There were a few loose stones lying on the cobbles, and she got herself a handful and threw them, hard as she could, screaming names back at them. They all thought she was mad, "the mad girl from Weaver's Hall" they called her. Well maybe she was.

They ran off. Tom stood there, breathing hard, his face flushed. "There was no need, Kitty," he said. "I could have beaten them both."

"Tom, you couldn't punch the froth off a Guinness."

He straightened his shoulders. "Well you're one to say. What happened to your face then?"

She turned away, side-on so that he couldn't stare. "Walked into the door, didn't I?"

"Has your daddy been banging on you again?"

"It was an accident, didn't I just tell you?"

"He's going to kill you one day, Kitty."

"You best be getting on to school, Tom."

"Maybe I'll walk with you."

"You go on now. I'm thinking I'm going to mitch school today."

"You can't be mitching every time you get a black eye now."

"I'll do what I like, Tom Doyle. Now you be getting on."

Tom worked his cheek with his tongue, like he always did when he was unsure. Look at him, standing there all posh in his uniform and polished shoes. She didn't know what he wanted with the likes of her anyway. He reached into his satchel, held something out to her in his fist.

"And what's that?"

"It's for you. You should buy yourself some shoes, Kitty."

She looked at what he'd given her. Half a crown. Half a bleedin' crown! "Where did you get this?"

"Never mind where I got it. It's yours now."

"You stole it from your ma, didn't you?"

"These cobbles must be hurting your feet something terrible. Look at 'em."

She held out her hand. "Can't take it."

"Why not?"

"You know what he'll do if I get money and I don't give it to him. And if I do, he'll only spend it on the drink. Besides, you shouldn't steal from your own ma. It's not right."

She pushed the coin back in his hand and went to walk off.

"Where are you going?"

"Out to Sandymount, I reckon."

"That's a terrible long way."

"Well I got all day, haven't I?"

"Maybe I'll come with you."

"You? Mitch school? They'll be sending you to Ardane, and you don't want that."

"Take my chances, I reckon."

She grinned at him. "Tom Doyle, you're a strange one. Come on then. Before the Brothers see ya."

Tom took one guilty look over his shoulder, hitched up his satchel, and followed her. And that was how it started: how they met the banshee and how the banshee saw all that death in Kitty's cards.

It was four miles out to Sandymount Strand, and by the time they got there, the tide was all the way out. Kitty said they should go cockling. Tom Doyle had never been cockling before, so she had to teach him. He left his shoes and socks on the beach, and they waded out into the mud, and she showed him how to look for the two little pinholes in the mud, how they'd have a blue mark around them. So you'd squat down and root that up and then take up your cockle.

After they had both got a good armful, they went out to the tideline to wash them in the seawater. She showed Tom how to eat them, screwing her knuckles into the shells to twist them open and then sucking out the flesh inside. They were sharp and salty, and she and Tom stood there in the ankle-deep sea, juice and brine running down their chins, and started to laugh.

By the time they'd finished all their cockles, the weather took a turn, the sun went behind a cloud, and Kitty looked up and said, "It looks like rain."

He acted like he hadn't heard her. Instead he said: "So why did he bang on you, Kitty?"

"He didn't bang on me. I told you. Yer ears not work, Tom Doyle?"

"You talked back at him, didn't you? I told you before, you got to learn to keep your mouth shut sometimes."

"We better go," she said. "We'll get soaked if we stay out here."

So they ran off and took shelter under the pier, and just in time, as the rain soon swept across the tide flat in gray sheets, and they had to huddle together by one of the pilings. But then Tom said he had better get his socks and shoes, and so he got soaked anyway.

"You'll have to explain to your ma how your uniform got covered in mud," Kitty said.

"Well, I'll think of something."

She watched him, a cowlick of wet hair hanging over one eye, that harried look he always had on his face like he had the whole world on his shoulders. He made her smile, this one. "You should be in school. You know you're not supposed to talk to us poor kids."

"Me dad works at the Guinness factory, same as yours."

"So how come you go to the private school then? How did you get these?" She nudged his shoe with her bare foot. He tried to tuck it under him, like he was ashamed of it.

"You know how."

"No, I don't. Nobody tells me."

A bit of rain dripped off a bang of his hair. "We got a shebeen."

"You?"

"Me mammy hides crates of porter in a manhole down the lane runs behind our place. Whenever she gets a customer, she gets one of us to run and get a couple of bottles and bring it in."

"Go on with ya."

"It's true, Kitty."

"What's she going to do with all the money, then?"

"Says she's going to send me and my brother off to London for a proper education. Says she wants me to be a hobnob, a doctor and such. Can you imagine?"

"Well that'd be a fine thing. When you come back in your carriage, you can throw me coins out the window. Or maybe you'll pay them to me in one of the kips. You'll be my favorite customer."

"Kitty, don't say that!"

She gave him a throaty laugh. He took everything so serious.

"You're meant for better than that life."

"At least those girls got money to buy nice stuff."

"It's not the life for you!"

"Look, it's stopped raining. I'll race you to the steps!"

They walked up to the docks, and Kitty found a coal sack lying on the jetty, and she darted around picking up the bits of coal that the men dropped when they were loading it from the boats onto the lorries. By the time she was done, she had nearly half a sackful, and her hands were black. They were too tired to walk back to the Liberties, so they scutted back to the city on the back of a Guinness dray. By the time they got off, Tom was shaking. He told her afterward he'd never done that before and he thought he should get killed.

For devilment as they passed Lalor's shop at the corner of Whitefriar Street, she helped herself to a carrot and a potato off the stall outside the shop. Tom didn't know what she was doing until after she'd done it, and when she suddenly took off, he ran breathless down the street after her. When they were clear, she turned and grinned at him, a potato in one pocket of her smock, a carrot in the other, the coal bag still over her shoulder. "Bet you wish you'd stayed in school now, with all your books, don't you, Tom Doyle?"

He put his hands on his knees to catch his breath. "Kitty, they'll send you to Glencree for doing things like that!"

"Sure I'm not old enough to go to Glencree. Anyway, I don't care, it would be away from me daddy. What about you, though? Be no one to fetch your mammy her porter! She'd have to fetch in help!" She laughed and pointed to one of the derelict houses on Peter Street, just the walls left standing, bloody places were always falling down, was what her father said. "Come on, we'll make ourselves a pot of stew."

They scrambled in among the debris, and Kitty produced a box of Pilot safety matches. She'd found them outside the pub one night when she went down to fetch her daddy and tell him to come home, his supper was ready. She got some old bits of newspaper, got a fire started, and when it was going she added a few bits of coal from the sack.

She found an old tin can, fetched some water from a pump in the street, and filled it up, put the potato and the carrot in. "Never mind the dirt and the skin," she said to Tom, "it'll do you good." She even had a cabbage leaf from the shop and tossed that in as well. And then they squatted there and waited for their stew to boil.

"So you're going to be a doctor then?" she said.

"I'll need to be. Someone will have to fix you up every time your da's been banging on you."

"He'll not be doing it forever." She found a stick and stirred their pot with it, though the water wasn't even close to boiling.

"And who's going to stop him?"

"When I grow up, I'm getting out of the Liberties, I swear. I was only jokin' about the kips. Going to do something with my life, I am. You're not the only one round here who wants to make something of themselves."

"Didn't say I was. So what are you going to do then? I mean, you're just a girl."

She pointed the stick at him and set him on his heels. "What do you mean, 'just a girl'?"

"I mean no offense now, Kit."

"That's the trouble with the world! Too many Tom Doyles in the world 'meaning no offense.' They think girls are good for cooking and cleaning and nothing else."

"I didn't say that!"

"I know what you said! Anyway, what if it wasn't like that?"

"What do you mean?"

"What if we had jobs, good jobs, and we could do what we liked, just as well as the men do?"

"The world isn't like that, Kitty."

"Then the world has to change!"

"Be careful with that stick, you'll have my eye out!"

"I'll have more than that if you don't watch your mouth."

"Jesus, Michael, and Joseph, you've got a temper. No wonder your daddy bangs on you!"

"And what about you, Tom, are you going to bang on your wife when you're a big grown-up man and a doctor and all? Is that what you plan to do?"

"Not if she's like you I won't, Jesus God no."

"Well that's more like it then." There were bubbles in the can now. Kitty gave it another stir. "You don't want to be growing up like that.

All right, now when this is done, we'll need some glass and a bit of cardboard. You're the man, so off you go, I'm just a helpless lass, I'll have to stay here and cook."

"What do you need glass and cardboard for?"

"The glass is to cut the potato with—what do they teach you in that fancy school? And cardboard is for plates. I'll not be eating it out of my hands, now will I?"

—⟫—

The potato and carrot were both half-raw, and the cabbage leaf was like eating hot seaweed, but Tom ate every last bit of it, like he was eating mash and gravy. Kitty watched him eat, smiled at that wrinkle he got between his eyes whenever he concentrated hard on anything at all.

"Did I tell you I heard the banshee again last night?" she said.

"Go on!"

"I did, Tom! A terrible sound it was. Like a dog howling."

"It *was* a dog howling."

"Like no dog I ever heard then. Me brothers heard it. They was scared too, even Sean, and he's older than any of us."

"Sean is scared of his own shadow. There's no banshee in the Liberties."

"There is too. Her keening is a terrible thing. And I know where she lives."

"You do not."

"Well I do, and I'll take you there, if you've the gumption for it."

"I don't believe you."

"Well they say seeing is believing, so why don't you come and see for yourself?" She saw the uncertainty in his face and grinned. "You're scared, aren't you?"

"I'm not scared."

"Sure you are. Written all over you."

"All right then, I'll come with you. Where is this banshee then?"

"She lives at the bottom of my street. I seen her sitting at the window every afternoon. She's got all this hair, long and thin and gray it is, just sits there combing it, and her face is awful, she's got green eyes and teeth like a mad dog."

"You're making it up!"

"Well come on then, I'll prove it to you," Kitty said, and she took his hand and pulled him to his feet, and dragged him along behind her.

Look at this Cork Street, she thought. *They must have been fine houses once, back when there was just one grand family living in each of them. Now they are as poor as you can get,* she reckoned. But you couldn't get much better, not in Dublin, least that's what her ma told her, not on what a man could earn down at the factory.

Well maybe her daddy didn't make much, but what wage he did get, he spent on drink. They might as well pay him in Guinness, she'd heard her ma tell the neighbors, save themselves the trouble.

It was a Monday and Mondays were washing day and there were line poles sticking out all the windows. The mothers were all out on their hands and knees, scrubbing the stairs and the front steps with black soap and a scrubbing brush. Being poor was no excuse for not having clean stairs, that was what her ma always said.

"She lives on the corner there," Kitty said to Tom. They both stood there at the curb; she saw him hesitate, then he marched across, determined to show her he wasn't frightened of any banshee.

She followed him, put her nose to the window, peered in. "I can't see her. She must have gone out."

Tom peered in as well, then of a sudden jumped back. "Jesus God, what's that?"

"That? It's just a sheep's head. Me ma gets them sometimes at the butcher's; you make great soup with them."

"Looks like the devil."

"And how would you kids know what the devil looks like?" a voice said.

Now it was Kitty who jumped. She would have run off, but Tom was in the way, just standing there with his mouth hanging open.

It was the banshee, her gray hair loose about her shoulders, her teeth all awry in her head, like old tombstones in a graveyard. She had a shawl wrapped around her shoulders, and she was bent over, like the men with the coal sacks down at the docks, only she didn't have a sack.

They were in for it now.

"What are you little devils doing looking in my window?"

"Nothing, missus. We was just looking at the sheep's head."

"You've seen sheep's heads before, and don't say you haven't." She grabbed Kitty by the shoulder. "You're Billy O'Kane's girl, aren't ya? I've seen you around. Look at the state of you. I can feel your bones through your dress here. Do they never feed you over there?"

"Me mammy does her best."

"Yer mammy doesn't have a great deal to do her best with. Your father's a useless excuse for a fella and no mistake. Well, don't just stand there. You'd better come in, and I'll get you some soup."

The old woman went in, and Tom made to follow. Kitty put out a hand to stop him. "It's the banshee!" she whispered.

"Doesn't look like a banshee to me. She said she's got soup, Kit. Come on, I'm starving. No offense, but your potato and carrot stew was shite."

It wasn't much inside—the banshee had just one room like everyone else, but there was just her living in it, no others, so to Kitty it looked like a palace except for the flies and bluebottles buzzing around the sheep's head. It lay on the table, half-unwrapped in the newspaper she'd brought it home in.

"Now sit down by the fire and warm up. It'll do you a bit of good."

There were two old butter boxes for seats on either side of the fire, and Tom didn't hesitate. There was a saucepan on the hob, and she ladled two bowls of soup out of it and gave it to them, with a hunk of stale bread each.

It was good soup too.

"What are they, missus?" Tom said.

"What are what?"

"Over there, on the table."

"They're my special cards."

"Why are they special?"

"Don't slurp your soup. Did no one teach you manners?"

"But why are they special?"

"I can read the future with them."

"Go on."

"Well you've a mouth on you. How old are you, boy?"

"Twelve."

"He's eleven," Kitty said.

"Eleven and you know it all, do you?"

"No one knows the future!" Tom said.

"Maybe not, but the cards don't lie, boy."

"So are you the lady that does the readin's?" Kitty asked her.

"Heard of me, have you?"

"I heard me ma talking about a lady that does readin's. Was it you told Bridie Chambers she was going to have twins and that her sister was going to get sick? She said it all happened just like you said."

"That doesn't mean anything," Tom said. "People have babies and get sick all the time."

"I suppose you wouldn't like to know your future then," the old woman said to him, "seein' as how you don't believe?"

Tom looked at Kitty and bit his lip.

"Sure he does," Kitty said. "He's all mouth and trousers, missus."

"Well then, maybe I'll read for him then." She drew the curtains to shut out the light from the street, then she lit the nub of a candle and put it in the middle of the table. Tom looked at Kitty, his eyes huge. "Bet you don't dare," she whispered, because she knew that would make him do it for certain.

The old woman picked up the cards and shuffled them and then told Tom to sit in the chair opposite her. He gave Kitty another look, put down his bowl of soup, and went over.

The old lady cut the deck in half, put the top half on the left, then put them together again, and handed them to Tom.

"Now you shuffle them," she said.

"For how long?"

"Long as you like."

They were bigger than any playing cards Kitty had ever seen, and they didn't shuffle easy, and Tom nearly fumbled some of them onto the floor. When he finished, he put them back on the table.

The old woman took the first ten cards from the top of the deck and laid them out in the shape of a cross on the table in front of her.

"They're funny cards," Kitty said.

"They aren't like an ordinary pack. The suits have fourteen cards instead of thirteen, and the suits are called cups, wands, swords, and pentacles."

"What about this one?"

"That's called the Hanged Man. It's a special card; it doesn't have a suit. Like this one, the Devil card."

Tom crossed himself.

"So what does it all mean?"

"It depends what your young friend here wants to know."

A twig fell in the grate by the fire. Both Kitty and the old woman looked at Tom expectantly.

"All right, then. Will I be a doctor when I grow up?"

The old lady studied the spread of cards. "Perhaps. The cards say you are going to be a great man one day."

"I'll be famous?"

"Not famous, not great in that way. I don't see that."

Tom looked at Kitty, then back at the woman.

"What else is it you want to ask me?"

"It doesn't matter."

"Come on, there's something else, it's written all over your face, boy. What is it?"

"It's nothing."

"You want to know about love?"

Tom shook his head, flushed scarlet.

"Well, let's see. Love." She fingered one of the cards and shook her head.

"What is it?"

"Love won't go easy on you, Tom. Not straightaway it won't."

"Well I don't care about that."

"Well you will, one day. The cards say if you want love, you'll have to learn to forgive, and that won't come easy to you. But after that, maybe it will be all right."

"Will I be living here in Dublin?"

"No, Tom, you'll be going away from here very soon, and you won't be back."

"Serious?"

"It's what the cards say, not what I say."

"Let me try," Kitty said.

Tom slid out of the chair, and Kitty climbed into his seat, still warm. The old woman handed her the cards. Kitty shuffled them and handed them back, watching her. It was like there was dust in the creases of the old lady's face, they were so dark and deep.

And when Kitty stared hard at her, she could see the candle flame in her eyes.

Kitty waited as the old lady laid out the spread on the table, placed a long and crooked index finger on one of the cards, moved it a little to the left, then back again.

A long silence. Kitty could hear kids out in the street; school had finished for the day, so she should be getting on home soon, or there'd be trouble.

She looked around at Tom. There was that frown line again, between his eyebrows, like he was worried, or scared, or both.

"So what do you see, missus?" she said.

The old lady swept up the cards, tapped them squarely, and folded them up in a silk, paisley handkerchief.

"What are you doing?"

"You best be running on home now."

"But what do the cards say?"

"The cards don't say anything."

"Yes they do!"

"You don't want to know what the cards say."

"But I do!"

Tom took her hand. "Come on Kitty. It's just a bit of foolishness."

"I want to know what the cards say!"

"Kitty . . ."

"I'll not leave here until you tell me what you saw in the cards!"

The old woman pursed her lips, and Kitty saw the banshee now, in her eyes, plain as day it was. "Don't you shout at me, young lady. You've got the O'Kane temper and no mistake."

"I want to know what's going to happen!"

The old woman leaned forward. "All right, then, but you won't be thanking me for it. You're surrounded by death, Kitty O'Kane. Death and water, death and fire, and your whole life you'll be surrounded by bad men. I don't see anything for you in the future unless you change what's in your heart. Now is that what you wanted to hear? Is it?"

And she blew out the candle.

"Well she didn't look like a banshee to me," Tom said.

Kitty stubbed her toe on one of the cobblestones, sat down on the curb, clutching at her foot, Jesus Mary, it was bleeding.

"Let me look at it," Tom said and bent down.

"I don't want you to look at it!" she said, and shoved him away.

"I was only—"

"One day when you're a grand man and a doctor I'll let you look at my bleedin' toe and not before!"

"What's gotten into you? Not the old lady, is it? That didn't mean nothing. No one can tell the future, it's all nonsense."

"It's not that."

"What is it then?"

"It's nothing! Go on home, Tom."

He stood there, kicked at the cobblestones, scuffing his fine leather shoe.

"What is it now?"

"You know what she didn't see?" Tom said.

"What?"

"That I'm going to marry you one day."

"What? Don't talk daft."

"I'm not daft, you'll see."

"Sure and you'll do no such thing," Kitty said.

"Why not?"

"I don't know why not! Now go home!" She jumped up and broke into a run, didn't look back until she reached the other end of Cork Street.

There was a fancy carriage pulled up outside one of the kip houses, some posh fella in a nice suit going in, the girls squealing at him out the windows. What a life.

She stood there a while in the dread gray light, breathing hard, staring up at her tenement house, the two third-story windows where they lived looked like eyes, like the old lady's, dark and mean. Her daddy would be home soon, drunk most like, wanting his supper, slamming his fist on the table if it wasn't ready.

It won't always be like this, she told herself. *One day I'll have a cup with a handle, and butter on my bread. And the world won't be the same neither, it'll be a better world, and if it won't get better on its own, then I'll make sure it does.*

She looked over her shoulder. Tom Doyle had gone.

She'd been mean to him. Well, she'd say sorry to him tomorrow.

But she didn't see him the next day; almost a week passed before she next spotted him in the street, and by then she'd forgotten all about the banshee. Another two months into winter, and Tom and his brother had gone, packed off to Liverpool on the ferry to start a proper schooling in England, just like he'd said. All that money from the shebeen—well, it had to be good for something.

Dare say I'll never see him again, she thought, *never mind marry him.*

It was all in the cards, wasn't it? Maybe you could change the world, but you couldn't change the cards.

CHAPTER 2

RMS **Titanic,** *Southampton, April 1912*

People talked afterward about how they'd seen her leave the dock on a soft April day, all the flags fluttering and handkerchiefs waving, the tugs tooting, what an occasion it was. All the second steward said later was that the harbor was full of ships because of the coal strike and that Captain Smith had nearly plowed into the *New York* on the way out to sea. He had almost sunk the *Hawke* in the Solent seven months before, when he was on the bridge of the *Olympic*. The captain was an accident waiting to happen was how the second steward told it.

Well it was just another sailing for Kitty; she had no time for being on deck. She was down in her cabin unpacking her things and getting her uniform on. And a fine thing it was too. On her first ship her cabin had been cramped and infested with roaches; it had been almost as bad as being back in the Liberties.

But that Tommy Andrews who designed the *Titanic*, he was a good man, everyone said so, and he made sure the crew were looked after, just like he did on the *Olympic*; he even made a quick visit below decks, and everyone called out to him as he made the rounds, thanked him for what he'd done. Kitty had time only for a brief hello to her new bunkmate, Elsie, and then it was off to work.

It was chaos as it always was on the first day, squeezing through the alleyways past stewards trying to maneuver steamer trunks through the crush. The pursers were shouting orders, and no one really had time to listen for the room bells ringing, everyone wanting drinks. And Holy God, the flowers.

There were boxes of flowers everywhere, mountains of them. Champagne and vases, that was what everyone wanted. The Astors' suite looked like a florist shop. "I need a dozen vases," they'd all say to her, "and make sure they're tall ones." The chief steward had already made it clear to her, "Ten vases, my girl, that's all you have for your section." Eighteen years old and she was already an old hand; she knew what to do, and most of the flowers that came on board found passage through an open port long before they found their owner. Even Kitty found herself doing it that day.

Kitty wasn't as round-eyed as when she started, though her eyes still sometimes strayed to the lace bedspreads and the mahogany furniture. Already she could tell the difference between Georgian and Queen Anne, not bad for a girl from Dublin. How the other half live, as her mother would say. Only it's not half, Ma. Not even half of a half of a half.

I wonder what it would be like to have money, she thought, *and the ease it brings.*

And the *Titanic* was something special, especially first deck. There were private viewing balconies for the best suites, lace bedspreads on the beds, and all the furniture looked as if it had come straight from a palace.

But she had no time for gaping, though she did allow herself a quick peek at old man Astor's new bride, she had imagined a blonde goddess after all she'd read in the newspapers, but she looked quite pale and listless to her, what in God's name did he see in her? It was a big scandal in the newspapers; he was not far off fifty, she was eighteen years old and, some said, already in the family way. But she supposed if you were a millionaire like him, there were different rules, or no rules at all.

She was looking after the Strausses, a lovely old couple; he talked to her like she was a friend of the family. And then, by contrast, there was Mr. Jack Finnegan, and his "wife."

A good-looking man, she noticed, and it looked like he thought so too. He gave her a lazy smile as she came in, looked her up and down as if she was something he might have for his dinner. This, even though the lady he was with—who looked to her more like a quick tumble than a wife—was standing right there among the steamer trunks and hat boxes.

He had a fob watch in the pocket of his brocade vest, and he was staring at it as if he had been timing her to see how long she took to answer the bell. She thought she'd never seen a man so vain in his appearance. He had on a double-breasted suit and spats, and there was a gold ring on the little finger of his left hand, with a diamond set in the heart of it, that glinted whenever he moved his hand.

"So you're to be our stewardess for the voyage," he said, and she knew the brogue, he was a Dubliner just like she was.

"Name's Kitty, Mr. Finnegan, sir," she said and gave him a little curtsey, same for Mrs. Finnegan, though she guessed she was no older than she was.

"Well, Kitty, and now that's a pretty name, I'm glad you'll be looking after us. Call me Jack." Brazen was the only word for it. He held out his hand, and she shook it; she wasn't accustomed to such informality from her passengers, but she could hardly refuse. He held her hand longer than he needed to, caressed it rather than shook it. "This is Mrs. Finnegan."

"You can call me 'ma'am,'" the Mrs. Finnegan said and shot Kitty a glance that let her know she'd like to claw her eyes out. She had a lapdog with her, a Pekingese, holding it in her arms like it was her firstborn. Kitty kept her eyes down and got on with her job. She showed them the wardrobes and the cupboards and checked that all their luggage had been safely delivered. "The first-class dining saloon and day room are all on D deck amidships." She went to the table. "These are the restaurant menus and first-class passenger lists, should you be needing them."

Jack took them from her and glanced at the inside page. He raised an eyebrow. "It says here that professional gamblers are in the habit of traveling to and from New York in Atlantic steamships. Is that true now?"

"It's just a friendly warning, sir. The White Star Line takes its responsibilities to its passengers very seriously."

Jack tapped the page with his forefinger. "It says I should avoid games of chance so that I am not taken unfair advantage of. Do I look to you like a man who would indulge in such immoral behavior?"

"Not at all, sir. I'm sure such warnings are unnecessary in your case."

He smiled and put the list back on the table. "Oh Kitty, I hope there are not going to be any undesirable fellows on the ship. I was told the White Star was a reputable company."

"It is, sir."

"I'm glad. I don't hold with criminal activity at all."

She looked at the luggage, still piled on the carpet in the middle of the floor. "Shall I help you put your clothes away, sir?"

"No thanks, Kitty, I'm sure Mrs. Finnegan can take care of all of that."

"Then is there anything else I can help you with, Mr. Finnegan?"

"Yes Kitty, there is." And he smiled at her and slipped half a crown into her hand.

She waited.

"I'd like a bottle of Heidsieck champagne, nicely chilled, and two glasses, and an ice bucket. Now will you do that for me, Kitty?"

"Yes, Mr. Finnegan."

"And I need a dozen vases for all these flowers," the Mrs. Finnegan said. "Tall ones."

Kitty took a deep breath. "Of course, Mrs. Finnegan," she said and got out as fast as she could.

———

Elsie was in the pantry; she put out an arm as Kitty walked in, and dragged her behind a door. "How are you holding up?" she said. She had a bottle of whiskey in her hand, and she put a tumbler in Kitty's hand and splashed two fingers into it. "Dutch courage, love. If another flamin' stuck-up cow asks me for a vase, I'll stick her roses where the sun don't shine, know what I mean?"

"I'm going to have trouble with one of mine. He's a wolf, ever I saw one."

"The one with the diamond pinky ring?"

"That's the one. Do you know who he is?"

"He's a gangster, love. Irish but lives in America. Don't you read the newspapers? Flash Jack, they call him."

"I never knew any gangsters, or not any that was good at it, only the boys back home that liked to fight outside the pub. There was never any money in that."

"Well, he's got plenty of it; you don't travel in first if you don't. Gawd, my bleedin' feet are killin' me already. Been doin' this long, have you?"

"Couple of years."

"Go on, you don't look old enough. What are ya, sixteen?"

"Eighteen."

"God love us, you're just a baby! Some of the crew on this tub, I reckon they was stewards on Drake's armada. Not a laugh in any of 'em. You Irish then?"

"Dublin. Once."

"Better watch out, Irish. You're too pretty by half. That toff of yours with the diamond on his finger gives you any trouble, you let me know, I'll sort him out for you."

They heard the chief steward outside, so they finished their Dutch courage, and Elsie wiped her mouth with her sleeve, put the bottle back on the shelf, and hid the glasses. Kitty went in search of a bottle of Heidsieck.

After she'd delivered it to the Finnegans' cabin, she got on with the rest of her work. The female staff were not permitted in the first-class dining saloon, but there was still plenty to do. The bells never stopped ringing; passengers wanting postcards, others needing their rooms cleaned and their beds made, even though they had only been on board a few hours.

It was past ten o'clock by the time she had finished. She was too exhausted to sleep, and she went out on the deck to get some fresh air. She stood at the rail and closed her eyes, breathed in the brine and the cold, reminded herself that anything was better than being back in the Liberties.

"A fine evening, isn't it?"

She looked around. There was a man sitting in one of the deck chairs; she hadn't seen him when she came out. He was wearing a blazer and a boater, dapper for third class. In her time on the Atlantic run, she had learned about American accents, and this one sounded like he was a Yankee, and a fancy one at that.

"'And that night while all was still, I heard the waters roll slowly continually up the shores . . .'"

"Is that poetry you're talking?"

"Walt Whitman. Have you heard of him?"

"I'm not one for books and writing and such."

"But books and writing are all we have. They keep us from barbarism."

"Well then they haven't done a very good job."

He laughed at that. "You have a point, I suppose. But let's not talk about man's inhumanity to man on a beautiful night like this."

"I shouldn't be talking to you at all, sir. I best be getting back to my duties."

"Back to your duties? At this time of night?"

"Well I have my passengers to look after. While they're awake, so am I."

"And how much do they pay you to be someone's slave?"

Kitty bridled at that. She peered closer into the dark, trying to see the man's face. "I'm no man's slave."

"Of course you are. The system has made slaves of us all."

I shouldn't be talking to a strange man in the dark like this, she thought. *I could get into trouble if the chief steward sees me. I should be away back to my cabin.*

But instead she heard herself say: "System? And what system is that?"

"Capitalism."

"Are you one of those anarchist fellas?"

Another laugh. "No, that's someone who doesn't believe there should be laws. I still believe in the law, I just think it should protect everyone, not just those with money. Don't you agree?"

"I wouldn't know about that. I never had much in the way of schooling."

"You don't need schooling to know what's right and what's wrong." He stood up and came toward the light. She still couldn't see his face very well, except that he had glasses, and that he was certainly not a great deal older than she was. "Lincoln Randolph," he said and gave her a little bow.

"Kitty," she said.

"Well Kitty. How did you come to be working for J. P. Morgan?"

"For who, Mr. Randolph?"

"Lincoln, please. And J. P. Morgan is one of the richest men in the world, some would say he owns the world. He certainly owns the White Star Line. He's your employer, did you not know that?"

"So what made you such a clever fella?"

"It's my business."

"What is your business?"

"I'm a busybody."

"I hope it pays better than being a stewardess for the White Star Line."

"And how did you come to be a stewardess, Kitty? There must be easier jobs for a pretty girl like you."

"Well sure, I could have got a job in a kip real easy, but I'd rather make a rich man happy, standing up."

"What's a kip?"

"It's a place fellas go to find true love with the woman of their dreams for half an hour."

"Ah, I've heard of such places, though I've never been. It's a cruel world, Kitty."

"Sure, and you're right there."

"It won't always be that way. There are changes coming."

"What sort of changes?"

"Changes in the way the world is run. We won't always live in a world where profit is the only thing that matters and the poor of the world lick the boots of a few."

"Well you could be right, but I'll settle for the vote and someone to make me a cup of tea at the end of the day, Mr. Randolph. Now I think I should be getting back below."

He took a step closer, and she saw his face in the light for the first time. *Not a bad-looking man, in a thoughtful sort of way.* He was wearing wire-rimmed glasses, and they made him look both kind and studious, even if he talked like the sort of man who would put a bomb under Parliament.

And before she could turn away, he took off his glasses and looked right into her face. "It was real nice to talk to you, Kitty. Real nice. 'What is that you express in your eyes? It seems to me more than all the print I have read in my life.'"

"Did you just make that up?"

"Wish I had. Walt Whitman again, I'm afraid. Good night, Kitty."

"Good night, Mr. Randolph," she said, and fled back to her cabin.

CHAPTER 3

Back in their cabin, Elsie was still awake, and together they finished their unpacking, putting out the little mementoes they had both brought from their last ships: Elsie her calendars and family pictures, Kitty the photograph of her little brother, Liam, and a small carved jewelry box Danny had given her.

"So who was the nice young gentleman?" Elsie asked her.

"What are you talking about?"

"Oh come on, Irish, this is a big ship, but it's not that big. I saw you talking to him as I came off watch."

"I've no idea who he was. He tried to engage me in conversation. You know what men are like; I couldn't be rude now could I?"

"Depends what deck he sleeps in."

"A passenger is a passenger."

"You must think I was born yesterday. Only natural, pretty little thing like you, I bet men can't leave you alone. Got anyone special back in Dublin then, have you?"

"I don't live in Dublin anymore, haven't been back there for years. And I don't know that I care to have a man in my life."

Elsie gave her a look. Kitty wondered how much she should tell her.

"There was a fella, he was a sailor, an officer he was, with Cunard."

"An officer!"

"I met him in Dublin. Ran off with him, I did."

"Were you in love with him?"

"I thought I was, but if you want the truth, I just wanted to get away from the Liberties and away from my father. Love is whatever you want to make it, I suppose. Besides, I was only a girl."

"You're hardly an old maid now. What happened?"

"You'll have to ask him that."

"Like that, was it?"

"Suppose I should be thankful. He got me this job, I wouldn't have it without him, and he got me out of Dublin into the bargain. Do I shock you?"

"Take more than that to shock me, Irish. Look, your business is your business, but if you want to know the God's honest truth, I wouldn't mind any sort of man, especially if he was rich, know what I mean? Be nice, wouldn't it—be a lady of leisure, not have to make beds and clean, no more 'Yes sir, no ma'am.' Lovely."

"You mean be a tart, like that so-called Mrs. Finnegan?"

"Well I don't know that I'd mind. I spend half my life on my knees anyway, and it's just another kind of polishing, innit?" She gave a breathy laugh. "Only the pay's better, and at least you can go to work without getting out of bed. Know what I mean?"

"That's a terrible thing to say!" Kitty said, but laughed anyway.

"No love, it's just life."

"Well, maybe you're right. But it shouldn't be that way."

"No, but it is, so we best just make the best of it." She started to get ready for bed, sat down on the edge of her bunk, and idly drew some strands of hair out of her brush. "Trouble is, I've not the looks to get myself a millionaire. You have, though."

"I'd rather die first."

"Oh, I wouldn't rule out your choices too quick, girl." Elsie cocked her head, heard the ship's bell ringing up on deck; six bells, an hour before midnight. "We'd better get some sleep. Mrs. Finnegan may be a tart, but I'll bet she's just the kind of trollop that'll want you to bring her breakfast in bed first thing. She'll be finishing her shift just as you're starting yours!"

Another breathy laugh.

Kitty was exhausted, but sleep did not come easy on the narrow bunk; their cabin was above the propellers, and she could feel the vibration of the screws and hear their muted drumming through her pillow. At least she and Elsie had a porthole; she could smell the crisp clean air, not like when she first started with Cunard, crew's quarters were deep in the bowels of the ship.

Still, it always took her a few days to get accustomed to being on a new ship, and for the longest while she tossed and turned, trying to get comfortable, till at last she gave up and just lay there, staring into the dark.

She thought about what Mr. Lincoln Randolph had said to her: *"How much do they pay you to be someone's slave?"* The nerve of the man! Who did he think he was, talking to her like that, and him traveling on third deck too.

Being a stewardess was no disgrace, better than being some man's mistress, a kept woman, like that tart who'd come on board with that Flash Jack, or whatever it was they called him.

But still, what he'd said kept nagging at her. Elsie was right; for all that she turned her nose up, Flash Jack's slutty little piece was the one sleeping in a nice wide bed with Egyptian cotton sheets, and she was the one in the cabin with another long day of making beds and carrying tea ahead of her. Sometimes a girl had to wonder if she was doing the right thing.

CHAPTER 4

Kitty was awake and in her uniform by six o'clock, before the first of her bells had started ringing. Elsie was right, Her Ladyship wanted breakfast in bed, out of spite if nothing else. And eggs soft-boiled, mind; if they didn't have soft yolks, she was sending them back, she made that clear enough.

Yes, Mrs. Finnegan.

And so to another day of scrubbing and cleaning and bell answering; fetching teas and making beds and polishing brass; eating hasty meals, standing up in a steamy pantry with the deck around her littered with the debris of the last meal. She cleaned cabins and bathrooms, swept and dusted; she arranged flowers, hung up clothes, fetched basins and cold cloths for the seasick. At night she turned down the beds, and on her way back to the pantry couldn't help but spare a single, bitter glance at the grand staircase, at the ladies on their way back from the dining room in their fine dresses, their arms bare, diamonds glittering at their throats and on their fingers.

At least you're not in the Liberties, she reminded herself.

Finally, a quiet moment. She looked around to see if any of the crew was watching her, made to go back to her own cabin, but instead took a wrong corridor on purpose, and headed down the alley past the engineers' quarters. The chief steward would raise the roof if he found out where she was, but he could never prove it was deliberate, could he?

She would just say she lost her way on the new ship.

It was the grandest liner she had been on since she started with White Star and the most stable; some of the crossings she'd made, the decks had been completely awash in bad weather, plates and bowls had to be placed on special racks on the dining room tables or they would end up in a madam's lap. On the older ships, it was like being in an earthquake for the entire crossing, even on first deck—the woodwork creaking and squealing, cabin doors slamming, crockery spilling from cupboards and smashing on the deck. She was seasick morning till night, all year round.

Third class on the *Titanic* wasn't like the other ships she had been on either. Usually it was bleak, airless, and overcrowded, and the noise from the boiler rooms was deafening. But thanks to Mr. Andrews even third class was almost sumptuous; there were glistening rows of white-painted cabins, even some laughing and singing. It did not have the refinement of first deck perhaps, but it was almost as good as first on some of the other ships she had served on.

Kitty found her way to the men's section, near the front of the boat, pretending she was on an errand, checking all the cabins as she went along. There were two double bunk beds in each of the cabins; most of the doors were still open with lights on, men in shirtsleeves sitting up, talking or reading.

Lincoln was plumped on his bunk in his braces and socks, a notepad on his lap. His spectacles were perched on the end of his nose. He peered over the top of them at her. "Well good evening!" He stopped writing and laid the notepad aside.

The other bunks were empty, the other men off somewhere. Lincoln didn't stand up for her, like a toff would, so she stood and leaned in the doorway, still half of her in the corridor for propriety's sake.

"Good evening, Mr. Randolph."

"Call me Lincoln."

"What are you writing?"

"An article about the suffragette movement in London. Do you know they've been smashing windows in Oxford Street? I'd say they mean business."

"An article? You mean like for a newspaper?"

"Something like that."

"Have you ever had anything published?"

"I write regularly for a newspaper called the *Masses*, and I've had several pieces in *Colliers* and the *Saturday Evening Post*. Have you heard of those?"

She shook her head. "Like I said, I've never been one for reading."

"That's a shame."

"So this article you're writing, it's for the Americans, is it? Do they care what happens in Oxford Street over there?"

"They don't care much for Oxford Street, but they do care about votes for women. It's a sore subject in certain circles."

"What circles?"

"Most circles, though it's mostly the men that are sore about the idea of it."

"So is that what you've been doing in England, Mr. Randolph? Writing?"

"Lincoln. And yes, that's what I was doing in London. I was in Paris as well, collecting material for articles."

"So what else do you do?"

"Well, that's about it."

"Nothing else?"

"No, that's how I earn my living."

"Why don't you write your articles in New York, then?"

"Well, I could, but my professor at Harvard always told me that if you want to write about life, you have to see life. And I want to see more of life than just New York."

"You went to Harvard? Isn't that one of them fancy universities?"

"As fancy as it gets, I suppose."

"So I ask myself, what's a man who travels third deck doing at Harvard?"

"And it would be a good question. The answer is, my parents sent me there—thought it would do me good."

"Your father has money, has he?"

"He has a cigar factory. The joke in the family is that the family fortune went up in smoke. No, you're right, I didn't laugh at that either."

But Kitty wasn't thinking about the joke; she was trying to make sense of Mr. Lincoln Randolph. "Your father owns a factory? So what in God's name are you doing down here then?"

He sat forward and dropped his voice in a mock whisper. "Because I don't think they would like my views on the upper decks."

"What are your views, Mr. Randolph?"

"Lincoln. Well to answer your question, Kitty—it is Kitty, isn't it? To answer your question, I'm not what you might call a great advocate of capitalism, even though I'm a product of it. Do you know what capitalism is?"

"Sure and I don't."

"It's the economic system we live and work in. Capitalism means paying your workers almost nothing for working intolerably long hours, and getting your customers to try and make up the shortfall in tips. That's it in a nutshell, I think. How much does J. P. Morgan pay you, Kitty?"

"I don't know this J. P. Morgan you keep talking about."

"You don't know him, but like I told you last night, it's him that owns this shipping line, and he's the one who tells them how much to pay you and all your fellow slaves on the *Titanic*. Come on, how much?"

"Two pounds, ten shillings a month."

"So you really couldn't survive without the tips, could you? It's starvation wages, Kitty, plus you have to buy your own uniform, don't you, and have it laundered?"

"I get an extra ten shillings a month for upkeep."

"Sure you do, if you have anything left over after you've paid for breakages. They charge you for breakages, too, don't they, Kitty? And do you know how much Mr. J. P. Morgan is worth?"

She shook her head.

"Somewhere between fifty and a hundred million dollars. Does that seem like an awful lot to you? Now how do you think he came to be worth so much money, Kitty?"

"I don't know, but I'm sure you're going to tell me."

"He makes so much because he pays you so little. You and tens of thousands of others who work for him. That's how he does it."

"Are you a socialist, Mr. Randolph?"

"Lincoln. Yes, I am, Kitty. Heard of socialism have you?"

"They say you people want to bring down the government."

"No Kitty, we just want to change the system and replace it with something better. You do know what a union is?"

"Of course I do."

"Well imagine a world where all the workers were in a union, where it wasn't just you going cap in hand to your employer, asking what wages he was prepared to pay you, instead you had every worker in the world standing behind you when you did it. What I dream of is a world where all the workers are organized into one big union so they can tell the J. P. Morgans of this world that if they want labor, then they'll have to give their workers a fair share of the profits. Imagine that! What if you weren't a slave anymore? What if you had power? What if a union made your work *valuable*?"

"You think that will ever happen?"

"It's the twentieth century, Kitty, it's the new dawn, a whole brave new world! Yes, I think it can happen and that, Kitty O'Kane, is what I write about."

"How do you know my name?"

"What?"

"I never told you my name was O'Kane."

"Well, I've been asking about you."

"Now why would you do that?"

"Why do you think I would do that?"

"I'm sure I don't know."

"Well, I'll leave it to you to figure it out." He picked up his notepad and started writing again. The fancy-pants upstart! Kitty would have liked to tweak his nose. Instead she turned to go. "What is it you want, Kitty?" She stopped, turned back. "You want to spend your whole life making up beds and cleaning up messes?"

"Of course I don't."

"No, I didn't think so either. Something tells me you want to leave a mark on the world, don't you?"

"How can I leave a mark on the world? I'm just a woman with no education, Mr. Randolph. Not like you."

"Lincoln. And I don't think it matters one good damn about education. All that matters is the fire in your belly."

Kitty studied him. He gave her a boyish grin, knew he had her. "I don't know about all this blather about capitalism, but a woman having a vote same as a man, now that would be a good start, if you want my opinion."

"Well, I do want your opinion, Kitty, or I wouldn't be talking to you. And suffrage is another thing that's going to happen, and you can be a part of it, or you can just stand and watch while you fetch and carry for people who don't give a damn about you." He grinned at her.

Kitty hovered for a moment. "I'd better be getting back."

"Nice talking to you, Kitty O'Kane."

"You too . . . Lincoln."

She made her way back up the gangway; her feet were an agony, her back ached, but a part of her was excited. Did men really think like that in Harvard? Did any man think like that anywhere?

Did Lincoln Randolph really think she could change the world?

Well she would think about all this some more tomorrow. For now, all she wanted to do was put her head down and get some sleep. She had perhaps just enough left in her to fetch a bottle of water from the pantry before she collapsed on her bunk.

"Ah, Kitty!"

She looked up. Her Highness sailed toward her, her little dog in her arms. Did the damned thing never walk anywhere? Didn't God give it legs?

"My dear, you do look so very tired. Are you going off-duty now?"

"I hope so, ma'am."

"Before you go, could you do just one more little thing? It's so lovely outside, and Jack and I are having just the best time looking at the stars, so would you mind giving Suzie her lamb cutlet and peas?" She dropped the dog into her arms. "Fresh peas, mind, and mash them for her, will you? You're such a dear. I knew you wouldn't mind."

She turned and flounced away, leaving behind a fog of French perfume and condescension. The dog yelped and writhed in her arms. Kitty stared after Jack Finnegan's fecking mistress and would have poked out her tongue at her back, but then she saw the chief steward watching her, so she forced a smile and headed off to the pantry, as if it really was no bother at all.

CHAPTER 5

The sky was blue, and the sea a lazy calm as far as the eye could see. They were four days out, and the ship had settled into a rhythm now. The service bells weren't ringing quite as often; the old soaks just sat in the saloons with their beers and cigars while the better sort patrolled the upper deck arm in arm, too much gentility for her by half, but she was too busy to have to watch it long.

Her Ladyship didn't have the same aversion to using her bell, she kept her busy enough. So in the morning when the bell rang yet again, Kitty knocked on the door and went straight in. She was surprised to find Jack Finnegan standing there in his shirtsleeves, his braces around his hips, and a drink in his hand. Straightaway she could tell it wasn't his first, and it wasn't yet lunchtime.

"Ah, Kitty. Can you clear away these glasses and plates from last night, please? I'm afraid Mrs. Finnegan and I have left rather a mess. And I need more cracked ice, if you please."

"Yes, sir."

Kitty got on with cleaning away the things, stacking them all on a tray. She could feel him there standing behind her, but she hadn't reckoned on how close he was. When she turned around, he was right there between her and the door.

A smile; well, it was more like a leer, really. "What's the matter, Kitty?"

"Nothing, sir, I'd best be getting on."

"There's no rush now, is there?"

"Mr. Richardson wouldn't like it if I'm dawdling about my work."

"Now who's Mr. Richardson?"

"He's the chief steward for first deck, sir."

"You let me worry about Mr. Richardson." She tried to squeeze past, but he leaned across the door, one hand on the jamb. His lips were shiny and wet, like liver. "You're a pretty little thing. All these red curls about your face." He reached out and touched her hair, nothing she could do about it without dropping the tray. "Slim as a reed too. I like that in a woman."

He tried to kiss her. She was shocked and stepped back, was proud of herself that she didn't drop the tray. He smirked and followed her retreat; she felt the bedroom door at her back, and there he was, a hand on the bulkhead either side of her now, no escape.

"Kitty, be nice to me, and I'll be nice to you."

"I'd rather just get this tray out of your way and fetch some cracked ice, if it's all the same to you."

She heard the cabin door open. Mrs. Finnegan stepped in holding little Suzie, and he took a step backward. His hands went in his pockets, but the flush on Kitty's cheeks and the look on his face—he somehow managed to look angry more than guilty—gave him away.

Her Ladyship took a moment, a smile frozen on her face, her eyes flicking between the two of them. "Kitty?"

"Just clearing away the table, ma'am."

"So good of you, my dear."

"She was just finishing up," Finnegan said.

"Kitty, now you're here, would you be a dear and bring us our breakfast down? It's much too noisy up in the saloon, and we don't like the people at our table. Do we, Jack?"

"But breakfast service is finished, ma'am."

"Yes I know, but I'm sure you can find something for us." She waved a jeweled hand at Finnegan. "You're such a dear. Isn't she, Jack?"

"Sure and she is."

"It's past eleven o'clock, Mrs. Finnegan," Kitty said.

"So it is. You spoil us so very much, Kitty. Run along, then."

Kitty heard the brandy snifter rattling on the tray. They all stared at it. Was she shaking because of Jack Finnegan trying to kiss her or this tramp talking down to her again? Perhaps it was both. Kitty hurried out as fast as she could.

⬥

A ghastly place, the pantry, at least Kitty always thought so, greasy and steamy and littered with the pots and plates left over by the cooks and the breakfast stewards. Mr. Richardson was standing near the hot press when she came in, was about to give the order to clear away.

"Sir, before you do that."

His head shot around. "Miss O'Kane?"

"Well it's Mrs. Finnegan on C deck. She says she needs to lie down in her cabin and would like breakfast brought to her directly."

His cheeks mottled. He took in what remained in the press, and made a quick calculation. "Well, I suppose there is the cold collation she might have and the peach compote. If she'd like a hot breakfast, she can have some grilled river sole and the oatcakes, if that's to her fancy."

"Thank you, sir."

He glared at her as if it were all her fault, and shook his head, despairing of the young gels they sent him these days, couldn't persuade their passengers to take their breakfast at the right time.

She saw Elsie make eyes at her. Kitty sidled over.

"He tried to kiss me," she whispered.

"Who, Mr. Richardson?"

"No, that gangster fella, Finnegan."

"What about Her Ladyship?"

"She was out of the room. Should I report it?"

Elsie shook her head. "You keep it to yourself, Kitty. No good ever comes of making trouble for a gentleman. Just try and stay out of his way, for God's sake!"

―――

The Finnegans' cabin was gloomy when she returned with the luncheon tray. The door to the viewing deck was closed, the lights dimmed. Kitty hesitated.

"I'm in here, Kitty," Her Ladyship called out.

She went into the bedroom. Mrs. Finnegan was sitting on the lace bedspread with her Pekingese on her lap. The curtains were drawn. It took Kitty a moment for her eyes to get accustomed to the light.

"Just leave the tray there, on the bedside table."

"Is Mr. Finnegan not having anything?"

"Mr. Finnegan has gone up to the saloon to play cards."

Kitty turned to go, hesitated when she saw the livid bruise on Her Ladyship's cheek, just below her eye. She had been crying.

"Shall I get you some ice for that?"

She shook her head.

"You should never let a man hit you, not ever."

"I fell. If anyone asks you, I fell. Now get out."

Kitty did as she was told. She almost felt sorry for her.

CHAPTER 6

Gray skies replaced the blue, though the ocean remained serene. It was an easier voyage than most she'd known on the Atlantic run. The water was like mercury under the misted stars.

But that night, the fourteenth, the air turned icy and drove the passengers inside, the gentlemen taking refuge in the saloons with their brandy snifters and cigars, the ladies retiring early to their cabins.

When Kitty had finished settling in her passengers for the night, she slipped out onto the third-class deck. It was late, and the cold took her breath away. There were ice crystals formed on the metal rails, and "whiskers around the lights," as the old hands called it.

She thought perhaps Lincoln Randolph had gone to bed, and so he should have done if he had any sense, but then she saw him sitting there, in the same deck chair as always, a blanket over his knees, a scarf wrapped around his face against the cold.

"Didn't think you'd be out here tonight."

"I was waiting for you," he said.

"What on earth for?"

"It's the best part of my day, talking to you."

"Well, then I feel sorry for you and the sad life you have. Did you finish your article?"

"I finished two and started on a third."

"Aren't we just the scribbler, then?"

"I told you, it's what I do."

"Not all day and every day, though? What is it you do when you're not writing? Is there a woman waiting for you back in New York?"

"I'm happily unattached. I don't hold with marriage. It makes a slave out of a woman and a monster out of a man. What about you?"

She shook her head.

"So do you have a job to go back to, Lincoln?"

"I told you, Kitty, I freelance my work. No man owns me; I won't allow it. I'll sell my articles to whoever will take them and then write some more."

"You won't be needing a union then."

"But there's plenty that do. There's big change coming in the world, Kitty, and I intend to be a part of it. Can you not feel it in the air?"

"Not tonight, it's so cold I've no feeling anywhere."

"Well, I'd say, even with a blue nose you're the prettiest girl I've seen in a long time."

"Would you, now? Well, pretty will get a girl in more trouble than plain, I've found."

"And you've a wit too. Wish I had more time to get to know you better."

"Well, we've three more days till we arrive in New York. Plenty of time, if that's what you want. But not tonight, it's too cold, and I'm too beat."

He stood up and let the blanket fall. She thought he was going to take her hand and wish her good night, maybe even a small bow as a gentleman might do, that would be a novelty. Instead he pulled her toward him and tried to kiss her. She let him, briefly, then she pulled away. "What do you think you're doing? I'm not that sort of girl."

"I couldn't help myself. Don't tell me you didn't like it."

"If that's the brave new world, I'll stick with capitalism, thanks very much. Now good night, Mr. Randolph."

"Well, I'm sorry if I offended you. Good night, Kitty."

He looked abashed, she thought, but not nearly as much as he should. She gave him a look and hurried belowdecks.

The alleyways were mostly deserted except for a few stewards on late watch, all of them yawning with one eye on the companion clock. Almost half past eleven. Late. She passed a few passengers on their way back from the smoking room, others stepping out for some fresh air before turning in. Well, they wouldn't last long out there.

It was warmer down in the cabin, but not by much. Elsie was already in her bunk, shivering under the blanket. "I can't get warm," she said.

"Give a thought for those two in the crow's nest," Kitty said. "What a night to be stuck up there. I've never been so bloody cold."

She scrambled into her own bunk for a few precious hours' sleep before she had to do it all again. She closed her eyes, thought about Her Ladyship and that bruise on her cheek, thought about Lincoln and how good it felt to have a man's arms around her again, even if for just a few moments.

She reached out a hand for the jewelry box. Her officer had bought it for her—only thing he ever got her—lovely it was, mahogany and inlaid with mother of pearl; he said it came from Hong Kong. She cradled it in the dark.

"So what's in there then?"

"I thought you were asleep."

"You got the crown jewels in there?"

"I wish."

"You're back late."

"Lady Astor wanted a nightcap."

"What about Mr. Randolph, did he get a nightcap too?"

"Don't talk filthy."

"Oh come on, Kitty, don't tell me you haven't been up on deck talking to your young man again."

"He's not my young man!"

"God love us, he's too handsome for third deck. I heard he was a writer and that his father's rich as Croesus. Come on, you can tell me. I won't tell a soul."

"Telling you and putting it on the front pages of the newspapers is just about the same thing!"

They both laughed at that, and Elsie had started to say something else when they felt the great ship shudder; there was a squealing so loud it was like the brakes of a thousand express engines. The hull vibrated for a few seconds, and then they heard the engines shutting down.

And then everything was still.

Elsie peered over the side of the bunk at her. "Sounds like something queer just happened, Irish."

Kitty lay quite still. There were voices in the passageway. One of the junior stewards knocked on their door and peered in.

"What's happened?" Kitty said.

"Been a little accident. Purser says they're going to fix it, and then we'll be on our way."

"What kind of bleedin' accident?" Elsie said, but already he was gone.

Kitty wondered what she should do. Absently, she got out of bed and started tidying the cabin, folding her clothes, putting things in their place. She could feel Elsie watching her. "What you doin', girl?"

Kitty didn't answer her.

Suddenly the door burst open. It was the chief steward. "My God, why are you girls still down here? Put on some warm clothes and your life jackets and get yourselves upstairs. You have to look after your passengers. Get them into blankets and eiderdowns and up onto the deck. Quickly!"

"What's happened?" Elsie said.

"We've hit an iceberg," he said, as if it was obvious.

And then he was gone. Kitty fumbled in the wardrobe for her uniform, and she and Elsie dressed in silence—neither of them could think of a thing to say. Kitty's teeth chattered, and her fingers were all thumbs. Finally she finished putting on her lifebelt and rushed out the door. She nearly tripped over a block of ice. How had that got down here? There were children playing in the passage, kicking around lumps of it as if they were footballs. The same junior steward who had come in earlier hurried past, shooing all the third-class passengers back into their cabins. "Just an engine problem," he shouted at them. "We'll be back underway shortly."

Kitty hurried up to first deck, checked that her passengers were all up and that they had their lifebelts on. "Is all this fuss necessary, Kitty?" Finnegan drawled at her. "They told me this tub's unsinkable."

"I'm sure it's just a precaution," Kitty said.

Her Ladyship asked her to get some warm milk for Suzie. Kitty stared at her. It all seemed so unreal. Finnegan was right, wasn't he? The *Titanic* couldn't sink. But as she ran toward the pantry, she saw Tommy Andrews coming the other way and she took one look at his face and she knew.

To hell with Her Ladyship.

Kitty went from cabin to cabin, reminding people to put on warm clothing and to take blankets and their valuables with them. Just a precaution, sir, madam, no reason to be alarmed. Have you got your lifebelt with you, please, sir?

Finally everyone on first deck was headed for the companionways, but taking their time about it—you didn't hurry the upper class. Some made jokes, some wanted to stay and chat. She saw several of the officers peering down, unwilling to alarm them, but she could tell by their faces, they just wished the passengers would hurry up about it.

She headed for the upper decks. There was music playing somewhere, from one of the saloons. It all seemed surreal. It was so cold outside, it took her breath away.

Sleepy passengers were milling around, fumbling with jacket buttons and lifebelt ties. Most of them acted as though it was a drill. Those gentlemen who had not yet gone to bed when it happened were standing around, smoking cigars, and murmuring to each other in low voices. She expected any moment one of them would ask her to run and fetch the porter.

She looked for'ard. Oh Jesus Mary. The *Titanic*'s bow was covered with huge blocks of ice.

One of the officers came around, ordering everyone to the lifeboats. "Just a precaution," he said. The music had stopped playing. She saw the orchestra six-piece step out of the saloon, locking the doors behind them.

There couldn't be any danger surely; the *Titanic* was as steady as a rock in the water. She might as well have been in dock. Then Kitty looked up at the bridge, saw Captain Smith up there, shouting at someone and waving his arms. She had never heard him raise his voice before, though they said when the *Olympic* had collided with the *Hawke*, he had raised an eyebrow.

That's when she knew for sure and certain.

Officers were ordering women into the boats, but most were unwilling to leave their men, especially when they saw the first boat being lowered, swinging wildly on its davit. It was only half-full, for God's sake.

"I'll not go without him," she heard a woman shouting. Her husband looked grim, kept pushing her away from him toward one of the officers.

She did a count of her own passengers, making sure she had them all.

The number 5 boat was ready to go down. Mr. Ismay was there, she heard him calling out: "Are there any more women before this boat goes?"

Officer Murdoch saw her. "Come on, jump in," he said to her.

"I'm just a stewardess," Kitty said.

"Never mind," Ismay said. "You're a woman; take your place."

Kitty clambered in. Mr. Ismay gave her a smile; he was sweating, she could see, even though it was a freezing night, and he had on only his slippers and pajamas under the blanket round his shoulders. Just as they were about to lower away, she remembered her jewelry box. Jesus Mary, she couldn't leave that behind.

She jumped back to her feet, grabbed Mr. Murdoch's arm, and clambered out.

"Where are you going, girl?"

"I'll be right back!" she shouted.

———

It was strange to pass by the staterooms, all lit up so brilliantly, their doors gaping open. There was expensive jewelry lying about on dressers, a pair of silver slippers lying on the carpet where they had been kicked off.

She passed a group of officers, still in their mess jackets, hands in their pockets, chatting quietly on the companion square as if they were waiting to go to lunch. They smiled at her as she went past. She knew them, of course: Tommy Andrews, Captain Smith, the chief purser, McElroy.

Farther down, the passageways were deserted. It was eerie; the steelwork was groaning and squealing. It was like being inside something that was dying. Kitty fought back her fear. *I'll not leave that jewelry box behind*, she told herself. *Now get a grip on yourself, girl.*

It was when she reached her cabin that she saw Elsie lying in the passageway. There was blood smeared on the deck. She must have slipped on the ice. There was freezing bilge water lapping about; if she'd fallen face down, she would have drowned.

"Elsie love," she said, and squatted down, rested her chin on her knees. Blessed Christ Jesus she was out to it; her eyes were rolled right back in her head, blood was matted thick in her hair. She had to get her out of there.

She was a big girl, Elsie, solid, and Kitty didn't have the strength for it. She dragged her as far as the companionway, but how was she going to get her up the steps? She shouted till her throat was sore, but there was no one around. The lights started to flicker. *Oh Jesus, help me, if they go out, we're really in trouble.*

"Elsie, wake up, now's no time for this fuss."

She sat her up, nothing she could do unless she had help. She yelled for help again, loud as she could.

"Is that you, Miss O'Kane?"

"Mr. Richardson! Thank the Lord! I'm down here!"

His face appeared in the companionway. His moustaches seemed to bristle with alarm when he saw her. "I told you to fetch eiderdowns!"

"It's Elsie, sir, she's had a fall!"

He came down the companionway. When he saw what had happened, he clucked his tongue as if Elsie was a dropped china plate. Then he bent down and hauled her over his shoulder. "I'll get her up top. You take care of your passengers like I told you, Miss O'Kane."

He started up the companionway. Kitty hesitated, then ran back down the passageway. "Miss O'Kane, where are you going? Come back here!"

The jewelry box was right there on her side table. She tucked it into her coat and ran back out. The lights flickered again. *The* Titanic *is going down,* she thought. *She really is going down.*

———

Up on deck the mood had changed, arguments had started over who would go into the boats and who wouldn't. Kitty peered over the edge of the port rail, just yawning blackness down there. Dear God in heaven, why did they have to get into the boats anyway? The *Titanic* seemed so steady. Someone pointed to lights on the horizon; there was another ship out there—help wasn't far away, surely.

One of the officers was walking around, reassuring everyone that all would be well. "There are plenty of boats in the vicinity," he said. "They'll be with us any moment now."

So why were they lowering the lifeboats? Another went down, there hardly seemed a soul in it.

Where were Mr. Richardson and Elsie?

There was a bang, and a distress rocket sparked into the sky. Kitty saw children pointing at it and laughing, like it was fireworks, and she had to admit, with all the lights on in all the cabins, the flare exploding against the black night, and all those millions of stars, why it did look very pretty, no mistake.

She climbed down the iron ladder to B deck, calling for Elsie and Mr. Richardson. Officers and men were getting more lifeboats ready. They looked tense, unlike the well-ordered groups of passengers wandering about.

So cold. She found an eiderdown lying on the deck and wrapped it around herself, climbed back up to the boat deck. More distress rockets arced into the sky. The lights on the horizon seemed to be getting closer. Some of the women were pointing even as they climbed into the lifeboats. The young officers were urging them to hurry.

Kitty started when she heard gunshots. Through the crowd she saw Fifth Officer Lowe point his revolver at a young lad who was hiding under some lady's dress on one of the lifeboats. She was pleading with Lowe: "He won't take up much room!" But Lowe ordered him off anyway. *Jesus God*, Kitty thought, *things have come to a pass when men start pointing guns at schoolboys.*

Another rocket went up into the night.

People were pointing, and Kitty turned to see what it was everyone was looking at. The sea was so calm that no one had noticed before, but now she could see that water was settling over the bow. Panic rippled through the crowd on the deck below her, and there was a surge toward the boats. Men started to fight for places, and Lowe held his revolver in the air and threatened to shoot any man that came too close.

Second Officer Lightoller ordered the boat down. Women were begging him to allow their men to take the empty seats, but poor Lightoller looked scared half to death; he wasn't himself. "Only women and children," he was shouting. "I'll shoot any man that tries to get in!"

There was a shocked silence as the boat was lowered into the water.

The women around Kitty started crying when they realized they would have to leave their husbands behind. Their men stood back, with stiff smiles.

Where was Elsie?

———✦———

Boats were being lowered more rapidly now. The blocks kept jamming, tilting the boats, some of them empty, some of them dangerously overcrowded. There were women and children screaming everywhere. *Titanic* was listing. Oh God, love us.

They were getting another boat ready. A quartermaster marshaled the women passengers behind Kitty in a line; a man tore his toddler's arms from his neck and handed the screaming little girl to her mother. He gave her a quick embrace and stepped back. "It's all right, go along. It's just a precaution. You'll be back here again in a few moments."

"I'll not go without you!" she screamed.

He turned away. Two sailors took her arms and dragged her screaming toward the boat.

Kitty thought she heard more pistol shots from the starboard deck. It was bedlam now. There were men throwing themselves at the boats, and the sailors were throwing them back.

They were trying to launch another of the boats from the promenade deck. Kitty saw her Mr. Astor hand his wife into the boat; he tried to get in with her, told the second officer that she was "in a delicate condition." But Mr. Lightoller ordered him off, and Mr. Astor waved encouragingly to his wife as he stepped back into an ever-increasing crowd of men. He lit a cigar and straightened his shoulders. He was still wearing his dinner suit.

A steward brought a crowd of Swedish immigrants up from the third deck, and there was a heated row. Then one of them dashed over to a lifeboat, the others followed, there was pushing, and she saw a punch thrown. One of the officers shouted instructions to lower away, and the lifeboat jerked downward into the dark, slowly at first, first one end up and then the other. A man dashed to the ship's side, and before anyone could stop him, he hurled himself into the descending boat. It rocked alarmingly, and he lost his balance and fell into the black water below.

One of the mailmen from the sorting office came panting up onto the deck. "The mail is floating up to F deck with the water." He said it as if he couldn't believe it himself. The music started up again, the orchestra in their lifejackets and overcoats had reassembled just aft of the first-class entrance.

Well, we have to have music to drown by, she thought. *On first deck they like to do things properly.*

Kitty fought her way to the starboard side. People kept pouring up the companionway from third deck. There was a big crush behind her; they all surged forward, and Kitty was pushed into a boat. She heard an officer screaming: "Women and children only! Women and children first!"

In moments the boat was full, and people were tripping over oars and tackle in the dark. A man tried to clamber in, missed his footing and fell.

The boat jerked down into the blackness below, past rows of brilliantly lit portholes, dark then light, then dark again. The men used their hands and the oars to keep the lifeboat clear of the hull. Clang, clang, clang, down she went. Their boat hit the water with a spine-jarring thud, a baby started crying somewhere at the back of the boat, no one else spoke.

Then the quartermaster in charge shouted, "Oars out," and the crew rowed away from the ship as hard as they could.

"There's too many on the boat," a woman beside her said. "Someone will have to get out." *Sure she doesn't mean herself or anyone from first deck, I'll bet. Would you like me to bring you a hot toddy before I step over the side?*

Kitty clutched her jewelry box tightly to her chest, rested her other hand on the gunnel—their lifeboat was so low in the water, her fingers were wet almost to the knuckles, and Jesus Mary the water was freezing. Anyone going into that would have no chance. The quartermaster shouted to the men at the oars to get them as far away from the ship as possible. "She'll suck us down under with her when she goes," he said.

This was not happening. It couldn't be real, it couldn't be.

CHAPTER 7

She had always wondered what the *Titanic* looked like, from a distance, had wanted to admire her the way the onlookers did that first day as the ship pulled out of harbor. She never thought she would have the chance, and never like this. The truth of it was the ship looked quite beautiful in her last moments, illuminated against a backdrop of a velvet sky spangled with ice-cold stars, brilliant white flares trailing sparks. Every porthole and saloon blazed with light.

She heard a murmur behind her; some of the women had started to pray. Others were weeping.

Kitty counted how many decks were still above water by the rows of lights she could make out. *One, two, three, four, five, six; wait no, it was five.* Perhaps she had miscounted. She couldn't be going down that fast, surely.

The quartermaster—it was Mr. Rowe—shone his torch around the inside of the boat. Some of the women were still in their nightgowns, had nothing on their feet. Two of the women were from first deck, one of them in a white silk dress trimmed with lace and covered with jaunty blue flowers, but Kitty didn't recognize most of the others. First class, third class, it didn't matter anymore.

Wait, wasn't that Mr. Ismay, there in the back, all hunched over in his blanket?

The baby was still whimpering somewhere in the dark.

The oarsmen were breathing hard, their backs into it; the quartermaster, urging them to greater efforts, kept telling them that they were still too close.

She counted the decks on the *Titanic* again; one, two, three, four.

She was going down by the head. Some of the women started to wail, not for the ship, she supposed, but for those they loved still on her.

Kitty twisted in her seat, looking for the lights she had seen earlier on the horizon. They should almost be there, but if anything, they seemed farther away.

She looked back at the rows of lights on the ship. Jesus God. One, two, *three*. Even from here she could hear those still stranded on her, screaming and crying out for help, saw men hurling themselves from the upper deck into the sea.

The *Titanic* lurched forward, and one of the massive funnels pitched off and crashed into the sea. There was a series of muffled bangs; she felt a shockwave roll across the water; the boilers exploding, she supposed.

The ship tilted straight on end, her stern upward, and her lights, which until then had not flickered for a moment, blinked out at once. They came on again for a single flash, and then she fell utterly to darkness. Her machinery roared down through the hull with a metallic shriek; it was her death cry, the strangest sound Kitty supposed anyone had ever heard in the middle of that vast black ocean.

The great ship hung like that, upright in the water until she broke in two, amidships, and her stern crashed back into the sea, sending up a huge tower of spray. Someone behind her started to whisper the Lord's Prayer.

Kitty closed her eyes to pray as well, like her ma taught her to do when she was a kid, but she couldn't do it. What good had praying ever done her, in the Liberties, or after?

It was a sight that would stay with her forever, the *Titanic* cut in half, the shadow of her stern and splintered upperworks floating in the darkness for what seemed like hours but could not have been more than a minute at most. Then with a swift and slanting dive, the rest of her slid beneath the waters.

For the first time that night, Kitty felt the faintest breeze in the air.

And then it started, the most chilling noise she had ever heard in her life: the cries of people struggling in the ice-cold water; not a hundred separate voices, but one long and continuous moan.

"We have to go back!" she shouted at the quartermaster.

"We can't," he said. "It's too dangerous."

"But those people!"

"You heard him," said a woman with a huge diamond necklace over her silk dressing gown. "We can't go back. We'll get sucked down with her!"

"But she's *down* now. Can't you hear them? That could be your bloody husband out there!"

"There's no more room," someone else said. "We'll sink if we take another soul!"

"They'll swamp the boat and drag us down with them," one of the oarsmen said.

"No, she's right," the woman beside her said. "We have to go back."

"Then you can swim back," the first woman said; and at a signal from the quartermaster, the men at the oars started to row harder, away from the wreck.

Kitty got to her feet, unsteady. "How can you bear to listen to that?" Kitty screamed at him, at all of them. "If we don't go back, you'll be hearing those screams the rest of your lives!"

"Sit down!" another of the women said—she had on a white silk dress.

"No, I won't sit down! I'm not your fecking housemaid now! I'm a human being, same as they are!"

The crew stopped rowing now; they were exhausted. They were drifting in an empty blackness, the shadows of the ice fields all around them, like shapeless beasts.

One of the men at the oars was a stoker—he was still black with coal dust, must have dashed straight out of the boiler room and been ordered into the boat, for all he had on was a singlet in the icy cold. He tried to light a crumpled cigarette he found in his pocket, but he was shaking so hard, he dropped it in the scuppers. Kitty put her eiderdown around his shoulders. He smiled and nodded his thanks at her.

She could still hear them out there.

"God in heaven, can you not hear them?" Kitty said. "For pity's sake, we have to go back!"

The quartermaster's breath froze on the air. He turned on his torch and swung it in the direction of the screams.

"She's right," the stoker said. "We have to go back."

But the other men on the oars shook their heads, sat there hunched over, huddled in blankets; they had done what they had been ordered to do, they weren't going back again now. Kitty turned to the woman beside her. "Are you with me?" She put down her jewelry box and picked up one of the oars.

The woman shoved one of the oarsmen aside. "At least we'll keep warm. Sophie, you can lend a hand too."

"Yes, ma'am."

"Who's Sophie?" Kitty said.

"She's my maid."

Another woman, without a word of English, joined them, two at each oar. The quartermaster took a change of heart and joined the stoker at the other set of oars. They started back toward the wreck.

<hr/>

But it took too long; when they first started rowing, the night had been torn with screaming, but it seemed that with every stroke of the oars, there were fewer and fewer shouts, and by the time they reached the first of the bobbing yellow lifebelts, the quiet was unnerving.

The quartermaster used a gaffe to hook the floating bodies toward the side of the boat. "This one's dead," he said.

"This one too."

"And this one."

Dozens of them. All dead, all of them. "It's no good," someone said.

It was quiet now, horribly quiet; there was just the sound of those at the oars trying to get their breath, the lapping of water against the side of their boat. Even the baby had stopped crying.

"Wait," Kitty said, "I heard something."

It was just a feeble flapping at the water, a hand slapping at the surface, no more than that. The quartermaster shone his torch into the darkness and spotted him among the floating dead, by just the merest movement of his head. He was barely alive, and one of the crewmen hauled him aboard.

Kitty snatched the torch away. Jesus God, she had seen better-looking corpses dead of consumption in the hospital in Dublin. But then he moved again—he was alive somehow—and they laid him in the scuppers. Kitty lay down next to him and put her arms around him.

"What are you doing?" one of the women said, somewhere in the dark.

"I'm warming the poor man up, I am."

"It's not decent!"

"For God's sake woman, he's practically dead!"

Someone threw an eiderdown over them. She realized later it must have been the stoker.

The quartermaster continued with the search, but the man was the only one they found still alive. The silence was utter.

Kitty tried to warm the man they had saved; it was like wrapping her arms around a block of ice, but it had to be done. If they could save even one life, she thought, then that would be something. At first he scarcely moved, but then he started to shiver, shaking so hard she thought he would break a bone.

The quartermaster's torch gave out, so her fellow passengers started burning any scraps they could find—hats, paper, money—hoping that a rescue boat might see them in the darkness.

Meanwhile Kitty lay in the scuppers beside their frozen survivor, staring up at the sky. The stars were like blazing chips of diamond up there, the frozen night endless.

Now she started to shiver as well. *This is it*, she thought. *I'm going to die out here. I was going to do so much with my life. Instead, there's just this. The banshee was right.*

❦

Dawn found them drifting among gray fields of ice.

It was a beautiful sunrise—there were faint pink mares' tails, and a new moon still hung in the sky with its crescent touching the horizon. A full-rigged schooner appeared beside them, then another, all sails set, fishing boats from the Newfoundland banks, Kitty guessed, standing by to help them. She was about to cry out and tell the others, even got herself sitting up for a better look, but as the sun inched higher in the sky, she could see they were not fishing boats at all, but icebergs, dozens of them, huge and peaked and glistening like shark's teeth.

Kitty looked down at the man beside her. He was so pale, she thought he had died in the night, despite their efforts to save him. But then she saw his eyes flicker. He couldn't speak, but somehow he managed to wrinkle the corners of his mouth into a smile.

Last night she had not seen his face clearly enough in the dark, and no one looked quite like themselves anyway, she supposed, not when they were dripping wet and nearly dead. But she recognized him well enough now.

"Lincoln," she said.

CHAPTER 8

The wind picked up with the morning, brushing aside a light mist. The sea rose with it, an icy spray that drenched Kitty as she lay shivering under the eiderdown with Lincoln; soon it was soaked through.

Several of the women were still praying aloud, been at it all night. *He won't help you, girls. At least, he's never helped me. When me dad took the belt to me, or my ma, where was God then?*

Lincoln still lay in her arms. Now and then his lips moved, and he muttered something she couldn't make out—it was the only way she could be sure he was still alive. She supposed it was only a matter of waiting to die anyway; if help was coming, they would have found them by now. As the morning wore on, she wished it could be over. Just fall asleep and die, if that was what it took. If only she could stop her body shaking like this.

She looked up at the others, not one of them moving now, even the ones who had been calling on the Lord. *See, I told you so.* Everyone all slumped against each other on the benches, wrapped in coats or blankets or whatever they had managed to salvage. The quartermaster was up in the bow, his head bowed on his chest, asleep too, or maybe dead of cold.

Around them mountains of ice marched remorselessly across a gray horizon.

And then she saw it, a rocket bursting in the sky. The quartermaster jerked awake at the sound of it, fumbled for his whistle. One of the wraiths on the benches pointed a finger at the horizon. There was a ship. The woman who had helped her at the oars, and Sophie, her maid, started shouting feebly for help. Kitty sat up and joined in. The quartermaster tried to blow his damned whistle, but it was frozen, or he was—they'd never hear that.

"She's stopped," someone said. "Why has she stopped?"

"They want us to go to her," the quartermaster said. "There's too much ice."

He shook the men at the oars awake. They were so stiff, they could barely move. It was going to be slow progress.

But it looked like they would make it after all. The women who had been praying through the night now started thanking the Lord for their deliverance.

Well, and there's a fine thing, Kitty thought. *The first time he's done a damned thing for me. But about time and glad of it, just the same.*

She looked down at Lincoln and smiled. He smiled back, more like a grimace really, but it was the best he could manage, in the circumstance.

CHAPTER 9

The Carpathia

Kitty sat on a bench, the jewelry box still clutched in her arms. The dots on the ice-strewn sea resolved into rowing boats and pulled alongside. She watched the survivors as they were helped up onto the deck, just as she had been an hour or two before. Most of them were women and all so wet and stiff with cold that they could not walk without being supported. They were shivering in dressing gowns, in cloaks and shawls, some even still in their evening dresses. The crew wrapped them in dry blankets and helped them onto benches and chairs; other sailors clustered around them with mugs of hot coffee. Doctors hurried from one to the other. Some were in such a bad way the doctors called for stretchers and had them taken belowdecks to the medical bays, as they had done with Lincoln.

Someone put a glass of brandy in her hand. Her hands were so numb, she could barely hold it. She swallowed some; it was so raw it made her choke as it went down.

She turned her gaze back to the ocean. They were surrounded by icebergs rearing like stark white hills from a vast gray plain. They made the empty sea look crowded.

She heard women wailing for their husbands. Kitty put her fingers in her ears and closed her eyes, couldn't bear it anymore. They all did that when they first got on board; those already on the ship rushed to the gangway as soon as a new boat was sighted, still hoping for a glimpse of husbands or brothers. But there were fewer boats coming now, and almost all the survivors were women, so there were not many joyful reunions.

"Kitty!"

She looked around. Elsie, her head swathed in a bloodied bandage, a blanket round her shoulders, came toward her, arms outstretched. "Flamin' hell. You're alive!"

"Elsie, Holy Mary, I thought you were dead."

They held each other. No words for this.

"Where's Mr. Richardson?"

"I remember he put me on one of the boats, but then I must have blacked out again. I don't remember anything much after that. I reckoned he must've stayed on board. You know what he was like, stickler for the rules."

"Dear God, no."

"He said you saved my life."

"I didn't do anything. He was the one carried you up to the deck."

"Blimey Kit. I can't believe it."

Over Elsie's shoulder Kitty saw two sailors carrying a man inside, a doctor hurrying after them. "Well saints preserve us," Kitty whispered.

Elsie turned around. "One of yours, Kit?"

"Didn't you see who that was? That gangster fella, Flash Jack."

"Doesn't look very flash now, does he?"

"That he doesn't. I wonder where Mrs. Finnegan is?"

"Reckon I can guess."

"It's the dog I feel sorry for," Kitty said.

Everywhere women sat curled in chairs, on benches, in chaise longues, or just curled up on the deck like heaps of jumbled clothes. They had on over-sized sweaters and baggy dresses or had just blankets over them, as they sat looking around in dazed grief; some had children clinging to them; some of them were crying; most stared in awful silence. Many of them had not a word of English, immigrants who had come looking for a new life, and now would have to face a future in a foreign country without their men.

The *Carpathia*'s passengers had given up their cabins and state-rooms; they had even given the survivors their clothes. But there was not enough room for them all. The crew had fixed up beds in the smok-ing rooms and the library, and there were mattresses lying everywhere.

As stewardesses, Elsie and Kitty had been given a cabin in the *Carpathia*'s crew quarters; it was dark and gloomy after the *Titanic*, but they were more than glad of it. When they got there, Kitty collapsed onto the bunk in her clothes, curled her knees up to her chest, and hugged the jewelry casket to her.

Alive. A miracle.

She felt for the key she wore around her neck under her dress and looped it over her head and unlocked the box. Inside were the bits of jewelry that Danny had given her before he took off back to sea, a cheap locket and a ring with a garnet stone.

She pushed them to one side, her fingers closing instead around a cockleshell, one she had kept from that day down at Sandymount, when all those years ago she had taught Tom Doyle to find them. She'd kept two of the shells, silly sentimental girl that she was.

She closed her eyes and slept for twenty-four hours.

<hr />

When she woke and went up on deck, the *Carpathia* was steaming back to New York. They had cleared the last of the ice, but now there was a dense fog.

She went down to the second-class dining room; it had been turned into a hospital to care for the injured and sick. Lincoln was awake; they had him on a mattress on the deck, but by now he was sitting up, drinking soup, and looking greatly recovered. When he saw her, he gave her a lopsided grin.

"Well, Kitty. So there you are. I was afraid you'd found some other devilishly handsome journalist to save."

"Don't be joking now. You're lucky to be alive."

"Then if I'm lucky, why would I be sad about it? I still remember your arms around me. I think that was what gave me reason to hold on."

"I did it for medical reasons."

"Then I'll jump in the sea more often."

"Another five minutes and you'd have frozen, like those other poor souls."

The laughter went out of his eyes. "Is it true what they say, only seven hundred survived?"

"I've asked around the crew, to see if there are other boats that found survivors. The *Carpathia* was the only ship that came to us." She lowered her voice. "Some of the poor women here are hoping that when they get to New York their men will be waiting for them, and no one has the heart to break it to them."

He closed his eyes. "Oh dear God."

"It's mostly women and children that survived."

"Well the officers said us men couldn't get in the boats, though it seemed to me a lot of them went into the sea half-empty. There wasn't enough even if they'd filled them, you know that? Not nearly enough boats for all those on the ship."

"Can you hear that, Lincoln?"

"Is that women crying?"

"It's been going on all morning. There's an Italian woman, she keeps crying out her son's name over and over. The poor woman is demented with grief. I can't stand it."

"You know they locked some of the doors in steerage, because they didn't want third class up on deck until first class had cleared the ship."

"Go on, Lincoln, that's not true."

"I tell you, Kitty, even in a shipwreck there's a rule for the rich and another for the poor. The poor bastards never stood a chance."

She looked at his arm; the doctors had splinted it as best they could; only his fingers stuck out of the bandages. "What's this you've done?"

"I must have hit something when I jumped into the sea. It's not my writing arm, so they can take the whole thing off for all I care." He lifted up the blanket, showed her his leg—another splint, and the ankle purple and twice its size. "It was a long jump from B deck."

"God, Lincoln, and I thought you were skiting. Are you in pain?"

"Not now you're here."

"That's enough of that now. Drink your soup, then get some rest. I'll come by again later."

He caught her wrist. "Doesn't it make you wonder?"

"What are you talking about?"

"Here you are, alive, all those others drowned. Don't you ask yourself why?"

"Because I'm a woman, Lincoln, and they put the women in the boats. It's you that's the miracle here."

"Still, you have to think about it. Life is so fragile, isn't it? God's given you another chance, Kit. What are you going to do with it?"

Kitty shrugged. She'd not thought about it.

"You can't just go back to things as they were."

"Why not? If there is a God up there, I shouldn't think he spends many nights sitting up, worrying about the likes of me."

"Kitty, it's a sign. You're meant for better things than this. Do you not want to make a difference to the world?"

"I've no money and no education, so how am I going to do that?"

"Maybe you need someone to show you how."

"Be like you, you mean?"

"Well, why not?"

"Go on, I can barely write my own name."

"There's a revolution happening, Kitty, and it's time you were part of it. I can see it in you. You're no ordinary woman, and you know it."

She looked in his eyes, the fiercest eyes she had ever seen; it was as if they were lit from within. He believed what he said, no doubt about it, and when she was with him, it was hard not to believe right back.

"Don't go back to the White Star Line. There's a better world for you, Kitty."

"And do what?"

"Stay with me in New York. I'll help you find a new job and a new life."

She pulled her arm free. "I'll think about it," she said.

"Good." That boyish grin. She wondered how many women he had used it on. He had a certain charm about him and no mistake, but charm had been her undoing before, and she didn't survive the sinking of that great ship just to throw herself into the arms of a different kind of disaster.

Oh Kitty, she thought. *Be careful, girl.*

CHAPTER 10

Strong winds followed by heavy seas, seasickness to add to the misery of grief and loss. The survivors on the overcrowded liner kept to their cabins, those that had them. Kitty spent most of her time in the second saloon with Lincoln. He had come down with a fever on the Wednesday morning and started to rave. He was better by the Thursday morning, but the doctors said he would have to be transferred directly to a hospital as soon as the *Carpathia* reached the dock.

It wasn't until the next night that the ordeal finally ended. They battled through choppy seas as they came closer to the coast, then sailed into banks of heavy fog. So they were miles up the Hudson River before the brooding New York skyline finally came into view, backlit by sheet lightning that flickered behind the storm clouds.

Kitty went up on deck and braved the cold and wet, stared up at the Liberty statue as they passed her, gripping Elsie's hand on the rail. Poor Elsie, her bandage was askew and stained brown with old blood; the doctors had told her she would be off to the hospital as well when the ship docked.

"What do you think it means, Elsie? Why us, when so many others died?"

"Blimey I don't know, Irish. Just lucky, I suppose."

"Lincoln said it was a sign."

Elsie puffed out her cheeks. She didn't hold with that kind of talk.

"It doesn't matter how rich you are, does it?" Kitty said. "Or how good you are. Mr. Richardson, Mr. Andrews, even Lord Astor—they all drowned, didn't they?"

"What are you saying, love?"

"There's not much to life, is there? Sometimes you just have to grab it, because you don't know what's going to happen tomorrow."

"We're lucky to be alive, I'll grant you that. As for the rest of it, thinking about it just makes my head ache."

"Do you think you'll go back on the ships?" Kitty said.

"It's me job, what else would I do?"

"Doesn't it seem like you've just been given a second chance and you shouldn't waste it?"

"What is it you're not telling me?" Elsie looked in her face and then gave a knowing smile. "It's your young man, isn't it?"

"He wants me to stay in New York; says he'll look after me, find me a job."

"Does he want to marry you?"

"I doubt it. He told me he doesn't believe in it."

Elsie laughed. "Well of course he doesn't. He's only after one thing, isn't he?"

"What if I don't want to get married either, Elsie?"

"Now listen here, Irish, I'm no prude, and falling in love with a good-looking young man is all very well. But what if you get in the family way with him? That's the thing you've got to think of."

"Oh, I don't have to worry about that."

"What do you mean, love?"

"Just take my word for it. It's the least of my worries."

"You're really thinking about doing this?"

"Maybe. I don't know. What have I to go back to, Elsie, except a boarding house in Southampton and two pounds a week for being a slave to people who want me to feed their damned dogs while they drink champagne in the first-class saloon."

Tugboats streamed toward them across the harbor, and soon they were surrounded. There were bright flashes as photographers shot off magnesium bombs; reporters were shouting questions across the water. The officers on the bridge ignored them, though a few of the passengers leaned on the rails and shouted answers to them. Kitty doubted if anyone could hear anything over the din of the tugs' horns, the drumming of the *Carpathia*'s engines, and the wash of the sea.

The *Carpathia* nudged slowly to her station at the Cunard pier, and the gangways were pushed across. The pier was packed with people—husbands and wives, sons and daughters, brothers and sisters, mothers and fathers, sweethearts. She could make out nurses in capes, uniformed police, a white knot of ambulance surgeons and embalmers, priests, a flock of black-garbed sisters of mercy. *Oh, we shall be needing mercy*, Kitty thought, *and more besides.*

What struck her most was the silence.

They let off the *Carpathia*'s passengers first. The captain knew what would happen when the *Titanic* survivors set foot on dock 54, and he wanted to clear as many passengers as possible first.

There were rows of people sitting under huge hand-painted letters corresponding to the initials of the names of the passengers they had come to meet. None of them knew if their loved ones were dead or alive. Women wept, but quietly, and the sound of the sobbing was more chilling than if they had all been screaming. Rain beat on the covered roof.

Finally, an officer led a sobbing woman passenger down the gangplank. She had an oversized dress that a *Carpathia* passenger had given her and a threadbare blanket around her shoulders. There was a shriek somewhere among the crowd, perhaps someone had recognized her; this was it, the first survivor, now they knew it was real.

Reporters shouted questions at the woman, but Kitty couldn't hear what she said to them, or if she answered them at all.

A low wailing rose from the crowd. It stopped for a moment as Bruce Ismay, the head of the White Star Line, went down the gangway. There was not a sound as he was led away in a cordon of officials; he was followed by a stoker with a huge moustache. Kitty recognized him, he was the one on the oars in her lifeboat.

The wailing started up again, grew steadily louder. It reminded her of those few minutes after the *Titanic* went down. The crying and shouting were almost a panic by the time Kitty went down to the quayside. She had waited for Lincoln; he had insisted she hold his hand as he came down on the stretcher. But as soon as she reached the bottom, she was jostled aside, doctors and nurses rushed in, reporters too, and he was hurried away through the crowd toward a waiting ambulance.

He reached out a hand through the crowd. "Find me in the hospital, Kitty! Don't you leave me now! Remember what I told you!"

There were others around him now. She guessed they were his mother and father—they looked suitably grim in a prosperous sort of way. There was a young girl too, his sister or his girlfriend. She knew nothing about him, she realized. Really, he was just some stranger she met on a boat.

The rich had taxicabs waiting outside the dock. Women, bent almost double with grief, were being helped into cabs by stone-faced gentlemen; couples clung to each other, with tears streaming down their faces. Newspaper writers, with pier passes stuck in their hatbands, were everywhere. One of them asked her what she remembered of the sinking. She stared at him as if he were talking to her in another language.

Elsie appeared at her side, steered her through the crowds. The White Star Line had a hotel in the city for them, she said.

"Let's get out of here, lovey."

A group of New Yorkers had collected clothing of every sort, had brought it down to the pier and spread it out on tables; it looked like a giant rummage sale, used clothes of every kind, for men and for women. Elsie held up an ankle-length dress with a lace collar and shook her head. "Blimey, I reckon this was in fashion when Queen Victoria was a girl." But there wasn't much else to laugh about—a gray day, and the memories of what had happened on this very dock the night before still haunted them both.

The woman who had almost thrown herself off the dock, shrieking a man's name; the small boy being led away by city officials, screaming for his mother, as he had been screaming ever since they pulled him from the lifeboat; the empty face of a young woman who spoke not a word of English, standing stock still in the middle of the dock as it emptied around her, staring up at the ship as if she could by force of willpower make her husband appear on the gangway.

I wonder what I look like, Kitty thought. *My hair a fright, wearing hand-me-downs taken off a damp table, with just a few cents in my purse that White Star official gave me last night to tide me over.*

They want me to sail to Southampton on the next ship out, go back to being a stewardess again, as if nothing happened.

"Elsie," she said, "I can't do this."

"What're you talking about, love?"

"I'm not going back to work for White Star."

"Love us, you're not going to go chasing after that fancy boy, are you?"

"I am, and you're probably right; it's a mad thing I'm doing, but my mind's made up. Do you have a few coins for a cab?"

Elsie dug in her pocket, forced some coins into Kitty's hand, everything White Star had given her. "You'll be needing this, then."

"I don't want your money, Elsie, you're as broke as I am."

"Take it anyway." She hugged her. "Where are you going?"

"To the hospital, I suppose. After that, who knows?"

"Promise me you'll stay in touch, Irish. Write to me care of White Star and send me your address, all right?"

"I'll do that, I promise."

"You just walk off, they won't take you back, you know. You'll be stranded here."

"I'll take my chance."

"Oh God love us, Kit. You're such a pretty thing. Take care of yourself."

Kitty walked through the arch and off the pier; there was a hansom cab outside, and she told the cabbie to take her to St. Vincent's Hospital. *Well, this is a big chance I'm taking, no mistake*, she thought as she climbed in. She had taken a chance with Danny, and he broke her heart, but he got her out of the Liberties, so she reckoned she had come out square on that deal.

Lincoln Randolph said she could make a difference in the world. *Let's see if he meant it.*

CHAPTER 11

Greenwich Village, Christmas 1914

Winter in Washington Square. A fine snow drifted from a sky the color of lead, dusting passersby and glistening on the black asphalt in long, cold lakes. The shop windows on Sixth were festive with red berries and ribbons and tinsel-decked trees; taxicabs scuttled toward Broadway; holiday crowds surged into the street from glowing subway entrances, laden with shopping.

Kitty went into Polly's on West Fourth. It was steamy hot inside, and she whipped off her hat and coat and headed for one of the corner tables where Netty was waiting for her. She was drinking coffee—it was what they all drank over here, no tea in America and certainly not in Greenwich Village.

"Kitty, where have you been?"

"They kept me working late at the office again. I swear to God, they go on and on about freeing workers from tyrant bosses, then they treat me like their personal slave." She wrapped her hands around the coffee mug to warm them.

"That bad?"

"I shouldn't complain, I know. I can type, I can even spell now, heaven help us. I guess I should be grateful, but Mother Mary, they get their pound of flesh."

"Did you read the book I gave you?"

"I haven't had time. I get home from work, I cook my tea, I fall asleep. I'd have more free time if I worked in a cotton field."

"Well it's almost Christmas."

"That's no consolation, Net. Looks like I'll be spending it on my own again."

"Where's Linc?"

"Still in Mexico. If I want his attention, I'll have to grow a moustache and revolt against the government."

"I saw his last piece in the *Union*. It was brilliant."

"He's brilliant, all right, he's just never here."

Kitty watched the snow swirling in the street. She'd been in America almost three years now, but she still wasn't used to it, the same language sure, but they had different words for everything; she'd learned that a scone was a biscuit, that sidewalk meant a pavement, and that autumn was fall. Still, she had a steady job—the pathway to her golden dream, as Lincoln had put it—and she was a part of Bohemia. Her apartment in Greenwich Village probably wasn't a great deal better than a tenement in the Liberties, but somehow it felt like a step up.

Because of Lincoln.

Though of course she could just be kidding herself there.

"So, when is he coming back?" Netty asked her.

"Should be home any day. That's what Henry said."

"You must be excited to see him again. . . . Kitty?"

She shrugged. How should she say this? Netty had known Lincoln a lot longer than she had; they'd been school friends, he had told her, back in Boston.

"What is it, Kit?"

"I don't know. I hear these stories. Sometimes Henry and the lads are in his office, laughing about something, and as soon as I walk in, it stops. And there's gossip."

"I shouldn't listen to gossip if I were you."

"But I do. Is it true, Net?"

Netty didn't have to answer, she only had to drop her eyes and look the other way, which is just what she did. So, it was true. "Kit, you're with a man like Lincoln, you have to make allowance for the way he is. It's not like being in Ireland. This is Greenwich Village. It's free love, isn't it?"

Free love, isn't that what Lincoln was always talking about? Kidding her about being pagan, about her old-world sensibilities, whenever they had a fight. Once he had called her a reactionary—it was months before she learned what the word meant.

He made free love sound like it was political, like getting married was something only the bosses did to keep the workers down. Well maybe he was right—he was clever, and he knew about things like that. And sure she did want to be a Bohemian, but when he said these things, talked about nobody owning anyone else, she thought he was talking about *other* people.

"A man's just a man, isn't he?" Netty said.

"Why is it different for a man?"

"That's the whole point, isn't it? You could take a lover while he's gone."

"But I don't want to!"

"Oh Kit, Mexico's a long way away, and he's coming home to you at the end of the day, isn't he?"

Danny all over again, Kitty thought. She shouldn't complain, though, should she? Danny got her away from Dublin, and Lincoln had got her away from being a maid. So, what was the problem?

The problem, she supposed, was that when she came here, she had dreamed of a second chance at life, and that didn't mean being a secretary sleeping alone in a drafty flat every night, waiting for another cheating man to come home.

"Do you love him, Kit?"

"What sort of girl would I be if I didn't?"

"Take my advice. You can't be a new woman and still think like our mothers did. What would be the point of that? Besides, there's this." She opened her bag and let Kitty have a peek.

"Oh no, not again."

Netty lowered her voice, though it was bedlam around them. "I thought it would look very nice in Gimbels' display window. Are you coming with me?"

"I don't know, Net."

"Come on. Just one brick is not enough for them to understand that we're serious."

"Oh Netty, if I spend any more time in prison, I'll lose my job."

"Henry won't fire you. They're on our side at the newspaper."

"He may be in favor of revolution, but he still pays my wages, and he gets an awful temper if there's no one there to bring him coffee and type his letters."

"You tell him from me, if he's not part of the solution, he's part of the problem. If he acts tough, get Linc to talk to him."

"Do you think all this is doing any good? You remember that march we went to in Washington? We got spat at and punched and kicked, and the police just stood by and watched. And what did the papers say? They called it a parade and talked about the hats we wore. What did that magazine say? 'For the marchers the ballot was important, but shopping is rarely far from a woman's mind.'"

"Are you going to give up, Kit?"

"No, I'm not giving up. You know I won't do that."

"Good. Most women in this country are asleep. It's time we woke them up, and this is the way to do it. Now finish your coffee and let's go."

They went outside. The cold was biting. As they were putting on their gloves, Kitty said, "Net, can I ask you one thing?"

"I think I know what it is. You're going to ask me about Linc and me, aren't you?"

"Did you?"

"It was all such a long time ago. He's coming home to you now. Isn't that all that matters?"

It was thrilling to ride the El—the elevated railway—as it curved through Manhattan's spine, from Greenwich and the theater district and Broadway right up to the Bronx. The carriages were often just a few feet away from the windows of office buildings and apartments, surely there was nothing quite like it in the world. It was spectacular; it was astonishing—unless you were underneath it, with the oil and grime dripping on your hair.

As they rattled up Sixth Avenue, Netty put her feet on the leather seat opposite her and gave Kitty a wink of encouragement. *It was all right for her*, Kitty thought. For all Netty's talk of Bohemia, her father owned half of Westchester County; she didn't have to worry about a job.

They got off at Herald Square. Gimbels took up half a city block on Thirty-Third, a block from Macy's. The streets were still packed with shoppers, the square clogged with motor cars and hansom cabs and trolley cars. It was perfect.

She and Netty stood outside one of the display windows, waiting for their moment, pretending to admire the latest fashion. For Kitty it was not just pretense; she was mesmerized by it.

"Are you ready, Kit?"

"Not this window, Net."

"Why not?"

"I like that dress. Do you see the one? What do they call that material again?"

"War crinoline."

"Well, if that's the worst that can come out of the war, then I'm all for it. I never had the figure for those other dresses. At least there's no more of those hobble skirts, I could never stand the damned things."

"Can we get on, Kit? We're not here to window shop; we're here to window *break*."

"If this was Dublin, they'd be scandalized."

Netty dragged her to the next window, but they saw a policeman watching them from the other side of the street, and Netty, linking arms with Kit, pretended to walk on.

A woman came out of the front doors and walked straight across the sidewalk in front of them. Her chauffeur was carrying her bags and boxes. Kitty caught a whiff of expensive perfume, and a vision in fox fur. The driver fumbled to open the back door of the Duesenberg without dropping the woman's shopping.

I know her, Kitty thought. She remembered a lifeboat, adrift among the icebergs; that night, the woman had been huddled inside a blanket, but underneath she had on a huge diamond necklace over her silk dressing gown.

"You heard him. We can't go back. We'll get sucked down with her!"

"Kitty!"

She turned around. Netty opened her bag, took out the brick, showed her the two posters she'd rolled up beside it. "Are you ready?"

"Go on with you then."

Netty hefted the brick in her right hand. She saw the concierge look over and shout a warning. Several women turned around and saw what was happening and started to shy away. "Votes for women!" Netty shouted, and threw the brick.

The front window of Gimbels seemed to melt inward; a woman screamed, everyone else seemed frozen to the spot. Netty pushed a poster into Kitty's hand and unfolded her own, held it up over her head. "Votes for women!"

Kitty did the same. "Votes for women!"

Gimbels' concierge ran over, grabbed Netty by the arm, and wrestled her to the ground. Kitty ran into the road, waving her poster at the passing motor cars and cabs. "Votes for women!"

The policeman was blowing his whistle; men were shouting abuse at them—she was accustomed to that. What she wasn't expecting was to see the copper get out his truncheon and go at Netty; she had her arms pinned, she was a woman, what was he thinking?

The first blow came down on her back, the other on her shoulders. Netty screamed and curled into a ball on the sidewalk. Even the concierge looked horrified.

Kitty dropped her poster and jumped on the copper's back; he yelled and fell on the icy sidewalk. She pummeled him with her fists, shouting curses at him; the concierge tried to drag her off, but she was having none of it.

Netty lay sobbing and howling on her side, there among the snow and the broken glass. Kitty was dragged away by the concierge, still yelling curses. She'd had enough of men hitting women, bullies they were, the lot of them—it was things like that that made her lose her temper.

⊷

The *Union*'s offices were on Fourteenth Street, as far north as you could go and still be in the Village. It was a fine day, cold and blue, and Henry and one of the writers and a junior editor were playing baseball in the alley. There was still a bit of snow on the ground, the last melt, last night's frost still shining on the rubbish cans.

Henry was shaping up to pitch when he saw her. He turned around and took off his mitt. "Where the hell have you been?"

"I had a bit of trouble last night. They only just let me out of the hoosegow."

His expression softened when he saw the pulpy bruise on her cheek. "What was it this time?"

"I didn't do anything, I swear. I was just standing there."

"I'm not the judge, Kitty. Tell me."

"Friend of mine rearranged a window display at Gimbels."

"What with?"

"A brick, if you must know. A brown one."

"That's all well and good, but I have a newspaper to get out, and where's my secretary?"

"Yes, I can see you're working your fingers to the bone, Mr. Liddell, but these things happen."

Henry nodded to the others. "Lunch is over. Back to work fellas." They fetched their coats and went back inside, leaving him and Kitty alone in the alley.

"Are you going to fire me?" she said.

"Now, why would I do that? Go home, Kitty, take the day off. That's a nasty bruise you have there."

"I've had worse."

"I'm sure you have." As she turned to go, he said, "It's not the way, Kitty."

"It's the only way." She wanted to just drop down on the cobblestones; every bone ached, the cops had given her a good kicking this time, but at least she wasn't in the hospital like Netty. "Have you heard from Linc?"

"He should be back any day. I need him to get over to Montana to cover the miners' strike."

"No rest for him then when he gets back?"

"He's a journalist; he can rest when he's dead." She remembered what Lincoln had told her on the *Titanic*: *"No man owns me, I won't allow it."* Even Lincoln Randolph had his price, though in his case the price was glory, not money. "Now go on, Kitty. I'll see you tomorrow."

"Thanks, Henry."

"And Kitty. No more bricks."

CHAPTER 12

She had been in New York almost three years, but it still overwhelmed her sometimes, looking up at the dizzying buildings and wondering if they were about to topple down, turning a corner and nearly getting her clothes torn off by the violent winds.

And the shops! It was not just that these Americans wanted to buy everything, it was the way they constantly thought of brand-new things to buy. If it was new, if it could be plugged into the wall, if you could wear it, they wanted it.

Greenwich Village wasn't like that, or at least, not as much as the rest of New York. It was a quaint jumble of coffeehouses, Italian groceries with sagging awnings, eighteenth-century gables, and Dutch attics with low rents. It was the home of artists and writers and the glamorous poor, as Kitty thought of them, men like Lincoln with disheveled hair and cheap suits and owlish glasses who talked about socialism and Communism and Dadaism, and other isms she had never heard of. It was the heart of Bohemian New York, the place you came to shock the rest of America.

Lincoln loved it there and in turn, the Village loved Lincoln right back.

Kitty crossed Washington Square, past the tea shops and studios on the south side, stopped to peer in at the window of the Peculiar Flower Shop, which didn't look at all like a shop but like an English country garden that had been picked up and dropped right there in the middle of the city. She went up an outside staircase, so rickety and creaky she was sure one day it would all come down and take her with it. She tripped over the black-and-white cat that was always sunning itself there and would never get out of the way even when it saw her coming.

The corridor was dim and quiet so that, even at this time of the afternoon, the blue flame in the gas jet in front of their room looked like a beacon on a gloomy sea. She fumbled for her key and went in.

Lincoln's studio was just a large room with a painted iron bedstead in one corner and was full of things that he had picked up on his travels and simply dropped on the floor and forgot about when he got home; some cow horns, a chipped vase almost as tall as her that could have been rescued from a Ming emperor's palace or from a vicarage, a pair of brown boxing gloves.

There was a letter pushed under the door. She looked at the postmark. It was from England, and she smiled and took it over to the table by the window to read it in the light.

There was a gas range with a kettle, and first she boiled some water to make herself coffee. For a moment she caught a glimpse of herself in the cracked mirror; Jesus God, she looked a sight, curls all astray across her face, a darkening bruise the size of a small orange on her cheekbone, just like her ma those times her daddy had taken the belt to her.

Only one thing to do, Kitty, my girl; that's avoid looking in the mirror.

She sat down with her mug of coffee, tore open the letter, and read it through quickly once, then again, taking her time over it.

> *Hello Irish,*
> *I hope this letter finds you well. You sounded a bit down*
> *when you wrote last time. I do worry about you, girl.*

Sounds like a funny thing to say I reckon, I never knew you for very long, it's funny how we're still in touch after so long, I suppose it's going through such a tragedy together. But I also felt like you and I could have been best friends if we had met each other before and I'm sorry we didn't get to spend more time together.

So I've got some news! That nice young fella I told you about, Bert, well he's asked me to marry him so we are going to tie the knot at Easter at the church in Hackney. I'd love you to be there and be my matron of honor, but I'll understand if you can't make it, it is a long way to come.

We are both very happy. He's a lovely young man and he treats me very nice. His dad has the local grocer's shop and he works there, delivering groceries and going to the market every morning. We are going to live with his parents at first until we get enough money together for a place of our own.

But that's not all! I'm going to be a nurse. I've had enough of being at sea, and Bert thinks it's getting danger-ous now, he says that one day the Germans will try and sink a British ship, the way things are going. I think he's right. Anyway I didn't want to be making beds and car-rying trays all my life.

Well, that's it for now. Do write soon and tell me what you're up to. Did you get my Christmas card? I sent it weeks ago. I hope you have a merry Christmas, I'll be thinking of you.

Your friend,
Elsie.

Kitty tucked the letter back in its envelope and stared out of the Dutch windowpanes at the bare, dreary yard across the way, at the crumbling bricks of the house next door. An ancient ivy vine, gnarled and decayed at the roots, climbed halfway up the wall. It had been in shadow most of the day, and the tenacious crystals of last night's frost still clung to the branches.

I wonder what it would be like to have a porch, a long garden, a view of the sea, listen to the waves at night instead of the couple downstairs fighting all the time.

There was just a single ivy leaf on the vine, rust-red at its stem, its edges tinged with the yellow of decay at the tip. It clung on, though, waiting for summer. How did it know the sun would be back? It couldn't, could it? It was just sheer bloody-mindedness that kept it hanging on, that was what Elsie would call it.

She heard whistling on the stairs. She would know that whistle anywhere. Lincoln threw open the door and stood there, grinning. He had a sombrero on his head, and he was not just tanned, he was mahogany, the most unlikely thing she had ever seen in the middle of a New York winter.

She ran up and threw her arms around him. He laughed at first, and swung her around, but then he saw the bruises on her face, and he dropped his bags on the floor and held her at arm's length, and the grin fell away.

"Kitty, what happened?"

"It's nothing," she said, and tried to hide her face in his shoulder.

"Those bastards," he said.

"It looks worse than it is. God, it's good to see you again! You've been gone forever."

"When did it happen?"

"I don't want to talk about it. I'll make you coffee." She twisted free and went to the range, put water in the ancient kettle.

"I told you, Kitty, you have to stop this."

"You told me to be a part of the struggle. I'm struggling." She crossed back to him and put a finger to his lips, put her arms around him, nestled her face into his chest. "God, I thought you were never coming home. Look at you, how brown you are. And what's this?" There was a livid scar on his forehead, freshly healed.

"I fell off a horse."

"What in God's name were you doing riding a horse?"

"I didn't get it riding a horse; I got it falling off a horse. God, I've missed you, Kitty." He pulled her closer, kissed her.

"I look a fright."

"You look damned good to me." He kissed her again, put both hands on her bottom, walked her backward, fell on top of her on the bed. He started to fumble with her clothes. The kettle boiled, and the whistle screamed. She pushed him off her.

"What's wrong?"

"The kettle, you don't hear it? And you've only just walked in the door."

"I missed you."

She took the kettle off the range. "Three months I haven't had a word from you, and now you walk in here and want to have your way."

"Is that wrong?"

"Well, you can at least take me to dinner first. I've been sitting in here on my own night after night while you've been out chasing Mexican bandits and God knows what else. My turn for some fun."

"You can be so bourgeois, Kitty."

"Well, heaven help us. I almost get violated by a scribbler in a sombrero who can't even stay on a horse, and suddenly I'm the one that's ridiculous."

Lincoln grinned. "Okay, baby. I guess all that can keep until later."

"I've never known it not to."

"You better get changed then. Time I got reacquainted with the Village, I guess."

"Every great fortune is a fundamental wrong. I don't give a damn about these so-called philanthropists. Anyone who gives a lot of money to the poor must have robbed them first . . . poverty is only the result of the workers not getting proper reward for their labor."

Lincoln had had some beers, and he'd forgotten about any kind of violation now, except that committed by the ruling classes. He was in full song. They were sitting in a cavernous, smoke-filled room at the rear of the Black Cat, and the noise was deafening, a joyous roar that bounced off the high rafters and the whitewashed brick walls. There was nothing to absorb the sound of hundreds of Lincolns shouting their vision of the brave new world that was coming.

Henry sat there, smoking and drinking whiskey, a tired smile on his face, like he'd heard it all before. Most likely he had. Kitty didn't know the man Lincoln was arguing with, some friend of Henry's who had dared to suppose that the world would collapse without some degree of private enterprise.

Lincoln fumbled to light another cigarette and leaned across the table. "The profit motive in the world economy is the cause for the war in Europe."

"But someone has to contain German militarism—"

"German militarism has nothing to do with it! Without a profit motive, Britain and France would not get caught up in this war. They own the world economy, and now Germany wants a piece of it. That's what this is about. Money."

Henry looked across the table at Kitty and gave her a wry smile. Henry loved politics but he wasn't *in love* with it, not like Lincoln was. He held up the bottle of wine, and she nodded. He refilled her glass.

"Sooner or later American boys will be fighting in Europe," Lincoln said.

"That won't happen."

"You don't think so? If that's what you think, you don't understand basic economics."

"So you think pacifism and appeasement are the answer?"

"No, what I'm saying is, why do we have a world where the poor have to pay so the rich won't lose their money? I think we need a war all right, but not a war in Europe; we need a class war, a war against the capitalists. If the workers are going to fight for something, they should fight for themselves!"

"And what about women?" Kitty said.

The two men stopped arguing and stared at her. "What?" Lincoln said.

"Shouldn't women fight as well? There's hundreds of thousands of us all across America; we're overworked and underpaid. It's men who have all legal rights over us and over our children. It's men who control our economic existence. It's men who hold the deeds to our property. Shouldn't we fight as well?"

Lincoln just stared at her, bleary-eyed.

Henry pulled his chair back. "I think she has you there, gentlemen. Now it's about time I get home, or I will definitely be in the firing line with the woman in my life. Thanks for an entertaining evening."

His friend—Kitty never discovered his name—decided to leave with him. After they had gone, Lincoln finished his beer and then stared at the froth in the bottom of his glass, looked disappointed that the argument was over.

The pianist started playing the latest fox-trot for a party of girls and young men from uptown. They had looked as if they were eager to dance all night, and after the first few bars, they all jumped to their feet.

"Too noisy in here," Lincoln said. "Let's go and get something to eat."

He stumbled when they reached the street, and she took his arm. It was bitter cold, and there was ice on the sidewalk. They walked past the Brevoort; at this time of night most of the uptowners were heading home. She saw a well-dressed couple get into a taxi; Kitty looked back over her shoulder at them for a moment, then walked on as fast as she could.

"Who was that?" Lincoln said.

"I thought I recognized him."

"Did you?"

"He was one of my passengers, on the *Titanic*."

"That was Flash Jack Finnegan."

"If you knew who it was, why did you ask me?"

"Just wondered how you knew him, that's all. Forget about it."

She wondered about that exchange later. Was Lincoln jealous? He had never shown any sign of it before. She didn't mind at all if he was, but it was always hard to tell what went on behind that lopsided smile.

━━◆━━

They walked a block to Fifth Avenue, a dark downstairs café; no Saks frocks and diamond bracelets and evening suits down here. This was the artistic set; younger, shabbier, immeasurably more interesting. There were girls, lots of girls, in bright-colored dresses, artists' models and actresses and mistresses and poets, girls with slender arms and pinched faces and Joan of Arc bobs, all of them smoking cigarettes.

A waiter found them a table, and Lincoln stared vacantly at the menu and ordered yet another beer. He looked up at her as if he were seeing her for the first time that evening. "That's a pretty dress."

"You noticed."

"You haven't worn it before."

"It's the latest fashion."

"You're showing a lot of leg."

"Just for you, Linc darlin'."

"Where did you get it?"

"Macy's. It's the only store Netty and I haven't thrown a brick at, so they're still nice to us. Cost me a month's wages."

"God, you're beautiful."

"So beautiful that you leave me at home unchaperoned for months at a time. Aren't you worried I'll find myself a lover?"

He shrugged. "I don't own you, Kitty."

"That's not the point, though, is it?"

"I'm not a nine-to-five man, honey. I'm a journalist. These pieces I did in Mexico, a lot of people read them. I've got a reputation now. I can't write things like that sitting at home, can I?"

It was true; Lincoln had become a minor celebrity, not only in Greenwich, but in the whole New York literary scene. He was being uncharacteristically modest; it was not only his dispatches from Mexico that had earned him his stripes; his piece on the *Titanic* sinking had been featured in the *Saturday Evening Post*, and for a time he had been feted with interviews by almost every newspaper in America.

The waiter brought his beer. Kitty had a champagne, "shampoo" as Netty called it. Lincoln took out a silver cigarette case, offered her one, and she took it. He raised an eyebrow at that.

"Well if you don't want me to smoke, don't offer me one."

"You've changed," he said.

"Wasn't that what you wanted?"

He smiled and took a sip of beer. "You know Henry was talking to me earlier tonight. He said he has some other things lined up for me."

"I know, the strike in Montana. He told me."

"No, that won't come to anything. Besides, I've told him I won't be going anywhere for him for a while."

Kitty waited. He took off his jacket, sat there in his braces, smoking. He always took his time to deliver bad news.

Finally: "I'm going to Europe, Kitty."

She drank her champagne, slammed the glass on the table. She hated it when she acted like this, couldn't help herself. "Europe?"

"This war in France, it's only just started. Mexico and Villa and Zapata, that's not going to mean anything in a few months. There's only one place for a man like me."

"How long will you be gone?"

"How long does a war last?" He leaned across the table. "I just have to be in the right place at the right time."

"I guess you'll do whatever you have to do."

Almost casually: "Come with me."

She wasn't sure she had heard him say it. "Come with you?"

"Sure. Why not?"

"You don't mean that."

"I thought you'd like the idea."

"You're drunk."

"I missed you so much these last couple of months. You were all I could think about."

He always looked so earnest when he said these things, she thought. It was hard not to believe him.

"Enough with typing Henry's bloody letters and showing off your legs for his advertisers when they come to the office. Enough of throwing bricks through shop windows for your conscience."

"It's nothing to do with my conscience!"

"We can write together. I know all the right editors. I can show you how it's done. I can *teach* you. You won't change the world breaking shop windows. You do it by changing people's minds, by writing the things they read in the newspapers. It's newsprint, not bricks, that will change the world, Kitty."

"I'll talk to you in the morning when you're sober."

"No, you'll talk to me now, Kitty O'Kane. Will you come with me?"

"You're mad."

"Maybe I am. But are you brave?"

He took off his glasses and grinned at her. Oh, that lopsided grin, that was how he always got his way in things. She kissed him right there in front of everyone, and a few people laughed and cheered, and afterward Lincoln whooped and slapped his knee and told anyone who would listen that they were going to be the best two damned writers in the whole world.

And then he shouted at the waiter for another beer and another glass of shampoo. No, damn it, bring another bottle.

Lincoln stumbled as he went up the stairs. He told her he needed to stop for a rest and then almost instantly fell asleep right there on the steps. If it had been summer, she would have left him out there, but it was winter, and he would freeze to death, so she slapped him awake and hauled him bodily the rest of the way to the landing and finally got him back on his feet. She had to hold him propped against the wall with one hand while she fumbled with the key to the studio with the other.

Jesus God, it was freezing out there, and here she was sweating like it was a hot day in June. "I swear to God, Linc, this is the last time I bring you home drunk."

He mumbled something back at her.

"Sure and I can't understand what you're saying."

He put his arms around her; he was a dead weight; she stumbled across the room with him, picking up speed until they reached the bed, and she fell on it, him on top of her. He gave a laugh, a low rumble deep in his chest, and started to fumble with her skirts.

"You can't be serious, Linc." His hands were everywhere, but somehow she managed to squirm out from underneath him.

"Kitty . . . I missed you . . ."

"Maybe you did, but you're no good to me in this state."

She got up and closed the door, lit one of the gas lamps, then came back to the bed. He was fast asleep. She stripped off his clothes, stared at him naked; God he was a fine-looking man, and she wouldn't have minded some strong arms around her tonight. He put out a hand, reached for her, and she was about to cuddle into him when she heard him murmur something, a name, a woman's name. She couldn't quite make it out, but it sounded Spanish.

Spanish, like that language they talked in Mexico.

It was late the next morning when he stirred, grunting like a bear and peering around like he was trying to see through thick fog. Kitty had been awake for hours, watched him with one elbow resting on her pillow, like he was something exotic, but dangerous, in a bell jar.

"God, how much did I drink?"

"The bar out of beer. Had to send to Canada for more."

"My head. Did I do anything stupid?"

"You asked me to marry you, don't you remember?"

The look on his face. "Did I?"

"No, but you should have done."

"You've a wicked sense of humor."

"Is that what it is?"

"I remember going to the Black Cat. It gets a bit hazy after that."

"Do you remember meeting Henry there? He had some friend of his with him."

"Right, yes. Wait a minute. I've got it now. It was his brother-in-law."

"Well don't expect any invitations to meet the rest of the family anytime soon. Then we went to another bar. You were complaining of a terrible thirst. Do you remember that?"

"Vaguely."

"You told me you were going to Europe, and then you asked me to come with you." She pulled back the covers, got up, and went to the range, found the coffee pot, and put it on the stove. "Jesus, it's cold!"

She could feel him watching her. "It's all right, I won't hold you to it. I know you didn't mean it."

"Perhaps I did."

"No, you didn't, Linc."

"Come here, Kit." She came back to bed, and he pulled her toward him. "You're all I've thought about these last two months."

"With all those dark-eyed *señoritas* everywhere you went?"

She waited for him to deny it. Instead, he said, "There's no woman makes me feel like you do."

"Oh Lincoln, you've kissed the Blarney all right."

"I mean it, Kitty. I might have been drunk last night, but this morning I'm sober, and I still want you to come to Europe with me. Drunk or sober, I don't say things I don't mean."

He pulled her down onto the pillows, and she felt him move his weight on top of her, easing himself between her legs. "God, you're the sweetest thing, Kit. I've never seen any woman as beautiful as you."

She closed her eyes, and he lifted up her nightdress; it was so good to feel his skin next to hers again, have a man's hands on her. Life could get awful lonely sometimes.

His fingers traced ancient scars. "Don't," she said. "They're ugly."

"They're not ugly. They're a part of you."

"They're ugly to me."

She let him do as he wanted, wrapped her arms and legs around him, drew him in. Was he lying about taking her with him? Danny had said he'd write, and he never did, and maybe Lincoln was the same. Still, she would deal with tomorrow when it came.

She felt his stubble on her neck, his warmth inside her. He kissed her, and she kissed him back and then made love to him while the coffee pot bubbled dry on the stove.

CHAPTER 13

Cunard Pier 54

A persistent cold rain was falling, mingled with snow. Lincoln put his arms around her, whispered something she couldn't hear with the porters yelling and people around her shouting and calling out good-byes. So different from the last time she had been here, that dreadful hush, all the people waiting in rows under those stark white letters.

"As soon as I'm settled, and I know I have things worked out, I'll send you a telegram. All right?"

She nodded, knowing that he wouldn't.

"You have the money for the fare now. Don't lose it."

His glasses had steamed over, and he took them off and wiped them on a handkerchief. He looked so young without them.

"If I don't see you again," she said, "thank you for everything you've done for me. You changed my life even if you don't know it."

"What are you talking about, Kit? I'll see you in a month, no more than two."

"Yes, but you know. If something happens."

"Nothing is going to happen to me."

"I don't mean that. I mean if you change your mind, I'll understand."

"I'm not going to change my mind, Kitty."

"But if you do."

"Just give me a few weeks to get settled, all right? I'll send for you." He held her again, the liner blasting its horn, any moment they would be pulling up the gangways. He let her go, bent down, and picked up his suitcase.

"Good-bye, Linc."

"I'll see you soon."

She watched him run up the gangway, but she didn't stay to see if he stopped at the rails to turn and wave. She ran outside, found a hansom, and jumped in the back. She sat there behind the portly, asthmatic cabby; she couldn't feel her nose it was so cold, stared at the horse's skinny haunches, shiny with rain. The cab headed toward the Village at a trot.

So what now for Kitty O'Kane? She wasn't the same girl that had left the Liberties; she had avoided the kips and the factories, and now here she was alone again in New York, but at least she had a job in an office and no drunken husband or hungry mouths to feed.

It wasn't much, but it was something. Besides, what did she think would happen? All that talk about changing the world, women getting the vote, her writing for fancy magazines, marrying a man who wouldn't beat her, living in a nice house. Well it was a fine dream, but it wasn't going to happen that easy.

She looked over her shoulder, saw the smoke pouring from the funnels of the great ship as she made her way up the Hudson, thought about Lincoln, in his homburg and his overcoat, heading down to steerage. He probably never gave her a second thought.

CHAPTER 14

"He wrote to you?" Netty said, with a kind of awe in her voice, as if the kaiser himself had sent her a Christmas card.

"A telegram and two letters."

"*Two* letters? Well there's a first for everything, I guess."

"I suppose so."

They were in Romany Marye's on Christopher Street, sitting at one of the wooden benches in the corner. They said Marye used to be an anarchist; whether she was or she wasn't, these days she made wonderful goulash, and it was cheap too. The restaurant was full of scruffy people who wrote, or wanted to, or painted, or had great thoughts. *I'll never paint or have great thoughts*, Kitty supposed, *but at least I can pay for my coffee.*

"So are you going to England?"

"Why not? He's kept his word. I'll keep mine." She could see it on Netty's face; she thought it was a bad idea. No one among his friends had thought she and Lincoln would last this long. "He says he'll teach me to be a journalist."

"You need proper schooling to do that."

"That's what I said to him. But you know what he's like. Still, that's the bargain. I told him I won't go just to be his mistress."

It was spring, but it was still biting cold outside and not much warmer in the restaurant. Netty pulled the collar of her coat up around her chin. They watched a thin young man with a threadbare scarf, bent over a bowl of soup, spooning up the broth with something like desperation.

"Who's that?" Kitty asked her.

"His name's O'Neill. Marye says he's a playwright, but I heard he dropped out of his course at Harvard. He's always in here. He never pays for his meals; Marye's told him he can pay her back when he sells one of his plays. She'll be waiting until she's old and gray if you ask me."

Netty's laugh turned into a hacking cough, and she winced.

"Are you all right, Net?"

"Got this cough, and I can't seem to shake it off. I've no heating in the studio, and winter just seems to go on forever."

"Perhaps you should move back home for a while."

"Oh, Daddy would love that. 'I *told* you so.' Besides, I don't think he'd take me back, not after what happened. How can a man not post bail money for his own daughter? Three days he made me sleep in that lockup." Netty put a hand on Kitty's. "If you must go to Europe, go somewhere warm."

Another fit of coughing, her cheeks almost purple as she gagged for breath. When the fit was over, she looked mortally embarrassed.

"You sure you're okay?"

"It's nothing, Kit. So when do you leave?"

"The *Lusitania* sails in a couple of weeks. Linc says he'll meet me in Liverpool."

"Aren't you afraid of the German submarines?"

"They wouldn't dare. Not a passenger ship. Besides, I've already had my sinking, thank you very much. It couldn't happen again."

"I don't know that I'd be willing to take the chance right now."

"You're thinking he's not worth it."

Netty looked unutterably sad. Kitty wondered what had passed between her and Lincoln before she had come along. "Well, there's nothing for me in New York," Kitty said.

"Do you love him very much?"

Kitty was about to say, of course, but she stopped herself. "I don't know," she said, and that sounded much more like the truth. How did any girl ever know if she was in love? Sometimes perhaps it was just telling yourself you were, because there was nothing better on offer.

She went to Macy's looking for a cheap fur coat to take with her to Europe. Her old one had worn through, and Lincoln had written in his letters that he planned to go to Russia as soon as he could and that the winters there would be even colder than the ones in New York.

The coat she wanted was on sale; according to the advertisement in the *Times*, they had "dignified" the price down to twenty dollars. "If Marie Antoinette should return to earth on Herald Square," it had said, "she would feel right at home in our corner window!"

Kitty supposed that the reduction had less to do with dead French queens and more to do with the fact that winter was almost over.

She had just reached the door, and she heard someone call her name—an Irish accent. She turned around and saw a young man walking up to her, a good-looking lad, and something about him was strangely familiar.

"Kitty. Kitty O'Kane? Is that really you?"

Oh Lord, she thought. *Who* is *this?* "Do I know you?"

"Your name is Kitty O'Kane? From the Liberties?"

"I might be. And who are you?"

"You probably don't remember me. You might remember my brother, though. Tom Doyle his name was. Is."

Kitty felt all the breath go out of her.

He held out his hand. "Michael, Michael Doyle."

He did look an awful lot like him, close up. In a moment she was back ten years, to a dirty street in Dublin, and Sandymount beach on a cold April day.

"You don't remember me, do you? I don't blame you. I used to tag along behind Tom when he went to school. I was under strict orders to shut up and stay out of the way! But he was always talking about you."

"What are you doing in New York?"

"Got an uncle lives here. Come to work for him I have. Dropped out of medical school, didn't have the brains for it, not like Tom."

Kitty felt numb. Tom Doyle! Until now, he was just a name from her past, icon more than man, and she never thought to see him again, or any of his family.

"You and Tom were at the posh school," was all she could think of to say.

"Well, it's not that we were ever that posh. You knew about the shebeen?"

"Yes, he told me about it. Always profit in drink, right?"

"That there is. Especially in Dublin."

"You look like you've done well. That's a nice suit you've got on."

"It's my uncle that's done well for himself. He has a business importing whiskey. He does very nicely, and he's training me to take over one day. Like you say, you can't go wrong with the demon drink."

"Another shebeen then?"

"This one's legal, and our customers don't have to come down the back lane."

"What about Tom?" she said, and her mouth felt suddenly dry. It was hard to get the words out.

"He's at medical school in London. Working at Saint Thomas' now he is, his first year out. I was at university a couple of years, but I'm not as clever as him. I dropped out. He's doing all right, though. You should see him these days; he's a couple of inches taller than me, played rugby for the university, almost lost his accent, a proper English gent."

A beat, while she composed herself and tried to sound casual. Then: "Is he married?"

Michael stopped smiling. "He got himself engaged last month."

She fixed a fierce smile on her face. "Good for him."

"He never forgot you, you know."

"We were just kids. What is there to forget?"

"He went back to Dublin looking for you. Your ma said you married a sailor."

"He did that? He went back to the Liberties?"

"Couple of years ago now. They said you'd disappeared. Liverpool they reckoned."

"I can't believe he'd do that."

"Wait till I tell him I saw you. He'll never believe it. Here, in New York of all places! Is it right, are you married then?"

She shook her head, a lump in her throat, thinking that Tom Doyle would go back to the Liberties and go asking for her. What a lad. *I wonder what he looks like now, if he still has that crease on his forehead when he's worrying something in his mind.* She remembered the cowlick that was always falling over his face. If she closed her eyes she could see him now, watching her stir that pot with the potato and the carrot in it like it was his ma's porridge.

"Where are you living now, Kitty?"

"I'm over in the Village with all them Bohemians."

"You should give me your address. I know Tom would love to write to you."

"Well I would, but I'm leaving soon."

"Where are you headed?"

"I'm back to England, to London."

"You should look him up then! He'd be over the moon." He reached into his jacket pocket, pulled out a fountain pen and a business card, and scribbled something on the back of it. "This is his address. Be sure to call on him."

"I'd better be going. I'm on my lunch break."

"Right then. Well take care, Kitty. Good luck in London." He took her hand. "What a stroke of luck. Wait until I tell Tom!"

She hurried out of the doors and ran for the El. It wasn't until she reached the station that she realized she still had the business card clutched in her fist. She stared at it. Tom Doyle, engaged now, a proper English gent fixing to be a doctor. *Good on you, Tom, and good on your ma as well to get you two boys out of it.*

She screwed up the card and let it drop into the gutter, into a puddle of dirty rainwater. Didn't even look at it. "Sorry Tom," she whispered. "But I'd only complicate things for you, and you don't deserve that."

A week later she was back at Pier 54 and climbing the gangway of the *Lusitania*. She tried not to think about the last time she did this. Couldn't help it, though, looking at the row of portholes, all she could think of was lifeboats lurching down into the dark, the sounds of those terrible screams. *Away with you, Kitty*, she told herself, *you've had your brush with the devil. It won't be happening to you a second time.*

It was the first day of May; another ten days and she would be in England to a new life, with Lincoln Randolph, and ready to change the world. She had with her a trunk of clothes, a new fur coat from Macy's, and a battered jewelry box with two cockleshells inside.

The start of a new life.

CHAPTER 15

May 7, 1915

The captain had been sounding the foghorn all that morning. It wasn't until midday that the fog finally lifted. The day was bright; the ship's speed seemed to have increased a little for the final push to England. Tomorrow she would be back in England. It would be strange to be on the other side of the Atlantic again.

After lunch, Kitty went up onto the second deck. She was hoping she might see the coast of Ireland off the port side. Ireland: whenever she thought about the place, it always reduced in her mind to a third-story tenement room in the Liberties. *"Pretend it's not happening, pretend you're on that ship, the sea wind is in your hair, salt and cold, and you're headed out to the white waves and only the gulls are screaming."*

Finally, I made it happen, she thought. *My life is not perfect, but at least I'm not back there.*

"On your own?" a voice said.

She turned. It was a woman; Kitty guessed she was in her fifties, a Boston accent. "I am. You?"

"Afraid so. I wanted my husband to come with me, but he couldn't get away from his work. What about you, are you married?"

Kitty shook her head.

"Pretty young thing like you?"

"I have a . . . friend, in London. I'm going there to meet him."

"Do you mean a lover?"

Well, that was forthright; but the way she said it was refreshing. Kitty liked her candor. "I suppose I do mean that."

"Well, good for you. You have the look of an independent young woman. To my mind, there aren't enough women like that in the world. What do you do?"

"I used to work for a magazine. The same one that my . . . lover wrote for."

"He's a writer? What's his name?"

"Randolph, Lincoln Randolph."

"Randolph? Isn't he the Communist that writes all those long rants that upset all the Republicans in Washington?"

"He's not a Communist."

"Isn't he? I thought he was. I met him once."

"You know Lincoln?"

"I write a little too." She rummaged through her bag, took out a plain white card. *Charlotte Reddings.*

"Oh my God! But I've read your articles in *Woman's Journal* and the *Pacific Monthly*. You're famous."

"No, not famous. My husband says I'm disreputable, which is something else entirely." Her eyes wrinkled mischievously. "I'm a little like your *friend*; I've made a profession out of upsetting people. I don't do it deliberately of course, I just happen to believe that women should have a better life in our society, and a lot of men don't like that, of course. Even some women object to the notion."

"Is that what takes you to England?"

"It is. I'm on a speaking tour. It's where I make most of my money these days. I wrote a book called *The New Woman*. Have you heard of it?"

"Heard of it? I read it, cover to cover."

"Did you? Well, I'm flattered. You should come to hear me next week. I'll get you a ticket if you like. It's somewhere in Marylebone."

"I would like that, very much."

Charlotte Reddings took off her glove and held out her hand. "I don't even know your name."

"Kitty," she said, taking her hand. "Kitty O'Kane."

"Now there's a pretty Irish name. So off to London, Kitty O'Kane? Did Mr. Randolph send for you?"

"Well, yes. But it's not the only reason."

Charlotte Reddings smiled and waited. *She sees through me like the front window of Macy's*, Kitty thought. "I'd like to learn to write."

"What do you want to write about?"

"The same things you do, Mrs. Reddings."

"Charlotte. Please. And why are you looking at me like that?"

"Like what?"

"You look shy of a sudden, and yet you don't look like a bashful kind of girl."

"Because the truth is, I've no cause to be thinking I can be a writer or anything like one. I've no education. I was brought up in the Liberties, in Dublin. We couldn't afford the newspaper. It's presumptuous of me to ever think I could write anything that could be good enough to print in a magazine, let alone a book."

"Oh, you think I'm a Vassar girl, is that it?" She grinned and raised an eyebrow. She leaned in. "Do I sound like a Vassar girl?"

"Not really," Kitty said.

"My mother's Boston Irish. I'm one generation out of the bog, Kitty O'Kane. My father left us when I was three; I went to seven different schools when I was growing up, couldn't have done more than four years of schooling. Learned everything I know from the public library. So, if I can do it, so can you." She leaned closer still, lowered her voice. "You have a literary lover. I'm sure he'll help you."

"He's helped me a lot already."

"And so he should. Look, you must already know how to type if you worked in an office. The rest is practice."

"It's not like I haven't tried."

"You must write about the things you know and the things that inspire your passions. What is it you know about, Kitty?"

"I know about a father who came home and beat up my ma and us kids every night. I know about a system that kept us down, my mother a slave, my father working all hours God gave him for a few pennies in his pocket. The bloody English selling us out to landlords who got rich, riding on our backs."

"Look at you! You get red in the face just talking about it. You must write with that sort of passion."

"I don't know I'm cut out to be a writer, though. I tell you, I'm not clever enough."

"It isn't about cleverness. I'm no Charles Dickens myself. I just want to change things, like you do. There's no good reason for women to be slaves to men or for any race of people to get put down by another. If you want to change it, there can never be enough men or women making that change happen. And we will change it, Kitty, even if it takes us a hundred years."

"I don't know that I can do it."

"But you want to, and that's the half of it. You know most people live and die, and they dream about a better world, but they never do anything about it. But you can."

"You sound like Lincoln."

"Well, we're not that different. He fights for the common man, like I fight for the common woman. Do you love him?"

Kitty was taken aback by the question. "He inspires me," she said, after a moment.

"Ah, now that is a careful answer."

"Well, how does anyone ever know if they're in love anyway?"

"If you ask the question you already have the answer. Answer me this then. Is it that you're just in awe of him?"

"I don't know."

"I suppose you'll find out for yourself in the end. Tell you what, why don't we talk about it next week? I have a magazine I publish back in New York, and perhaps if you write something for me, I could think about publishing it. The pay is lousy, I warn you. We've only fifteen hundred subscribers. Holding unorthodox opinions is no sure path to riches."

"I don't care about the money."

"Well, you should because it's money that will give you your freedom as a woman. Don't ask Lincoln to give it to you." She squeezed her hand. "Don't give up, Kitty. If I can do it, I'm damned sure you can."

Kitty smiled; perhaps Lincoln was right then.

"Well, I must go and work on my notes for my speech. I should work out what I'm going to say when I talk to these people next week. It's been nice talking to you, Kitty."

Charlotte Reddings smiled and made her way back inside. Kitty turned back to the sea, closed her eyes, let the wind blow through her hair.

Charlotte sounded so much like Lincoln, with her passion for wanting to change the world. Kitty had never really supposed that Kitty O'Kane from the Liberties might shout back at the devil, despite what Lincoln said. But wouldn't it be something if she could do for working women what Lincoln was doing for the working man? Use words to change people's minds about things.

She heard a shout and opened her eyes. Someone was pointing to something off their starboard bow. It looked like a low, black ridge. There was another shout, more urgent this time, from one of the sailors.

He was pointing to a white fizz streaming through the clear water toward them, and immediately she knew what it meant.

"Torpedo!" someone shouted.

Jesus God, no. This couldn't be happening, not again.

There was a huge explosion, and it felt as if they had rammed at full speed into a wall. Kitty saw a spout of black water heave into the sky around them, and then it washed down over the decks, drenching her. The *Lusitania* shook from bow to stern and heaved to one side.

CHAPTER 16

Kitty rushed down to the saloon to get her lifebelt and found the chief steward blocking her way. There were dozens of lifebelts piled behind him.

"You have to go back up to the deck, ma'am," he said.

"I need a lifebelt."

"I'm sorry, but there isn't one for you," and he took her arm and forced her back toward the companionway.

"I need a lifebelt," she said, and she felt the ship starting to keel over.

"I'm sorry, ma'am, there aren't any left."

"They're right there! I need a lifebelt!" And she tried to shove past him, but he threw her back. Just then the ship listed right, and a rush of water poured down the companionway. "You have to go back," the steward said with a tight little smile, and then there was water rushing into her mouth and carrying her down into the bowels of the ship and it was dark and cold and she couldn't breathe.

Kitty sat up in her bed, arms flailing, gulping at the air. She kicked the bedclothes onto the floor and stared around the room, trying to remember where she was. She got up and tugged aside the curtains.

There was the clatter of horses' hooves down in the street, the chink of milk bottles on the doorstep. She tore aside the net curtain, her heart still banging painfully in her chest. "It's all right, Kitty," she murmured under her breath. "It's all right."

She looked around the room, wondered where Lincoln was. The bare floorboards were cold on her feet, even though it was supposed to be summer. She moved her stockings that were hanging in front of the gas fire. It would be good to light it and warm the room up a bit, but Lincoln would go mad at the expense.

Right then she heard him bounding up the stairs. He was whistling, must be pleased about something. As he strode in, he gave her a perfunctory kiss on the forehead and threw the newspapers on the table: the *Mirror*, the *News of the World*, even the *Express* so he could see what it was the Tories were saying.

She didn't tell him about her dream; he mustn't know she was still having nightmares. She went to the kitchenette and spooned some tea into the pot. "I'll make it, Kit," he said, although he never understood why she liked it. "Maiden's water," he called it. It was the one thing he always complained about: he couldn't get a decent cup of coffee anywhere in the country.

She sat down at the table, started to look through the papers. The headlines were all about the war and the battles at Ypres and Gallipoli. The *Express* made it sound as if the Germans would capitulate any day, but Lincoln had taught her to read between the lines. *"The papers over here will only tell you what Lloyd George wants you to know,"* he had said. *"If the public knew what was really happening, the war would be over tomorrow."*

The *Daily Mirror* had an article about suffrage. Denmark and Iceland were preparing to give women the vote. The Right party had been decimated at the elections, and the Social Democrats were preparing amendments to the constitution, with women's suffrage as one of them. It only needed the king to ratify it now.

"It's twelve thousand women," Lincoln had said. "And it only applies to women forty and over."

"But it's a start."

He looked doubtful.

The News of the World was filled with advertisements about Pears soap and Bovril, and a scandal piece: "Courted Two Lovers: Airman has to pay damages. Did not end with old before starting with new!" There was a regular serialized story: "The Laughing Mask."

She found a short piece about William Jennings Bryan resigning in the wake of the *Lusitania* sinking. He said he was utterly opposed to Woodrow Wilson using the incident to drag America into the war: "It is not likely that either side will win so complete a victory as to be able to dictate terms, and if either side does win such a victory it will probably mean preparation for another war."

Her eyes drifted to the feature article on the facing page.

"The Unkillable Kitty O'Kane," by Lincoln J. Randolph.

She read the headline again.

"Jesus God, you didn't."

She looked up; he was watching her, a smile frozen on his face. He brought her a cup of tea in a chipped mug and put it in front of her. He looked so damned pleased with himself. "I've made you famous."

"This isn't about making me famous. This is about making you famous."

"You haven't even read it!"

She read it through, quickly. She supposed the facts were right; how she had survived both the *Titanic* sinking and then the sinking of the *Lusitania* by a German U-boat, all in the space of three years. There was even a photograph, one they'd had taken together the year before in a photographer's studio in New York.

"What's wrong?"

"You make me sound like a hero. When the *Lusitania* sank under us, a sailor threw me a lifebelt, and I put it on. That was it. It was very much the same on *Titanic*."

"That's not the point, Kit. How many people survive two famous shipwrecks? And anyway, you weren't just thrown in a lifeboat the second time. You said so yourself, it was only your lifebelt that saved you;

you were floating in the water for over an hour. Come on, it was a miracle. It's a story everyone wants to read."

Her dreams were nothing like what had really happened; the chief steward had actually sought her out with the lifebelt that had saved her life. Lincoln made her sound like a hero, but she was nothing like one. After she put on the lifebelt, she had just stood there, frozen with fear.

She thought about the banshee; maybe there was something to the cards after all.

"Some good people were drowned that day. Just because I survived, that doesn't make me a hero. It just means I'm lucky."

"Exactly. *Damned* lucky. *The unkillable Kitty O'Kane.* You must admit, it has a ring to it."

"Why didn't you ask me, before you wrote this?"

He shrugged.

"You were frightened I was going to say no," Kitty said.

"Would you have said no?"

She didn't answer him. Damned right she would have said no.

"No harm done, Kitty. A little bit of fame, it will help get your foot in the door with editors when you start writing yourself." He tried to put his arms around her, but she pushed him away.

"I feel like you've used me."

"If I want to use you, there's better ways." And there was that boyish grin again.

"I'll have people staring at me in the street now."

"A good-looking girl like you, they stare anyway. And who recognizes anyone from a photograph in the newspaper? You could be Kaiser Wilhelm."

"Then use the kaiser's photograph! You shouldn't have done it!"

"For God's sake, Kitty, I'm a writer. I have a story right in front of me, what do you think I'm going to do?"

"Well I'm glad I'm good for something!"

It isn't the article, she thought. *He's right, it does no harm. It's that I'm sitting here and feeling useless, like a kept woman.*

He sat her on his knee, and she put her head on his shoulder. "How long are we staying here, in London?"

"I want to introduce you to a few more editors before we leave."

"I've met them all. Half of them look at me like I'm not there, and the other half look at me as if my *clothes* aren't there."

"We need to go out and buy you a typewriter before we leave."

"Leave for where, Linc? You've been telling me for weeks, the War Office won't let you anywhere near the front lines."

"It's true, they won't. This is going to be the most heavily censored war in history."

"So is it Russia we're going to then?"

"Not just Russia. If we can't write about the Western Front, then we'll write about what's happening all over the east, in Greece and Serbia and Bulgaria as well."

"But who will want to know about those places?"

"People here and in America have to be educated! This war is going to change everything. The old order is getting thrown out; there's revolution coming all over Europe. I want to be at the heart of it when it happens."

"People don't want to be educated, Linc. They aren't interested in revolutions."

"In America they are. Because a lot of Americans were born in places like Russia and Germany. And Ireland. There's things happening in Europe no one there knows about—the uprisings in Greece; men, women, and children getting slaughtered in Serbia. People aren't being told! They read what Churchill and Lloyd George want them to read, but they don't know the truth of it. So, I've decided to tell them. We leave next week."

"Next week?"

"I've heard the British are going to send an expeditionary force to Thessaloniki."

"And where in God's name is that?"

"It's in Greece. From there we can get into Serbia, cover the war there. After that, we'll find a way into Russia. That's where the fire's going to start, Kit. The Bolsheviks will take Russia out of the war, and as soon as they do, the whole house of cards will collapse." He jumped up, went to his satchel, took out two hardbound books. "I got these yesterday. You have to read them."

Kitty looked at the spines: *Capital: Volume 1* and *Socialism: Utopian and Scientific.*

"This is Karl Marx; this is Engels. You want to change the world, Kitty? This is how you do it." His eyes were shining; she could almost feel the heat coming off him. "We're in the middle of history, Kit, the world is never going to be the same. It's time for change! Lloyd George and Churchill want everyone to think they'll win their little war and things will go back to the way they were. But the whole of Europe is convulsing, and no one knows about anything more than a few trenches in France. But we're going to tell them!" He gripped her hands. "Are you with me?"

"Why me, Linc? Why didn't you take up with some clever Vassar girl with glasses?"

"Because they've never been dirt poor like you; they don't really understand what it is we're fighting for. Do they?" His arms went around her waist. "Do you love me, Kit?"

She nodded, because she didn't quite trust her voice.

"We're going to change the world!" he said, and this time at least it was dreams he was drunk on, and not beers, and so she let him carry her back to bed. He made love to her with such passion that he left her sore the rest of the day. Still, she supposed if the unkillable Kitty O'Kane could survive two shipwrecks, she could endure one overenthusiastic lover.

She got off the Underground at Leicester Square and made her way toward the Strand. As she crossed Charing Cross Road just opposite the National Gallery, a cyclist rang his bell at her; he had a basket on the back piled with greens, on his way back from Covent Garden, she supposed. When she looked down, she found dung on her new shoes. Damned horses. The city would be a sight cleaner and safer when there were just motor cars.

There were recruiting posters up everywhere:

IT IS FAR BETTER TO FACE THE BULLETS THAN TO BE KILLED AT HOME BY A BOMB.
JOIN THE ARMY AT ONCE & HELP STOP AN AIR RAID.
GOD SAVE THE KING!

Lincoln had laughed when he saw them. "Would anyone like to tell me the respective odds of getting hurt by a bomb thrown out of the basket of some goddamned balloon against running the full length of a boggy football field toward half a dozen machine guns? You Limeys are rich!"

She hurried along the Strand, past the buskers and sandwich-board men to the Lyons teahouse. She went into the food hall—oh, so elegant with all the mirrors and dark wood and potted palms. It was packed, waitresses in black dresses and white aprons rushing to serve cream cakes and pots of tea. Elsie was already there; she waved to Kitty from a table in the corner. She was in her nurse's uniform—all blue and cream, and freshly pressed, it made Kitty feel drab.

Elsie was the first person she had come looking for when she reached London, after she'd recovered from her ordeal on the *Lusitania*. They had kept in touch with letters, but they hadn't seen each other since that day at the docks; Elsie squealed like a schoolgirl when she saw her, and hugged her and wouldn't let go, never mind all the people.

Elsie had already seen Lincoln's article in the *News of the World*; she'd even taken a cutting. She took it out of her purse, told Kitty she was going to show it to all her friends at the hospital. "Never thought I'd ever know somebody famous!"

"I'm not famous, Elsie. I'm yesterday's news already. Sure and I saw someone on the way here, using the *News of the World* to eat their fish and chips out of."

"'The unkillable Kitty O'Kane'!"

"Away with you, let's get a pot of tea."

A Gladys in a black dress and white apron came over, and they ordered teacakes with their tea. She scurried off, and Kitty took off her hat and gloves and put them on the table.

"Can't believe it happened to you twice, love. Not a day goes by I don't think about *Titanic*."

"You think I don't?"

"I don't know, to be honest. You're the only one I've ever talked to about it, proper like. The only one who understands, I suppose."

"Elsie, it all gets mixed up in my head sometimes. Ever since I've been back in London, I've been having these bad dreams; the ship's sinking, only I can't remember which ship I'm on."

"I had dreams, too, for a long time."

"When did they go away, for you?"

Elsie fidgeted. "They didn't."

Their fingers touched across the table.

Kitty said, "I remember, after the torpedo hit, there was this second explosion, and that was what tore the ship apart. I saw the four funnels fly clean out of the ship, and I thought: I'm going to die now after all, and it seemed almost funny to me, to survive *Titanic* and then to drown at sea anyway. The ship went over so fast; the lifeboats were crashing into the passengers on the other side of the ship. A seaman threw me a lifebelt, and I put it on and then I just stood there. I felt frozen. There was a lifeboat getting lowered on my side, and another seaman just pushed me into it. But something went wrong with the pulley and the boat turned upside down and I fell into the water. Next thing I remember, I was floating among all this wreckage, and the ship had gone. I saw a collapsible boat and I swam toward it and a while later I remember them dragging me on board another lifeboat. But then I must have passed out again because I don't remember much else. A minesweeper took us all into Queenstown."

Their waitress reappeared with a huge silver tray—the poor girl was rushed off her feet. She put down a pot of tea and a plate of buns, then hurried to the next table with cream cakes and sandwiches.

Kitty crumbled off a piece of teacake and put it in her mouth. "I met someone on board, a woman called Charlotte Reddings, a lovely lady she was, and a great writer, someone you could really look up to. Yet she drowned and here I am, eating sweet buns with you."

"Well I'm glad you're here."

"Doesn't make sense to me."

"It's one thing surviving one shipwreck, girl. But two! It must mean you're meant for something."

"Well, I wish I knew what that thing was." She looked at the tea. "Will you be a mother?"

Elsie smiled. "I hope so, soon."

"Are you?"

"No, not yet."

She poured the tea.

"How's Bert?"

"He's busy with the shop. His dad was busier than a one-armed paper 'anger while we was away on our honeymoon. Bit crowded upstairs with us and his mum and dad and his three brothers, mind."

"Have you been looking for a place of your own?"

Elsie didn't answer. She fumbled in her bag for a handkerchief.

"Elsie, what's wrong?"

"It's all right, I'm just a bit emotional at the moment."

"What is it? Is it Bert?"

"No. Yes. Well, he's talking about joining up. Says all his mates are over in France, and he should be too."

"That's ridiculous."

"What, fighting for your country?"

"Is that what it is?"

"Well, of course it is. What else does a man do when his country needs him?"

"His family needs him more."

"What if everyone said that?"

Kitty swallowed back her answer to that. What good would it do, trying to explain to her what Lincoln had taught her about how wars were just about profit. Elsie wouldn't understand. Instead she said, "Oh, but Elsie, you're just married."

"I know. Bert reckoned it would all be over by now. Who would have thought this war would have dragged on like it has?"

"Do you think he'll really go?"

"There are two types of men in the world, Irish, those who get in the lifeboats and those who don't. If he'd been there on the *Titanic*, Bert would have been one of those that wouldn't have got in the boat. He says he'll feel like a coward if he doesn't join up. I'm terrified one day I'm going to come home and he'll have his papers in his hand."

Kitty stirred a lump of sugar into her tea—it was so weak she could almost see the sugar sitting at the bottom of it. "How's the nursing?" she asked Elsie, thinking she should change the subject before she said something she shouldn't.

"I love it. I'm still training, like, but it's a lot more interesting than being a stewardess. A lot more rewarding too."

"You're over at Saint Thomas', isn't it?"

Elsie sipped her tea and nodded.

Kitty hesitated, still stirring her tea long after the sugar had dissolved. "This may sound daft . . . but do you know a doctor called Doyle?"

"There's lots of doctors over there."

"This one will be young. My age."

"There's a new intern by that name. He's handsome too. All the young nurses are making eyes at him."

"Does he sound Irish?"

"Not as Irish as you, but a bit. Why are you asking?"

Kitty shrugged as if it was a matter of only casual interest. "I knew this young fella, a long time ago, back when I was a kid in Dublin. I heard he was working there."

"Shall I ask him if he remembers you? Perhaps it's the same one."

"No, don't do that. Like I said, I hardly knew him."

Kitty turned the conversation again. They talked about the latest Zeppelin raid, on Stepney, and Elsie told her how a house not half a mile from their shop had been hit by one of the bombs.

They finished their teacakes and got an extra cup each out of the little silver teapot.

"What about you, Irish? What's next for you?"

"Lincoln says the War Office won't let him go to the places he wants in France and even then, they want to censor everything he writes. So, he's planning on going to Greece."

"Greece? Gor' blimey, that's a long way."

"It is. And he wants me to go with him."

"You're not going to, are you?"

"Have you not heard of a lady war correspondent?" Kitty laughed. "No, neither has anyone else. Everyone says I'm stupid to even think about it; they say it's too dangerous, but I'll have Linc with me. The really stupid thing isn't that I'm a woman; it's that I have no proper training. That lovely woman on the *Lusitania*, the writer, she told me I should just write from the heart and that editors love that."

"Well, I guess if she was a great writer, like you say, then she would know."

"Lincoln has been telling me the same thing."

"Is he finally after making an honest woman out of you? It's been long enough."

Kitty stared at the tablecloth, didn't answer.

"You can't live in sin forever."

"I don't see why not. Marriage never did my ma much good. Besides, perhaps I don't want to get married and have children; there's other things I want to do."

"Well I don't know about that. I'm not a *Bohemian* like you. But I don't like you going off to Greece. You can't keep tempting fate, girl."

"Haven't you read the papers? I'm unkillable."

"No one's unkillable for long, girl."

"Well, like you say, perhaps it's what I'm meant to do."

"You remember that Mr. Richardson? Our chief steward? Gave up his life for me, he did, put me in the lifeboat and then stood back. He said, 'Elsie, you go along now, and make sure you make this life count.' And I reckon I have. I reckon I've paid him back. You know how?"

Kitty shook her head.

"I'm happy. I wasn't happy then, but I'm happy now. That's how I've honored what that poor man did."

"I can't, Elsie."

"Why not? Just find a nice man and settle down, Irish. Pretty girl like you won't have any trouble. What's wrong with being happy?"

Kitty shook her head. Was that why she'd survived both those ships going down, so she could just get married and be somebody's wife?

"I want to make a difference, Elsie. When I see my name on a magazine piece or a newspaper article telling the whole world why women should have a vote and why workers shouldn't have to slave all hours so rich men can get even richer, why young men shouldn't bleed and die while other men buy another big house and a fancy car—when I do that, then I'll know my life has been for something!"

She could see what Elsie was thinking, but it was different with her and Lincoln. She wasn't expecting him to look after her forever.

"I don't want to be like my mother, Elsie. I don't want to do this just for me; it's for my sisters as well, for my ma, for every woman in the world. For every little girl lying on the floor with strap marks on her back."

"Not every woman in the world wants you to fight for her, Irish." Elsie felt in her pocket for her watch, peered at it. "I'd better be getting back to work. I still have to get across the bridge, and if I'm late Matron will have a fit."

They walked outside into the sunshine together. Summer was finally come to London. Kitty saw a paperboy across the street. Another battle was going in a place she couldn't pronounce, Krithia.

"Bert doesn't have to go," she heard herself say.

"I don't want him to go neither, but his country needs him."

"It's not his country that needs him, it's some banker in the city."

Elsie gave her a sharp look. "You sound like a bleedin' Communist you do." It was a joke, perhaps, but she had made her point. She kissed Kitty hurriedly on the cheek and headed across the Waterloo Bridge.

"It's what you've got to fight against, Kit," Lincoln said that night as they lay in the big iron-framed bed in their flat. "Not just men, but other women. They won't like you for being different."

"She's only looking out for me. She's a friend to me, no mistake."

"But you scare her, the way you live."

"Well, living in sin I am—she said as much—being with you. No ring on my finger."

"And what difference does a bit of paper make?"

"Well if I was worried about that, I wouldn't be here, would I?" She rolled toward him. She ran her hand along the line of his jaw, felt the sharp stubble under the pads of her fingers, stared at the hazel flecks in his blue eyes, magnified by his glasses. "Just promise me something," she murmured.

"What's that?"

"When I was a kid, growing up in the Liberties, my daddy used to take the belt to me and to my ma. I can still feel it, still hear it; it makes this special kind of sound as it whips through the air. It's not just the physical hurt of it, it's the hate that comes with it, the humiliation, the sheer bloody terror of it."

He held her closer.

"A man will never lay his hands on me like that again, not ever. Promise me, Linc, promise me you'll never do that, you'll never use your fists on me."

"You know I won't, Kitty."

"Promise me anyway."

"I promise."

He took off his glasses and put them on the bedside table. He slipped his hand under her nightdress, up her thigh and to her hip. He pulled her toward him. She saw that look come to him, the hunger.

"Never ever hurt you, Kit," he said, and kissed her.

"Make sure you don't," she murmured, and kissed him back.

<hr />

The next night they were standing in Waterloo Station, the steam from the train engine curling under the iron girders above their heads. Porters rushed past with trolleys piled high with people's luggage; the platform was packed with soldiers saying good-bye to their sweethearts and wives and kids. Kitty and Lincoln pushed their way through the din toward one of the carriages.

It wasn't really like going away, because she had never had a place she could call a home, not like others did. Her life had always felt like drifting to her—you couldn't call the Liberties any kind of place you'd long to go back to. Liverpool, New York, London; there couldn't be a home, or happiness, until she'd done what she had promised herself she would do.

She would save every little barefoot girl cold and hungry in the Liberties tonight, the Liberties and every damned hellhole like it.

CHAPTER 17

The Border between Russia and Occupied Poland
Chelm to Petrograd, September 1917

They ate sour black bread and drank weak coffee and stared at the rain beating mournfully against the train windows. A man with a wiry black beard and a greasy bearskin hat started a desultory conversation in Russian with Lincoln. After a while he shook his head and stared at them as if they were both mad, then turned away and stared out of the window in sullen disapproval.

"What was that about?" Kitty said.

"He asked me what we were doing in Russia. He says he's a commissar with one of the Petrograd Soviets."

"Did you tell him a man in his position should buy a new hat? I swear there's a host of God's little creatures moving in it."

"It didn't seem like a good time to mention it."

"A commissar. Does he know what's happening with the war?"

"He's heard that the Germans have crossed the Dvina, and Kerensky is building trenches to try and stop them. But he thinks the Cossacks might take the city first anyway. It sounds like a real mess. He asked me what the hell I thought I was doing, taking a helpless woman into the city right now."

"A helpless woman."

Lincoln smiled. "I told him the helpless woman had spent the last two years with me in every battleground in Europe, getting shot at, arrested . . . how many times is it, Kitty?"

"Three times."

"And that the king of Bulgaria had pinched your bottom. So I didn't think the Germans or the Whites scared you very much."

"Did that shut him up?"

"Not really. He said Kerensky isn't the king of Bulgaria and that we'd both be dead by morning."

The carriage wheels squealed as they pulled to a stop at a cheerless border post. Kitty peered out. Jesus God, all the color seemed to have been drained out of the world.

As they stepped down out of the carriage, she got her first glimpse of Russian soldiers. They were great giants of men, with huge moustaches and beards, in ragtag, dirt-colored uniforms without insignia or decorations or epaulettes. They each wore a simple armband of red cloth, and stood around in small groups or slumped on their haunches in ones and twos around the platform, their rifles and ammunition belts slung over their shoulders.

Lincoln said, "Give me a minute," and went over to a group of soldiers with a pack of cigarettes, offered them around, talking to them in his schoolboy Russian. Meanwhile Kitty and the rest of the passengers were herded into a cold and badly lit room, where sullen-faced guards demanded passports and started rifling through luggage. A squad of soldiers holding bayonets stood watching.

Most of the other passengers were Russians; they appeared to be accustomed to the bullying, kept their eyes down when the customs guards shouted questions at them and tossed back their passports, and hurried to unlock their trunks and suitcases when told to do so. The guards rummaged through the luggage, looking for something to steal.

When it was Kitty's turn, the guard tipped up her bag, emptied the contents on the trestle table, started rifling through. What was her nationality; what was her religion; what was she doing in Russia?

He started taking out her medicines and her cosmetics and putting them to one side. Her jewelry case was added to the pile.

"You're not having that," Kitty said to him.

He stared at her.

She leaned over and took back the case. He tried to wrench it from her arms, but she fought back. Everyone else in the room turned their heads away; the other guards stopped leaning on their rifles; one of them shouted at her and fumbled for the revolver he carried in a holster over his greatcoat.

"Shoot me then, you big lump of lard, but you're not having the jewelry box!"

But suddenly Lincoln was there, smiling, telling everyone to calm down, saying things in Russian she didn't understand.

Then he turned to her. "Hey, what's going on, Kit?"

"Tell that arse he's not having the jewelry box. He can have the iodized throat tablets, if it's that important to him; he can have the Pond's vanishing cream, though I swear it'll do his ugly mug no good; but he's not having this!"

"He has a gun, Kit," Lincoln said, through gritted teeth.

"He can stick his damned gun where the sun don't shine, tell him. I don't care."

The guard made another grab for it. Kitty clung on, shouted right in his face. "You're not having it!"

He let go and took a step back. The soldier with the gun tried to step in, but Lincoln stepped between him and Kitty, handed the man the rest of his cigarettes and a crumpled ball of rubles. He crammed the rest of Kitty's things back into her bag, still smiling, never once taking his eyes off the guard, talking the whole time. She hadn't realized he knew that much Russian.

Then he took Kitty by the arm, maneuvered her out of the shed and back onto the platform, as far away from the guards as he could. He stood there breathing hard, looking back over her shoulder to see if any of them had followed.

"What in God's name was that about?" He stared at the case she was holding in her arms. "What the hell is in there anyway?"

"Never you mind."

"Is it the Irish crown jewels or some damned thing?" His face darkened.

"It's my personal things, and he's not having them."

Lincoln shrugged and turned away, defeated. "You're going to get me killed, I swear."

"So, what did the soldiers say?"

"Best I can make out, the Germans have taken Riga; the whole fucking front is collapsing. They say Petrograd is under martial law. The czarists are marching on the city; there's a counterrevolution under way; the city's under siege. Everything's gone to hell."

"So, now what do we do?"

He grinned. "It's bad news for the Russians. I didn't say it was bad news for us. This is what we came here for! We're right at the heart of the biggest damned news story there is right now!"

"As long as we're not dead by morning, like the gentleman said."

"Well if you stop shouting at border guards, it might give us an outside chance."

⟢⟐⟣

They arrived in Petrograd in the middle of the night. The station was soon empty. They stared at their luggage and each other. "Now what?" he said.

"Well, if you were any real gentleman, you'd go outside and get us a cab."

They heard footsteps farther along the platform, and a massive silhouette appeared between them and the solitary gas light on the station entrance. Kitty smelled the massive bearskin hat before she recognized its owner.

He said something to Lincoln and then picked up his suitcase.

"Damn, he's offering us a ride," Lincoln said.

He led them outside. A huge gray car was parked in the forecourt. There was a young soldier behind the wheel. They climbed in. "He said there's only one hotel in the whole city that's still open, the Hotel Angleterre. He wants to know if we have a reservation. Do we, sweetheart?"

"Tell him I booked the honeymoon suite months ago."

Another quick exchange. "I said we didn't have a reservation. He said it's okay, it's empty."

They all crammed into the back seat. Kitty tried not to breathe too deeply; their rescuer's coat had the smell of a wet and muddy sheep, and his hat was as ripe as a three-day-old corpse.

They set off through the black and deserted streets. There seemed to be sentries at every block, but the young soldier at the wheel shouted the password out of the window, and he was waved through.

It was just past three in the morning by her watch. Suddenly every church bell in the city started to ring.

"Do you think that's to welcome us?" Lincoln said.

The commissar leaned over to Lincoln and growled something in his ear. They both laughed.

"Do I want to know what that was about?" Kitty said.

"He was complimenting the king of Bulgaria for his taste in bottoms."

Lincoln and his new friend were still deep in conversation when they pulled up outside a shabby four-story building just off Nevsky Prospect. Kitty left them to it and trudged up the steps of the hotel. The porter was asleep at the desk, and it took several minutes of banging on the door to wake him. When he finally let her in and Lincoln rejoined her, they signed the register, and the old man took their passports and put them in the safe. He shuffled up the stairs, ignoring the lift. "He said it's broken," Lincoln said over his shoulder.

They went up three floors and followed the porter along an eternity of worn and faded carpet. They reached a set of white-painted double doors. He swung them open and pressed a button on the wall. Kitty blinked under the blaze of an old-fashioned crystal candelabra.

It could have been one of the czar's minor ballrooms, she thought, just the size of it, with its gold leaf and mahogany paneling and dusty crimson draperies. It smelled musty and damp, as if no one had used the room for a hundred years. There was a four-poster bed in the far corner of the room, and next to it an enormous bathtub, cut out of solid granite, with four brass claw feet.

The porter handed Lincoln the key and left, shutting the door.

Kitty went to the window. The dark silhouette of St. Isaac's Cathedral loomed up toward the sky. The noise of the bells was deafening. She could see the bell ringers inside the church, lit by a thousand candles, the bell ropes tied to their elbows, knees, feet, and hands, bouncing up and down like marionettes. With each movement they added another note to the madness of the desperate city's predawn sonata.

Kitty and Lincoln kicked off their boots and crawled into the bed, fully dressed. Kitty realized the jewelry box was still in her pocket. She tucked it under the bed, put her arms around Lincoln, and fell asleep.

CHAPTER 18

Kitty got out of bed and went to the window. Lincoln was still asleep, one arm limp over the side of the bed. She wiped a thin sheen of ice off the glass. Her breath froze on the air. Outside, Petrograd looked gray and grim.

Little Kitty O'Kane in Russia. Who'd have thought it? But another part of her wished she was back in Lyons teahouse, eating teacakes. Her stomach growled at the thought of food.

Two years now she had been traveling. She had never thought to see so much of the world, or that she would see so much death either. It had sounded like an adventure back in London, when she'd been describing their plans to Elsie. But these last two years had scored the soul out of her. The excitement, even the fear, had long gone; these days she just felt numb. She'd seen things she wished she'd never seen; she and Lincoln had written story after story, trying to tell it all. And what good had it done? The world had not changed, not a bit of it, if anything it had moved another ten steps closer to hell.

God knew, she had tried. She had had her first piece published, in the *Union*, and that had been followed by a handful of others. More than she had ever dared dream, but nothing to shake the world either. Had anyone even read them? Did anyone else even care?

Lincoln kept telling her not to give up.

She heard him stir and looked over her shoulder, saw his eyes blink open. He smiled and sat up, fumbled into his boots. He came and stood behind her, wrapped his arms around her.

He nuzzled her neck. "So, we're finally here," she said.

"We're finally here."

"What's that building over there, the one with the gold spires?"

"That's the old Admiralty building. Peter the Great built it, and it marks the very center of the city. Those blue-green domes over there are the Turquoise Mosque. It's still being built."

"It's not like I imagined. Apart from those two places, it's all so drab."

"Well, it's a city, not a health spa. Scared?"

"A bit," she said.

"So am I." He smiled and ran a hand through her hair. "But first I'm hungry."

<hr>

They breakfasted in the grand dining room of the Hotel Angleterre. Soldiers with muddy boots and gaunt faces slouched in and out, looking utterly at odds with the mirrors and the red velvet chairs; it wasn't long ago that only officers and their ladies would have been allowed inside.

The Tartar waiter stood back while they looked through the four pages of the menu. When they had finished reading them, he took them out of their hands, and said: "All we have is black bread and *chai*."

Lincoln shrugged and smiled at Kitty. "Well what luck. That's exactly what we'd chosen, isn't it, Kitty?"

Kitty looked around the room. A Cossack in a gold-and-black uniform, with earrings in his ears, was scowling at them. She turned away.

"He probably thinks we're Germans," Lincoln said.

"I've been accused of being many things, but never a German. So, what are our plans?"

"Have you heard of Madame Ballanskaya?"

Kitty shook her head.

"She's like a Russian Emmeline Pankhurst, I guess. She has radical ideas about family and marriage and society, like your friend Charlotte did. Only if the Bolsheviks take power, her radical ideas will become government policy."

"So how does a woman get to run things in a place like this, for the love of all that's holy?"

"The important thing, I guess, is that she backs the winning side. She's an unlikely Bolshevik. Her parents were aristocrats; they sent her to Paris to be educated, but all that happened was that she became radicalized."

"A little like yourself."

He grinned. "I guess so. Anyway, she was arrested and imprisoned three times by the old regime, and that gave her a lot of credibility with Lenin and Trotsky. She wants to combat illiteracy, and she has some sweeping ideas about new marriage and labor laws. Just the sort of things you want to write about."

"What about you, are you going to the palace, talk to . . . what's his name, the eejit you said runs this place?"

"Kerensky."

"Yes, him."

"I don't think so. His days are numbered, Kitty. Think I'll come with you out to the Bolshevik headquarters and see if I can talk to Trotsky. That's where the story is."

"You really think his people can take over?"

He leaned over the table and took her hands in his. "This is where it's going to start, Kitty. The workers are deserting the factories; the soldiers are deserting the army; the talk is there's going to be a revolution, the real thing! These people got rid of the czar! What next? If it can happen in Russia, it can happen in Germany, it can happen in England."

It was impossible not to believe when she looked into those eyes.

"What is happening here is the blueprint for how we're going to change the world. Our job is to tell people what's happening now and then show them what's possible in the future. As writers, we won't let the governments and the bosses tell people what to think anymore!"

"I'll do my best, Linc, and I'll hope you're right."

"Everything we've talked about, Kitty—about unions, about abolishing capitalism, a new order, a new society—I think the Bolsheviks are the ones to make it happen!"

God, I hope so, she thought. *After all we've been through, I want it to mean something.*

Their breakfast arrived: soggy black bread and bitter black tea.

Lincoln sipped at it and winced. "The one thing I miss about capitalism," he said, "is a decent cup of coffee."

A concierge stood outside one of the big hotels, sporting a ragged peacock feather in his hat, a gold sash across his uniform tunic. He looked bedraggled and cold, grimly waiting to salute a carriage with a grand duke or a duchess that would never arrive.

The only color in the drab city was from the red flags that hung from every building, every statue. There was even a socialist flag tied to Catherine the Great's scepter in the little square before the Alexandrinsky Theater. Elsewhere, there were ugly blotches where imperial insignia had been torn down.

On every corner, there were long lines of people without proper coats, waiting in the bitter cold to buy bread. They stared empty-eyed at the couple as they passed.

Bread shops with no bread, tramlines but no trams. Lincoln asked an old man how to get to the Smolny Institute.

"Walk," he said.

———◆———

They trudged along the boulevard for over an hour before finally they saw the graceful cupolas of the convent, the barracks-like façade of the Smolny Institute beside it. It was an intimidating building, two hundred yards long and three stories high, the imperial arms still carved insolently over the entrance. Not long ago it had been a convent-school for the daughters of the Russian aristocracy, the place where they received a "proper" education. It had been patronized by the tsarina herself.

Now it was headquarters of the Bolshevik Party.

There were guards at the outer gates, demanding to see credentials. Kitty and Lincoln took out their credentials and got in line. Ahead of them was a slight man with a mop of dark, wavy hair, wearing thick glasses. He looked like a college professor. There was a pretty, sparrow-like woman with him. He was speaking to her in French.

The guard put out a hand and stopped them. The slight man made a play of searching through his pockets, then gave the guard a shrug, said something to him in Russian, and tried to go through. He was shoved back. There was an argument.

"What's happening?" Kitty asked Lincoln.

"This is Trotsky. It's him. This is the guy I wanted to interview!"

"Why won't they let him in?"

"He said he's forgotten his pass, and the clod on the gate doesn't know who he is! Said he's never heard of him!" Lincoln started to laugh and then said something to the guard. He was a huge man with a beard the size of a bath towel. He growled something back.

The argument lasted half an hour and when the guard finally let Lincoln and Kitty through, Trotsky was still at the gate, arguing with him. They made their way up the long wooden sidewalk from the outer gate, passed several cannons and an armored car. The first snowflakes fluttered down from a gray, windless sky.

Inside, crowds of people milled around the dark and cavernous hallways. Soldiers straight from the front lines, sailors from the nearby Kronstadt naval base, factory workers from Moscow—all tramping up and down the marble tiles in their muddy boots. And everything in semidarkness. Kitty counted a few offices lit by dim bare bulbs, but mostly the grand schemes of the Bolsheviks went on in a kind of clamorous twilight.

They passed a ballroom with fluted columns and silver candelabra. It was host now to Soviet delegates from all over Russia; Kitty saw them through the open doors, shouting and waving bits of paper at each other.

Soldiers slept on chairs and benches in cold and unlit rooms. Others stood guard outside committee rooms, checking passes. She wondered what the refined young ladies who had once glided along these hallways to their French lessons would think of it now.

A Red Guard led the way up the stairs to the second floor. They went down another dimly lit corridor, to a pair of huge double doors, and he went straight in without knocking.

Madame Ballanskaya's office was a lofty white room lit by glazed-white chandeliers holding hundreds of ornate electric bulbs, although only two of the bulbs appeared to be working. It must have been a lecture hall once, for there was a dais behind her desk, with an empty gold frame above it from which Kitty supposed an imperial portrait had been sliced out.

She had expected a severe-looking woman in a drab peasant's smock, like the female commissars she had seen elsewhere in the building, but the woman who looked up from behind the desk was instead wearing a lacy shirtwaist with a long narrow skirt, and there was even a show of calf between her boots and the hem. She wore a tweed cape, as if she had just stepped out of the pages of a French fashion magazine. Her dark hair had been bobbed.

Lincoln greeted her in his stilted Russian, but to Kitty's surprise the woman fixed Lincoln with a cool stare and answered in flawless, if heavily accented, English. "I am sorry, what is your name again?"

"Lincoln. Lincoln Randolph. This is my colleague, Katherine O'Kane."

Madame Ballanskaya looked at her as if she was something she had found on the bottom of her shoe.

"Miss O'Kane would like to interview you," Lincoln said to her.

She raised a single, provocative eyebrow. "What about you? You do not wish to interview me?" She looked him up and down—the greatcoat, the stubble, the hair flopping into his eyes. If she had licked her lips, she could not have looked more predatory.

"I was hoping to talk to Comrade Lenin," Lincoln said, and pushed his spectacles further up his nose.

"Lenin doesn't talk to anyone. You should try Trotsky."

"I've already talked to him. He's still out there at the gate. The guards won't let him in."

She seemed to think this was very funny. "Every week he does this. You would think such a brilliant man, he wouldn't forget his pass. I don't know how he even dresses himself; I think his wife does it."

"Well, I'll leave you with Kitty," Lincoln said. "She's been really excited about meeting you. I'll meet you back down in the hall," he said to Kitty, and left.

The guard led Lincoln out of the room, shutting the double doors behind them.

"Is that your husband?" Madame Ballanskaya said.

"My colleague."

"No, I think the way you look at him, he's your lover. Is he any good?"

"He's a wonderful writer."

"I mean, in bed. Is he a good lover?" Madame Ballanskaya fixed her with a look. She had intense, black eyes and the bearing of an empress. *But underneath she's a trollop*, Kitty thought. *I've known lots of them.* "You don't know if he is or not?" she said to Kitty.

"I just don't think you should be asking me that question."

"You want to ask me all your questions, but you won't answer one of mine."

"We don't ask those sorts of questions where I come from."

"So, you are bourgeois. I thought so. Or perhaps you are frightened some woman will steal him from you if you tell everyone what a good lover he is." She put aside her papers and replaced the top on her fountain pen. She indicated the chair opposite her desk. "Please, sit."

Damn you, Kitty thought. She had put her off balance.

Madame Ballanskaya sat back and crossed her arms. "So you write for the newspapers in the West. What do they know of the revolution over there?"

"Not much. And what they do know scares them. They're scared that it might happen in New York or London."

"It will happen in New York and London, eventually. History tells us that revolution is not an isolated event because it is not about overthrowing governments, it is about spreading new ideas."

"Well, it's not like the world doesn't need new ideas." Kitty leaned her elbows on the desk. "They tell me all women have the vote here."

"Of course."

"We're still fighting for the vote in England and in America."

"*We* are still fighting?"

"I've been arrested three times for demonstrating."

"So, not *too* bourgeois then?"

"I know what it's like for a full-grown man in a policeman's uniform to hit you with a wooden baton. So no, not *too* bourgeois."

"I know of the suffragettes, of course. Your Emmeline Pankhurst was here with a British delegation a few months ago. She brought the

American and British ambassadors with her and a lot of reporters, like you. They met with Minister Kerensky. You know this Pankhurst?"

"I know of her. She's a great woman but I don't agree with everything she says."

An arched eyebrow.

"She wants women to stop the struggle for suffrage until after the war," Kitty said. "It seems to me that makes her as much a part of the establishment as those we're fighting against. She thinks the war and the lot of women are two different issues. But they're not."

"I said this also to Pankhurst when she was here. But I think she does not understand socialism. In fact, I did not find her to be revolutionary at all, just rather stiff woman with a taste for the drama. Is this what you wish to ask me about?"

Kitty took out her leather-bound notebook and her pen. "Well, to start with, I think my readers would be very interested to know how the revolution here will serve women."

"The first thing your readers in the West must understand, Miss O'Kane, is that our revolution does not mean just new government. It is about completely new way of life. It is true that now the czar is gone, women have the right to vote, and Bolshevism means equal pay for equal work for both men and women. But that is just the beginning."

"But the right to vote and the right to equal pay are two things that Western women can only dream about right now."

"That is because Western women are not just enslaved by men, they are enslaved by their own minds."

Kitty felt herself bristle. "You think so?"

"Let me tell you little bit about myself. My parents sent me to study in France when I finished school, and I made the most of my opportunities. I learned about life in the West, and I learned how to read Western books and converse with Western intellectuals. I can speak thirteen languages. But the most important thing that I learn was that changing laws is nothing. To really bring about revolution we must change the way that people *think*."

"And you found that out through reading books? It's one way, I suppose. Myself, I found out about it by growing up in a tenement in Dublin."

"So you come from the peasant class then?"

Kitty took a slow, deep breath. "Peasant class? I never got to aim quite that high." She checked her notes, the questions she'd scribbled down. "So what will the Bolsheviks do for women, Madame Ballanskaya?"

"Do you believe in marriage, Miss O'Kane?"

"Well I'm not married, so I'm not in a position to offer an opinion right now."

"Bolshevism believes that marriage, even the traditional family unit, is a pillar of our oppressive past. Under Communism, men and women will work for society, and in turn they are supported by society. Children will be wards of the state, not belong to their families. That is the only way men and women can free themselves of the oppressive system."

Kitty stopped writing in her notebook, thought about Elsie and her Bert in their grocer's shop in Stepney. "Not every woman in the world would agree with you there."

"That is because most women in the world are stupid; they think to choose between one form of oppressive government or another is freedom. But in the end, it makes no difference. Only revolution is different."

"You don't believe in the family at all then?"

"You come from very happy family, Miss O'Kane?"

Kitty didn't answer.

"Every woman has right not to be afraid that one day she and her children will be left with no food, no shelter, no money. Men are unreliable in this regard; they use their economic power as weapon. It is only the state that can guarantee a woman her freedom."

"What about love?" Kitty said.

"I do not dismiss it. It possesses a uniting element which is valuable to the collective. But women must forget this idea that their well-being can be entrusted to the hands of another. Then she becomes just another form of property. Bolshevism will allow women, as well as men, the right to own property, and divorce will be possible upon request. Isn't that the Utopia you dream of, Miss O'Kane?"

The interview lasted more than an hour. When it was over, Kitty walked blindly away along the corridors, and was soon lost. She felt angry and frightened and didn't know quite why. Hadn't that damned woman just promised the kind of world where there would be no more tenements, no more drunken daddies, no more bruised little girls?

So why did she feel like this?

And where was Lincoln? Where was the way out of this damned place?

Thirteen languages!

Damn her and her thirteen damned languages to hell.

CHAPTER 19

Kitty tore a chunk out of the black bread with her teeth, washed it down with bitter black tea. She stared at her typewriter, blew on her fingers to try and warm them. Still not October, what would it be like here when winter came?

The floor was littered with screwed up balls of paper. How to explain Madame Ballanskaya for readers of the *Union*? Did she report her interview verbatim, or did she put herself in the piece, express a little of her own revulsion at this cold-eyed version of Bolshevik ideals? But if she did that, she would have to understand why the woman made her so angry.

Perhaps it would be better just to describe the Bolshevik's utopian dream without hinting at her own unease. The idea of equal pay and instant divorce would shock even the most liberal of the *Union* readers on its own. Her own undefined sense of unease was getting in the way of a good story.

Lincoln smoked as he tapped away in the other corner of the room. He looked up, saw her staring at him. "What is it?"

"I can't do this," she said.

He stubbed out the cigarette and came across the room. He held out a hand. "Let me see."

"I've only written three paragraphs."

"You've been sitting here all morning."

She tore the page out of the typewriter and handed it to him. He peered at her over the top of the page. "What's wrong, Kitty? I thought she was perfect for you. Social and economic equality for women. Isn't that what you believe in?"

She shrugged and nodded.

"So, what's wrong?"

"If I could put into words what's wrong, I would. That's the problem, though, isn't it? I can't, because I'm a lousy writer."

Lincoln tapped the page with a fingernail, pursed his lips, then looked back at her. "You're too earnest. Too many details. People don't want to read that. You have to put more passion in it, Kitty."

"You think I have no passion?"

"I know you have passion, you just haven't let it out onto the page."

"I don't like her, Lincoln."

"Who? Madame Ballanskaya?"

"She looked at you like a bear looking at its dinner."

"You're imagining things."

He read the rest of what she had written, pushed his spectacles farther up his nose, and frowned. "'The satisfaction of one's sexual desires should be as simple as getting a glass of water.' Wow, did she really say that?"

"According to her, love is only valuable as a 'uniting element which is valuable to the collective.' She's not exactly Walt Whitman."

"I guess it's only another angle on what we say about free love in Greenwich Village."

"On what *you* say about it. But that's not all. The family unit—everything is units with that woman—the family unit will wither away once the second stage of Communism becomes a reality."

"Henry could make a great headline out of that if you can get it written."

"You agree with her?"

"Well, it's not that far from what your Charlotte Reddings was talking about, God rest her soul."

"Charlotte still believed in love and family."

"How do you know that? You only talked to her for a few minutes, Kitty."

"I read her book. Did you?"

Lincoln shrugged.

"That Ballanskaya woman is so damned smug."

"Well, she's smart, she has a reason to be smug."

"I know she's smart. She must have told me so a dozen times. In thirteen languages. And no one has a reason to be smug, Lincoln."

"But maybe she's right."

"Or maybe she isn't. But she's willing to test out her theories on real people, and not just one or two—she wants to play with the lives of millions of people."

"I didn't know you were so in love with the domestic life. You never got too nostalgic about yours."

"This has nothing to do with my feelings one way or the other."

"Hasn't it?"

"What does that mean?"

"Look, you asked my opinion, Kitty, I'm giving it. Just get it written."

"I should just write down what she said and leave it at that?"

"Well you still have to slant it toward your readers."

"Women still love their families, even in New York."

"You know what I mean."

He went back to his desk.

She put another blank page into the typewriter. Perhaps Lincoln was right, he was the darling of the left-wing press, after all, and what was she? A hopeful with no more than a handful of articles to her name after almost two years at it.

She was still earning less than Elsie got for changing bedpans. She certainly was no Charlotte Reddings yet; no newspaper column, no speaking tours.

She was about to try again when she heard the crack of rifle fire. They both looked up at the same time. "It's a long way away," he said, "it's on the other side of the city." And they went back to work.

Day after day of drenching rain. People shivered, dead-eyed and dripping, in the bread lines, which grew longer each day. Even before dawn women appeared on the iron-white streets, waiting hour after hour in numb despair for milk or candles or kerosene, some of them with babies bundled in their arms.

Kitty sat at her typewriter, wearing every piece of clothing she had, her breath forming little clouds in the air. There hadn't been any heating in the hotel for days. At night she worked by the light of a solitary candle, which was almost burned down to a nub.

Not everyone was suffering. From the window she could see the Nevsky Prospect lit up like Broadway; from up there she could hear roars of laughter and the pop of champagne corks from inside the gambling halls. A dancer called Karsavina still performed to packed houses at the Mariinsky Theatre, even though her audience wore mostly rags, and many had foregone eating that day just to buy a ticket.

Pretty young whores in fake jewels and furs smoked cigarettes in cafés, accepting free drinks and bargaining hard before agreeing on a price. It was love, of sorts, that they were selling, and perhaps it served as a unifying element for the collective, just as Madame Ballanskaya had said. Hard to concentrate with the rumbling of cartwheels down in the street. The art treasures were all being removed from the Hermitage; Lincoln said they were even stripping the tapestries from the walls of the Winter Palace. Every night the wagons went by, laden with priceless old treasures bound for the Kremlin in Moscow. They were even moving the machinery out of the factories.

She stared at the blank page. How to explain to people in America the complexities of the revolution? Kerensky, the man who had replaced the czar, was now in turn under threat by the Bolsheviks, supported by their ragtag army of Red Guards and the imperial sailors from the naval base at Kronstadt. On Kerensky's side were the Cossacks and the officer cadet corps, the Junkers. How to make sense of all the other factions and who they sided with, what they wanted? Even Lincoln was hard pressed to explain it all to her sometimes.

She heard him coming along the hall, the thump of his boots muffled by the carpet. The door burst open. He came in, tracking mud across the carpets, swinging his arms against the cold, almost lost inside the greatcoat and bundled scarf and fur hat.

"How was it?" she said.

"The Council? Everyone was just screaming at each other across the chamber. The Bolsheviks walked out. Then Kerensky tried to make a speech and he got shouted down. I saw him in the corridor outside, sitting on a bench, crying. I think he's having a breakdown." He pulled up a chair and sat down, almost straightaway he jumped to his feet again, so excited he couldn't keep still.

"I think it's really going to happen, Kit. Everything we've ever talked about. We're about to witness history!"

She couldn't type anymore, could barely feel her fingers. Finally, she calmed him down, and they got into bed fully clothed, piled all the spare coats they had on top of the bed. But she was still shivering.

Lincoln put his arms around her, his own body shaking with cold. They listened to the crack of distant rifle fire echo across the roofs.

Made throwing bricks through shop windows look like a child's prank, this. "I'm scared, Lincoln," she said.

"So am I." His voice was muffled by the blankets and coats.

She lay there staring into the dark, sleet weeping down the window, fog freezing and thick as a shroud over the city. What a cold, gray place to change the world.

CHAPTER 20

The next evening, as she made her way back to the hotel, a battery of artillery rumbled past, the horses' hooves clattering on the cobblestones. A company of cadets followed, in military caps and greatcoats, stern and stiff, so different from the rough and ready guards. Soldiers with bayonets had been posted in front of the state bank, and there were mounted militiamen on every corner.

People elbowed each other to read one of the multitude of proclamations that seemed to cover every smooth surface. "Stay Home." "Come Out and Support the Government." "Support the Workers." "Support the People's Republic."

Rumors flew; Kerensky had gone to the Council of the Republic to offer his resignation; the Junkers were preparing to assault the Soviet; the Germans were just five miles away.

Night fell, and everyone was still out on the street. Knots of people murmured under gaslights. The sound of gunshots echoed over the rooftops from the other side of the river. A wave of people flooded toward the square.

Lincoln had gone to attend an emergency meeting of the Council earlier that morning, and he still wasn't back. She was afraid. He had told her that he expected trouble there from the sailors from Kronstadt, the naval base for the Baltic fleet. They had sided with the Bolsheviks and were expected to try and disrupt the meeting.

When she got back to their hotel, the porter gave her a letter. The English stamps with the head of George V seemed so quaint here. She looked at the postmark. The letter had been posted almost two months before.

She took it upstairs to their room. She flicked the light switch on and off a few times, nothing. She tried the tap in the washstand in the corner, but there was no water either. She lit a candle, sat down at the table and tore open the envelope.

> *Dear Irish,*
>
> *It was so good to get your last letter. I hadn't heard from you in so long and I was worried about you. I still have the piece you wrote for the News of the World about the war in Serbia, it's pinned up on our wall at home, I tell everyone I know a famous writer! They are impressed.*
>
> *I can't believe the places you've been. Who'd have thought? I always thought there was something special about you the very first time I laid eyes on you on the Titanic. My goodness, so much has happened since then!*
>
> *I don't have good news. My Bert is back from the war, I think I told you in my last letter I had news that he'd been wounded, well he's home now thank the Lord. He didn't lose an arm or a leg like some of these poor blighters, it's his mind that's wounded, bless him, shell shock the doctors call it. He just shakes all the time, sometimes he can't even hold a spoon to feed himself and he has nightmares something terrible, wakes up screaming sometimes, scares our little Jackie, it does, I've had to send her away to stay with her aunt and uncle.*
>
> *To be honest, I wonder if Bert will ever be right again. There doesn't seem a lot the doctors can do for him*

but we hope and pray for the best, at least he's alive and that's a blessing.

I'm still working at Saint Thomas', we see a lot of the returned soldiers in here, some of the injuries make you want to cry. The doctors are wonderful here and they do what they can.

Talking of doctors, you remember that intern you asked me about? Well he's married now, got a little one on the way they say. Most of the doctors don't talk much to the likes of us nurses, but he is a bit different I have to say, he always smiles at us and is very friendly.

I don't know if this letter will ever reach you, but this is the address you gave me, I suppose God willing I'll hear if you end up somewhere else. I do worry about you, and I say a prayer for you on Sundays at the church though I know you don't believe in that sort of thing.

Take care and write to me when you can.

Your friend,

Elsie.

Elsie. She imagined her sitting in the Lyons teahouse in her uniform and her cape, writing the letter before she rushed off to her shift at the hospital. It made Kitty angry when she thought about Elsie's husband. What did the war have to do with him, with any of those poor boys?

She reread the second to last paragraph. So, Tom was married now. She was happy for him; she imagined him with some demure and pretty English rose, him in his suit with a gold fob no doubt, and a homburg, distinguished now and everyone doctor this and doctor that. *Good for you, Tom.*

She heard a jingling outside in the street and looked down out the window, saw Lincoln jump from a sleigh and rush inside. When he came in, his face was flushed with excitement.

"I was right; it's started," he said, almost out of breath. "Some Kronstadt sailors with guns rushed into the Council and ordered everyone home. The Bolsheviks are getting ready to take over. There's going to be a fight, Kitty. Get your coat."

"Where are we going?"

"They're getting ready to storm the Winter Palace. Come on, we can't miss it."

It was dark down in the street, just a single yellow streetlight on the corner of the Nevsky. A knot of Kronstadt sailors stood in the middle of the street, talking in low voices and smoking cigarettes. An armored vehicle was parked nearby, black oil smoke from its exhaust freezing on the air, two Red Guards sitting on the turret, watching them.

The whole city seemed to be holding its breath.

There were muddy leaflets scattered in the slush underfoot. Lincoln picked one up. He held it toward the half-light of a street lamp, squinted as he tried to read it:

Citizens! The Provisional Government is deposed. State Power has passed into the organ of the Petrograd Soviet of Workers' and Soldiers' Deputies.

"Is it true, do you think?"

"I don't know, Kitty. Maybe."

It all felt a little unreal. She could see lights blazing on the Nevsky, the trams were still running, people going to the theater and the movie houses and the cafés as if the revolution had never happened, as if tonight would not change the world.

Kitty gripped Lincoln's arm.

"Look," she said. "There."

A mass of sailors was surging toward them along Voskressensky Prospect, Red Guards marching behind them. They were carrying rifles and bayonets and wearing the red armbands of the Bolsheviks over their greatcoats, the entire makeshift army headed in the direction of the Winter Palace. A motor truck rumbled past; Lincoln recognized one of the guards from the Smolny, standing on the back; he shouted to him in Russian, and the man waved a revolver and shouted something back. She didn't understand much of it except one phrase: "The game is on!"

The truck slowed at the intersection, and Lincoln grabbed her hand and pulled her toward it. "Come on," he said. "This is it!"

They scrambled to climb aboard. The guards laughed and shouted encouragement as they pulled them up.

Kitty could hear more rifle fire in the distance.

A Red Guard with a long black beard and a black cape, grinned and called out something to Lincoln.

"What did he say, Linc?"

"He said we're all going to get killed."

"Wonderful."

"He also said tell the beautiful lady to take off her yellow hatband. It's a perfect target for snipers."

It was cold without it, but she took off her hat.

⚔

They bounced along the dark streets, Kitty clinging to the wooden tailboard to keep from being jolted off. The wind froze her face. She felt a thrill of exhilaration; little Kitty O'Kane from Dublin, and here she was, seeing history being made! No, more than that: she was a part of it.

They drove helter-skelter down a wide black avenue; there were bonfires glowing in the dark, and soldiers loomed out of the darkness, shouting and raising their rifles. Were they warning them or cheering them? She could hear gunfire coming from the palace. *I could die tonight*, she thought. *But I'm here, and I don't care.*

As they reached the streets around the palace, it grew eerily quiet. The only lights came from the Duma, which was lit up like Herald Square. Another bonfire had been lit on the corner of the Ekaterina Canal, and a squadron of armed Kronstadt sailors were waiting there. Half a dozen of them jumped out into the road, hands aloft, blocking the way, yelling furiously at the driver to stop. The truck drew to the side of the road, and they all climbed out.

"The sailors are saying we can't go any further," Lincoln said. "All the entrances to Palace Square have been cordoned off. He's heard that the Junkers have surrendered and Kerensky has gone into hiding, but no one seems sure."

"That's it then?"

"The hell it is. I'm not missing this. This is one of the greatest moments in human history." He showed one of the sailors his credentials, and it was like magic; the man grinned and let them through the cordon. They ran toward the main arch. Some Bolshevik soldiers were milling about underneath it; it seemed like they weren't sure what to do. Lincoln had a hurried conversation with the sergeant in charge.

"He says it's too dangerous to go any further. He's waiting for orders and reinforcements."

"We've come this far, Linc. We can't stop now."

She grabbed Lincoln's hand and pulled him after her. The sergeant shouted at them, and there was the crack of rifle fire. She didn't know if it came from the palace or from the Bolsheviks. Hell with them all. Lincoln was right, they couldn't miss this. They ran through the arch and past the Alexander Column. There was more rifle fire. Was it snipers or the Red Guards inside the palace celebrating an unexpected victory?

Dozens of rifles had been thrown onto the cobblestones; she supposed the Junker sentries had run off and left them there. She slumped behind a barricade heaped with boxes, barrels, an old bed-spring, a wagon. Lincoln dropped down beside her. Her heart was in her mouth.

"Are they shooting at us?"

"I don't know!"

They were just fifty paces from the palace itself. There were lights on at every window, and she could see scores of people rushing around inside.

"There's a door," Lincoln said.

"Let's go then," she said. They ran across the cobbles, and Kitty was surprised to find the door unlocked. They hurled themselves inside.

They were in some kind of storeroom; there was another door on the far wall, and they could hear a muted roar on the other side of it. Lincoln edged the door open.

They peered out. Kitty caught her breath; she had never seen anything quite like it. She could make out two massive Corinthian columns that seemed to go all the way to a heaven far beyond the crystal chandeliers. *Just one of those*, she thought, *is about the size of our tenement in Dublin.*

The patterned parquet floor shone like a mirror. Or what she could see of it, anyway. It was covered with rows of filthy mattresses and a litter of cigarette butts, hunks of black bread, and empty bottles of French champagne. She supposed this was where the Junker cadets had been garrisoned.

There were packing cases scattered everywhere. Kerensky's men had still been packaging up the palace treasures when the Junkers had surrendered. Now the Red Guards were prizing them open with bayonets or bashing in the lids with their rifles, pulling out tapestries, Etruscan vases, ornate table clocks, one man even an antique gilded harquebus.

The looting had started already.

"Oh my God," Lincoln breathed. "It's true, it's all over. It's all over!"

The palace servants, still wearing their blue-and-gold uniforms, were pawing desperately at the soldiers, tugging at their sleeves. "No, you can't touch that. Put that down!" The soldiers just shoved them out of the way. Kitty saw a Red Guard carrying a massive table with a mosaic top under one arm, a curlicue chair under the other; another pretended to fan himself with a folding ivory-and-lace fan.

A commissar ran in, holding a pistol. "Comrades! Don't touch anything! Don't take anything! This is the property of the People!"

"Well, look who it is," Lincoln said.

"I can smell his hat from here," Kitty said.

It was Lincoln's friend, the commissar from the train. A head taller than most of the men around him, his wiry black beard quivering with indignation, he cut a fearsome figure. He drew an ancient pistol from his belt and held it in the air. He fired two rounds into the vaulted ceiling.

"Stop! Put everything back! Don't take anything! This is the property of the People!" he roared again.

He went over to one of the looters and knocked the bundle of damask and tapestry out of his arms; he pointed his revolver at two men carrying a massive bronze clock, and they gingerly lowered it to the floor. He paced the hall, making sure everything was crammed back into the wooden crates, then ordered some of his own men to guard them.

"Revolutionary discipline, comrades!" he bawled at them.

The shout was taken up along the corridors, up and down the stairs: "Revolutionary discipline, comrades! This is the property of the People!"

It was then that he saw Lincoln and Kitty, watching from the doorway, and he brought up the revolver and pointed it directly at them. "You! Come out!" Lincoln put his hands in the air and did as the man said. Kitty followed.

"Is he going to shoot us?" Kitty said.

"Maybe. I don't think he's recognized us yet."

"Say something!"

Lincoln started to talk to him, but the commissar's eyes were wild, unfocused. He kept on shouting and waving the gun. Kitty felt her bowels turn to water.

He herded them toward the door. Other guards were running in now, shoving everyone with the butts of their rifles. "Clear the palace! Everybody out of the palace except the commissars!"

Terrified cadets, wearing the red shoulder straps of the Junker schools, were being led through the corridors at gunpoint by the commissar's men. Kitty supposed they were being taken prisoner. They were herded into a long line in front of the side door along with a handful of Cossacks.

The commissar took up position behind a long wooden table and had two of his soldiers search everyone in the line, whether they were a Junker or a Cossack or a Red Guard.

There was a cadet in front of them, a tall boy with red cheeks and an improbable waxed handlebar moustache. The Red Guards went through his pockets and looked under his coat. They found a cracked porcelain plate, a champagne cork, a coat hanger, and a worn sofa cushion. He had on a gold ring inlaid with a small emerald, which he claimed was his, but they took it off him anyway.

"The treasure of the Romanovs," Kitty said.

The commissar noted these items on a piece of paper with his pen. "Now, will you take up arms against the People anymore?" he said to the cadet.

The Junker shook his head, sullen.

"Well?"

"No," he said, and the commissar nodded, and one of the soldiers shoved the boy out of the door. It seemed he was free to go. He stared in dumb surprise, and then the door slammed.

"I told you, didn't I, on *Titanic*!" Lincoln whispered to her. "I said this would happen! And we're here at the heart of it! A new start, Kitty. No more capitalism! Unions and votes for women, everything we always dreamed of and wrote about! This is it, it starts today! Today the Winter Palace, tomorrow Buckingham Palace. Next week there will be red flags all along Nevsky Prospect; next year they'll be all along the Unter den

Linden and the Champs Elysées! And we're here, Kitty, we're here to see it all begin, just like I promised!"

A new world, as easy as that.

He held his hands in the air as one of the guards searched him for loot. The other guard stepped toward Kitty, but the commissar stopped him. He would do the search himself. He grinned at her with broken teeth, then ran his hands up and down, under her coat, very slowly, and finished by giving her bottom a hard squeeze. She yelped.

Then he turned to Lincoln, patted his chest, and said something to him. "What did he say?" she asked.

"Well Kitty, he said that now he's the same as the king of Bulgaria."

CHAPTER 21

The refectory on the ground floor of the Smolny where young ladies had once practiced their table manners was now a mess hall for Red Guards in muddy boots, and stubbly-faced factory workers with tobacco-stained fingers. Kitty and Lincoln paid their two rubles and stood in line with a bowl and a greasy wooden spoon to get their ration of steaming cabbage soup ladled from an immense tin washtub.

For another five kopecks Kitty could get a cup of tea as well. It wasn't the Ritz, but it didn't need to be, she reckoned. She never ate this well in the Liberties.

The war had not ended with the storming of the Winter Palace; according to Lincoln, that was just the start. The Bolshevik insurrection was spreading through Russia like a wildfire. He had already rushed off pieces on the storming of the Winter Palace to the *Union* and *Collier's* and the *New Yorker*.

"This is going to make me famous," he told her. "No, better than that. Notorious!"

So this wasn't about a better world then; just a better world for Lincoln Randolph.

They sat down on a bench at one of the long, rough wooden tables. "Kerensky's marching on Petrograd," he said, tearing off a slice of soggy black bread from the communal plate in the middle of the table. He dipped it in the watery soup.

"But he has no army."

"He has the Cossacks."

"That's madness," Kitty said. "They're the very people he's been fighting all his life. They supported the czar."

"Well, this is one crazy country. Hey, I got a letter here for you, the *Saturday Evening Post* by the look of it."

Kitty tore it open, read it through quickly. Another rejection.

"They didn't like it, huh? Which piece was that?"

"The Death Battalion."

He shrugged and spooned some more soup. His glasses were steamed up, and he wiped them on his sleeve.

"What?" she said.

"Sorry?"

"That face. What did it mean?"

"Kitty, that piece was very emotive. I told you that."

"You said being emotive was my strength."

"Yeah, but don't overdo it."

Kitty took a deep breath. "You told me to let my passion come through in my writing."

"I didn't mean you should get so carried away. There's a difference between passionate and hysterical."

"In your professional opinion then, that was what was wrong with it? A regiment made up entirely of women throwing themselves at German machine guns at the battle of . . . what was it? Smorgon. Then when they get home, they have their own soldiers make fun of them for being girls and try to rape them—that was too *emotive*?"

"Maybe." He returned his attention to his soup.

Well she had let herself be emotive about Madame Ballanskaya and still sold the interview to the *Union* and then a piece called "Marriage and Motherhood in Russia" to *Collier's*.

But no one had bought her article on the storming of the Winter Palace, just as they had turned up their noses at her stories about the slaughters in Serbia and Bosnia. That apparently was the province of war journalists like Lincoln. A woman couldn't be a war journalist. No editor would say as much, but that was what it came down to in the end.

Meanwhile, Lincoln's own piece on the storming of the palace had been syndicated across America as well as Britain. He was even talking about writing a book about the revolution now sweeping across Russia.

For all her work and her very minor celebrity, she was still earning less than she had at the *Union*, typing Henry's letters. She was still reliant on Lincoln for her survival. What an irony. Madame Ballanskaya would like that.

"Perhaps I should go home," she said.

Lincoln stopped eating. The look of dismay on his face surprised her. "You want to leave me here? Kitty, no. I don't know what I'd do without you."

"Do you really mean that?"

"Well, sure I do."

"You've never said that before."

"Goes without saying."

"Nothing goes without saying, Lincoln. You're a writer; you should know that."

Just then—speak of the devil—Madame Ballanskaya herself walked into the hall, head high and arms swinging, like a man. God knows, she wasn't built like one. Heads turned among the younger Bolsheviks as she went past; Kitty even saw Lincoln's eyes flicker for a moment too.

When Madame Ballanskaya had her peasant's soup and a glass of tea, she came over to their table and sat down next to him, so close that they were almost touching. Lincoln did not protest, although he paid her no attention either.

Madame Ballanskaya stared at her with an expression Kitty couldn't quite read. *I wonder if she read the interview I published in the* Union, she thought.

Lincoln finished his soup quickly, and he and Kitty left. He had ignored the Ballanskaya woman a little too pointedly, it seemed to her. *Lincoln might not know what he'd do here without me*, she thought.

But I damned well do.

———

The trams were not running that day; they headed back from the Smolny on foot. A biting wind cut through the streets; Kitty could smell snow. They were almost back to their hotel, on Nevsky Prospect, when they heard the tramping of boots.

"Look," Lincoln said.

Mass upon mass, the Bolsheviks were heading out of the city to face Kerensky's Cossacks, thousands of them. At the front were the Red Guards with cannons and motor trucks full of soldiers; behind them the latest recruits, straight from the factories by the look of them, none of them marching in step, and not just men and boys, but women, even children in worn-out boots and thin, ragged coats. Some of them were only armed with spades.

They carried a red flag with coarse gold lettering: "Peace! Land!"

There was a Junker standing behind them. "Look at them!" he said to Lincoln. "They will run like sheep when they have to face real soldiers. Do you think a single one of them can fight?"

CHAPTER 22

That night Red Guards patrolled the streets, or squatted around little fires on the street corners. As dawn broke, Kitty got out of bed and peered through the curtains. There was no one about. *Somewhere out there, beyond this hulk of a city, Kerensky and his Cossacks are waiting. I wonder how long the revolution will really last?*

The snow had turned to sleet, and the ruts in the roads had iced over. An army truck fishtailed down the Morskaya. By some miracle, overnight the heating had been turned back on in the hotel. If it only lasted an hour or two, it was still something.

Lincoln's side of the bed was cold; he hadn't come home again last night. Lately he had taken to working late at the institute and sleeping on a bench in the halls or on the floor in Trotsky's office.

She dressed and sat down at the table by the window with her coat over her shoulders and a blanket over her legs. Even when the heating was on, the room was never really warm enough.

She stared at her typewriter.

Now don't be hysterical, Kitty. And don't write about the war.

If she couldn't write about the war, what was there to write? She ran her hands across the cover of the one book she had dragged with her all the way across Europe, through Greece and Serbia and beyond the Pale.

"*The New Woman*," she said aloud. She wondered what Charlotte would say if she could see her sitting here now. "*Write with passion,*" she had said.

"*Write with less passion,*" Lincoln said.

Write about what you know.

Poor Charlotte. She should be here, Kitty thought; *I should have been the one who drowned on the* Lusitania. *Charlotte was the one who could write, the woman others listened to. Here I am in the middle of the greatest social upheaval in recent history, and all I have is a growing pile of rejection letters, months old, look at them all; the* Louisville Herald, *the* Baltimore Sun, *the* Buffalo Evening News.

She heard a muffled footfall in the corridor; it had to be Lincoln, they were the only guests left in the hotel.

He looked like hell; he had three days' growth of beard and was deadly pale. He threw off his hat and poured himself a brandy and lit a cigarette. He tossed a letter on the desk. "This was down at reception," he said.

She ripped it open, barely glanced at it before tossing it into the metal wastepaper bin beside her. "*McCall's*," she said.

"Which piece was it?"

"The one about the Winter Palace. I think my account was too emotional for them. I have to learn to downplay the most important revolution in human history."

He shrugged. "They just want different things from you. What about when we were in Constantinople, that piece you wrote about the secluding of women in the Middle East, and how it's only one step away from what happens in America. The *Saturday Evening Post* bought that."

"In other words, women shouldn't write about politics or war because they can't get their pretty little heads around serious subjects."

"If you have unpopular opinions, don't expect to be popular."

"You're popular."

"Notorious. And yes, before you say it, that's because I'm a man. It's what you're fighting against. But I'm on your side, Kitty, don't forget that."

The fight went out of her. "It's like I haven't seen you for days," she said.

"It was only one night. There was a late-night meeting of the Soviet; I couldn't afford to miss it."

"Don't you ever get tired of it?"

"Tired of it?"

"We've been doing this for two years, drifting from one war to another."

"This is not just a war, Kit. You said it yourself. This is a turning point in history, happening right here, now. How can you get tired of that?"

"I don't know," she said. "I just do."

"Don't get discouraged. You're still learning."

"Just sometimes I think it would be nice to stop, build a life somewhere."

He sighed and sat down beside her the desk. "Kitty," he said. "Kitty."

"I want to go home."

"Where's home?"

"I don't know. Where is home for you, Linc?"

"We can't leave now." He drew her face toward him. "Come on, Kit. Don't lose heart. You mean the world to me; you know that, don't you?"

He kissed her on the mouth, then pulled her toward him. She knew what he wanted and her fists came up and she tried to push him away. Why was he making love to her right now? Because he was overcome, or because he wanted to change her mind? He shoved the blanket on her knees aside and onto the floor. He pulled up her skirts.

"Not now," she said.

"I missed you," he said, and his hand cupped her breast and squeezed.

"That hurts," she said.

His breath was ragged on her cheek. He put his hand under her legs, scooped her up, and carried her to the bed. It felt wrong; she didn't want to do this right now, but if she made a point of it, there would be another fight. *Let him just do what he wants*, she thought, *perhaps it's easier.*

The bed was cold, the bolster was trapped under her back. Lincoln was on top of her; his hands were everywhere; he hadn't even warmed them up. He was tugging at her underwear, pulling her drawers roughly down to her knees.

"Let's get under the covers," she said, but he didn't seem to hear her. He pushed her knee to the side, was fumbling with his trousers, trying to get them down. She was trapped underneath him. Two faded cherubs blew kisses at each other across the flaking paint of the ceiling.

She felt him hard against her leg, and her skirt ripped. He tried to force himself inside her; he licked his fingers and made himself wet. But he still hurt her. And then he was inside her, jaw clenched, eyes shut; she could feel his breath quickening in her ear. She concentrated on the molding on the ceiling. The edge of his belt buckle bit into her thigh, and her hands closed into fists around the quilt.

There was something angry about the way he hammered away at her. What had happened to him? She felt as if she wasn't there, that she was watching herself from the other side of the room. Then he juddered and gasped and it stopped.

His face was inches from hers, his skin flushed, his eyes unfocused. He pushed himself backward so that his weight was off her, and pulled up his trousers and buttoned them. He didn't say anything, just lay there staring at the ceiling.

Kitty found her drawers on the floor and stood up, smoothing her ripped skirt down back over her legs. She retrieved her blanket and coat and went back to her typewriter, in the corner. After a while she heard him start to snore.

She stared at the blank white page.

CHAPTER 23

There was another, smaller mess hall upstairs at the Smolny, reserved for the bureaucrats. There was thick, yellow butter for the bread, and tea was served in a glass. Now that Lincoln had ingratiated himself with the leading Bolsheviks, he and Kitty had started taking their lunches there.

Lenin went there, too, but he always ate alone in a corner. He was a little round man, quite bald, with a head too big for his shoulders. "Never seen him eating with anyone," Lincoln said. "Shuts himself away in his office most of the time." He had managed to interview him only once in all the time they had been in Petrograd and had not been impressed. "As cold a man as I ever met," he said.

Trotsky came in and joined them, as he often did. He had Madame Ballanskaya with him. Unlike Lenin, Trotsky was never on his own, was followed everywhere he went by an army of clerks and toadies. As she sat down, Madame Ballanskaya gave Lincoln a smile.

Kitty saw the look that passed between them. *Jesus Mary, not again.*

Trotsky was more animated than usual. One of the Red Guards brought him his lunch, and he picked up his spoon but then pushed the bowl away almost immediately. The man never stopped talking, and if he had an idea he had to express it, and eating got in the way of holding court. But even though her Russian was improving, he talked too fast for her to catch most of what he was saying.

"I don't know how he does it," Kitty said. "He looks exhausted."

Madame Ballanskaya leaned in. "Comrade Trotsky has been working in his office twenty-four hours a day for weeks. Often he sleeps at his desk."

"Well he looks all in to me. I wouldn't be surprised if he has a nervous breakdown."

"That cannot be allowed to happen," she said. "That is why Comrade Randolph has agreed to help us."

Kitty looked up at Lincoln. He couldn't meet her eyes. "Help? How?"

"You haven't told her?" Madame Ballanskaya said.

"There hasn't been a moment," Lincoln said.

Madame Ballanskaya sighed theatrically and said she should be getting back to work. She left the hall, took her glass of *chai* with her.

"What's going on, Linc?" Kitty said.

"Look, it's nothing. Trotsky needs someone to help him with . . . you know, talking to the press, getting stories out about the revolution. One man can't do it all."

"You've agreed to this?"

"Sure, why not?"

"But we're journalists, not Communists."

"I'm not giving up being a journalist. In fact, this will make our lives easier. I'll have the inside dope on everything that happens here."

"You're going to be Trotsky's mouthpiece? But isn't that what you told me was happening in England at the *Times* and the *Express*? Journalists just spreading lies for one side or the other."

"Perhaps the truth is, Kit, I am not a journalist. It's a means to an end. Changing the world is what matters to me; I don't give a damn if that makes me a great journalist or not."

"Oh, don't kid yourself, Lincoln Randolph; you care all right, what the world thinks of you. Besides, we can't change things by lying to people."

"I'm not lying to anyone. Anyway, let's be honest, no journalist is ever entirely neutral. That piece you wrote for the *Union* about Tatiana wasn't exactly—"

"Who?"

Was there a bit of color in his cheeks? "Madame Ballanskaya."

"Since when are you on first name terms with her?"

He shrugged. "Well, if we're going to be working together . . ."

"You're going to be working with her? I thought you were working for Trotsky."

"I'm going to be working with all the Petrograd Soviet."

"I cannot believe you've done this. That woman knew about this before I did."

"Do I have to clear everything with you first?"

"Yes, you do. Because we're in this together."

"Is that what it is? I thought I was helping you, Kitty, not the other way around."

That stung. But it was the truth, wasn't it, even if she didn't want to hear it. "Then do it because . . ." She was about to say: because you love me. But did he? Love had never been mentioned. She thought she was Bohemian, like Netty and all the other young women from the Village, didn't need a man to take care of her.

But love, now. Well in the end, everyone wanted to be loved, didn't they?

"You don't own me, Kitty, I don't own you. Remember?"

"Sure," she said, "I remember."

He slammed his tea glass down on the bench so hard she thought it would shatter. "Don't owe you anything," he said, and got to his feet and stormed out.

She rode the tram back to the Angleterre alone that night. Lincoln stayed late for another meeting of the Soviet and didn't come home.

When Lincoln walked back in the next morning, Kitty had her suitcase open on the bed, was throwing her clothes into it. Lincoln didn't say anything straightaway. He sat down and watched her pack.

"You're leaving."

"No point in staying."

"Because of one little fight?"

"Is that what it was? I thought it was because you were having an affair with Tatiana the Great."

"What are you talking about now? We have a professional relationship, nothing else."

Kitty slammed down the lid of her suitcase. "I'm getting nowhere, Linc. Not with you, not with my typewriter. Kidding myself on both counts."

She tried to lift the case off the bed. Damn, it was too heavy for her. She dropped it on the floor, and it spilled open.

"Maybe that's a sign."

"It's a sign I need a new case is all."

He stood up finally, put a hand on her arm. "Kitty, don't go. Please. I was wrong. I'm sorry. I shouldn't have said those things. I didn't mean it." He put his arms around her. "No one said this was going to be easy."

"No one said it was going to be this damned hard," she murmured back, but her voice was muffled by his coat.

"I never promised you a bed of roses with me, did I? But I said the world was going to change, told you right there that very first time, on the ship. Come on, Kitty. You can't leave me now."

He pulled her toward the door. For a moment, she thought about pulling away. Was this still what she wanted? For no reason, she found herself thinking about Tom and London and another life, a milkman coming up the path, a gas fire, a man who came home to her every night.

You can't have both, Kitty. You can't be a good little wife and change the world as well. What is it going to be?

CHAPTER 24

A week later they were sitting in what the Bolsheviks called a *trak-tir*; it reminded Kitty of one of the dank bars where Lincoln and his Bohemian crowd used to hang out in Greenwich. It was dark and noisy, a heaving mass of workmen and soldiers, all shouting at each other through a haze of tobacco smoke.

Lincoln sat at the end of the table, in animated conversation with his new cronies. Kitty's Russian wasn't good enough to keep up with much of what was being said, so she watched Lincoln shouting and gesticulating at his new comrades with a sort of bemused detachment.

The Bolsheviks were in full control of Petrograd now. Kerensky had tried to retake the city, but the Red Guards had not run like sheep—as the Junker had said they would—and Kerensky had been stopped at Tsarskoye Selo. Lenin was talking with the Germans about a truce. The revolution appeared safe, for now. Already Trotsky was planning not only for a new Russia, but a new world. Lincoln said they were to be a vital part of it; they would explain and export the revolution through what they wrote. The next war would not be a war of guns and horror, he said, but a war of ideas. At last it was time for working men and women everywhere to stand up and be heard.

Someone squeezed into the empty chair beside her. It was Madame Ballanskaya. In her long skirts and fox furs she looked as out of place here as the czarina. Yet the crowd around them seemed to defer to her, shuffling their stools away to give her more room, shifting their cigarettes so the smoke did not drift into those cool gray eyes.

"Comrade, so nice to meet you again," she said to Kitty. "I am surprised to find you still here."

"Why wouldn't I be?"

"Revolution is not for the fainthearted." A casual smile. "So how are your stories received in the West?"

"The editor at the *Union* was happy with our interview. He said it drew a lot of letters from his readers."

Madame Ballanskaya lit a cigarette. "Really?" She exhaled a stream of smoke, and her eyes never left Kitty's face. "I thought it was a little . . . pointed."

"You read it?"

"I have all the American newspapers sent to me. I read them in English of course."

"In English? I thought you'd have them translated into Assyrian for you."

Not even a smile. "I thought your commentary was very clever, using your own bourgeois points of view as counterpoint."

Just one good slap is all she needs, Kitty thought. *I could put her on the floor among the tea stains and the cigarette ends. Haven't had a good catfight since I was in school, but I wouldn't mind one right now.* Kitty lowered her voice. "Was I being bourgeois? Or did I just think you were a snooty little hoor? We have them in the West as well. They're not exclusive to the revolution."

Madame Ballanskaya's expression did not change. Kitty wished now she had bitten her tongue—that famous temper of hers was going to get her in trouble again.

"Where else have you published your work, Comrade? Apart from, what is it? The *Union*?"

"The *Philadelphia Public Ledger* took my piece on marriage and motherhood in the new Russia. Did you read it?"

"No. It wasn't syndicated." She leaned closer. "In fact, it is very hard to read your work because much of it isn't published at all. A short piece in the *New York American*. Yes, a few articles in the *Union*, but it is a free magazine, hardly the *New York Times*. Besides, the editor is a friend of Lincoln's, so he has no choice but to take your articles; am I correct?"

"It's hard to find much sympathy for left-wing viewpoints during a war."

"Yet Comrade Randolph does it. Let's face it, if it were not for him, you would not have survived as a freelance writer. He is the one taking care of you. You write about economic freedom for women, but you have none yourself."

She's right, and that's the worst of it, Kitty thought. *I'm just a snooty little hoor myself. I have my pretensions, but I was raised in a tenement room in Dublin, and everyone can see it. I didn't go to school in Paris, and I don't speak thirteen languages; I'm an impostor.*

She felt her cheeks burning. She wanted to knock this beautiful, snarling monster off her chair, but she wouldn't give her that satisfaction, not in front of everyone.

Instead she stood up, put on her coat, and walked out.

———

There was a tram headed toward Saint Isaac's Square, and she jumped on it. As it moved off, she heard someone yell her name, and she looked back and saw Lincoln running along the track behind. He grabbed a rail and jumped up on the running board.

It took him a moment to get his breath. He held on to the rail as the tram swayed from side to side. "Kitty? What's wrong? Why did you walk out like that?"

"That . . . damned woman."

"What woman? You mean Tatiana?"

"I only know her as Madame Ballanskaya. But I'm not in the inner circle, now am I?"

"What did she say to you?"

"She said I don't belong here and that I should go home. Not in so many words, of course, but I got her point."

The other passengers—Red Guards, workers, delegates—stared in mute astonishment at the two westerners arguing at the top of their voices in their strange language. She didn't mind them. They couldn't understand her, and she wouldn't have cared if they could.

"Come on, Kitty, we've talked about this before."

"And before I always let you persuade me to stay. What for, Linc? So women like that can laugh at me?"

"You're not going to quit now, after all we've been through?"

"You bet I am."

"You can't! You're just starting to earn a reputation for yourself!"

"As what?"

"As a writer!"

Kitty laughed and tossed her head. "According to her, I'm a joke."

"Don't listen to her. You said you wanted to change things; you said you wanted to make a difference. Do you think that just happens overnight?"

"What do you care what happens to me, you work for Trotsky now."

"What the hell did she say to you?"

"She knew my publishing history, damn well near enough. Now how did she know that?"

"They know everything about both of us. We're foreigners; they keep dossiers on us."

"What she knows didn't come out of a file."

"I don't understand why you're so upset."

"She said that I couldn't survive without you, Linc; that if it wasn't for your connections, I'd have had nothing published. Maybe she's got a mean mouth on her, but you know, it's hard to argue with her."

"Have I ever complained?"

"This isn't about you! Not everything is about you!"

"You're acting crazy. Why do you take any notice of her?"

"I wanted to be more than this! Ah Jesus God, we've gone past our stop."

They leaped off when the tram slowed at a corner and started to trudge back through the snow. "It's not like I mind, Kit."

"Maybe you don't mind. I mind."

"You can't go back!"

"Why not? What good is all this doing? How can a girl like me ever be a writer for a fancy magazine? I'm just making a complete idiot of myself!"

She saw the look on his face; really, he was like an open book.

"*Colliers*, the *Post*—they rejected my latest pieces, didn't they?"

He wouldn't meet her eyes.

"Why didn't you tell me?"

"I didn't want you to get discouraged."

"How many other rejections have you been keeping from me so I don't get 'discouraged'?"

He didn't answer.

She walked on, faster. She heard him shouting after her as she turned the corner of Morskaya and St. Isaac's Square, but she kept her head down. *Damn him. Damn them all.*

Just as she was walking past the German Embassy, the man walking in front of her dropped onto the muddy snow, and a moment later she heard the crack of a rifle shot echo around the street. Blood pooled onto the snow from the man's head.

"Kitty, get down!" Lincoln hammered into her from behind and forced her face down into the snow. Some Kronstadt sailors who had been on guard outside the Hotel Angleterre rushed down the street, shouting, *"Provokatsiya!"* This was supposed to be over. Kerensky must have infiltrated snipers into the city. More rifle fire; a shadow moved on the rooftop of the telephone exchange on the other side of the street. The cabmen in their padded coats who had been sitting idly around the square were panicked into action, and whipped their horses into a gallop to get out of the square.

Lincoln pulled Kitty to her feet and dragged her toward their hotel, but the front doors were locked. Lincoln hammered on the glass, but the porter had vanished. A bullet kicked up the snow a few feet away.

"It's no good," Kitty said. They started to run. If they could reach the corner, they would be safe. Everyone around them had the same idea, and they joined the melee stumbling through the snow back up the street.

An armored car roared around the corner at full speed and stopped directly in front of them. Kitty shrieked and covered her ears as the machine-gunner fired at the roof of the telephone exchange. The noise was deafening.

The snipers fired back. One of the sailors yelled and crumpled, clutching his leg. Kitty stopped and turned back for him.

"Leave him!" Lincoln shouted at her.

"I can't leave him!"

Lincoln swore and nodded. They dashed back down the street.

The boy's left leg was shattered. She held his head in her lap, and he looked up at her, his eyes wide with almost childlike surprise. He didn't seem to be in pain. His blood soaked into the mud and slush of the street in a widening pool, and his face turned very pale. His eyes rolled back in his head.

More sniper fire echoed around the street. Lincoln threw himself down beside her, forced her head down next to his. A man in an expensive bearskin fur coat lay next to them. He kept saying, over and over: "I'm sick of this revolution! I'm sick of it!" A peasant woman lying on their other side crossed herself and whispered prayers.

The machine gun in the armored car hammered again. "Now!" Lincoln said, and he pulled Kitty to her feet. He grabbed the sailor's arm and dragged him behind them toward the corner. The sailor's comrades dashed out and helped haul him the last few feet to the corner.

Kitty fell against the wall, and Lincoln collapsed beside her. "You all right?" he said.

She nodded.

He was staring at the top of her head. He took off her fur hat. He gave a little laugh, no humor in it, just astonishment. There was a bullet hole through the top of it. He poked his finger through it, wiggled it at her. She stared in dumb astonishment.

"Now how the hell did that not blow your pretty head off, Kit?"

She took the hat from him. When did that happen? The bullet must have passed a cigarette paper's width from her head, and she didn't even hear it or feel it. Saved again. But for what?

"Oh Kitty, you really do have nine lives," he said.

She laughed too, then she started to shake all over, couldn't stop it. He held her as she cried.

~◆~

Kitty stared out of the window; it was quiet down there now. The snipers were holed up inside the telegraph station, besieged by Red Guards and Kronstadt marines. She could see them on the Morskaya, crouched behind makeshift barricades of barrels and boxes. Soldiers peered from the street corners, occasionally firing volleys at the high windows. Half a dozen bodies still lay strewn in the snow.

She picked up the fur hat she'd been wearing that afternoon, stared at it again.

I don't know that I can do this anymore, she thought. *Another inch to the side and I'd be lying down there in the street like a bundle of rags, just like them. What difference would it have made?*

The door opened, and Lincoln came barreling in, brushing snow from his coat. "It's a platoon of Junkers; they took over the telegraph station this morning. Trotsky says they were hoping to start a general uprising, but now they're completely cut off. He doesn't think they can even hold out till morning." He came over, held her. "Are you okay?"

She nodded. But she wasn't okay, not really—she still felt numb.

"That was a brave thing you did with the sailor."

"Is he going to be all right?"

"I don't know; I never saw him again after the sailors dragged him off and put him in a car."

"Well I'll say a prayer for the lad, even though I don't believe in it. Sure, it can't do any harm. He was so young. Not much older than my little brother in Ireland, I'm thinking."

He sat her down on the bed. The heating was off again, and it was frigid inside the room. They both still had their gloves and coats on, and there was ice on the inside of the windows.

"Kitty, about what you said earlier this afternoon. You're not going to leave me now, will you?"

"I'm not doing any good here."

"You've got to keep going. Promise me."

"How did she know so much about me, Linc? Did you tell her?"

"I swear, on my mother's life, it wasn't me. I told you, the Bolsheviks have files on every foreigner in Petrograd."

She nestled under his arm. "You really think I can do this?"

"I know you can," he said.

He was a convincing rogue. She had to believe him now, didn't she?

CHAPTER 25

They woke to find new-fallen snow heaped on the sill outside their window. The mud was gone. The gray city was transformed overnight: the somber government buildings along the prospect had been turned into ice palaces. But when Kitty stepped out of the hotel, the reality of a Russian winter was not quite as appealing. The coachmen in the square sat shivering under ice-stiff blankets on the running boards of their droshkies. The cold was savage. Through the clouds the sun appeared almost translucent. When it finally broke through the clouds, just after noon, its reflection on the snow hurt her eyes and made her squint.

And this was just the start of it. She had dreaded the cold enough in Dublin. The thought of a Russian winter terrified her.

By January, life in Petrograd had reached a desperate pass. There was no coal for the power plants, and the city lived in perpetual darkness. The shops had run out of candles, and Kitty took to buying holy candles in the church, meant as offerings to the shrines of the holy saints, and bringing them back to the hotel under her coat so that she had enough light to write by.

Lincoln now preferred to work at the Smolny. Trotsky had given him his own "office" on the top floor, an annex to his own, and had it cheaply partitioned like a poor artist's studio. There was a desk; a hard, wooden chair; and a cot to sleep on. No pictures on the wall, not even a window.

But at least there was light, he said, at least enough to write by. When the trams weren't running, he slept there as well.

"I'm not walking home in the snow, Kit," he said to her. "You could stay out there with me."

"So everyone can see you've brought your mistress with you?"

"It's not like that."

"That's what Madame Ballanskaya thinks."

"Who cares what she thinks?"

I do, Kitty thought. But she didn't say it.

CHAPTER 26

Kitty set off from the hotel through the snow. It was bitter, her feet and hands ached, even through her boots and fur-lined gloves. It was so cold she felt ill from it. As she turned the corner onto Nevsky Prospect, an icy wind almost knocked her off her feet.

She swung onto the step of a streetcar, its platform so bent down from the weight of the people she could hear the undersides of it scraping along the ground. Soldiers were already out in the streets trying to keep the tracks clear to Smolny.

When she arrived at the institute, she waved at the two guards huddled by a fire at the main gate. They knew her well enough by now they didn't even ask for her pass.

There were two more guards outside Lincoln's office, burly fellows with enormous beards. She smiled at them, and they waved her through. One of them made a joke to the other; she didn't catch it, but she could imagine what he said.

Lincoln was bent over his desk, scribbling notes in the margins of a typewritten report. He barely looked up as she came in; the light caught his glasses and accentuated the lines that had appeared on his face. He waved a hand casually to the chair on the other side of the desk.

"You didn't come back again last night," she said.

"I didn't finish till after midnight."

She sat down, watched him work. There were strands of gray in his hair; she hadn't noticed them before. "You'll make yourself ill working these hours."

"I'm checking over some things for Trotsky. He's written a history of the revolution; I'm helping him edit it. Then I have a piece I'm writing for *Collier's*, and I have this other piece on internationalism for Henry. What do you want me to do?"

"At least you've got magazines to write for."

"What?"

"You know Lenin has shut down every single newspaper in the city except for his own."

"It's not his newspaper, it's the People's."

"Which people?"

"Come on, Kit, not now. I'm busy."

She put her hand over the report to make him look up at her. "I'm serious."

He threw down his pen. "Do you know what's happening out there? The Germans, the Whites, Kerensky—we have enemies on every side. They *had* to shut down the newspapers; they can't let their enemies fill the people's heads with lies at a time like this."

"Isn't this the kind of repression they were supposed to be fighting against?"

"Propaganda is more dangerous than Zeppelins and machine guns. The Provisional Revolutionary Committee had to do something. These are temporary and extraordinary measures to prevent the lies and misinformation coming from the czarists and the bourgeoisie. When it's over, then we can have freedom of the damned press again."

"Jesus God, now you're scaring me. You sound like Lenin."

"Hell, what did you think a revolution was? Did you think we would all sit around and work out our differences over a cup of tea? We believe in this revolution, in the future that Russia can have, but it isn't going to happen unless we win this war first. Things won't magically work out right away. It may not be happening quite the way we wanted it to, the way we talked about and hoped, but at least it's happening."

"Have you heard of the Cheka?"

"Sure I've heard of it."

"It's the secret police."

"Or to give it its real name, Kit, the All-Russian Extraordinary Commission for Combating Counter-Revolution.'"

"The secret police."

"Forty guys."

"Forty men who have been given control of the Sveaborgesky Regiment, as well as a group of Red Guardsmen and a cohort of very enthusiastic sailors from Kronstadt. That's quite an impressive start for a temporary and extraordinary measure."

"Every country has an agency charged with maintaining its own internal security."

"I know. The British had one in Ireland; they called them the Black and Tans. They used to pull men's fingernails out in Dublin Castle and beat them to death with rifle butts. My uncle was one of the victims."

"Whose side are you on, Kit?"

"I thought I was on the side of women getting a say in their country's future and men getting a fair day's wage for their work. But it doesn't seem to be working out like that."

"The French Revolution took five years, and that country is only the size of the Ukraine. This is going to take time, that's all."

She wanted to believe him; she wanted to believe him so badly.

"How's that piece you're doing on the new marriage laws?" he asked her.

She shook her head.

"Let me finish this, and we'll work on it together. I'll see you back at the hotel later."

She felt so tired. She got up and left him to Trotsky, and the revolution, and the brave new world.

———

Kitty stared out of the window of the streetcar as it crawled through the cobbled streets. The wind hurled flurries of snow against the bleak buildings. Mud had frozen into deep, black ruts.

She got off outside Saint Isaac's and hurried along the avenue, her head down against the wind. The snow was soaking through her boots. Some deserters from Kerensky's army sat on the steps of the church selling cigarettes. She didn't know how they didn't freeze to death.

She had almost reached the hotel when she heard shouts coming from one of the side streets. She hesitated, knowing that it might be dangerous, but curiosity got the better of her.

She went around the corner; there was a truck parked in the middle of the street, and beside it a squad of Kronstadt sailors were gathered around a man in his shirtsleeves. They had him down in the mud, among a litter of broken glass. They were kicking him with their heavy boots.

She knew straightaway what it was—one of the liberal newspapers had their offices in this street, and a small press. There was a racket coming from inside the building. She looked through the shattered window, saw a dozen other sailors inside, smashing the desks and cabinets into firewood with axes while their comrades took to the printing press with sledgehammers.

So this was Lincoln's All-Russian Extraordinary Commission for Combating Counter-Revolution. They were just as she had imagined them.

A man with huge moustaches and a long black leather overcoat was overseeing the beating. He looked pitilessly at the middle-aged proprietor at his feet. The kicking was going on and on. The man was screaming in a shrill voice, and there was blood all over his face, his wire spectacles lay twisted and smashed in the snow.

"Stop it!" she shouted at the man in the overcoat, and she ran over and grabbed one of the sailor's arms and tried to pull him away.

He swung his arm free and shoved her backward. "Mind your own business unless you want the same treatment," he said.

The proprietor had curled into a ball. He had his hands over his face; he was squirming and trying to get away. She knew what it was like to wriggle like that; it was what you got for answering back. They wouldn't stop until you stopped moving, that was the trick. You had to get past the pain; when you went numb, they didn't want to kick you anymore. She wished she could tell him, but he was probably too old to learn the trick.

"Don't go in there!"

One of the guards put out a hand to stop her, and she knocked the rifle aside and shoved him as hard as she could, both hands on his chest. He was so surprised, he took a step back, and in that moment she was through the door and into Lincoln's office. *Temporary and extraordinary measures?* Perhaps he should come see for himself just how extraordinary they were.

But Lincoln was not at his desk. She heard noises from behind the flimsy curtain that separated his cot from his office. She pulled it aside.

Madame Ballanskaya's cashmere shawl lay on the floor, along with her dress and her drawers. Her very unrevolutionary tortoiseshell clips lay scattered around the parquet floor. Lincoln lay not quite naked on the bed; he still had his boots on and his trousers, which were around his ankles. Madame Ballanskaya sat astride him, in the feminist position, as perhaps she'd call it, her rather large breasts swinging.

They stopped what they were doing when they saw her, and Madame Ballanskaya waited a moment to catch her breath. She looked at Kitty with a curious smile.

"Is there a problem here, comrade?" she said.

CHAPTER 27

There were crowds of shabby-looking soldiers at the train station, fighting to get on board the carriages. They were wrestling with each other at the doors; others had smashed the windows to get on board. Kitty stood there with her suitcase in hand, buffeted by the press of people. She shoved her way to the gate, desperate. She couldn't go back; she couldn't.

There was a little girl sitting against the wall near the ticket office, one dirty hand outstretched to the passersby. Winter, and she had no shoes. There was a purple bruise on her cheekbone, and her lip was cut, an old scab on it. *I was going to save you once*, Kitty thought.

A Red Guard appeared in front of her and barred her way to the gate. "Your papers," he said. "Show me your papers."

He flicked through the pages of her passport, then nodded to the two soldiers with him. "Please," he said, "you must come with me."

"What's wrong? I have to get on that train," Kitty said.

"You are under arrest."

"What for?"

He shoved her toward the soldiers. "You must come with us," he repeated. Kitty thought for a moment about trying to run. But it was impossible, not in this crowd, and where would she run to? This was Petrograd, for God's sake.

She let them lead her back out of the station and toward the waiting truck.

⎯⎯

They took her back to the Hotel Angleterre. Lincoln was waiting for her in their room. He was wearing his commissar's cap, a new affectation, and the fur coat that Trotsky had got for him. He was sitting on the bed, elbows on his knees, staring at his boots. The snow had melted off them and formed a large, muddy stain on the carpet.

The soldiers left her there and shut the door.

"Did you do this?" she said.

He didn't answer her.

"Did you send those men out to arrest me?"

"I swear, I didn't."

"Don't swear anything to me anymore. Your word doesn't count a damn with me now."

He looked up, his cheeks hollow. "I'm as much a prisoner as you are."

"So we're prisoners now, then? Is that what you're telling me?"

He nodded.

"So much for the fecking revolution, then."

He hung his head.

"What is this about?"

"Tatiana."

"You mean the Ballanskaya woman? She did this?"

"Yes."

"Because of you and her?"

"No, this is about you, not me. What in God's name did you say to her?"

"She has that much power?"

"Yes. I thought I told you that."

"This is why I'm here? God in heaven."

"I'm sorry about this afternoon. I didn't mean to hurt you."

"Oh, fuck off."

"Please, Kitty. It wasn't what you think."

"Wasn't what I think? I thought you were fucking her. Or she was fucking you. One or the other, I'm pretty sure it's what it was. I've seen it done before."

"I thought you were—"

"Thought I was what?"

"I thought you understood about these things. About people not owning each other."

"Well perhaps I'm not the revolutionary that you are, Lincoln. I hope you and that damned woman will be very happy fucking other people together."

"It's not like that."

"Well, what's it like?" She looked around the room: the frost on the glass; the stiff, ancient drapes; paint peeling off the cornices; the stupid bath that there was never enough hot water for. What a sad place; what a sad couple.

She laughed.

"What?"

"Here I was, going to change the world. I can't even get on a train."

"It will be all right, Kitty."

"No, it won't be all right, Lincoln. Or maybe it will be for you. You have Trotsky and Tatiana the Great."

"I'm under arrest as well."

"What for? Did your performance not meet her exacting standards?"

"I went after you; I couldn't bear the thought of staying here with-out you. But apparently, I'm indispensable to the revolution. I am requested to stay in Russia for as long as they need me."

"'Requested'?"

"It's the kind of request where, if you don't agree to it, they shoot you."

"I'd like to feel sorry for you, but it's beyond me right now."

He held out his hands toward her.

"You have to be joking, Lincoln."

He dropped onto his knees. "Please, Kitty. Forgive me. I'm lost without you. I'm begging you here."

She had always vowed that this would never happen to her; she thought about her father, always so sorry after he'd done something when he was drunk, always swore he'd never do it again. Now here she was herself, like her mother, betrayed by being in love with a man.

"Get up, Lincoln."

"Please. We're in this together now."

"No, Lincoln. We're in it, right in it, but not together. You can stay at the institute with the lovely Trotsky and the lovely Tatiana. You'll not come back into my bed. Oh, and next time you're making pillow talk, you can tell that hoor to get me a visa back to England."

Lincoln pushed his glasses up his nose. He looked disappointed. "Are you going to give up that easily?"

There was a vase on one of the tables, a sickly green color. It looked old, and it was badly chipped. It had been annoying her since the first day. She picked it up and hurled it as hard as she could at his head. He saw it coming and dodged it, but narrowly.

"Get out," Kitty said. And he did.

CHAPTER 28

Lyons Corner House, the Strand, London, November 1921

Six years since she had seen Elsie; it might as well have been a lifetime for the changes it had brought in her. It was not just the touch of gray in Elsie's hair and the lines around her eyes, but the energy of her. Her smile when she saw Kitty was not as quick, and her movements were slow and tired, like she had been doing the night shift every night since 1915.

It made Kitty wonder what Elsie saw when she looked at her.

"Kitty!"

"Elsie, it's so good to see you again!"

She was surprised by how fiercely Elsie held to her; she could feel the bones in her shoulders; she had lost a lot of weight.

It was crowded in the teahouse and steamy hot. The rain was pouring down outside, but of course, it wouldn't be England without the rain and everyone flapping umbrellas and complaining. Kitty and Elsie threaded their way through the crush to a corner table, ordered cups of tea and a teacake to share.

"I can't believe it's you," Elsie said. "It's been so long. Never thought I'd see you again. You look beautiful as always."

"I'm the color of a dishcloth and skinny as a rake."

"Oh, get away with you. Now come on, we've only got an hour. Tell me what's been happening to you, love?"

She wondered where to start. When she thought about it, six years really was a lifetime. There were things she had seen, been a part of, that would never leave her; she had written about them, but she had never actually talked about them, not with anyone. God knows she tried to not even think about them.

How could she tell Elsie about that village in Serbia where they had come across the bodies of a hundred women and children all chained together, their heads struck off and lying in a separate heap? Or feeling the bones of the dead crunching under her feet as she walked through what was left of the Austrian and Serbian trenches, listening to the eerie howling of the wild dogs in the woods around her?

How could she even begin to describe what she'd done? How could she explain what it felt like to watch that young sailor bleed his life away in front of her in the snow, or stand by helplessly while the Cheka beat the newspaper publisher half to death in the street? All that casual violence.

Now she was back in London, it all hardly seemed real, even to her. Like telling someone about a nightmare you had once. Only her nightmares were real.

No, she couldn't tell Elsie about those things.

And then, after all that, these last three years a virtual prisoner in Russia. Another lifetime gone. And what had she to show for it? A few articles published in the *Union* and *Irish World*, and she wouldn't have sold those if it wasn't for Lincoln.

But she tried as best she could to describe to her friend all those months following Lincoln around godforsaken countries, places that she'd never heard of before she left England: Greece, Serbia, Turkey, the Pale in Bessarabia; about fighting with a Russian border guard over two cockleshells in a cheap wooden box; told it as if it was all just a lark. Elsie shook her head in wonderment as Kitty talked about a life spent sleeping in train stations and filthy boarding houses. She gasped when she told her about her close call in the street in Petrograd. She mentioned her meetings with Trotsky and Lenin, even though Elsie said she had never heard of them.

And then there was Lincoln. What could she tell her about him?

So instead she tried to tell her what it was like to spend three years living in an empty hotel.

"Must have felt like you were in prison," Elsie said.

"I was; a prison with chandeliers and creaking floors, but a prison just the same. I could go wherever I wanted in Petrograd, but there was no way out of the city unless I felt like walking to Finland."

"I can't imagine it."

"No one can imagine it, Elsie. There were people literally getting tortured in the streets. You just can't believe what you're seeing."

"What about . . . Lincoln?"

"He's still in Russia, last I heard. He's writing a book about the revolution there."

"Is he going to stay there?"

"He has no choice at the moment."

"Is he one of these, what did you call them—Bolsheviks, then?"

"The American government says he is, though he's the darling of the Bohemian set in Greenwich Village. If he ever goes back to New York, he'll get torn to pieces at the docks—the police trying to arrest him, and the society matrons trying to drag him off to one of their literary luncheons."

Elsie patted Kitty's hand. "I always thought you were going to marry him, love."

"He always said he wasn't the marrying kind. I should have listened to him."

"What's going to happen to him?"

"It's not up to him anymore. They won't give him a visa to leave. He's their mouthpiece to the West, really. He's too valuable to them at the moment."

"The poor man."

Kitty decided not to tell her about Madame Ballanskaya or any of Lincoln's other indiscretions. What was the point? "Yes," she said. "The poor man. It's a tragedy."

Kitty didn't like talking about Russia or any of it. She would have bad dreams tonight, just from having relived it again, even for a few minutes. She turned the conversation around as soon as she could.

"What are you doing these days? Are you still a nurse?"

"Yes, still at Saint Thomas'. I'm the breadwinner in our family now, suppose you'd say."

"How's . . ." Kitty tried to recall his name. "Bert."

"Much the same. Shell shock, it sounds so harmless, don't it? Like an attack of nerves." Her voice trailed off.

"He's not getting any better?"

"He spends hours just sitting in a chair staring at nothing. He's tried to get a job, but no one wants him, not like he is. Can't say I blame them." Elsie forced a smile. "At least he's all in one piece."

"Does he ever talk about what happened to him?"

"I try to get him to talk to me about it, but he won't. Hardly a word since he's been back."

Well, that I understand I suppose, Kitty thought. "What about . . . you had a little boy, didn't you?"

"No, a little girl—well, two now. I was carrying Amelia when he went away to the war."

"It must be very hard," Kitty said.

Their cups of tea arrived. After the waitress moved away, Elsie said, "It's funny how life turns out. Always thought one day I'd get married and have a family and live happily ever after. Never expected a cakewalk, of course, but didn't expect it to be like this."

Kitty squeezed her hand.

"Terrible thing, war," Elsie said.

Kitty wondered what to say to that. She felt a familiar rage building inside her. This was what she wanted to change, the order of things, people like Bert having their lives broken to make rich men richer, powerful men more powerful, and women like Elsie left at home to pick up the pieces afterward.

They crumbled pieces off their tea cake and stared at the rain.

"We got the vote at last. Did you read about it?" Elsie said.

"Not the same as the men."

"No, but it's a start. All that agitating, it did make a difference."

"I hope so, Elsie."

Elsie sat up straighter, as if she was trying to shrug off her melancholy with a shake of the shoulders. "Mustn't be too gloomy. We got our health, that's the main thing. So, what about you, Kitty? What's life got in store for you now?"

"I don't know, Elsie. I've got a job, working in an office just off Piccadilly Circus. I live in a boarding house in Bayswater. Just a room, but it's luxury after Petrograd."

"What about your writing? I thought you were doing well."

"Oh Elsie, I could never make enough to live on. Besides, now we have the vote, there's nothing to write about, is there?"

Elsie glanced up at the clock. "I'd better be getting home, get the kids their tea. Walk with me to the bus stop."

They stood huddled together under their umbrellas, standing back from the road, away from the splash of the tires from the buses and automobiles on the Strand. Not near as many horses as before, Kitty noticed.

Elsie fumbled in her purse for change for the fare. "Remember that doctor friend of yours?"

"Tom? Is he still at Saint Thomas'?" Kitty tried to sound unconcerned.

"He's an intern in the surgical ward now. Clever young man. He'll go far, mark my words."

"You said in one of your letters that he was getting married."

"Yes, poor man."

"Poor man?"

"Tragic."

"Why Elsie, what happened?"

"Lost his wife and baby to that Spanish flu a couple of years ago. Terrible thing, really was, so many people I knew passed away. More people died from that than they did in the war, they reckon."

"Oh, poor Tom."

"Yes well, happened to lots of people, no consolation, though, is it? Not when it's someone you love. Here's my bus. Take care, Kitty. Oh, it was so good to see you again. Let's do this again soon!"

The bus arrived and Elsie jumped on. As Kitty watched it set off along the Strand, all she could think of was: *Tom Doyle, he's just a mile or two away, just over there in Lambeth. What I wouldn't give to see him again.*

———※———

"So Milly comes down the stairs, I said to her, 'What on earth are you wearing, gel? You are not going out like that!' I don't know what has gotten into her lately. Bad enough she cut her hair like she did, but these ridiculous fashions these young gels are wearing these days. The sooner she finds herself a husband and settles down the better."

Balfour took his homburg and Burberry raincoat from the coatrack, glanced over at Kitty.

"I wouldn't employ a girl if she looked like that. Would I, Miss O'Kane?"

Kitty looked up from her Remington. "No, sir."

"Women today. This is what we get for giving them the vote!"

Balfour's client laughed and then looked at her, gave her a smile. God, the look in his eyes. *They don't like us raising our hemlines*, she thought, *but they can't wait to lift them up themselves.*

"We're going out to lunch," Balfour said. "What's wrong with the typewriter there, Miss O'Kane?"

"The keys are a bit stiff, sir."

"Must be the cold weather. Don't break a nail!"

The door closed. Kitty looked across the office. Chandler, the junior clerk, was smirking. Last week he had asked her out to go for a drink with him; she'd said no; she supposed he liked seeing her put back in her place.

Keep your mouth shut, Kitty. Remember you need the money.

<hr>

A paperboy was shouting out the news as she made her way toward the Underground. She found a coin in her purse and bought the newspaper. She scrolled down the front page quickly; the *Dáil* in Dublin had ratified the Anglo-Irish Treaty to make Ireland a free state. Ulster in the north had been given the option to opt out.

So, at last. They were going to give her country its independence, make Ireland free again. *Well we'll see if that's the way it all comes out*, she thought. It wasn't done yet. You could never trust the English.

By the time she got to Lancaster Gate, it was already dark; the gas lamps were on in the street, though they weren't much use in the fog. It was bitterly cold. The branches of the trees looked like claws.

Mrs. Ratcliffe looked out of her door as she passed.

"Good afternoon, Mrs. Ratcliffe."

Mrs. Ratcliffe nodded. Satisfied that Kitty did not have a man or a bottle of gin with her, she went back inside, and her door clicked shut.

A girl dressed in a bathrobe and her hair wrapped in a towel dashed across the landing. Kitty heard laughing from one of the other rooms, and a girl came out holding a curling iron and ran in after the first one. She heard them talking about the latest thrash they were going to. They had given up inviting her; they knew she always said no.

They all thought she was odd, and she didn't give a damn.

She went into the room she shared with a girl called Suzy. There was a chest of drawers and an overstuffed armchair piled high with clothes; an ancient dressing table that they had to share; a wardrobe with one loose door, which was on Kitty's side. A thin curtain ran along the center of the room and divided it into two, with a single bed on each side.

In the very corner was Kitty's "desk," really just a narrow hallstand with a Remington typewriter balanced precariously on top of it. Kitty threw her bag and coat on the eiderdown and sat down on the edge of the bed. She would try and get something written before Suzy got home; her incessant chatter would make it impossible to get anything done after that.

What she had told Elsie wasn't exactly true; she hadn't given up quite yet; she was busy outside working hours writing an article for the *New York American*. The editor had liked one of her pieces on Trotsky and had asked for a rewrite. It would mean a nice paycheck if they accepted it; more than that, it would give her some much-needed confidence and be an important addition to her writing credentials.

Downstairs one of the girls had put a record on their new phonograph, one of the latest popular tunes: "Ain't We Got Fun." Kitty thought about Elsie, about the people she had seen standing in bread queues in Petrograd, about her family back in the Liberties.

Fun for some, she thought. *When it's fun for everyone, and the world is a fairer place, I'll stop writing and come downstairs and dance with you.*

CHAPTER 29

She arranged to see Elsie again about a week later at their usual Lyons on the Strand. Kitty was early, so she got a table and sat down to study the menu. A lamb cutlet was only seven pence. She would treat herself.

But when it arrived, it was the smallest cutlet she had ever seen. Could have come off a rabbit. Even with a sprig of parsley beside it, it looked lost on the plate. She immediately regretted her recklessness. Lots of things a girl could buy with seven pence. She picked up her knife and fork and promised herself she would at least savor every bite.

"Well, if my eyes don't deceive me, it's the unkillable Kitty O'Kane."

She nearly choked on the first mouthful. When she looked up, there he was; fifteen years, perhaps more, but she knew it was him straight away. Tom Doyle, in a sharp suit and hair damp from the rain, the cowlick falling over one eye just as she remembered.

"Elsie told me I'd find you here."

Kitty stared at him, couldn't find her tongue.

He sat down. "You don't mind?"

"Tom." It was all she could manage.

"She told me you were just back from whatever godforsaken place you went to. But she didn't tell me you'd been struck dumb. Now that's a great pity. I remember Kitty O'Kane always had plenty to say for herself."

"Oh my God."

"Now that's a start, but not what I would call true eloquence."

"What are you doing here?"

He smiled.

"Did Elsie put you up to this?"

"I didn't need putting up to anything. Sure and she told me that she'd seen you, and I said I'd like to come along with her one day and see this grown-up Kitty O'Kane all for myself. But she was unavoidably detained at the last moment."

Kitty swallowed, dabbed at her mouth with her napkin, almost knocked over her water glass.

"I see you've gone to town on the establishment's culinary delights. And why not, it's almost lunchtime." He raised a hand to the nearest Gladys, who smiled at him and bumped aside one of the other waitresses in her rush to get there first with a menu.

"It takes me half an hour to get a waitress to serve me in here."

"You just have to smile, Kitty. People love a smile."

"I can grin like a Cheshire cat, and it does no good. But then I'm not a handsome young doctor, am I?"

"Now that's got nothing to do with it, Kitty. The sun has turned your head."

"There's not much sun in Russia."

"So that's where you've been? I thought it was wildest Africa. You look as pretty as I remember, all the same. So Russia, was it? Have you turned to Communism yet? Careful, you almost spilled your water there. Now that's the second time. What's wrong, Kitty, do I make you nervous?"

"I can't believe it's you!"

"Well it is, at least the last time I checked. It's glorious to see you again. It's been too long. Now you look hungry. How about the smoked salmon?"

"I could never afford that."

"Then allow me. Do you want another cup of tea, Kitty?"

"Elsie should have warned me."

"That I drink tea?"

"That you were going to come. I can't *believe* she'd do this to me."

"Are you sorry?"

She shook her head no. Tom smiled and absently held up a hand, and the waitress was back in a moment. When she had taken their orders and gone, Kitty said, "So what were you doing calling me that?"

"Calling you what?"

"You know what. That thing they wrote about me in the newspapers."

"The unkillable Kitty O'Kane? I never saw it in the papers, to be honest. Elsie told me about it. She still has the cutting, I believe, though it's a bit yellow by now. You've lived a remarkable life."

"Well, none of it was my doing. I was just unlucky, or lucky—it depends how you look at it."

"She said you're a writer now."

"She's skiting. I'm a secretary in a solicitor's office."

"But you've had articles published in big magazines and in newspapers."

"A handful, that's all."

"That's a handful more than most, especially for a girl from the Liberties. Are you all right, Kitty?"

Oh God, she was staring at him again. It was really him, her Tom Doyle, the earnest schoolboy who stole half a crown off his own ma for her, the greenhorn who didn't know how to catch cockles or steal from a greengrocer shop. He'd grown so tall and confident and handsome. Here he was, a surgeon at a big London hospital, and he made her feel like she was somehow the special one.

"She's full of you, that Elsie. Once I got her started, she couldn't stop. She was telling me about some of your adventures. It sounds like you've been everywhere. Russia for heaven's sake. Now, I've heard the Bolsheviks eat their own children. That can't be true, can it?"

She was reluctant to talk about it at first, but he had a way about him this Tom Doyle, so she told him about Russia, the things she couldn't tell anyone, not even Elsie; how she had gone to Russia thinking the revolution would be a beacon for change for the rest of the world and how the dream had turned into a nightmare in just no time at all.

"So it's true what the papers are saying?"

"There's four million people died there last year, Tom, died from starvation and typhus while there's others live in palaces, only now the rich have commissar's uniforms instead of epaulettes and braids. But that's not even the worst of it."

"And what's the worst of it?"

"Do you remember what the British did to us, Tom? Do you remember hearing your dad and your uncles talk about the Black and Tans? I thought those brutes were as bad as any man could get. But they were nothing to what I saw over there. Have you heard of the Cheka?"

He shook his head.

"It's a secret police force. Trotsky and Lenin were behind it. The things that they do to people who stand up to them, it's unspeakable, just unspeakable. I feel sick just thinking about it. Some brave new world."

"It must have been hard for you, traveling around like that, on your own."

She felt her cheeks blush hot. She wondered if Elsie had told him about Lincoln. "There were other journalists with me; we stuck together for safety."

Did he believe her little white lie? She wanted him to think well of her, and she didn't think her past would thrill a man like Tom. She wished she could tell him the whole truth, but she couldn't.

But Tom didn't ask her any more about that part of her life. He let her talk about her adventures, and before she knew it, she had eaten all her smoked salmon and most of his and drunk three cups of tea and been to the ladies room twice and was still talking, about how things had to change, how there had to be equal votes for men and women, women of all ages, and that if Churchill and Lloyd George didn't let the Irish have their independence as they said they would, then there was going to be trouble, because she knew her own people and they had had enough.

Finally, when she stopped talking, she felt exhausted and a little embarrassed, and she sat back and waited for his censure. He looked at his watch. That was it, then. He was going to make his escape. She didn't blame him. Her ma had always said she could talk the hind legs off a donkey.

Instead he said, "I don't have to be back at the hospital for another hour. Do you feel like a walk along the river? It's even stopped raining for us."

"You want to?"

"Well I wouldn't say it if I didn't, now would I?"

⟡

It was cold down by the embankment, and Tom pulled the collar of his coat up around his ears and thrust his hands deep in his pockets. The fog still hadn't lifted, and she heard the hoot of barges moving up and down the Thames.

"So, it's a doctor you are now."

"I'm training to be a surgeon."

"You're going to be an important man then."

"I don't mind about the importance, Kit, that's not what it's for. It's about saving lives, or those lives that can be saved, at least."

Kitty hesitated, wondered how to say it. "Elsie told me about your wife. I'm sorry."

He didn't answer her straightaway. Finally: "Funny thing is, she was perfectly well at breakfast time. By evening she was in her last throes.

Have you ever seen anyone die of the Spanish flu? It's a terrible thing. They drown right in front of your eyes, and not a damned thing you can do."

"It must be terrible."

"The little lad died a couple of months later. Still only a baby, he was."

"Oh, Tom."

"We still don't know what it was. He sickened for a few weeks, and then he just died. The doctors at the hospital called it flu, but it wasn't. I think he just missed his mother."

"I can't imagine what that must have been like for you."

"No, then it's best not to try."

"When did it happen?"

"It's two years now. Or yesterday. It depends on whether you're looking at the calendar or into my shaving mirror. Do you know what I mean?"

She didn't know what to say to him. They walked in silence for a while. Seagulls cried mournfully through the gray.

He stopped by the Needle, leaned against the stone. "A lot of people have suffered these last few years. I'm not the only one."

"Doesn't make it any easier."

"No, but it stops me dwelling on it, when I'm tempted. Life has to go on, doesn't it?"

"I suppose it does, though sometimes you have to wonder which direction it will go in."

"Yes, all ways just lead off into a sort of fog." He took out his fob watch. "I'd better be getting back. It was so good seeing you again, Kitty. I can't tell you how much."

"It was good seeing you, Tom. Take care."

She put out her hand. He studied it for a moment, then took it and pulled her a little closer. "Do you know how much I've thought about you over the years?"

"I've thought about you too."

"Have you really?"

"To quote a great man, I wouldn't say it if I didn't mean it."

"I know it sounds crazy, standing here in the rain and saying this . . . but do you fancy a trip to the seaside?"

"Are you mad? What, now?"

"No, not now. Sunday. It's my day off."

"Sure and it's the middle of winter."

"I like the seaside in winter. Not as many people. Reminds me of Sandymount. Besides, it's just a day out. Get out of London for a few hours, enjoy the bracing salt air."

"Are you sure?"

"What is there to be sure about? It's only a trip to the seaside."

She laughed. "Where, then?"

"We'll go to Southend-on-Sea. I'll meet you Fenchurch Street Station, ten o'clock, Sunday morning."

"All right then. I'll see you then."

And he smiled. He made her shiver inside with his smile.

"I'll buy you a stick of rock," he said, and bounded away across the street and up the road toward Waterloo Bridge.

CHAPTER 30

Another cold day, but at least the sun was out, pale and distant in an ice-blue sky. Kitty was wearing her good Russian fur coat, with a woolen hat pulled down over her ears; not her most glamorous look, but the wind felt as if it had come straight across the North Sea from Petrograd.

People were running along the platform for the train. She looked up at the station clock; the train would be leaving in another two minutes. Tom was late. She wondered if perhaps he had changed his mind. Had she talked too much the other day? Why would a bright and upcoming doctor want a Communist former suffragette on his arm anyway?

Besides, she was assuming too much. They were just friends, from the old days. That was all it was.

He wasn't coming.

She saw him running up the steps to the station, so handsome in his careless way, the fur collar of his jacket pulled up around his ears. He was out of breath. "I'm so sorry," he said. "There was a holdup on the Underground. I was afraid I'd miss you. Do you have a ticket?"

She showed him her ticket stub, and they hurried along the platform until they found an empty compartment and jumped in. Just as he was shutting the door, she heard the guard blow his whistle.

"Just in time!"

"I thought you weren't coming," she said.

"Why would I not come?"

"I thought perhaps you changed your mind."

"I've changed my mind about many things in my life, Kitty, but not about you." He unbuttoned his coat and settled back in the seat.

The train made its way through the East End, past slums with barefoot children that reminded her of the Liberties. After a few miles they left the city behind, headed into the Essex countryside, past sleepy villages, Pitsea and South Benfleet, the shrimpers lying on their hulls in muddy creeks. When they stopped at the station at Leigh-on-Sea she could see all the way over the Thames to Kent.

"This is nice," she said.

"All that mud. Reminds me of Dublin."

She smiled.

They got off the train at Southend and walked down High Street toward the seafront. Most of the shops were closed, but they passed a news kiosk with a handwritten placard:

"IRISH TROUBLES SET TO CONTINUE."

Tom bought a *News of the World*, quickly scanned the front page. "Knew there'd be trouble when Churchill persuaded Lloyd George to water down the treaty."

"It was too good to be true, anyway. They've had their boot on our throats too long to take it off now."

"Well they've a nice lapdog here in Michael Collins. But de Valera and a few of the others aren't going to go along with it, says here they intend to fight for full independence."

"So there's going to be a war," she said.

"Let's hope not. Ireland has had enough of war this last five years."

"Some people have never had enough of war."

He tucked the paper under his arm. "Well, let's not talk about it now. Not on such a fine, bright day."

Fine, but cold. The wind hit them as they reached the Palace Hotel on top of the cliffs and almost knocked them over. They headed down Pier Hill, past the sunken gardens. Down at the stony beach, the tide was out, almost as far as the end of the pier; she could make out the ominous gray silhouette of a warship in the channel, steaming past the Isle of Grain. There were a few other brave souls like themselves, braced for the cold, down on the promenade. No pleasure yachts today; they had all been pulled up onto the beach.

"Want to walk out to the end of the pier, Kitty?"

"It's bloody freezing, Tom."

"You've just come back from Russia. Sure, this is nothing. There I was, thinking you'd be wanting to sit in a deck chair."

"You're mad, you know that?"

"We can wait for the train, if you want."

"And what would be the point of that? Come on then, it's only a mile. I'm sure I can still manage it."

There were few others game for walking out beyond the pavilion. The pier-train went past them when they were halfway out, just two other couples huddled inside. The cold didn't deter the kids of course; she looked down in the mud, and there were two rascals down there, thirteen- or fourteen-year-olds in long shorts and vests, searching for crabs or tiddlers.

"Do you remember when we did that, Tom?"

"How could I ever forget? That time at Sandymount was the first cockle I ever ate."

"You were a good lad. I remember how you used to stick up for me."

"You made a lot of trouble for yourself in those days, Kitty—things you used to shout at those boys."

"I never did."

"You threw stones over the street and yelled at them for being posh."

"That's a lie."

"I saw you do it!"

"Well, I don't remember now. I know you were never like that. You were always nice to me."

"Well I was in love with you, wasn't I?"

He didn't look around at her when he said it; it was like he was talking about the weather. She dared a glance. Right there was the question that had been in the back of her mind ever since she met up with him again, the one she hadn't dared ask herself: Was Tom Doyle still in love with her?

And if he said he was, what would she do about it?

"Have you ever been back there, Tom?"

"Dublin? Not since my ma died."

"She did? I didn't know that. I'm sorry."

"A few years back now. Drank too much of her own liquor. Me and my brother owe her a lot. That shebeen she ran on the sly, I don't know how she got away with it all those years, but without it there would have been no university for me or for him. Sure and when she died she left us the house and a pretty sum besides that she had salted away; she was a hardworking woman and never spent a penny on herself."

"She sounds like a proper saint."

"Not many saints sell as much liquor to people as she did. And by all accounts she had a string of men coming in and out of the house after we were gone. But no matter what other people said about her, she was good to us. That's all that matters, I suppose."

Everything was closed up at the end of the pier; shutters rattled in the wind, seagulls huddled on the rails, feathers puffed out. There was a striped Punch and Judy booth, battered by the wind.

"Did you ever watch a Punch and Judy show?" Tom said.

"I was in one. I was the baby that was dropped and every character that walks in that Punch takes a whack at."

"I knew about it. I think a lot of people knew."

"And no one did a damned thing because it was the same in their house. I don't know why people think Punch and Judy is so funny. It's not."

"What happened to him?"

"Me daddy? He's dead now they tell me. I reckon the drink did for him."

"Did you go back for the funeral?"

"The only reason I'd have gone back would have been to make sure he was dead and the coffin lid was nailed down good and tight."

"And your ma?"

"I don't know, Tom."

"You've not been back ever?"

"No reason to. She wrote me a few letters in the first couple of years after I left. But I haven't heard from any of them in years."

"Look, this place is open."

There was a tent with a placard set up outside:

"Madame Rosa, Fortune-Teller to the Stars! Career, love, happiness, luck! It's all in the cards!"

"Jesus God, I'm not going in there."

"Why not? It's just a bit of fun."

"Do you not remember that crazy old woman at the bottom of our street?" Kitty said.

"Sure I remember her. She scared the living Jesus out of me." Tom hovered outside. "You sure you don't want to try your luck a second time?"

"It's all nonsense, Tom."

"Is it? She knew you were going to be on the *Titanic*."

"She didn't know!"

"Sure she did. That's why she wouldn't read your cards that day."

"Maybe she did, maybe she didn't. Either way, I'd rather not know the future, thanks very much. I'll make my own path and hope for the best."

"So are you going down the right path now, Kitty?"

"I won't know till I get to the end of it now, will I, Tom Doyle? Now can we get off this pier? I've not been as cold since Russia!"

⋙

They found two deck chairs and sat on the pebbly beach and watched the tide edge in, the winter sun glittering on the wavelets. She wished Tom would hold her hand, at least do something to show her how he felt about her. His sudden reappearance in her life confused her. He represented a life she could never have; the woman a man like Tom would marry was someone she could not be. And yet . . . and yet, she realized that he was everything she ever wanted. This was selfish of her, though. She shouldn't let herself get carried away, or him.

"So, tell me what you're doing these days," he said.

"Oh, I'm busy and important I am. I make cups of tea, type letters, and smile at the clients when they come in. And you think being a surgeon is hard!"

"Why are you not writing anymore?"

"Well I would, but there's little things like paying the rent and eating that get in the way of it."

"Elsie said you were doing well with it."

"Oh, the rags I wrote for, you were lucky if you got a free copy of the magazine as payment. Writing for those big magazines, now that's not so easy for a girl from the slums of Dublin. I had to teach myself, mostly—the gall I had, me without any education to speak of. And when I did get something written, Lincoln would always say it was too emotional. He said I should be more hardheaded, or no editor would look at it."

205

She saw a shadow pass over his face. "So you showed everything you wrote to this Lincoln?"

"Well, yes. He was like a mentor to me."

A suggestion of a smile, the corners of his mouth moved, or was it a grimace?

"Most people in America didn't care much about what was happening in Russia, anyway. Unless there was battle. And that didn't help me much either; there isn't an editor alive who thinks a woman could ever write about a war and make any sense."

"You were in Russia a long time."

"Four years, just about."

"Why did you stay all that time?"

"I tried to leave after Lenin took over, but it was too late." *He must know I'm hiding some of the story from him*, she thought. But she went on with it anyway. "When I tried to get away, the Bolsheviks wouldn't allow it. They refused to give me a visa, took my passport away."

"Why?"

"They said they didn't want me coming back here and writing 'misinformation about the revolution,' was how they put it. They started censoring everything I wrote. I was virtually a prisoner. Eventually a friend of mine managed to get me out."

"This Lincoln Randolph?"

"Yes, Lincoln."

"What happened to him?"

"He's still there."

"Are you sorry?"

"For what?"

"For going to Russia."

"Well it's easy to live your life looking backward, they say. I really thought the Bolsheviks were going to change the world, and I was going to be at the vanguard of it, writing about it to people back here."

"You were going to be one of the heralds of the new Utopia."

"Something like that."

"That's what you want, is it Kitty?"

"Is that wrong, Tom? To want to see a world where children don't starve to death, where women don't get beaten by their husbands every Saturday night and have a say in things just as much as any man. I'd like to think there'll come a day when men don't work every hour God gives them for a few shillings while other men do nothing except shout at them to work harder."

"No, it's not wrong to wish for it, Kitty."

"But you don't believe it can ever happen, do you? You think I'm just a stupid, hysterical woman."

"Because I don't agree with something you say, doesn't mean I think that you're stupid. You're far from that. You're a dreamer perhaps, but the world needs dreamers to make things happen."

"I just wanted to make a difference."

"Yes, I understand that. I do too."

"There's so much trouble in the world, Tom, so much suffering."

"There is and there always will be. That's the way of it."

"But it shouldn't be."

He leaned forward, his hands on his knees. There was a lovely crease at the corner of his eyes when he smiled at her, just as he was smiling at her now. "You remind me of my wife, God rest her soul."

It wasn't quite what she wanted to hear, she supposed. She nudged some pebbles with her foot.

"She was quite the idealist. It was what attracted me to her. She had a spirit about her, just like you do. I think you would have liked her."

"I doubt that, Tom."

He raised an eyebrow.

"I think perhaps I would have been jealous."

"Jealous?"

"Did I say something funny, Tom Doyle?"

"It's just that she always said that about you. She was jealous."

"Of me? She never knew me."

"I suppose I used to talk about you sometimes, when I talked about growing up in Dublin. She said you and I must have been more than friends. I said how was that possible, she was only ten years old when I left."

"I remember I was devastated when you'd gone. Had to fight the big kids on my own."

"I doubt that, Kitty. You were always the kind of girl that could look after herself."

"Well you were still my hero, for what it's worth."

"Elsie said you were a suffragette for a while too."

"I marched a few times, got myself arrested. Nothing hundreds of other women didn't do."

He smiled, turning his homburg over in his hands. "She was a suffragette as well."

"Your wife. She marched?"

"Sure she did. Got herself arrested, too, when she was sixteen, assaulting a police officer, or that's what they said. The judge let her off with a fine, seeing as how the police sergeant was six foot four and she was barely five two."

"What had she been doing?"

"A few older women had a plan to break into the Houses of Parliament, and she decided to go along. A regular tearaway she was."

"And what did you do?"

"Oh, this was all before we met. But she reminded me of you. She had a temper as well."

"I do not have a temper, Tom Doyle!"

"My God you do. I'd as soon cross you as fight Jack Dempsey."

"Are you laughing at me?"

"A bit." But then the laughter went out of him. "So I've told you about Evie. Now you tell me something about this Lincoln Randolph."

"How did you know about him? Did Elsie say?"

"He was the one wrote the article about you. And he has something of a reputation, in the papers. He was the one you went to Russia with, am I right?"

She nodded. She reminded herself never to underestimate Tom's intelligence again.

"Was he your lover?"

He searched her face, looking for the truth, but that was the last thing she wanted him to have. She heard herself say: "He was just a friend, Tom. He helped me a lot. We were both dreamers, as you like to call it." What a terrible lie. *The Good Lord himself will come down and burn you to a crisp with hellfire.* Wasn't that what her mother used to say to her whenever she caught her out, though how God should ever get hold of hellfire, she never quite explained.

Could he read the blush in her cheeks?

"I didn't think anyone outside of America had heard of him."

"I like to keep abreast of things. I don't just read the *Times*. I'm familiar with Lloyd George's view of the world. I like to read other points of view as well."

"You're a constant surprise, Tom Doyle."

"I like to think so. Is your Mr. Randolph still there?"

"In Moscow the last I heard, reporting on the famine. He was a good journalist once, hard-nosed. He's just a mouthpiece for Trotsky these days." She blew on her hands. She couldn't even feel her nose. "I never forgot you, Tom Doyle, and that's the truth of it."

"I never forgot you either."

"But you went and got yourself married."

"And would be still, but God saw fit to take my family from me. And I can't change that. I can't change any of the things I've done, good and bad, and neither can you. But now here we both are, and we've come to a fork in the road at the same time. Almost seems like fate. That's what the banshee woman would call it."

"You like all that stuff, don't you?"

"I do when it suits me." Another smile, gone as it quick as it came. "What is it you want, Kitty?"

She didn't know how to answer him. The truth of it was she didn't know what she wanted anymore. She felt caught up inside, like there were two voices inside her, both yelling at each other, and she couldn't make out what either of them was saying over the din.

"I don't know, Tom."

"You have the vote. The Bolsheviks were a false dawn. Life has changed a bit for the better, hasn't it, and you've done your share."

"It's only the start of it."

"No, the start of it was Adam and Eve. The end of it, that nobody knows. It's getting cold. Let's go back, shall we?"

They walked along the beach, the pebbles rolling and grinding under their feet. There was a starfish down on the hard sand. Tom picked it up and tossed it into one of the muddy pools by the tideline. Then he found another and did the same thing.

"You have to leave the Liberties behind, Kitty."

"It's not about the Liberties. It's not about me daddy either."

"I never said anything about your dad. But it is about that, anyway."

"I don't care about any of that; it's all in the past."

"If only that were true." When he looked at her like that, it was as if he could see right into her soul. "There's so much trouble in the world, Kitty, and there always will be. You can't save everyone."

He found another starfish, carried it down the beach, went squelching through the mud to find another pool to drop it in, to keep it from drying out before the tide came back in.

"You're ruining your shoes, Tom."

"They're only shoes."

"They're only starfish."

"You tell that to the starfish," he said.

She trailed after him along the beach. He kept finding more, throwing them back in.

"What are you doing, Tom?"

"What I can."

"There's hundreds of the damned things on this beach. You can't save them all."

He bent down, picked up another, and tiptoed through the mud until he found a pool of water deep enough to drop it in. "No, but I saved that one, didn't I?" He walked back up the shore to the pebble line. "You do the little that you can, then you go home and live your life. You can't spend your whole life going up and down the same beach. Otherwise it never ends."

"I just want to count for something before I'm done."

"You do count, to me." He stepped closer. "You can't change the world, Kitty. Best you can do is change yourself."

CHAPTER 31

"So what are you going to do, Kitty?"

"I don't know, Elsie."

They'd finished their cups of tea and were lingering over the free glass of water. The waitress cleared the cups away, clattering them onto the tray, letting them know she was waiting for the table.

"What is it you want? Every single nurse in the hospital is itching for him to ask them out, and here you are keeping him at arm's length."

"It's not what I want, it's what *he* wants. And I don't think I can give it to him."

"And what would that be, love?"

"A wife."

"Well I can see how he's being unreasonable."

"He had a wife."

"And she died, through no fault of his, poor man. It's been over two years, and he's been through enough, surely? He wants to start again, and who could blame him?"

"I don't know that I can be what she was."

"Well then move aside, lovey, there's plenty that do."

"So many times I should have died, Elsie. When the *Titanic* went down under us, and the *Lusitania*, and those times in Russia when I was lying face first in the street with bullets whistling around my head.

It's a miracle I'm here. And for what? There has to be more for me than just cooking a man's dinner and having babies."

Elsie put down her glass so hard that water spilled on the tabletop. A few people turned and stared. "How dare you!"

"What?"

"What is so wrong with being a good wife and a good mother?"

"Elsie, I—"

"Do you know how hard this is? You say it like it's something just anyone can do, like it doesn't . . . how dare you demean my life!"

"I'm not demeaning it . . ."

"It's easy to care about the whole world, Kitty, isn't it? But let me tell you, it's a lot harder to care when you have to do it one person at a time!"

Kitty didn't know what to say to her. She hadn't meant to hurt her—that was the last thing she had wanted. The words had been out of her mouth before she'd had time to stop and think.

Elsie fumbled in her purse and slapped her threepence on the table for her share of the bill. "You don't know how lucky you are."

"Lucky? You never grew up in the Liberties."

"The Liberties was a long time ago, Kitty. Now you're just a beautiful young woman with the chance to live a better life than most will ever see. But you don't see that, do you?"

She got up and hurried out of the tea shop. Kitty called after her, but Elsie didn't even turn around.

Kitty wandered aimlessly past Charing Cross Station and down toward the embankment. She needed time to think. There were soldiers in khaki uniforms begging in the street, their war medals pinned to their chests, caps upturned on the sidewalk. Most of them had a trouser leg or a sleeve pinned up and a sign: "Wounded in the War. Wife and Four Children to Support. Please Help."

She dropped some coins into a cup.

What had gotten into Elsie? Kitty had never seen her act like that before. She hadn't meant to demean her; that wasn't what she meant.

And how could she say she was lucky? Lucky to grow up in the Dublin slums, lucky to have a father who beat her with a belt any time he had a pint of porter under his belt? She'd like to see her try it for a day. Well all right, it couldn't be easy having a husband who couldn't work, and two small girls to look after—but the whole point of what she had been trying to do was to open people's eyes to that, show people that men shouldn't have to go to fight other people's wars, that women shouldn't be the ones left at home to pick up the pieces.

She was on Elsie's side.

Her life had been about fighting for women like Elsie, not demeaning them. Couldn't she see that?

Yet it nagged at her.

How could Elsie say she was *lucky*?

Well, because she had been, if she was honest with herself. She had survived the *Titanic* and the *Lusitania*, and the sniper in Petrograd. What was that if it wasn't luck? Just because she couldn't make sense of all the things that happened to her didn't mean it was all bad. Elsie was right. It was just the way you chose to look at it.

No, if she'd had to stay in Dublin—that would have been unlucky.

Mares' tails flew across the sky; a north wind whipped at the damned Union Jack flying over the Parliament farther down the river. They were talking up another war in there, more torment for those left behind in the Liberties. Damn them all, those mean-eyed men in there with their cigars and fobs and pinstriped suits.

She hurried back up the steps. She had to get back to work.

CHAPTER 32

Kitty caught the tube from Bayswater to South Kensington. It was a short walk from the station to the address he had given her, a terraced house just off Old Brompton Road. She stood outside the front door, her hand on the brass knocker, gathered herself. Then she took a deep breath and knocked.

She had expected Tom to open the door, but instead a young and pretty woman in a maid's cap and apron met her at the door.

"Is Mr. Doyle at home?" Kitty said, brightly.

She felt herself coolly scrutinized. Then the maid stood aside and, without a word, led the way inside.

Kitty followed her into a drawing room. "He will be down in a moment," the maid said with a strong French accent, and left the room.

There was a coal fire burning in the hearth, and Kitty warmed her hands. She looked around; she had the sensation of disturbing another woman's nest. The floral cushions on the leather chesterfield, the lace antimacassars on the leather wingback chair in the corner were a woman's work. There were framed photographs on the mantel; she recognized Tom's mother from Dublin, and his brother, Michael, the two of them standing together on a city street—it looked like Broadway.

Tom bounded through the door. "Sorry if I kept you waiting; I seem to be making a habit of it." He looked wonderful, as he always did, that glorious smile, sparkling brown eyes. He was wearing a Fair Isle sweater and slacks, the first time she had not seen him in a suit. "Can I get you anything? Tea? A sherry?"

"Do I look like a girl that drinks a lot of tea, Tom?"

He laughed and called for the maid, whose name was Jeanette. He asked her to fetch two sherries.

"She's French," he said.

"She's very young and French."

"Yes, she is. I think I've scandalized the entire neighborhood, keeping her here. She was my wife's choice. I kept her on after Evie died."

"For continuity's sake."

"You can think badly of me all you like, but it won't do any good. God and my maid know differently."

Jeanette brought them their sherries, and he held his glass up in a toast. "To the Liberties," he said. "May we never see it again."

"Who would have thought those two little kids standing up to their ankles in mud at Sandymount would wind up drinking sherry in a fancy house in London. It pays well, being a doctor."

"A doctor's salary doesn't pay for all this, Kitty. I'm still only halfway through my residency."

"It's your wife's?"

"Evie's father bought it for us as a wedding present."

"That's very generous. Most people get a kettle."

"Well, he's very rich. She was his only daughter, and he decided if she was going to marry an Irishman, then he was going to make sure she lived close by, where he could keep an eye on her. As it turned out, it did no good. There's some things even money can't save you from."

"That's sad."

"Yes, it is. I doubt the poor man will ever get over it."

"And you?"

"I've a life of mixed blessings, Kitty. I'd a mother who paid to put me through medical school by selling strong drink and died an alcoholic. I had a wife with a rich father who gave me a nice house, and then

I lost the family it was all meant for. God has a queer sense of humor, does he not?"

"Oh yes, he cracks me up every time."

It seemed that Jeanette was cook as well as maid, and a very good one. There was a consommé first course followed by beignets of sole. Kitty thought about black bread and tea in the refectory of the Smolny Institute; the watery vegetables and boiled meat that were standard fare at the boarding house. So, this was how some people lived. Tom had done well for himself; here was someone who really had left Dublin behind.

He brought out a bottle of wine, a French Semillon in keeping with the theme of the night, and poured some into her glass, proper crystal. It was pale as straw and smelled faintly of lemon.

"When will they be making you a proper doctor then?" she asked him.

"When I become a proper doctor, as you call it, I'll not be a doctor anymore, I'll be a mister. Doctor Thomas Doyle will be just plain Mr. Doyle again."

"Now that doesn't seem fair."

"Well you see, back in the Middle Ages surgeons were barbers with no medical training. So, when the College of Surgeons wanted a royal charter, back in the eighteenth century I think it was, the Royal College of Physicians insisted that no one could be a surgeon unless they had a medical degree first. So what they did, they got their doctorate, then as soon as they got their diploma from the College of Surgeons, they reverted back to 'mister' as a direct snub to the RCP. It's childish I know, but it's been going on for centuries, so why stop now?"

"And that's what you want to be is it, a surgeon?"

"Another two or three years, and I'll have my fellowship."

"So how did all this happen, Tom? Where did you go when you left pretty little Dublin town?"

"Well, until I was sixteen, I was at some fancy boarding school in England. Went to university in Canada after that—I think my ma thought it was cheaper. But I didn't like it there, and after I got my doctorate, I was lucky enough to get an internship back here in London."

"You were lucky you missed being in the war."

"No, I didn't miss it. I enlisted when I came back."

"Now why would you do something like that? Why would a good Irish lad want to fight wars for the English?"

"If I knew then what I know now, I guess I wouldn't have done it. But I did, and I was shipped out with the medical corps, and learned a great deal very quickly at other men's expense."

"You were in France?"

"Flanders, a little place called Passchendaele. Not that I'd want to talk about any of that over dinner."

"At least your job was to put men together again, not tear them apart."

"I don't know that I put many men back together, Kitty. Some folk think it's a glorious thing to be wounded fighting for your country, like it's only the dead that are unlucky. They don't really understand what a bullet does, shattering bones to tiny pieces, lacerating nerves and muscles that no surgeon can ever repair. I've seen men with gunshot wounds; they go through agonies that last month after month, and for some of them you know the pain's going to last a whole lifetime. It's all hidden behind hospital walls where people can't see it. I've had men, strong men, beg me to end their lives; others grab the anesthetic from my hand and press it closer to their face, begging me to stop when I change their dressings every day. I don't believe that war is a way to resolve anything. Or that with that last one still fresh in their minds, my fellow Irishmen want to start another one."

"Then what are they to do, Tom?"

"I don't know, Kit, but I'll tell you this: anything worth dying for is worth living for." He picked up his wine glass. "Anyway, enough of that now. Tell me about your adventures, I'm sure they're far more interesting."

At his gentle coaxing, she told him about some of the things that had happened before she got to Russia; of being held under house arrest by Russian Cossacks in the English Hotel in the Pale, discovering later that she and three other journalists had been ordered to be shot as spies.

"Shot?"

"Lucky for us, the Cossack commander was drunk when he got the orders, and they had been rescinded by the time he had sobered up."

"Oh my God, Kitty. You live a charmed life."

"Did I tell you I went to Serbia?"

"No, you didn't."

"We wanted to cover the fighting there between the Serbians and the Austrians. Not many people know about it. But getting there is just awful. You have to rub yourself head to foot with camphorated oil, then put kerosene in your hair. It's disgusting. Then you fill all your pockets with mothballs, you even sprinkle them through your luggage."

"But why?"

"Everyone does it. The country is absolutely riddled with typhus and spotted fever, and they say it's the only way to protect yourself."

"This was all before you went to Russia?"

"Four years I was there. I thought it would be a few months at the most."

"If they didn't want you to leave, why didn't they put you in prison?"

"They didn't have to. You can't do anything there without the Cheka finding out about it. If they don't want you to go, you don't go. Believe me."

He shook his head. She liked it, the admiration her stories elicited from him, though it all sounded more glamorous than it ever really was.

"Did you meet this Lenin fella?"

"Short. Round. Cold. Possibly mad."

"That's it?"

"I only heard him speak once, in the Soviet at the Smolny in Petrograd. Damn near put me to sleep."

"Trotsky?"

"Intellectual. Intense. Pleasant. Would murder his own grandmother for principle."

"Someone must have impressed you."

"I had tea with the king of Bulgaria once. Me, Kitty O'Kane from the Liberties."

"You wouldn't drink tea with me."

"You're not the king of Bulgaria. It's like this, I was staying at the Grand Hotel in the capital of the place, I can't remember its name . . ."

"Sofia."

"Okay, thanks, Mister Doctor. Anyway, I was staying there and it's like the strangest place you ever been to in your life. If you want to interview the premier of the country or one of the ministers, you go next door to the café, and you get one of the bellboys to call them up on the telephone. So, I went down there and asked them to call the king. And he came!"

"Did you get a big story out of it?"

"No, all I got was my bottom pinched."

"Well, Kitty, you can hardly blame him for that."

"Really? So how is it you've never tried?"

"Like you said, I'm not the king of Bulgaria."

"I wouldn't let that put you off. He has a very nice uniform, but I've seen better in pantomimes. Other than the hat, he's not such a fine figure of a man."

"This must all seem very mundane to you now," he said. "Being back in London."

"I suppose it does. That doesn't mean I miss it. There are some things I can live without. I don't know that I relish being shot as a spy or dying of typhus. Have you ever seen someone die of it?"

"I'm afraid I have."

"Well like you said, we shouldn't speak of it at dinner."

"Speaking of which, here's afters," he said. "Or dessert, as Jeanette makes me call it."

Jeanette took away the plates, and served crêpes flambéed in Grand Marnier. It had been a long time since Kitty had eaten any meal quite like it. She told Jeanette just how lovely it all was, and got a cool smile in response.

"I don't think she likes me," she mouthed at Tom after she'd gone.

"She's very protective of me," Tom said. "It'll be all right once she gets to know you."

"And how long will that be?"

"Oh, a year or two. No more than three."

Kitty asked him about Michael, told him how she'd bumped into him in New York years before.

"Yes, he wrote and told me."

"Couldn't believe it when I saw him. He looks so much like you."

"Not so much these days." He leaned back and patted his belly. "He married an Italian girl; all he does is eat. Still, he seems very happy."

"Is he still in America?"

"Our uncle retired, and he's running the business now. But we've stayed close. He got straight on the ship when Evie died; he was here when we lost little Eion. Don't know what I'd have done without him. But he's away back there now."

"Eion? That was your little boy?"

"Wasn't a year old when he left us. I still can't make sense of children dying, Kit, but I guess I'll have to, now I'm a doctor, and it happens all the time. I can't feel sorry for myself when I see these things happening to other people every day."

"Do you have photographs, Tom?"

"You want to see them?"

"If you don't mind that."

Tom had a study just off the hall, with a rolltop desk, a shelf of medical books, and a small hearth. There were several framed photographs on the mantelpiece; one was of Tom with a pretty young woman with long, fair hair; another of the same woman in a wedding gown, standing alongside Tom; between those, another photograph of a small child with a single tooth and tufts of dark hair.

Kitty winced, felt something clutch at her heart.

"This one was taken on our wedding day, outside the Saint Thomas of Canterbury in Rylston Road. And this one was two weeks before she died."

"Tom. I'm sorry, I shouldn't have—"

"It's okay."

"You've been through a lot."

"So have you, Kit."

"What was she like?"

"Evie?" Tom shrugged, seemed to consider how best to answer her. "She had a good heart, kind. And she was clever, too, you could never put one past her."

"She was beautiful, too, I can see that for myself."

He nodded.

"How did you meet her?"

"She was the daughter of one of the hospital's benefactors. We met at a fundraising dinner. I was an intern, green behind the ears; I couldn't believe she'd even noticed me. Her father opposed the match every step of the way, well why wouldn't he, didn't want his daughter marrying some uppity bog Irish. But defied him, she did; I still don't know why."

"Sounds like she had spirit."

"You know me, Kitty. I didn't want a meek little woman who would bake scones and look decorative at dinner parties."

"What was she doing when you met her?"

"She was a classics teacher at Saint Paul's Girls' School." He saw the face Kitty made and said: "She was educated at Roedean and then got a law degree at Girton College in Cambridge. But of course it was no use to her because they won't let women practice law in this country. She was also—and you'll like this a little better—a member of the Heretics Society *and* the Women's Social and Political Union. I think if you'd ever met her, you would have gotten on famously."

"You're an unusual man, Tom. Most men would run a mile from a woman like that."

He looked so sad. Without thinking, she reached up and touched his face. He smiled at her, put his hand on hers. *God, I could lose myself in those eyes*, she thought. She felt her face getting hotter and knew she had to get out of the room.

"Kitty."

She stopped suddenly in the hallway and turned, and he almost bumped into her. They looked at each other.

Then he leaned in and kissed her. It was the kiss she had always wanted from him; it went on and on.

"Excuse me, Doctor," Jeanette said.

Tom pulled away.

"I'm sorry, I came to get the dishes . . ."

"Yes, right you are, Jeanette. No apologies necessary. Please. Carry on."

Kitty looked at her over Tom's shoulder. The poor girl was blushing like her head was on fire. She squeezed between them and noisily started to clear away the plates in the dining room.

Kitty looked up at Tom. "I think I need another sherry after that."

After Jeanette had finished cleaning up the plates and glasses, Tom told her that she was excused for the night and that she should go to bed.

After she'd gone, Kitty said, "I think you've scandalized her."

"It seems I've a talent for scandalizing. Everyone in the street thinks she's my mistress."

"She is rather young and pretty."

"She's not my type."

"What is your type?"

"I'm looking at her, Kit."

Kitty wondered what it would be like to kiss him again, have his arms around her, take off her clothes for him. Jesus God, yes, she wanted that. But what would he do if she suggested it? Would he think she was wanton? She realized there were things she could do with a man she didn't love that she would balk at doing with Tom.

"Do you ever think about a husband, a family, Kit?"

"I think about it."

"I sometimes think that little Eion . . . look, I know this sounds mad, but I think that perhaps his soul is still waiting there in heaven to come back. He couldn't have been here such a short time for nothing. Do you think that's possible?"

"What if . . . what if your new wife couldn't have babies, Tom?"

"Are we talking about you, or just generally?"

"Let's say you had the mad notion to marry me, and you would be mad, you know that. But suppose. What if I couldn't have them?"

"A healthy young thing like yourself?"

"Well, you never know, do you now?"

"I'd be willing to take the chance."

"Would you, Tom? Would you really? With little Eion up there waiting for you?"

She looked up at the clock on the mantel. It was getting late. She wanted to kiss him again, but she knew she wouldn't, not now. "I think I should be getting home."

"So soon?"

"Mrs. Ratcliffe has a curfew for us girls. If I'm not home by ten o'clock, she'll lock me out."

"I'll walk with you to the high street, find you a cab."

"It's all right, I'll get the tube."

"I won't hear of it."

The streets were shrouded in fog creating halos around the gas lamps, and magnifying the sounds of their heels on the pavements as they walked up to Old Brompton Road. They heard the clip of horses' hooves and saw a hansom coming toward them through the mist. Tom waved it down.

He pulled her toward him. "I had a wonderful night."

"So did I."

"Have lunch with me next week. There's a place near Piccadilly Circus, the Café Royal. Meet me there on Tuesday, one o'clock."

"That would be lovely. Good night, Tom."

"Good night, Kitty."

And this time she was the one who pulled him toward her. She kissed him on the lips, let herself melt into him, but then it scared her how good it felt, and she pushed him away again, and climbed into the cab. She gave the driver her address in Bayswater.

Tom pressed some coins into the cabbie's hand. The man flicked the reins, and they clattered off into the night.

She saw the curtains move in Mrs. Ratcliffe's bedroom as she got out of the hansom cab. It clipped on, was soon lost in the fog. It was only after the cab had gone that she was aware of a man on the other side of the street, watching, his collar pulled up around his face. She ignored him and hurried up the path to the house.

"Kitty."

She spun around, her heart in her mouth. "Lincoln?"

He stood at the gate, still in shadow. "Is that the way you say hello to me?"

"I couldn't see you in the fog. . . . Is that really you?"

"What's left of me."

"When did you get back from Russia?"

"A few months ago."

"Jesus God. How did you find me?"

"It wasn't easy. . . . God you're a sight for sore eyes. I've missed you so much."

He took a step toward her and tried to put his arms around her, but she backed away.

"What are you doing here, Linc?"

"What do you think? I came back to find you."

"You're a liar."

It was him, and yet it wasn't. He looked deathly pale, and thin. God alone knew what torments he had been through in Russia after she left. She had seen his byline in the *New Republic* and the *Guardian*, knew from what he'd written that he must be out of there, all those stories of millions dying of starvation in the new Utopia. By the looks of him, he had nearly been one of them.

She had supposed he'd gone to enjoy his infamy in the Village, had never thought he would come back here.

He reached for her a second time. "It's too late," she said, and pushed him away and ran inside.

CHAPTER 33

Balfour came out of his office slapping the *Times* against his thigh, threw it down in front of Chandler. "What do you think of that?"

"Mr. Balfour?"

"We give the Paddies a treaty, make them a free state, and this is how they respond."

Chandler gave Kitty a sly look. *Don't fire up now*, she told herself. *They're goading you and you know it. Just ignore the bastards.*

"They've accepted the treaty, haven't they, sir?" Chandler said.

"Collins has. But this de Valera fellow says they won't. Wants all thirty-two counties to have dominion status. As if the Irish could ever govern themselves! The only thing they know how to do is get drunk and beat their wives!"

"You know all about the Irish do you?" Kitty heard herself say. It was out of her mouth before she could stop herself.

"What's that, Miss O'Kane?"

"I thought they'd abolished slavery. Had you not heard that rumor, Mr. Balfour?"

"What in God's name are you talking about, gel?"

"The majority of Ireland are Catholics, but it's only Protestants that can sit in the Parliament and make the laws, and you can only vote if you own land. Does that not sound like slavery to you?"

"The Irish have a better life than most, and they should be grateful for it."

"A better life than who, Mr. Balfour? You? You've had it all handed it to you on a plate, your money, your education. Oh, and let's not forget being a man. Now that was a lucky stroke of chance. You get to vote and take whatever job you like. Now that's something to be grateful for."

"Who do you think you're talking to?"

"I know who I'm talking to. A jumped-up lardy bigot who's never known hardship and never gone hungry in his entire life."

There was a dreadful silence. Chandler started to laugh, then put a hand over his mouth to smother it. Balfour's cheeks turned the color of beetroot.

He tried to control himself, but when he finally spoke, it came out as a squeak. "Miss O'Kane, I think you should collect your things and leave. You can collect your wages from the front desk on Friday. Now get out of here."

Oh, but God I need this job. Well, too late now.

Me and my big mouth! Kitty felt every eye in the office as she took her things out of her drawer and put them in her purse. She took her hat and coat from the rack and went to the door.

She looked around the office. "Now don't tell me you haven't all been itching to say that to the pompous pot-licking little bog jumper!"

And she walked out.

She strode purposefully toward the Underground. It was only when she was on the platform that she slumped against the tiled wall and closed her eyes. She let out a long sigh.

"Oh Jesus God, girl, what have you done now?"

⇒

Kitty sat by the window in the Café Royal, could not help but feel astonished at where her life had taken her. A pale winter sun hung over London, and the granite and marble arcades threw deep shadows over Regent Street. How it had all changed since she first left. Now the bankers and society matrons rubbed shoulders in the street with bright young things in tight, calf-length skirts and cloche hats, their boyfriends in loose-fitting Oxford bags, their hair slicked back like matinee idols.

The bread queues, the Cheka death squads, the bodies left lying in the street; it all seemed so far away now.

"What England needs is a revolution," she said.

Tom smiled and tore a bread roll with his fingers. "You think the Bolsheviks will take over?"

"Not the Bolsheviks, God help us. But something. There's veterans begging on the street, and there's young men who look like they've never even seen a rifle, riding around in fancy cars, with their silk scarves flying everywhere. Does that seem right to you, Tom?"

"No, it doesn't seem right to me, Kitty, it never did. But what are we going to do about it? They're starving by the millions in Russia, so the newspapers say. I don't much fancy that either."

The waiter arrived, turtle soup for Tom, consommé for her. Tom gave her a wry smile. "I know what you're thinking, Kitty, and if you can come up with a way to get the consommé to the starving in Russia, I'll do it."

She laughed at him, at herself, for being so transparent. "What is it you want with me, Tom Doyle? I'm not the woman for you."

"You'd best let me decide that."

She picked up her soup spoon, put it down again. "I'm not her, Tom. I know you think she was like me, and maybe there's parts of her that were. But she didn't grow up in the Liberties, Tom. She didn't have that to live down."

"What are you talking about, Kitty?"

"I'm not the one for you, Tom. There's things you don't know about me."

"Such as what?"

"I can't give you what you want, I can't be a demure little wife . . ."

"I don't want a demure little wife."

"Tom, this is moving too fast. I have to think about this. The last thing I want to do is hurt you."

He shook his head. "There's an easier life than the one you have, Kit. Don't you yearn for it?"

"So that's it, Tom? You're my meal ticket out?"

He took her hand, but she pulled away.

"Tom, I just can't. Don't ask me. Please."

If only she could make him understand, because there would never be another Tom Doyle for her. Perhaps she should just tell him the truth, and face the shame of it.

"I love you, Kitty," he said.

She couldn't say it back to him, even if it were true. The look of hurt and bewilderment on his face tore her heart. She barely touched her soup, barely looked up through the rest of their lunch.

———✦———

Afterward he said he would walk her back to her office, and she let him. She couldn't even bear to tell him that she no longer had a job to go. She liked how much he had admired all she had done, and yet she knew that admiration would last just a few minutes more. She didn't want him to pity her, as well as despise her.

This is for the best, she told herself. *In the end, it is.*

They stopped outside a door shiny with black enamel paint, gold plaques on the brick. One of them said: "Sloane & Balfour. Solicitors."

"What's wrong, Kit?"

She turned and looked up at him. She hadn't planned to do this here, with people and buses and hackney cabs passing. She hadn't planned to do it all.

"There's something you have to know about me, Tom."

He must have an idea of what's coming. She watched him ready himself.

"How did you think I got out of Dublin? I didn't have a ma who owned a shebeen or an uncle in Canada. It was a sailor, Tom. His name was Daniel and he was a second officer on a merchant ship and I went with him to Liverpool and I lived with him in sin, but he helped me find a job and he got me out of Dublin and I'll never thank him enough for that."

"Kitty, I—"

"Wait, let me finish. Lincoln wasn't just a mentor like I told you, wasn't just a colleague. You knew that was a lie, didn't you? You just didn't want to believe it. I was his lover, was his lover since I was eighteen near enough. You really want to marry a girl like me?"

She was right. She knew that if she told him, it would change everything, and when she looked at his face, the look in his eyes, she knew it was true.

She might as well tell him everything.

"There's one more thing; while I'm at it, I might as well tell you it all. When I was in Liverpool, I got pregnant to Dan, but by then he'd already left me. So, I stopped the baby. God forgive me, I just couldn't face doing what my ma did. I couldn't. I know it was wrong, but don't worry, God punished me for it, for the damned abortionist nearly killed me and now I can't ever have a baby again. So you see Tom, I can't be what you want me to be, not in any way."

People were staring at them; the man with his head bowed, the woman with tears running down her face. *What a spectacle we are for a bright winter's day.* She had to get away. "I'm sorry, Tom. I'm so, so sorry." She kissed him on the cheek. He didn't move; it was like kissing a statue.

A bus pulled up to the curb. She jumped on; she didn't know where it was going, but it was somewhere, anywhere away from here. She heard Tom shout at her; he started to run after the bus as it pulled away. She shook her head at him and then turned and sat down on one of the wooden seats and didn't look back.

She handed a few coins to the conductor, barely glanced at the ticket, stared out the window at the men and women walking up and down the street; all of them had a story, she supposed, and hers was just another one.

You made mistakes, you had to pay for them. That was the way of the world.

CHAPTER 34

There was a knock on her door, and Mrs. Ratcliffe put her head around. "Miss O'Kane, there's a gentleman downstairs has asked to see you."

"Tell him I'm not here."

"He's been hanging around in the street all morning. I think you should talk to him and let him know this is a respectable area."

She looked out of her window. Jesus God, it was Lincoln. She put on a shawl and ran down the stairs.

He was leaning against one of the lampposts in the street right outside. There was a litter of cigarette ends around his feet. He looked awful. He was wearing a torn Russian greatcoat, and there was three days' stubble on his cheeks. He looked desperate, even dangerous—no wonder Mrs. Ratcliffe was concerned. "What in God's name are you doing, Linc?"

"Waiting for you."

"How long have you been standing here?"

"I don't know. I got here just as the sun came up. I had to see you. I can't stop thinking about you, Kitty."

"You have to stop this."

"Come for a drink with me."

"It won't do."

"Just come for one drink, and I'll leave you alone. I promise."

She bit her lip.

"Please Kitty. After all we've been through. Just one drink."

"All right. Just one then."

He grinned. "That's my girl."

She went back inside to get her coat.

———

Just a handful of customers in the Queen's Head, an old man in the corner with a half of Guinness, an old lady with a bag of crisps and a gin. She was complaining loudly to the barman that the salt in the little blue salt packet was wet, just one solid lump. He was ignoring her.

He put down his *Daily Mirror* and looked over his half-moon glasses at them as they walked in. "What will it be?"

He was surprised when they both ordered vodka. Said he would have to look to see if he had some.

"Old times' sake," Lincoln said to Kitty.

The saloon bar was gloomy and overheated and smelled of stale hops. The gas lamps were on, though it was only just past two in the afternoon. The dull yellow light reflected on the mahogany paneling.

Lincoln rolled himself a cigarette. It was an affectation he had picked up in Russia, but now it looked as if it had become just a regular habit. She noticed the tremor in his hands.

"So what are you doing home on a Wednesday afternoon?" he asked her.

"I got fired."

He grinned. "What did you do?"

"What do you think?"

"Something to do with that famous temper of yours! So now what are you going to do? Does your landlady know?"

"Not yet. When she asked why I was home, I said I had two weeks' holiday coming. I'm not sure she believes me."

"So now what?"

"I don't know. Find another job, I suppose."

"That won't be easy, not without a reference." He threw back his vodka, Russian-style, and went to the bar to get another. The barman looked alarmed. She wondered what they would make of Lincoln in polite Boston society now.

"What about your boyfriend?" he said as he sat down.

"What about him?"

"Will he help you out?"

"How did you know about Tom? Have you been spying on me?"

"Spying is what I do best. I'm a journalist, Kitty. No one has secrets from me, not even Lenin."

"No, Tom's not going to help me."

"Has he given you the push?"

"Perhaps."

"He's mad."

"No, what it is, he's too good for the likes of me. What about you? What happened with your countess? Did Tatiana the Great kick you out?"

"You know the Russians. They're so temperamental."

"Did she find you with another woman?" A pause. "She did, didn't she? Oh, Jesus God."

"It wasn't like that."

"You can't help yourself, can you? You don't even close your eyes when you're kissing, in case something else comes along."

"That's not fair."

"No, but it's accurate. I can't believe I stuck with you as long as I did."

"I'm sorry. I mean it. I know it's too late for us, but I just want you to know I'm not the same man you left. I've woken up to myself. You were the only one I ever loved, you know."

"Is that supposed to make me feel better?"

He leaned closer. "'Whoever you are, now I place my hand upon you, that you may be my poem. I whisper with my lips close to your ear, I have loved many women and men, but I love none better than you.'"

"Oh Linc. They're just words, you know. And they're not even yours."

He spread his hands in a helpless gesture, like he was somehow the victim of it all. "Walt says it better than I can."

She swallowed the vodka; it burned all the way down. One taste of the foul oily stuff, and suddenly she was back in Russia, that damned cold and violent country. "How did you get out? I thought the Foreign Ministry were never going to let you go. You're their prize asset. In the *Times* they call you a Communist, did you know that?"

"What do I care what they call me? Anyway, maybe they're right; maybe I am a Communist."

"After everything you've seen?"

"Just because the Bolsheviks are crazy doesn't mean their ideas are." He ran a hand through his hair. He had changed, she thought. It wasn't just fatigue; though exhaustion, physical and spiritual, was etched into the lines in his face with a chisel; and it wasn't just the months of malnourishment. There was a desperation about him. He looked like an escaped convict.

"Come to Ireland with me," he said.

"What? Come to—what? Are you mad?"

"You've heard what's happening there."

"And what of it?"

"You want to see things change, don't you?

"Once I did. Look what good that did me."

"This is different! It's Ireland, Kit. How can anything be more important than the place you're from?"

"There's nothing for me in Ireland."

"There's going to be a war there. You know it. I know it. The whole world knows it. The Irish want full independence, not these crumbs

Churchill is offering them. And if Ireland can win its freedom, then next is Egypt, India, the whole damned empire."

"I don't care about the empire."

He moved closer. "But you care about Ireland. You've seen what the British did there, firsthand."

"What do you want me there for?"

"Nothing means anything without you there, Kit."

"Oh, go on with you."

"Don't give up, Kitty—not on yourself, not on the cause. You know it's not over. Wars aren't about guns anymore, Kitty, they're about who can tell the best story! You saw it for yourself. What was the first thing that Lenin did after the Bolsheviks took over Petrograd?"

"He took down all the other newspapers! And it was wrong!"

"Isn't that what the British are trying to do now? They don't want people like us there, telling the other side of the story. You and me, we can be the voices telling the real truth of it! Remember that newspaperman you saw the Cheka beating up in the street? Do this for him! I have the contacts. And people here are a lot more interested in what happens in Ireland than they are in what happens in Russia. This time we can do something, and we can make it count."

"I'm not interested."

"I think you are." He put his hand over hers. "We're birds of a feather, you and I. We understand each other. We may not be saints, but we can still do something worthwhile. You know I'm right, don't you?"

And perhaps he was. All her choices were gone, weren't they? She had seen them slip away in Regent Street, seen the truth in Tom's eyes. Lincoln knew it too; she could never be anyone's wife, not now, not without feeling she had given up on that little girl cowed in the corner in that house in the Liberties.

There really only was ever one choice, and that was to go back.

CHAPTER 35

Dublin, Ireland, Spring 1922

March, and the first leaves were budding on the trees. Kitty and Lincoln headed down Haddington Road to their lodgings on Northumberland Road. It was a short bus ride out of the city center, but the boarding house Lincoln had found for them was cheap, and cheap was all they could afford.

They were on their way back from their weekly briefing from Erskine Childers at Sinn Fein. Childers produced the *Irish Bulletin*, a mimeographed sheet that was the main source of information from the Irish side on what had been happening in the Troubles, as the British liked to call them. It categorized incidents under headings such as "Arrests," "Armed Assaults," and "Raids," mimicking the way a police inspector might write a report to his headquarters. He knew how to get a message across, Childers. His reports were easy to read, and sometimes conflicted wildly with the official briefings from the British at Dublin Castle.

They had been two months in Dublin now, and the situation was far from settled. Although the Irish republican party had signed a treaty with the British for independence, the British had watered it down— they wanted Ireland as a dominion of the empire with George V still their king. The Irish who had fought the British in the Black and Tan War were now split among themselves about whether to accept what the British were offering or go back to the barricades.

For one heady moment the previous year, Ireland had seemed on the brink of finally gaining her freedom, but now the country was about to tear herself apart again, just as Lincoln had said. Clever bastards, Churchill and that Lloyd George, they had worked out that if they couldn't defeat the Irish, then the next best thing was to let the Irish destroy each other. Now the Irish were arguing with each other, Michael Collins and the Free Staters on one side, de Valera and the republicans—Sinn Fein—on the other, holding out for complete independence.

Kitty and Lincoln were passing the gray stone gate of the Beggars Bush barracks. The British had handed it over to the Free State army earlier that year, after they signed the truce. It was strange not to see the bloody Union Jack flying over the gate. Instead of the Black and Tans, two painfully young Irish lads stood sentry wearing the Free State uniforms that Childers himself said he had come to despise. The new Free State army was there to enforce Churchill's damned treaty, he said, them and Collins had sold out to the British.

"They're traitors to Ireland! Free State? British lackeys, simple as that."

She could see how Lincoln would think that. But to her they looked more like pimply young boys fresh out of school.

One of them handed the other a cigarette, and they both hunched over to light up.

"You wouldn't see the British Army guys doing that," Lincoln said.

"Doing what?"

"Leaving their posts for a smoke."

"They're just lads."

She turned up her collar against the wind. Dublin was a cold and depressing place in the winter, all gray skies and grim stone. It felt strange to her to be back; almost like she had never been away, and that scared her.

"Do you think Childers is right, that it's going to be civil war?"

"I don't see what else it would be."

"But they can't turn on each other now. All these years fighting the Black and Tans, getting the British out of here. They have to work out a compromise."

"If Lloyd George had only held his nerve for another month or two, your Irish boys were all but done. If he hadn't caved in and called a truce, it would have been all over anyway. These young Irish boys are sick of fighting, and hardliners like Churchill know it, that's why he's not going to let them off the hook."

"Collins is right," Kitty said. "Staying in the dominion is not what they wanted, but it's better than nothing. Churchill will never give them full independence."

"That's not what Childers thinks. He's with de Valera."

"There's not many others that are."

"But there's enough."

"Are you going to write that?" she asked him.

"Sure I am. De Valera needs all the help he can get. Are you with me on this?"

"I'm not sure anymore what I'm going to write."

"What do you mean, you're not sure?" Lincoln said. "This is the fight, Kit. We have to tell people the truth."

"Everyone seems to have their own truth, don't they?"

"You really want your people to accept this treaty, bow down to Churchill and Lloyd George and the rest of them?"

"Maybe it's not complete independence, but it's halfway to it, and it means no more young boys have to die. If they want full independence, they'll have to keep fighting the British for another ten years, and they don't have the men or the guns or the stomach for that. So what choice is there?"

"The choice is not to give in!"

Their raised voices had caught the attention of the two sentries on the gate. One of them called out to her; they weren't sure if Lincoln was molesting her.

Kitty waved to the boys on the gate to let them know she was all right. "Maybe those lads over there have just had enough of killing and seeing their friends and brothers killed. Have you considered that? And what do you care anyway? You're not Irish."

"I care about freedom."

"You didn't care much about it in Russia. Except your own, of course." She turned away, frightened to see him like this. In Serbia, in Greece, early on in Russia, her heart had been in it, but coming back here had been a mistake. The truth was, she was tired of it all. Nothing was going to change; nothing ever did.

She turned away from Lincoln and kept walking. A truck turned the corner of Haddington Road, coming from the Mount Street bridge. Something told her it was trouble—the speed it was coming, bouncing over the potholes like that toward the barracks gate.

Three other trucks rolled up the street behind it.

One of the sentries shouted a warning and raised his rifle. "Get down," Lincoln said, and threw her to the ground. The other sentry fired off a shot just as the first truck skewed across the road. Armed men in greatcoats and flat caps poured out of the back of it; bullets cut through the air above her head, the noise deafening.

Kitty kept her face pressed against the wet pavement, turned to the side, facing the gate. She saw the young sentries drop to their knees and aim their rifles, but before they could fire another shot, one of them fell down, screaming, clutching at his leg. His mate started to crawl toward him, a volley of bullets stuttered into the bricks above his head, and he changed his mind and wriggled back through the gate.

All she could see were the boots, dozens of them, as they ran past her, over her. Another volley of gunfire echoed around the courtyard inside the barracks as the battle continued. The boy with the bullet in his leg was still screaming.

Finally, she raised her head. She saw one of the republicans, no more than a schoolboy himself, walk up to the wounded Free State soldier. He aimed his handgun at his head.

"Don't do it!" Kitty screamed, and started to get to her feet.

Lincoln grabbed her and pulled her down again. "Kitty, for God's sake!"

The boy fired the gun twice, and the young sentry lay still. The lad turned away almost casually and strolled through the sentry gate.

Kitty tore free of Lincoln's grip and ran toward the young sentry. There was nothing she could do. She knelt down and cradled his head in her hands. Jesus God, he couldn't be more than sixteen or seventeen years old himself. His eyes were open, the gray of the clouds in them. He had freckles across his nose.

"Oh my God. What have they done to you, boy?"

Lincoln stood over her, screaming things at her, but she couldn't hear him over the sound of the shooting on the other side of the wall. He grabbed her arm and pulled her to her feet, dragged her away, keeping close to the barracks wall until they were well away.

"What in God's name did you think you were doing?"

Kitty stood over the basin, pouring warm water from the jug, washing the blood from her hands and arms, staining the water red. It had gotten everywhere, on her blouse, on her coat, even on her shoes.

"Did you not see what he did? The boy was wounded; he'd dropped his gun. It was murder was what that was. Cold-blooded murder."

"And how was it going to help him, you running up like that?"

"He was some mother's son."

"They're all some mother's son."

"What in God's name was he thinking to do a thing like that?"

"What do you expect, Kit? This is a war."

"It's not a war! A few months ago, those two boys were on the same side. I understood them shooting at those fecking Black and Tans, but this was two Irish boys. They could have been cousins!"

"The sentry was fighting for a government that's going to sell them out to the British."

"Or maybe he was just a young lad that was sick of all the killing. Maybe Collins just wants the best deal he can get, and the republicans should give him a chance and see what happens."

"My God, what's wrong with you?"

"It's funny, I was going to ask you the very same thing."

She started shaking, couldn't seem to stop. Lincoln took her in his arms and held her. He smelled of tobacco and cheap whiskey, but somehow even that was comforting. She stood there in her slip, shivering in his arms, staring at the bloody water in the basin.

"I love you, Kitty," he whispered. *God in Heaven. What?* It was the first time he had ever said that to her. *Why now?*

He cupped her breast in his hand, eased the other hand under her slip. A long time since she had let him touch her. But she needed this; she needed him to hold her. She ran her hands through his hair, over his collarbone, felt the ridge of his shoulder blade stark against the skin—all the softness she remembered of him gone now.

"Tell me you love me," he whispered.

But she wouldn't; she couldn't. He pulled her toward him anyway and onto his lap, drawing her slip over her stocking tops. He was gasping and muttering under his breath. She unbuttoned his shirt. He was so thin she could see his ribs.

She undid his trousers, yanked them down to his knees. She eased herself down onto him. He felt so hot when he was inside her; everything else was so cold.

She had to save something from this. Time was slipping away from her, with every slow sliding stroke, slipping away. She stared over his shoulder, at the basin by the window and her woolen hat lying on the worn carpet, and blinked slowly, wondering what on earth had happened to Kitty O'Kane, the one who knew what it was all about.

She had to get her back, somehow. But how?

Dublin Castle was more a Georgian palace than a fortress; all that remained of the medieval fortress that had once stood here was the bastion they now called the Record Tower. For almost two centuries now, the castle had symbolized British dominion over Ireland; it was the headquarters of the British garrison, the lord lieutenant of Ireland had his state apartments there, and it was where the chief secretary for Ireland had his offices.

Even after all these years of being away, she felt as if she was a traitor just stepping inside the place. She remembered how her father and her uncles used to have a name for men they thought were a little too fond of the British: "Castle Catholics."

And for all the gilt and grandeur and elegance of the Latin inscriptions and heraldic devices, the castle had a dark history. Just two years before, three IRA men had been tortured and shot in one of the cells.

Kitty had made an appointment with the undersecretary, but he had kept her waiting in a drafty corridor for over two hours now. A British officer sat behind a desk at the reception, scratching away in a heavy leather-bound ledger with a pen. He barely glanced at her.

When she asked him how much longer the undersecretary would be, he raised an eyebrow and said in a cool voice that the undersecretary would see her as soon as he was available.

Even Lenin had not kept her waiting so long.

She took out her notebook and stared at what she had written the night before. It was a draft of a piece about the shooting they had witnessed at the Beggars barracks. *"What are you going to write, Kitty?"* Lincoln had asked her. *"Are you going to say that a republican shot that Free State trooper in cold blood? Is that how you're going to say it? Because that's what Lloyd George would love you to write."*

"But it's the truth," she had said. *"Now you're censoring the news, just like the British did in the trenches. What's the difference?"*

"You're too emotive," he had snapped back at her. *"You write like a woman would write. You'll never sell any of your stuff if you're always so emotional about things."*

It was what he always said when he didn't like a point she was trying to make.

She looked up at the warrant officer. He gave her a chill smile. *Which will be the greater humiliation*, she thought, *sitting here all day or walking out without my interview?*

"I know you, don't I?"

She turned to the voice. It had been ten years, but as soon as she saw him, she was back on the *Titanic*, in a stewardess uniform, watching him smoke a cigar while she put flowers on his table.

He was dressed much as he had been then, with immaculate precision, in a charcoal double-breasted woolen suit, diamond tiepin, polka-dot tie. He had a fur-lined Ulster topcoat draped over his shoulders. The diamond pinkie ring on his left hand caught the light as he puffed on his cigar.

"Where have I seen you before?"

"I'm sure I don't know."

He stood over her, thinking. "I got it. The *Titanic*! You were our stewardess."

"You remember that?"

"I never forget a pretty face. Well, how about that. Ain't it a small world? What are you doing in Dublin Castle?"

The warrant officer looked up, curious.

"I have an appointment with the undersecretary," Kitty said.

"Does he need a new maid?"

"I'm a journalist these days."

"A journalist! Well don't that beat all. How did a girl like you become a journalist?"

"Like me?"

A beat. "A former stewardess."

"The same way anyone becomes anything. You work hard."

"Yeah? Is that the secret? I must remember that." He gave the warrant officer a conspiratorial wink. For the first time, the soldier looked uncomfortable.

"Is Bernie keeping you waiting?"

"Bernie?"

"Undersecretary Masterson."

Kitty looked past him at the officer on the desk. "I've been here since nine thirty."

He took out his fob watch. "Two hours! Goddamn. Now that's most uncivil of him. Let me see what I can do."

He turned on his heel and walked back down the corridor, his heels clicking on the marble. A few minutes later he was back with another junior officer in tow. "Miss O'Kane?" the officer said. "Mr. Masterson will see you now."

Jack Finnegan smiled at her.

"Thank you," she said stiffly to him, not sure if she wanted to be indebted to such a man.

"It's not what you know; it's who you know." He touched the tip of his homburg. "We'll meet again," he said and went off down the stairs.

Kitty smiled at the warrant officer who looked away, furious.

She followed Masterson's lackey down the corridor. One for the Irish.

CHAPTER 36

Summertime was coming to Dublin. The streets were crowded, everyone taking the air along the quays or window-shopping up Grafton Street. Hard to imagine that there was a war coming.

De Valera's republicans had taken a stand. Three months ago they had taken over the Four Courts, as well as Kilmainham Gaol and the Kildare Street Club in the center of Dublin. It was a direct challenge to the authority of the so-called Free State and Michael Collins, and he would have to do something or lose all credibility. For now, he and de Valera were waiting for the results of the coming elections. If de Valera's candidates won enough votes, Collins might still be forced to back down.

"Do you remember that night in Turkey?" Lincoln said to her as they walked. "We had dinner in the Municipal Garden at Pera, there was a band playing ragtime on the terrace. They'd hung electric lamps in the trees, and the moon looked huge, yellow as butter. There was the Horn right there below us, and the lights of the ships, and you could just make out the towers of the old city all glittering in the moonlight. What a night that was."

"I remember it."

His voice dropped to a whisper. He leaned closer. "Do you remember making love to me that night? It had never been like that for me before. You were so—"

"That was a long time ago."

"Not so long, Kitty."

"If I was so special, Linc, what about all the other women in between?"

He tried to take her hand, but she moved a step away.

"You believed in me once," he said.

"That was before I found Russia's minister for women's affairs belly dancing on your lap and her knickers on the bed stand."

"I told you, she was nothing to me. You're the only one that ever mattered. We've made a difference to the world, you and me."

"Have we? It doesn't feel like it. Does anyone care, do you think?"

"Look over there," he said, nodding at a young boy selling newspapers on the corner of the street. "It's the only real education anyone has these days. Newspapers. People like us, we're the future."

"And what are we doing with all this power? Telling them they should go to war again."

"We have to show people the right way to think."

"God Jesus, listen to yourself!"

"We can't give up the fight. We can't let them win."

"They already have, Lincoln. Nothing we did, nothing we wrote, made a damned bit of difference."

He stopped and looked at her. He looked like a little boy that had just been scolded by his mother. She'd hurt him, though she'd not meant to. What was wrong with him? He should be content—the book he had written about the Russian Revolution had just been published, and overnight he had become the darling of the smart set in London and New York. At least Lenin had been good for *him*.

Kitty was riding on his coattails now; the *Republican* had taken her pieces, and the *Irish Times* in America. He had been right: people on both sides of the Atlantic were interested in Ireland the way they never were about people starving in Petrograd. Little Kitty O'Kane from the Liberties was a proper writer now.

Funny how it just didn't matter that much to her anymore.

"You can't let me down now, Kitty," he said. "You can't walk out on this."

She hurried on, Lincoln walking fast to catch up.

Kids were playing soccer on Saint Stephen's Green, people feeding bread to the ducks. She sat down on one of the benches by the bandstand, smiled at the little children with ice cream–sticky faces. Lincoln, breathing heavily, sat down next to her.

They were like that for a long time, not saying anything. "Promise me you won't let me down."

"Let you down?"

"I need you, Kit."

"You didn't need me in Russia."

"That was a long time ago."

"Because it was a long time ago doesn't mean it never happened."

"What are you going to do, go back to your fancy doctor in London?"

"I can't," she said. "Even if I wanted to."

"And what do you want?"

"I don't know what I want anymore," she said. After a while she stood up again. "I need to be alone for a while, to think."

She walked away through the park, and this time he didn't follow her. She headed back through the town toward the Liffey, staring at the familiar places that she had grown up with. She stopped halfway across the Dublin Bridge, watched smoke rise into the sky from a Guinness boat out by Butt Bridge as it made its way toward the Irish Sea, seagulls swooping and crying over the stern. She could smell the brewery farther upriver.

The sun glittered on the dome at the Four Courts. Hard to imagine the republican lads in there, staring out of the windows with their guns and their slit-eyed determination. The bells of St. Michan's pealed over the city, and barefoot kids from the tenements skimmed stones on the surface of the river.

She'd been so many places over the years: New York, Petrograd, Constantinople, London, Belgrade. She'd survived wars and ships sinking under her, even an order for her own execution.

Somehow she had made it through it all. But the one thing that truly terrified her was going back to the Liberties. She had been in Dublin six months, and it was the one thing she knew she still had to do.

CHAPTER 37

The weather had turned foul again. Rain slanted through the streets, rivulets of dirty water rushed down the gutters, clogging the drains. The old Georgian house watched her approach, warily, like a dog at a gate. She could smell it even from the corner.

There were kids everywhere on the stairs, just as she remembered. Different kids, of course, but maybe the rats were the same. Angry voices from the other sides of doors, husbands yelling at their wives—that was familiar. She climbed the stairs slowly, almost turned back. Would her ma still be here? Over ten years now, the last letter Kitty had from her ma was when her father died, when Kitty was living in Liverpool with Danny. She hadn't even written back.

Perhaps her ma was gone too. And what about Mary and the boys?

She knew these steps so well, how many times had she been up and down them as a kid, running to fetch water from the pump in the yard for her ma, or to use the drop toilet—she could still remember that particular stench.

She hesitated outside the door. *Don't be scared; your daddy's dead now*, she thought. *In the ground these ten years. He can't hurt you now.* She took a breath and put out her hand. Jesus God, she was shaking.

She knocked on the door.

She almost didn't recognize the old woman who opened it. Gray she was, and bowed down by life. Wisps of hair hung loose around her face, the rest was tied back, too much of it to bother with. There were deep lines in her face, and she wore a shapeless gray dress. It was her hands that caught Kitty's attention, raw and calloused from work, a crone's hands.

"You don't recognize me, do you?"

"Yes I do, Kitty. You never forget your own."

Suddenly there were tears in the old woman's eyes. *Not just any old woman*, Kitty reminded herself, *it's my ma, she's my ma.* She started to move toward Kitty, then held back as if she thought her daughter might step away from her. When Kitty embraced her, she felt her tremble. She felt so frail, so thin.

"I never thought I'd see you again, girl, never thought we'd see you back here. You'd better come on in."

It hadn't changed much, still smelled of cabbage and mold, like she remembered. There used to be a straw mattress for all of them in the corner; there was a bedstead now, so going up in the world then. Washing hung on a line across the middle of the room, a broken and peeled statue of Jesus sat in the hearth, heartily satisfied to see so much suffering, she supposed. There was an enamel bowl on a wooden crate in the middle of the room, for washing clothes and washing people and washing dishes.

The sash windows were rotting in their frames, and the doors barely hung on their hinges. Most of the cornices had come down by now; they were for rich people once.

Two huge pairs of eyes watched her from the corner. Two girls: one was no more than twelve, a little sister she never knew she had, and the other must be Mary, she reckoned. She was just a baby in filthy nappies when Kitty left; now here she was all green-eyed with a mess of red, curly hair; she could have been looking at herself at that age.

Except for no bruises on her. Now that was a blessing.

Her ma put a kettle on the hearth. "I'll make us tea." She rubbed her hands on her apron. "You'd remember Mary. The other one is Joan. Say hello, girls. This is Kitty. I've told you about Kitty, right?"

Kitty tried a smile; the two girls just stared.

"So, what are you doing back in Dublin?"

"Working, Ma. I write for newspapers now."

"God preserve us, you're joking me."

She shook her head.

"Well, fancy that. Truth is, after you went off, I never thought I'd hear from you again. Such a shock it is, seeing you here. Never thought you'd go off and make something of yerself. The newspapers! Who'd have thought such a thing?"

Make something of myself. Is that what I've done? Kitty thought. She hadn't told her ma the whole truth of it, but then she supposed that not ending up with a room full of kids in a tenement in Dublin, well that was making something of yourself, wasn't it?

"Did you hear about your father?"

"You wrote me."

"You never wrote back. Wasn't sure that you got it."

"How did he die?" She saw the tears come to her mother's eyes at the mention of him, and it made her angry. "God's sake, don't cry for that bastard."

"He was your father."

"I know what he was. You said it was a heart attack."

"He was drinking down the pub on the corner, and he just went over, God rest his soul."

"No, not God rest his soul, God damn him to *hell.*"

"Kitty!"

"I'm not sorry for saying it; he was a brute. Where's Sean?"

"He went away to the Great War. Never came back."

"Oh Jesus. He was only a kid!"

"Half the men in the street died over there."

She asked about the others: Ann was out working, she said, got herself a fella now. "You know young Michael died. He would have been just crawling when you left. The doctors said it was something wrong with his lungs. Poor little mite, he was never a strong lad. I've still got a lock of his hair, there's nothing else left of him."

"What about Liam?"

"Liam! I don't know what I'd do without Liam. You'd not recognize him now; he's a big, strong lad. He spent two years in Mountjoy after the Rising."

"I might have known he'd join the republicans. He was always the one with the fight in him."

"It was hard with no money coming in. Ann helped out, went into service; she's a good girl that one."

"Where's Liam now?"

"He works at the docks. He'll be home soon I should think, if he doesn't stop at the pub. Bit of his father in him there. His wages keep us going here, but he'll be off and wanting to marry himself soon, I shouldn't wonder."

She brought her tea, milky with no sugar, and Kitty didn't ask for any.

"You got yourself a fella, Kitty?"

"I have; he's here with me. He's a writer too. Famous in his way, he is. He's American."

Now why did she tell it like that, and to her mother? Made it sound like Romeo and Juliet or some damned fool thing. She saw her ma glance at her finger, looking for a ring, and when she didn't see one, she bit her lip, but she didn't say anything.

"It's so good to see you again, Kitty. I've said that many prayers for you over the years in the church. I always lit a candle for you on your birthday."

"I should have written," she said.

There was so much to say, to tell her. But where to start? She couldn't tell her the truth about Liverpool. And how could her ma ever understand about Lincoln and Russia and New York and the rest of it? She might as well tell her about going to the moon.

Besides, none of it mattered, did it? That wasn't what happened. What was really important was what happened long before any of that.

"Did you want to see where your father is buried, Kit?"

"Only to spit on the grave, Ma."

"Now Kit. He wasn't a bad man; it was the drink that did it. He wasn't always like that."

She couldn't believe it. All these years she'd been away and all her mother wanted to do was to talk about him. It made her blood boil. "Why didn't you protect me, Ma?" *The look on her face. She knows what I'm talking about, all right.* "Did you never think to leave him?"

"And go where? What would you have had me do? Life gives you a hand; you have to play it."

"I didn't. I chucked the hand and walked away."

"Easy for you to say, you didn't have children needed looking after."

"I still have the scars on my back from his belt."

Her ma looked down at her lap, screwed her apron up in her fists. *Just say something, Ma. Anything.*

The door burst open, and for a moment Kitty thought it was her father standing there, the smell of Guinness on him, sleeves rolled up, those huge shoulders and the broad brown leather belt at his trousers. *God, he even looks like him.*

It was only when he spoke that it was different; he had a soft voice and a calmness about him. He stopped halfway into the room, looked at her ma and then at her.

"Who's this now?" he said.

"Do you not remember Kitty?" her ma said.

"Kitty?" It took a moment, but then it came to him. "Well. So back now, are you?"

She got to her feet. "Hello, Liam. Last time I saw, you were only up to your ma's knee."

"Well that was a long time ago now." He looked down on her; he was a good head taller, a big man like his father. "What brings you back?"

"She's working for the papers now," her ma said, eager. "She's writing about the Troubles."

"Oh you are, are you? The newspapers are no friends to us."

"Not all the newspapers are against you. The ones I write for are on your side."

"And what side is that?"

She had expected a warmer welcome from him. She remembered little Liam, standing up to their daddy whenever he took out the belt.

"I've no love for the English either, Liam."

"It's not just about the English now, though, is it?" He went to the slow fire in the hearth, picked up the kettle with a rag, poured himself some of the stew that had been cooking there. "How long you back for then?"

"I don't know. I thought I'd pay a visit."

"Kind of you to think of us."

"Liam," her ma said.

"So it's the war that brings you back, then?"

"People have to know the truth of what the British are doing here."

"Listen to you. You still care about us, do you? Or does it just make a good story?" When she didn't answer him, he said, "I spent time in Mountjoy."

"Ma told me."

"Did she tell you what they did to Sean? Couldn't believe it myself. It's one thing to die, but he was fighting for the wrong fecking side."

"Liam!"

"Ma, sure and the girls have heard the word before."

"Why did he join?" Kitty said.

"You know Sean. He was behind the stable door when they were giving out the brains."

"That's no way to talk about your brother, God bless his soul!" Ma said.

"You know it's true." He pulled a wooden crate toward him and sat down. "Never thought we'd see you around here again. How long is it, ten years? Maybe more. I couldn't believe it when you left. She'll come back, I used to keep saying to my ma. She wouldn't leave us."

"I had to go, Liam."

"Well, it's done now, isn't it? All in the past." The last word, he almost spat it out. He sat there in his shirtsleeves and boots, looking indestructible, but then they all looked like that until the bullets tore them in half.

"Are you still with the republicans?" she asked him.

"Why wouldn't I be?"

"Have you not done your share? Your ma's lost two boys; you won't let her lose another one?"

"What does it matter to you? You don't live here anymore. Sure I'm going to fight, if we have to. We've come this close. If we give up now, what will happen?" He studied her with hard, green eyes. "Is that what you're going to write for the newspapers, what a good thing it is to have the British tell us how run our own country?"

"Anything worth dying for is worth living for."

"And who told you that? Only thing to make anyone understand your point of view is a gun in your hand, I reckon."

"Us women got the vote, and we didn't have guns."

"No, but you threw your fair share of bricks if I remember right. Being reasonable never helped anyone."

Kitty let it go. There was no changing a man's mind when he was determined to die; she had learned that much in the last few years. She looked at the two girls, still silent, looking scared of their own shadows, the two of them. *I hope Liam doesn't use his belt on them*, she thought.

"I heard you was on the *Titanic* when she went down," he said.

"Now where did you hear that?"

"A little bird told me. Is it true?"

"Kitty, you never told me that," her ma said.

"Well, it's true."

"You're one of the lucky ones," Liam said.

"I've been lucky a few times since as well."

She wanted to tell them more, but the look in Liam's eyes stopped her. She realized he hated her. He must have looked up to her more than she ever knew, had wanted her to stay and look after him and his brothers. All these years she thought it was her mother who would have blamed her for abandoning them, and it wasn't, it was Liam.

"You heard about our dad?" he said.

"I heard. Heart attack."

"Is that what you told her?" Liam said to Ma. "It was no heart attack, Kit. He was dead drunk and stepped in front of a Guinness cart, right under the horse. Took him three days to die in the hospital."

"Jesus." She looked at her ma, but she was staring at the floor.

"Were you there at the end, Liam?"

"Was I? Fook! Ma went to see him. I don't know why." He put his thumbs in his braces. "Threw him out I did."

"Threw him out?"

"Bastard hit me one too many times. I always swore I'd do it, and one day I did. He was taking off his belt, and I clobbered him, hard as I could. He started sobbing like a baby. I threw him down the stairs and told him if he ever came back I'd kill him. I meant it too. I'd have swung for him."

"Jesus God, how old were you?"

"Fourteen. Taught me well, didn't he?"

"Good on you then."

"Well someone had to do it."

She looked at her ma. She wondered what she'd felt about that—was she relieved or was she sorry? She supposed the truth of it was Ma loved that brute. *Loved him more than she ever loved us. I just never wanted to accept that*, she thought, *but you can't twist what is into what isn't.*

And that was her answer, the one she'd been looking for. It had been right there the whole time. She just didn't want to see it.

"I'd best be going," Kitty said.

"Will you not stay and have dinner with us?" Ma said.

Liam shook his head. "It's best she's going now, Ma. Sure she has things to do."

Kitty got up and her ma followed her to the door. Liam stayed where he was.

"You will come back, Kitty?" her ma said. "Whenever you can."

"Sure I will." She pressed a handful of bank notes into her hand when Liam looked away. Her ma shook her head, tried to give them back, but didn't try too hard. God knew she needed them and after all this time, well it wasn't nearly enough.

"I'm sorry for what I did, Liam," she said over her ma's shoulder. "But I had to get out."

"Well, I guess everyone has their own side of it," he said. "But you shouldn't have come back. I'm glad you got out of here, but there's nothing here for you now. You've just upset everyone. Now go on and good luck to you."

She felt the house watching her as she walked to the corner in the rain. *"I'm going to marry you, Kitty O'Kane!"* So much for childish dreams. The reality of it was her little brother was getting ready to fight a war no one could win, and she was living with a man she didn't really love. She looked back for the last time and swore she could hear the old house laughing at her.

She bought a newspaper, stood huddled in a doorway by the tram stop, reading it. The rain was coming down harder now; summer in Ireland, she thought bitterly. And the English complain! The newspaper was calling men like Liam "irregulars," like they were mutineers. Months before, they were the country's saviors.

Perhaps Lincoln was right; she couldn't just be a spectator when her brother was about to make himself a martyr. Someone needed to speak for him and men like him.

But then what, when it was all over?

A car slowed down, pulled up to the curbside. It was a blue Rolls-Royce, the silver lady on the bonnet something she hadn't seen in this part of Dublin before, not anywhere outside the Dublin Castle. The passenger in the back seat wound down the window. "Now you're getting wet, Kitty my girl. Would you like a lift?"

"Mr. Finnegan?"

"You'll get soaked through in this. Here, get in."

He swung the back door open. She hesitated.

"You'll catch your death out there."

She closed her umbrella and got in.

Finnegan patted the seat beside him. What a motor car; she had never sat in the likes. As she got in, she smelled tobacco, leather, and Finnegan's expensive cologne. Finnegan tapped on the driver's shoulder; he was a big paddy who looked more like a bruiser from Temple Bar than a chauffeur. "Drive on, Seamus."

"I live up around Beggars barracks," Kitty said.

"I know where you live, Kit."

"Mr. Finnegan, I—"

"The name's Jack."

"Have you been following me?"

"Not following, as such. I'm keeping an eye out for you, as friends should for each other."

"Keeping an eye out for me?"

"This is not an accidental meeting, Kitty. I felt I needed to warn you."

An expansive grin. Kitty huddled farther into the corner of the seat. He was a big man, big around the shoulders and belly, and he spread himself in his seat like an emperor. His knee was touching her leg, but she couldn't move any farther away, not even in a big car like this.

What on earth made her get in an automobile with this man?

"Warn me about what?"

"You know your boyfriend's making trouble for himself?"

"He's a journalist, trouble follows him about."

"Being a journalist is bad enough in Dublin these days. But I don't mean that. I mean his activities with Sinn Fein."

Kitty laughed.

"Oh, it's no laughing matter, Kitty. I'm serious."

"He's not in Sinn Fein!"

"You don't think so?"

"He's one for causes, but he writes about them, he doesn't fight them."

Another smile. But Jack Finnegan, she realized, was one of those men whose smile was a warning. There was no warmth in it; it was rather a baring of the teeth. "I see you've been visiting old haunts."

"You *have* been following me."

"Just taking an interest. Your ma could do with a little help, especially if young Liam gets himself into trouble again. It won't be easy for her, living in a place like that with three girls still at home."

"What do you know about Liam?"

"You keep asking me how I know things as if I never grew up in Dublin. A man like me could make life a lot easier for you and your family, Kitty. All you have right now is trouble, and this boyfriend of yours is only going to make more for you."

They pulled up outside the old Victorian house on Northumberland Road. Finnegan wiped away the condensation on the window with the back of his hand. "Life can be an uncertain thing if you don't have money. And you don't, do you, Kitty? A beautiful young woman like you, it's a terrible shame. It could be a lot different, if you wanted it to be."

"Can you let me out please, Mr. Finnegan?"

He swung open the door. She had to squeeze past him to step out onto the curb.

"I always get what I want in the end, you know."

She turned and leaned in. "Why me?"

"I've wanted you from the moment I first saw you. Now here you are. Some would call it fate."

"Thank you for the ride, Mr. Finnegan."

"You let me know when you get tired of living like this."

"I'm my own woman, but thank you."

"There's no point to all this, you'll see. Nothing will change. When this is all over, the only thing that will be different is that your young man will be dead." He shut the door, and the Rolls-Royce pulled away from the curb, the tires splashing rainwater on her woolen stockings.

CHAPTER 38

She thought Lincoln would interrogate her when she got back, must have seen her out of the window, that he would want to know how it was she came home in a Rolls-Royce. But he wasn't in their room. As she climbed the boarding house stairs, she found him on the landing talking to two young men with thick Irish brogues, both wearing greatcoats and flat caps.

They finished their conversation before she got there. They pushed past her coming down the stairs.

"Who were those fellas?" she said, but Lincoln didn't answer; he just turned and went back inside their room. "I said, who were those fellas?"

"Sit down, Kitty."

She stared at a bundle lying on the rickety wooden table, something wrapped in a torn piece of canvas. He unwrapped it. It was a pistol, a Browning LE, he called it. It was covered in a thin layer of oil and looked brand-new. He took out the magazine and a handful of bullets from his jacket pocket and filled the clip before clicking it back into place.

"What in God's name is that?"

"It's a lovely gun, isn't it?"

"What are you wanting a gun for?"

"Well, what do you think?"

"So that speech about the power of the press, about how we were making a difference, that we were the only ones who could educate people about the truth—all so much nonsense you were spouting, was it?"

"I've been doing a lot of thinking, and it occurs to me that perhaps men like Childers are right. In the end the only answer is one of these."

"You're joking me now."

"I've made up my mind, Kitty. I guess we all have to decide which way we're going to go in the end."

She stared at him, sitting there in his vest, his braces around his hips, that look in his eye. She supposed she should have suspected this from the start, when he came back from Russia—what had happened there had changed him, deep inside. It had started when he went to work for Trotsky. Everything else was inevitable after that, wasn't it?

"Kitty, if Collins and the Free State win this election, the republicans aren't going to just accept it. It's going to be war, and I'm not going to stand in the wings and write how the brave Irish boys have been screwed over by the English yet again, this time betrayed by their own brothers. Oh, it will make a fine story, for someone, but I'm not the one that will be writing it. This time I'm going to be in the story, making a stand for what's right."

"Make a stand? What in God's name are you talking about? This fight has nothing to do with you."

"Kitty, my great-grandfather didn't come to Boston because he wanted to see the world. Did you never hear about the potato famine? That was the British did that, near on seventy years ago. Did you know they were still exporting food from Ireland while a million Irish died? That's what my grandfather was running from, the fucking British. Well he made something of himself; we're respectable now, a good, solid Boston family who could afford to send their son to Harvard. But it's not forgotten. Not by me, not by anyone in our family. Do you understand me now, Kitty?"

"I thought it was all just a game to you."

"Maybe back in the Village it was a game, but it's not a game now."

The look on his face scared her. He took off his glasses, took her face in his hands, kissed her as passionately as she had ever been kissed by any man. There was an animal savagery to it. He carried her to the bed, threw her down, yanked down her drawers. He didn't say anything to her. No whispered endearments these days, no Walt Whitman.

He ripped down his trousers and turned her over, gripped her by the hips, pulled her skirts up around her waist. She let him do what he wanted; it wasn't lovemaking, was it, him in his undershirt, pumping away with such fierceness in him. It was like this was the last time, like he wanted to leave his seed behind in something before he left the world.

The Lincoln from the Village days never made a sound in bed; now he was grunting so loud she heard the landlady banging on her ceiling with a broom.

He was hurting her now. She tried to pull away from him, but he was too strong. When he finished, he shouted out so loud she thought they could hear him in the Beggars Bush barracks.

Afterward he lay face down in the pillow, snoring. She got out of bed, feeling tender and a bit shocked by what had just happened. She went to the window, stared at the rain on the glass, the light from the gas lamps forming halos in the condensation.

She thought about Jack Finnegan, and what he had said to her, the offer he had made; it was tempting, of course it was, but that was a road she would never take.

And she thought about Tom, darling Tom, but there was a future she could never have, even if she gave all this up.

And now Lincoln was going to war. She surely couldn't go down that road. But if she didn't join him, then what in God's name could she do?

Two days later the election results were announced; most people had voted for Collins and the Treaty, but the result wasn't as decisive as many had hoped. With no clear winner, the wrangling went on. The republicans were still in control of the central law courts, and the British government was demanding that Michael Collins clear them out or face reoccupation for being in breach of the treaty. If that happened, any chance of a Free State would be gone. De Valera had pushed Collins into a corner.

"It's virtually an ultimatum from the British Cabinet telling the Irish to turn on each other," Lincoln said.

But in the end, it wasn't the election or the ultimatum that brought the civil war.

It was early in the morning, and she was barely awake, when she heard Lincoln pounding up the stairs in his boots. He must have gone out early to get a newspaper. He threw the *Irish Times* on the bed.

"Look at that," he said. "It's going to be on now."

She sat up and stared at the headlines. Sir Henry Hughes Wilson, Chief of the Imperial General Staff and a hardline Unionist who had just won election as the member for North Down, had been shot dead outside his house in London. The British government was blaming de Valera and the breakaway Sinn Fein. They had suspended the withdrawal of British troops in Dublin and demanded that Collins' Provisional Government take immediate action.

"It's time to decide, Kitty. What are you going to do?"

She didn't answer; her thoughts were a turmoil.

"You can stay here and write about it, if you want. But for me, the time for all that is over."

"I'll not pick up a gun," she said.

"You don't have to. They'll be needing nurses as well as fighting men. You've seen enough, in Russia, you'll not faint at the sight of blood; they'll need someone like you. So, are you coming with me?"

"Where are you off to?"

"Those fellas you saw here the other day, they say they can get me into the Four Courts before the Free Staters cordon it off, but only if we go now. I'll join the garrison there, that's where the fight will start. Kitty, I've the chance to do what my grandfather couldn't do, and that's fight back against the bastards. So, what's it to be?"

CHAPTER 39

They waited for evening, walked quiet through the twilight. They avoided Lord Edward Street and Dublin Castle, the Free Staters had set up roadblocks at all the major intersections and were searching everyone going in and out of the center of the city.

Instead they skirted to the east and crossed the Liffey by O'Connell Bridge, keeping to the backstreets. The light was beginning to fail by the time they made their way onto Mary's Lane. Kitty could hear the gulls wheel and cry over the Smithfield Market ahead of them.

They stopped at the corner of the lane that led to the back of the Chancery. Lincoln took the pistol out from his coat and peered around. "It's safe," he whispered, and they headed down to the gate. His two republican friends had given him the password, and he whispered it through a gap in the gate. It inched open, and then they were inside.

That easy.

Well, that's it, Kitty thought. *I'm in the war now.*

CHAPTER 40

The Four Courts was over a hundred years old, a vast complex of buildings that once housed the four courts of Ireland: the Chancery, the King's Bench, the Exchequer, and Common Pleas. It was a landmark in Dublin, the beautiful Round Hall and dome as gracious a landmark as the city had.

It had never been built as a castle, and Kitty realized it would be almost impossible to defend it for any length of time. There were many entry points, and each one had to be barricaded. The republicans had done what they could, setting up sandbags, barbed wire, trenches, and mines all around the perimeter. Even an armored car, stolen in a raid on a Civic Guard barracks at Kildare, had been parked outside the front gates of the Courts, its machine gun trained on the approaches.

Inside, the men were preparing and cleaning rifles and machine guns, laying out spare parts for them. All the windows and doors had been barricaded with sandbags. They were quickly briefed by the republican in charge of the garrison, a senior Sinn Fein man called O'Connor. Lincoln was given an old RIC carbine and taken upstairs to man a position overlooking the quays. Kitty was sent down to the basement where a doctor was setting up a field hospital.

A *Cumann na mBan* nurse by the name of O'Riordan was laying out supplies; bandages, iodine, gauze, and lint. She frowned at Kitty when they brought her over. "Have you done this sort of thing before?"

Kitty shook her head. "But I won't faint away if that's what you're thinking. I've seen men cut in half with machine guns and more dead bodies than I care to remember."

"That a fact? Where did you see this then?"

She told her, and the nurse nodded and said: "Well I'll guess you'll do then."

"Not much choice is there, anyway, by the looks of it."

A flicker of a smile. "I guess there isn't."

There was an old black range against the far wall, and Kitty helped the other nurses prepare a hot meal; there wasn't much, enough for soup and some tea. The men ate their dinners in the dark; the power had been cut off, and all they had was a few candles. News began to filter through that an attack was imminent, probably before morning. Some of the boys could still not believe it, that the men they'd fought with less than a year ago would turn their guns on them. Collins wouldn't go through with it, some of them said.

It was a bluff.

Kitty was touched by their innocence.

<hr />

Lincoln didn't come down for his soup, so she got a mug of it and went looking for him, found him standing at his post overlooking Chancery Place and Inns' Quay, cleaning his rifle. Some sandbags had been piled on top of a heavy oak desk with a loophole for the muzzle.

He thanked her for the soup, took it from her without taking his eyes from the street.

"So, it looks like it's going to really happen," he said.

"Looks like it."

"Father Albert is in the Round Hall giving everyone absolution."

"I didn't think things were that bad," Kitty said. "Are you going down for it?"

"No, are you?"

"Not likely. If God's a Catholic, nothing I do now is going to change his mind about me. But if he's a socialist, then he won't want me mixing with the likes of them."

"How are things downstairs?"

"The field hospital is a few benches shoved together, and they've set up a munitions factory in the Records Office, a couple of fellas with glasses trying to make grenades out of tin cans. Your friend Trotsky would have felt right at home."

She could hear the Free State trucks moving into position behind the Courts, bringing more troops to the Bridewell police station on the other side of the courtyard. Lincoln pointed out the lights in the upper windows where the sniper and machine gun positions were being set up. There was the tramp of soldiers' boots on the cobbles, lights moving on the other side of the river.

"They're bringing up their big guns over there," he said. "There's one on Winetavern Street and another on the quays on Lower Bridge Street. They would have got those from the fucking British. They've armored cars and a couple of Stokes guns into the bargain."

"What are they?"

"Stokes guns? They can put a mortar round down your chimney and pick out which side of the hearth to land it on."

"Jesus God, we've no chance, do we?"

"Not much of one. Dare say they don't plan to send the troops in until all that's left of us is a few piles of rubble."

She sat down next to him, put her head against the sandbags. "Is this it, then?"

"You'll be all right Kitty; they won't hurt the women."

"Well I'll tell that to the Stokes mortars when they drop down the chimney. It'll be a comfort."

"You're the unkillable Kitty O'Kane, remember?"

"No one's unkillable, Linc."

He fumbled in his pocket for his cigarettes. He lit one. She had to help him; his hands were shaking. "Look at that," he said. "You'd think I'd be used to it all by now."

"You don't have to do this."

"A bit late for changing my mind, Kit."

"This isn't your fight."

"Oh, but it is." His face was illuminated for a moment by the glow of his cigarette. "Do you have any regrets?" he asked her.

"Oh plenty, but I don't see the point of going through them now."

"I don't mean that. I meant do you have any regrets about meeting me?"

"And where would I be if I hadn't? Still turning up beds on a cruise ship or some lady's maid to the rich folk. You showed me things in life I'd only dreamed about."

"But this isn't the Utopia we talked about."

"To have a dream broken, first you have to touch it. It's no bad thing to be disillusioned. It meant what you dreamed about in the first place was just that, an illusion and nothing else."

"It isn't a dream, Kit. It's just that sometimes you have to make a sacrifice to make a dream happen."

"Well, what good is the sacrifice if you never live to see it?"

"There's something called the greater good."

"Anything worth dying for is worth living for."

"And who told you that?"

"Never you mind," Kitty said.

"You know I love you, don't you Kit? Never meant to. Happened while I wasn't looking." He reached for his pocket, took out a hip flask. It was empty. "Not even a last drink."

"You can't shoot straight if you're full of whiskey."

"I can't shoot straight anyway."

She laughed.

"I just want you to know, if we don't make it out of here, I'm glad we met. I hope you never regret what happened between us in years to come."

"Go on and finish your tea. I've got to be taking the mug back."

"God bless you, Kitty."

"Good night, Linc."

She spent that night wrapped in the scarlet and ermine of a judge's robe she found in one of the courtrooms. Her pillow was a law book she found near it; it looked and smelled old, a relic from the days when the first Englishman came to Ireland and started all this bloody trouble in the first place.

She felt for the jewelry box in her pocket; it made her think about the banshee and the sheep's head and a pot of soup bubbling on the range and the playing cards all wrapped up in a silk handkerchief. *I don't see anything for you in the future unless you change what's in your heart.*

Sure and what was it that the banshee had been trying to tell her all those years ago? What was it that she had to change? Oh, she had tried to change everything but herself, set the whole world to rights, but if she was honest with herself, Tom Doyle was the real cause she never gave up on. Yes, she had loved Lincoln in her way, she supposed, but she suspected now that she had only been with him to prove to Tom that she deserved him. Her writing for lost causes was the ladder, and there Tom was waiting at the very top, with his stethoscope and his nice suit and his lovely smile, his arms wide. And when she finally stepped on that top rung, it would mean she was worthy of him.

The trouble was she hadn't ever believed that she did deserve him, not really. Not bashed-up, barefoot little Kitty O'Kane from the poor school; and not the woman either, with her sinner's past and scarred womb.

Oh well. It would all be over tomorrow.

CHAPTER 41

It started at ten past four in the morning.

The pounding of the gun woke her, and then she heard something like an express train going overhead. Something crashed into the East Wing, shaking the whole building. Plaster cracked and fell from the walls; a light fitting fell from the ceiling and smashed on the floor. A huge crack opened in the bricks at the gable end.

Several of the nurses had screamed, but now there was an eerie silence, and then they heard another of the Free State guns boom across the river.

"It's really started," Nurse O'Riordan said.

⟡

Their first wounded was a young lad shot by a sniper in St. Michan's bell tower as he was running back to the main building from one of the outlying courts. The boy was both lucky and unlucky—the bullet had missed him, but had ricocheted off the cobbles and hit him in the ankle.

Kitty helped one of the nurses carry him down on a canvas stretcher from the Round Hall. He was screaming fit to burst a lung. Broken glass crunched under their feet as they ran; all the windows had been smashed in by machine-gun fire and shellfire. She had a glimpse of the sun rising over the city, streaks of red giving way to yellow and orange;

the flash of rifles and machine guns on the far side of the Liffey looked almost pretty if you didn't know what it was.

They put the boy on a bench in the basement, and the doctor, a man named Ryan, got to work on him. There was no sedative except a little tincture of opium, and she and Nurse O'Riordan did their best to keep the boy quiet while the doctor worked on his shattered leg. She remembered what Tom had said to her; a bullet didn't sound like much until you realized what it could do to the bones and muscles underneath. Without proper care, the lad might not ever walk again.

I hope all this is worth it, she thought, fetching water and towels, mopping up the blood as best she could, trying to shut her ears to the screaming. *I hope all this is one day going to be worth it.*

The shelling went on right through the day; when there were no wounded to treat, every minute seemed like years. They all listened to the crash of the rifles and machine guns, watched dust shake from the ceiling every time another shell smashed into the building. She was sure that the whole place was going to come down on top of them.

There were three more wounded, all injured by the shelling, and she helped the other nurses get them down the stairs and clean up the wounds best they could and then quieten them down enough that Ryan could work on them.

There was nothing to eat, just a few biscuits and some tea. Nurse O'Riordan put the tea in a flask, and Kitty volunteered to go upstairs and give it to any soldiers that wanted it. They leaned against the walls or the sandbags and grabbed the tea from her with shaking hands and crammed the biscuits in their mouths, then went back to the windows and kept firing at any Free Staters fool enough to raise their heads.

<hr/>

Evening fell on the shortest and longest day of her life. So far none of the garrison had been killed; Ryan had treated five men with bullet and shrapnel wounds, and they were recovering on benches or on stretchers in the first aid post.

The shelling had not stopped. She couldn't block it out; even with her hands over her ears, she could still feel it. Every time a shell landed, the whole building shook, and the concussion seemed to go through her whole body, right to the core of her. *I'll go mad if this keeps up much longer*, she thought.

The West Wing was all but down. They were under fire from virtually every direction; there were British snipers in the church towers and on the roofs of the tall buildings on the other side of the river, a Lewis machine gun on a tower in the Jervis Hospital. Free Staters had infiltrated across the Liffey bridges into the maze of side streets behind the Four Courts. There was talk of the Republican Dublin Brigade breaking through the cordon and sending in reinforcements. She didn't believe a word of it.

CHAPTER 42

With the West Wing just rubble, the Free State artillery was concentrating now on the East Wing. She helped the other nurses drag a man off one of the benches; he had been hit in the head by a chunk of stone; Ryan had finished with him, said there was nothing more he could do for him. There was a priest standing right behind them, ready to give him the final absolution.

O'Riordan grabbed Kitty's arm. Another shell landed, and the whole room shook; Kitty saw the nurse mouthing words at her, but the incessant shelling had made her ears ring; she could hardly hear anything.

"What is it?" Kitty shouted.

"I need your help to get one of the wounded down here!"

She still couldn't hear her. O'Riordan had to mime what she wanted; Kitty followed her up the steps, dragging a canvas stretcher. The sound of rifle and machine gun fire was louder up here; it was bright, almost too bright; shells had punched huge holes in the walls. A piece of masonry fell from the ceiling; it missed her by only a few feet; if it had hit her, it would have crushed her like a beetle.

The men were crouched down. She saw shadows moving through the smoke and dust down on the quays. God in heaven, how much more could they take of this?

One of the men was waiting for them; he grabbed O'Riordan's arm and pulled her after him into one of the rooms, shouting at them all the while to hurry. They crawled the last few yards. A burst of machine gun fire tore the plaster off the walls above their heads.

There were three men in the room, two of them were hunched against the wall; she thought they were dead until they moved their heads. They weren't even flinching at the shell bursts anymore.

Lincoln lay covered in a thick layer of dust; the blood on his scalp and ear startling against the ghostly mask of gray. Their bottle of iodine and their little bundle of bandages would not help him now.

"Oh Linc," she said, "what have you done to yourself?"

There was blood everywhere; his hair was matted with it. His glasses lay shattered in the rubble of brick next to him. She thought he tried to say something to her when he saw her, but perhaps she only imagined it. She held his head in her lap as O'Riordan examined the wound. She looked up at Kitty and shook her head.

She watched the light fade from his eyes. He had no last words for her.

The soldier who had led them up there grabbed Lincoln's rifle and threw it at the two other men. "For God's sake what are you doing? Start shooting, you pair of bastards!"

Empty-eyed, one of them twisted around and did as he was ordered. The other man just kept staring at the far wall, murmuring something over and over under his breath.

"Are you all right?" O'Riordan said to her. "Did you know him?"

She nodded. "A little," she said. She felt in Lincoln's pocket, found the pistol the IRA lads had brought him, tucked it away in her jacket pocket.

⊰―⊱

She didn't remember much after that.

By Friday, there was a fire raging out of control in the headquarters block. Around noon, the munitions factory, downstairs in the Records Office, exploded.

Kitty had been crouched in the corner of the first aid post when it happened. Her back had been against the wall; she was watching Ryan and the rest of the nurses work on some other poor boy. As the masonry cracked and tumbled around her, she thought: *This is it. This is the end of me this time.*

A dead silence; even the machine guns fell quiet. Kitty choked on the dust. As it started to clear, someone shouted to them down the stairs: "It's over! O'Connor's run up the white flag."

Kitty went out with the doctor and the other nurses. They took the wounded with them, eight of them on stretchers, and three bodies covered with towels and sheets. What was left of the garrison was huddled in the Round Hall. What a mess it was. The Corinthian columns were pockmarked with shrapnel; most of the statues of the Irish judges and lawyers that had stood in the niches in the walls were lying in pieces on the floor.

Some of the boys had lit a fire under the dome; they were throwing their rifles and guns into it, watching them melt, anything but leave them for the bloody traitors who had brought them to this.

There were ambulances waiting amid the rubble outside on the quay. Kitty looked back at the building, could scarce recognize it through the smoke. There were throngs of people watching from the other side of the river and on the bridges. There was ash in the air, it was as if it was snowing; the paper from the Records Office, someone said. "One thousand years of Irish history is what you're breathing in, ladies," Dr. Ryan said.

⸻⟶

They took them to the Mater Hospital in a fleet of ambulances, the priest coming with them, still muttering his prayers over those the doctor thought might not make it. Afterward some Free State soldiers took them to the Four Courts Hotel to be fed.

Not that she or any of the other nurses had much appetite. Kitty looked at the young guard who was supposed to be watching them, a fresh-faced boy, couldn't have been more than eighteen years old. He had left his rifle by the door; he had probably never fired the bloody thing, just some fresh recruit they had sent off to guard the women, she supposed.

She felt the weight of the pistol in her coat, curled her finger around the trigger. She could have left his brains on the pavement, poor boy, but that wouldn't have brought Linc back, would just have meant another grieving mother to follow yet another coffin to the cemetery. So instead, when the boy wasn't looking, she turned around and went home.

She stood on the Dublin Bridge, watched the smoke rise from the ruins of the old courts, the smell of it acrid even from there. The great copper dome of the Four Courts rumbled and crashed to the ground.

She went back to Northumberland Road, let herself in with her key, went up the steps to their room. She almost imagined seeing Lincoln there, sitting in front of his typewriter, a cigarette stuck to his bottom lip.

She put a fresh piece of paper in her Remington and started typing: "Today, in Dublin, my lover died in my arms."

That's too emotive, she heard Lincoln whisper to her.

"To hell with you, Lincoln," she said out loud. "This time I'll write it my way and to hell with you."

CHAPTER 43

Mountjoy Prison, Five Months Later

Kitty was in a cell with four men. It was getting dark, winter drawing in; hard enough in this place in summer, God alone knew how she would make it through another week in here in the winter. Just a candle, four brick walls, and a threadbare blanket.

They were singing a republican song in a cell down the corridor. The guard hammered on the door with his rifle and told them to shut up. It made them sing all the louder, beating on the wall with their tin mugs. She closed her eyes and tried to sleep.

Next thing she knew two screws kicked open the cell door and hauled her to her feet. She had given up protesting; she let them drag her down the corridor. *What is it now?*

"You have a visitor," the screw said, and he pushed her into a room, made her sit on a wooden chair. The only other furniture was a table, leaked candle grease all over it. A guard with a rifle stood by the door.

She smelled her visitor's cologne before she saw him. Then he strolled in, waving a silver-topped cane like Churchill inspecting the troops; he had a silk scarf around his neck, looked immaculate as he always did. He smiled at her and sat down, took a cigar from his pocket. The guard lit it for him. He sat back, puffed appreciatively at the flavor of it, and smiled at her.

"Kitty. You don't seem surprised to see me."

"Nothing much surprises me anymore."

"It's sad to see you brought to this pass. Pretty woman like you."

"What is it you want, Mr. Finnegan?"

"Jack. Please. I think we know each other well enough by now."

"Seeing as how you seem to know everything and everyone, can you tell me what I'm doing in here?"

"Well according to the arrest report, the civil guard found a pistol in a drawer when they raided your lodgings in Northumberland Road. I find that hard to believe."

"Do you now?"

"Was it yours?"

She shook her head. "It belonged to an associate of mine."

"Can he vouch for that?"

"He's dead."

"That's unfortunate."

"I forgot the damned thing was even there."

"But how did it get there?"

"I put it there."

"You're not helping your case." A genial puff of the cigar. "You should be more careful."

"Are you here to gloat, Mr. Finnegan?"

"You see, what I don't understand is why you stayed on in Dublin after you wrote that piece for that big magazine in America. How did it begin again? *Today, in Dublin, my lover died in my arms.* Especially when it was syndicated like it was; a lot of people read that; it got a lot of currency. Made a lot of people very upset. You embarrassed them, Kitty, is what you did."

"I just told the truth."

"Maybe it was the way you said it."

"My former colleague, may God rest his soul, always said I was too emotive. It seems to me now that I wasn't emotive enough."

"Personally, I liked the piece a great deal. Very powerful. But it marked you out as a troublemaker with the government here, you see. And now you've broken the law, they're not inclined to be lenient."

"I never fired a gun in my life."

"I don't think they care. The Special Powers Act lays out a list of offenses that are punishable by death, penal servitude, or deportation. One of those offenses is possession of a firearm. The talk is, they want to shoot you. Did you know that?"

Kitty couldn't get her breath. She felt the blood drain out of her face.

"It's times like this, you see, that you need friends."

"Friends?"

"I could help you out, you know. You really want to die in this little squabble? It's pointless, don't you think?"

She stared at the floor.

"Oh, look at you, Kitty. What a mess you've made. When they stand you up against the wall in the yard, and you hear the firing squad lift the bolts on their rifles, will you know what it's all been for? You can shout at the devil all you like, but in the end it all finishes up the same. The only difference is whether you're alive or dead, and that's about it."

"What is it you want from me, Mr. Finnegan?"

"I think you know."

He was right, she did know. It was a stark choice in the end.

"What happened to your wife?"

"My wife?"

"On the *Titanic*."

"That was so long ago," he said. "I can't even remember her name."

"I thought she was Mrs. Finnegan."

"That was then, this is now."

"Perhaps in a few years, you'll be saying the same about me."

"But that's not today, is it? And today is all I'm worried about." He leaned forward and took her hand. "Your hands are cold, Kit. They need warming by a good fire. Be nice to me, and I'll take care of you in turn. It doesn't have to end here, for nothing. Come to New York with me, you can have a good life there."

She blinked slowly, thought about O'Connor and the rest of his ragged men stumbling out of the smoking wreck of the Four Courts, shell-shocked, heads down, defeated. *No matter how hard you fight*, she thought, *sometimes the odds are just too great.*

"You can get me out of here?"

"I have good friends here," he said. "Men in the government who owe me a favor. I only have to say the word."

But Kitty couldn't say the word. She couldn't even raise her eyes from the floor.

"Say it. *Please help me, Jack.*"

He waited. The silence stretched. But finally: "Please, help me Jack," she said.

He laughed and banged a fist on the table, delighted with himself. "Good then. The deal is done."

CHAPTER 44

Finnegan's, Greenwich Village, 1924

The walls were papered with book jackets; Kitty could make out Joyce, Yeats, Wilde. There was a huge mahogany fireplace—fake of course, they didn't need a fire down here, everyone was sticky with sweat. The crowd was shoulder to shoulder, young men flashing money, women in skimpy, fringed dresses, hemlines almost to the knee. They all flashed their suspender belts and garters when they sat down.

Modern girls had bobs or Marcel waves now. *I should get one*, Kitty thought. *For something to do. Because I can.*

The club was a wall of noise, a Negro band playing a popular number called "Toot, Toot, Tootsie," all trumpets and brass, while the girls jiggled bare arms and legs. The cigarette smoke was thick as a London fog.

Looking around, Kitty made out a heavyweight boxer who had fought earlier that evening at Madison Square Garden; several newspaper reporters; the mayor of New York as well as several Tammany Hall contenders.

Like Jack said, a man needed friends. You never knew when you might need one.

One of Jack's waiters brought her a martini. She watched Jack over the rim of her glass. He was sitting, talking to a man she'd never seen before. He seemed Italian; he was heavyset, with small eyes and a big forehead. He looked like a rat looking out from under a ledge.

Nice friends he has, she thought.

The conversation looked like it was getting heated; the Italian guy was waving his finger at Jack. She saw Jack's minders moving in, another couple of guys in sharp suits did the same, took up positions behind their boss's chair. Jack's visitor yelled something and stormed out. Jack leaned back in his booth, laughing, like he hadn't a care in the world. But then he always did that, whether he'd just won twenty grand on a horse or the police had just raided one of his clubs.

A girl came over and sat on Jack's knee; she had on a black choker and a tight sheath dress. Jack had recently taken a liking to flappers, but she'd never seen this one before. Jesus Mary, they were getting younger all the time. This one had the eyes of a cat and the cropped black bob of a movie star.

Jack smooched with her for a while, then pushed her off his lap and came over. "What's gotten into you?" he said to Kitty.

"I'm bored."

"You're bored? You know who we got in here tonight?"

"Who?"

"Half of fucking New York, that's who. How can you be bored?"

"Who was that?"

He grinned. "The girl? She don't mean nothing. You're still my number one girl, you know that."

"Lucky me. But I don't mean the tart, I meant the gorilla in the pinstripe suit."

"Oh him? Business associate."

"He looked dangerous."

"Just some greaseball, don't you mind him."

"I think I'll go home. Will you be home tonight, Jack?"

"Why, you jealous?"

"You can sleep with whoever you want; it saves me the trouble. Just don't wake me up when you get home."

It wasn't the answer he was looking for. He leaned over the table. His breath was rank with alcohol and cigars. "If it wasn't for me, they'd have put you up against a wall, don't forget that." He straightened up again, and a smile spread across his face. He patted his belly, which seemed to be taking up more space these days. "Why don't you stay and have another drink. Loosen up. You don't have to be an uptight bitch all the time, do you?"

"No, I don't have to, it's a choice. I'll see you in the morning, Jack." She left her martini on the table and headed for the door. She could feel him watching her. Like he said, he always got what he wanted. But that didn't mean he was going to like it.

<hr />

From the street, a casual passerby would never know one of New York's most famous speakeasies was just a few feet away, and she supposed that was the point. There weren't many lights on at this time of the morning, most of the brownstones were in darkness. There were a few Rolls-Royces, Duesenbergs, and Buicks parked discreetly farther down the street; her bodyguard hurried her toward a Packard. He opened up the rear door for her and then climbed in the passenger seat.

The driver started the car, and they drove off in silence. Kitty watched the somber silhouettes of midtown Manhattan fly by in the darkness; the Flatiron, the MetLife Tower, Grand Central, the Plaza Hotel.

It started to rain, and she stared through the rain-spattered glass. For no reason at all she started to think about Tom, what he was doing, who he was with. Two years since she had seen him that last time. She hoped he was happy. He deserved that much.

"If it wasn't for me, they'd have put you up against a wall, don't forget that."

Jack was right, that's exactly what they would have done. This had seemed a better alternative right then; if she had had the guts, she would have spat in his eye, let them shoot her if that's what they wanted. But she was weak; she didn't have the courage to go through with it; she didn't believe—not like Lincoln had believed.

You can't change the world, Tom had said to her, but you can change yourself.

They headed into Brooklyn. A horse clattered along in front of them, tossing its blinkered head. Her driver veered around it, the street black and empty. A truck pulled out of a side street, cut them off. Her driver cursed and stamped on the brake.

"What the fuck is he doing?" he shouted, and realized only when it was too late what he was doing.

But Kitty knew and had already ducked her head down. She heard the roar of pump-action shotguns, saw the windscreen glass shatter. The Packard rocked as a hundred pellets slammed into it. Five, six volleys, then silence.

Someone yanked open her door, a man in a flat cap with a handkerchief tied around his nose and mouth to hide his face. He pointed the shotgun straight at her. *"Ma che cazzo!"* he said and lifted the barrel. *"Scusate, signora,"* he said, and he and his partner ran off.

Kitty sat up. Her driver and bodyguard were sprawled horribly in the front, the blood looking black in the darkness, spread all over the upholstery and the roof and what was left of the windscreen. She heard the truck drive off, but she didn't move, just sat there, staring into the distance, waiting for someone to come and get her, a neighbor perhaps, the police.

There was gore on her dress and on her legs. It had sprayed everywhere. Everyone else's luck running out. But she was still there, covered in the blood of others, wishing she was somewhere else. Nothing had changed, had it?

"I'm sorry, sweetheart," Jack said to her. "That wasn't meant for you, it was meant for me."

"Well, of course it was meant for you!" Kitty screamed at Jack. "They could have blown my head off if they'd wanted. Do you think I don't know it was you they were after!"

One of Jack's lackeys had brought her home from the precinct. The cops had grilled her, but what could she tell them?

They thought she was holding out on them. "You know your boyfriend's the biggest bootlegger this side of the Atlantic?" one of the detectives had said to her.

"Of course I do, I'm not stupid."

"What are you doing with a guy like that?"

"I don't know," she had said. "What are you doing working for the cops?"

The older cop shook his head. "You know he has a lot of enemies?"

"Apart from me?" she said.

She told them what she could, that she'd seen Jack arguing with some guy. "Where?" they said, but she wasn't going to fall for that. No, she didn't know who it was, but she described him to them, and one of them said, "Pasquale," like that should mean something to her.

"Is he a bootlegger too?"

"What do you think, lady?"

What Kitty thought was that Jack should have known something like this might have happened. What was the point of saving her from one firing squad just to let her get killed by another one?

Eventually they let her go. They knew she was just Jack's moll, and she knew it too. They told her to tell Jack to expect a visit. She said not to bother, he would probably come down to the precinct in the morning with his lawyer, as usual.

She got home just on dawn. Jack was patrolling the front parlor, a glass of whiskey in his fist. It clearly wasn't his first. He came toward her with his arms out.

"Don't fucking come near me," she said.

He wanted to know what the cops had said, what she had told them.

"Everything I know," she said. "But as I don't know very much, then you don't have to worry, do you?"

"They won't get away with this," he said.

"For God's sake, Jack. I don't give a damn about you or your business. Just don't get me involved in any part of it."

She poured three fingers into a glass and then changed her mind and took the whole bottle upstairs with her. She went into the bedroom and locked the door behind her. It wasn't until she knew no one could see her that she dropped onto the bed, buried her face in the pillow, and cried. Damn this all to hell. She had failed at every damned thing.

She had once vowed she would save every hungry little girl crouched on the floor covered in blood and bruises. She would right the past by saving the world.

Save the world? She couldn't even save herself.

CHAPTER 45

There was the crisp bite of autumn in the air; the street vendors were selling hot pretzels in the park. She had a new driver now, Manny, a burly, taciturn man much like the first, except this one, of course, was alive. Irish, Jack said, though she could never tell because he hardly spoke. A new car, too, a shiny black Marmon.

As they drove down Fifth Avenue, the buildings changed from Beaux arts limestone glories like the Plaza to fancy department stores selling everything from fur coats to soft furnishings. She was just a few blocks from the Flatiron and Washington Square and the Village, but she was a world away.

This was her new life now. No more rejection letters from magazine editors, no more stuffy solicitors or patronizing bosses; no worlds to change. Dropping her spare change into the caps of the panhandlers along Broadway was the closest she came to her social conscience now. She didn't like this new Kitty nearly as much as the old one, but at least she was warm, and never hungry and, for all the good it did her, alive.

Manny parked in the street, and she went into Macy's, looked over the new season's fashion. A sequined pencil sheath caught her eye; its headdress came with a garnet and a peacock feather. *I wonder what Jack would think of me in that*, she thought. *He probably wouldn't even notice.*

For no reason she could think of, she thought of the bedraggled peacock she had seen screaming in the shattered window of the royal palace in Belgrade, after the Austrian guns had done their worst. She remembered a group of soldiers standing underneath it and imitating it, as if they thought it was funny.

Perhaps the feather came from the same bird.

No good, her heart wasn't in it. She didn't need another dress, or more shoes. The day stretched in front of her, endless, barren. She caught a glimpse of her own reflection in one of the store mirrors, someone's fancy woman in an ermine wrap and a black Milan straw turban. Who was she? No one she was likely to mix with.

She took a side door out of the store so that Manny wouldn't see her, walked aimlessly along the street. She was filled with a kind of panic, as if she had woken up in a strange city, and for a moment she felt completely disoriented. She thought she could smell the hops from the Guinness factory in Saint James's Gate, hear the kids playing in the Liberties. She forced herself to be calm, stepped back against a Macy's window, took a deep breath, waited for whatever strange moment this was to pass.

"Kitty?" A voice from the past.

She looked around. It was Michael, Tom's brother, not her imagination. He still lived round here somewhere, wasn't that what Tom had said? He had grown a little around the middle, otherwise he still looked like he had the last time she had seen him, how many years ago?

He smiled at her, though he looked a little uncertain. "It is you? Tom said you were back in New York."

She couldn't think of a thing to say.

Michael took off his homburg, held out a hand. "Good to see you again."

"Hello, Michael."

"You're looking well. In fact, you look spectacular."

"Do I? Thank you."

"You didn't think to get in touch?"

"I'm sorry."

"Well, never mind. I understand."

At last she found her voice. "Tom wrote to you?" He nodded. "What did he tell you about me?"

"Just that he'd heard you were here. He says you're married now."

She didn't answer. What could she say to him? No, I'm not married, I'm just some gangster's whore. *Better to say nothing and not let him and Tom think worse of me than they already do.*

"How is Tom?" she said.

"Tom's Tom. He always talks about you in his letters. He's not over you, Kit. You know that?"

Again, what could she say? They stood there in the street, looking at each other.

"Well, look at you. Wait till I tell Tom I've seen you."

"Do you have to? Tell him, I mean."

"Why wouldn't I?" Then: "Oh Kitty, what happened between the two of you? It's a terrible shame is what it is. He's coming over next week, did you know that, come to visit me and his uncle. It's our uncle's sixtieth. We're having a big party over at my house in Brooklyn."

"I can't believe he still thinks well of me, never mind wants to see me."

"Tom would never say a bad word about you. He never has. Look, I know you're married and everything now—"

"I can't, Michael . . ."

"But he's staying at the Plaza. He arrives on Friday, if you change your mind."

"Take care, Michael," she said, and hurried away.

They were driving back to the Bronx along Sixth Avenue, when she told Manny to stop the Marmon. "Let me out here."

"The boss says—"

"I don't give a damn what Jack says. Now let me out or I'll jump out and you can explain to him why I ended up in the hospital in your very first week on the job."

"Where are you going?"

"To feed the fecking ducks. Now mind your own damned business, you big Irish monkey!"

It had been a fine morning when they started out, but there was a storm blowing in. She walked head down, into the wind; piles of leaves swirled around her; women with perambulators and little children hurried past her, heading the other way, for the gates.

The wind had formed little wavelets on the lake; even the ducks were scurrying for shelter. It was going to rain. She stood there, her hands in the pocket of her coat. Any minute and the wind would take her turban, and then where would she be? *Would you be so special then, Kitty O'Kane, with your Marcel wave blown all over your face and soaked through like something they dragged out of the Liffey?*

God what was she doing? Of all days to see Michael. What must he have thought? *Maybe it was better they put you up against the wall at Beggars Bush and shot you along with the rest.*

She remembered Tom's face that afternoon she told him about the abortion, about Lincoln, about why she couldn't have his baby. God in heaven. How could he still think well of her?

Shot at and sunk and pitched up all these places, her bottom pinched by kings, her news stories in American magazines. Perhaps once she would have thought it a fine life. But she was supposed to have made a difference. And nothing had changed; Lincoln was dead, the Russians were still starving, the Irish were still fighting among themselves.

Oh, but we women got the vote. But then, Tom's wife had done as much for that as she had and still managed to marry a fine man and have a baby.

Manny sounded the horn. He was standing on the running board, signaling for her to get back to the car. God in heaven she was a prisoner, not much different from Mountjoy was it, just the walls were bigger, and she didn't have to pee in a bucket.

She went back to the car. *I can't live like this.*

CHAPTER 46

Jack had lived in New Jersey for a few years, but he said his neighbors were too noisy, and he was getting too much attention from the local police, so just before he brought Kitty back from Ireland he had moved to the Bronx. Their two-story brownstone was unremarkable from the outside, as it was meant to be; it was only when you got inside that you discovered it was unlike any other house in the neighborhood.

Jack had decorated it to his own taste: Egyptian-inspired lamps, Turkish rugs, gilt mirrors, dark-red tapestries on the windows. She supposed it was how an Irish thug would have decorated Versailles. There were onyx ashtrays scattered everywhere, and they were full of cigar stubs; the place reeked of them. The kitchen had every modern electrical appliance available—waffle irons and toasters, even a popcorn maker.

The house even had its own stand-alone garage where Jack's men played cards and shot pool.

She had come a very long way from the Liberties, but now it hardly seemed worth it.

When she got home, she put a record on the new gramophone player and poured herself a brandy from a crystal decanter and stared at herself in the gilt mirror that Jack had hung in what he liked to call the smoking room. The mirror was massive, as big as the pool table in the garage.

She patted down the curl on the side of her head, wondered how Michael had recognized her through all this rouge and lipstick. She was embarrassed that he'd seen her in the turban. *He knows what you are*, she thought. *You didn't have to advertise it.*

She took her drink upstairs to the bedroom. Ghastly. She wondered who had decorated it, perhaps the Mrs. Finnegan from the *Titanic*, or one of a dozen in between. It was painted in hot-pink and orchid, the double bed, the wardrobe, the chest of drawers all in heavy walnut. It wasn't a bedroom, it was a boudoir.

The strong liquor had made her lightheaded. She closed her eyes, tossed her gold-and-black brocade shawl on the bed and accepted an invitation to dance from the king of Bulgaria, and twirled around the room.

The king asked her to marry him, but she politely declined, informed him that she was promised to a famous London surgeon. "His name is Sir Thomas Doyle," she said. "He has saved the king's life on countless occasions."

She went to the dressing table, took out the little jewelry box she had hidden in one of the drawers, opened it with the key she kept in the locket around her neck. She took out the shells. She could still smell the sea on them, or perhaps that was just her imagination.

She heard the door slam and then a screech as someone took the record off the gramophone. Jack, back early, and in one of his moods. He came storming up the stairs.

She finished her drink and waited. The storm had hit. The rain slammed against the glass like children were throwing gravel at it.

"Who was the guy?"

"Hello, Jack, you're home early. How was your day?"

"I said, who was the fucking guy?"

"What?"

"Don't get cute with me. Manny told me he saw you outside Macy's talking to some jerk."

"Manny's been spying on me?"

"He works for me, he don't work for you. Now who was the guy?"

"He was an old friend from Dublin."

"Old friend? You don't have old friends, you hear me?"

"What the hell is wrong with you?"

He pointed a fat, ringed finger in her face. "You don't screw around on me, you understand?"

"But it's all right for you to screw every tart that walks into Finnegan's."

He bunched his hand into a fist, and his arm jerked back.

"You hit me," Kitty said, "and I swear to God I'll kill you. No man is ever going to hit me again and get away with it. I'll wait till you're asleep and I'll put an ice pick through your heart and don't think it's just words because you know it's not."

They stared at each other.

"You stay away from other guys," he said. "You hear me? You don't do anything unless I tell you first. You're just a broad, remember that!"

Perhaps she never would have gone to see Tom if he hadn't said that. But he did, so then she couldn't stay away.

It was Friday morning a week later. Kitty peered through the curtain, a foggy morning. Fate on her side: she saw Manny asleep in the Marmon out in front of the house. She put on a plain dark coat and a broad brimmed hat, something like the old Kitty would have worn, and hurried down the stairs. She went out through the kitchen, winked at the cook, who winked back, and went down to the lane at the back of the house. Then she walked down to 149th to catch the El.

She settled herself in an overstuffed floral armchair, and a bellboy appeared with a plate of potted crab and cucumber sandwiches and a pot of tea. She had no intention of talking to Tom, not really; she just wanted to see him, just one more time. Her plan was to sit in the Palm Court, in the corner, where no one could see her, but where she could see him. That was all. She didn't want to hurt him anymore, didn't want to ruin his life. He must have a wife by now, or at least a fiancée.

There was a pianist somewhere, playing "I'm Nobody's Baby."

She had checked the newspaper for the day's sailings. The *Brittania* had docked that morning at nine o'clock. She guessed it would take Tom at least two hours to clear the customs hall and get a cab from the wharf. Meanwhile she would sit here and drink her tea and eat her sandwiches and pretend to read her newspaper.

Not much good news, but then there never was. Someone called Zinoviev was calling for intensified Communist agitation in Britain. The *Daily Mail* had published his letter, and now everyone in England was up in arms about it.

It was stuffy, and she loosened the buttons on her coat. Underneath she had on a black dress and a sheer overskirt; it fell to a few inches above her ankles, just enough to show them off, if a man happened to look. She had a red sash around her hips, a white rosette to the side. She imagined that if someone was watching her and knew of her plan to remain anonymous, they might have asked why she had gone to so much trouble dressing that morning.

She would perhaps have answered that she always dressed well, no matter the occasion, that Jack expected it of her.

Because she wasn't dressing like this for Tom. She just wanted to watch him cross the foyer, take one last look at him, then she would go home and let him get on with his life.

When he had not arrived by noon, it occurred to her that Michael had told her the wrong hotel, or the wrong day, or simply that Tom had changed his mind and arranged to stay somewhere else. The busboy asked her if she wanted more sandwiches, more tea. She shook her head no, just bring me the check.

Well, that serves you, my girl, she heard her mother say. *Nothing good ever comes from bad intention.* Only, was it bad intention? What if Michael was right, what if he still thinks well of me, despite everything?

The doorman touched his cap as she walked out. *What money and a few graces will do*, she thought. *Was a time I would have walked past here and not even dared look through the windows.* She smiled at the memory and, lost in her own thoughts, walked straight into Tom Doyle.

He looked more confident than she remembered, and prosperous, in his camel hair coat, a pair of gray kidskin gloves in his hands. He started to apologize for bumping into her, then saw who it was. "Kitty."

"Jesus God," she said. "Where did you come from?"

A bellboy took his suitcase from the back of the cab. *Of course*, she thought, *the ship was late berthing because of the fog.*

He was staring at her openmouthed. "What are you doing here?"

"I'll be honest, I don't know. I just wanted to see you. I didn't mean for you to see me."

"Michael sent me a telegram. He said he'd seen you. He said you ran off. You've been making a habit of that."

"I wasn't sure you'd want to see me again."

"Because of London?"

"Of course, because of bloody London. I don't know how you can bear to look at me, never mind talk to me."

"After your little speech there in the street, you never gave me a chance to tell you how I felt."

"I didn't need to. It was all over your face."

"Can we not stand out here talking about this? We don't want to give everyone a free show. How about we go inside and have a drink?"

"This is New York, there's only tea."

"God, the bloody Volstead Act. I forgot. They're barbarians, these people. We can't talk about this over tea."

"There's coffee."

"American coffee is even worse than their tea. Come on, let's walk."

"What about your luggage?"

"They'll take care of it, that's why I'm paying this hotel so bloody much. Come on, Kit."

He took her by the arm, and they crossed the road to Central Park, dashing between the horse-drawn cabs. The fog had started to clear, the sun burning it away to leave a washed blue sky.

———✦———

"I looked for you, do you know that? I went back to the boarding house, but they said you'd left and they didn't know where you'd gone. The next thing I know Michael sends me a copy of an article he's seen in *New Republic*, about the war in Dublin, and it has your byline on it. A double page, right in the middle of the magazine."

"You read that?"

"Didn't everyone? I still remember that thing you said: 'Every good British citizen likes his wars to be fought at a distance and, if possible, in the name of God.' I still quote it to friends."

"That article got me into a lot of trouble when it came out."

"I suppose it did. But it was a good piece of writing. Your Mr. Randolph would have been proud of you." He took off his homburg, pushed that comma of hair out of his eyes. "Is that why you left London, because of him?"

"It wasn't how you're thinking."

"How was it then?"

"I just didn't think you'd want to see me again, after what I told you."

"I wish you'd let me do my thinking for myself, instead of you doing it for me."

He stopped walking, turned her to face him. His eyes looked right through her. She had never seen him angry before, but he was angry now. She didn't blame him.

"You must hate me, Tom."

"I don't hate you. But I'm wary of you. You have too many damned secrets, always have, ever since the Liberties. It wasn't anything to be ashamed of, back then. It was your father, not you."

"There's things to be ashamed of since, though, isn't there? I've made a real mess of things."

He took her hands. "You're freezing."

"Cold hands, warm heart, my mother used to say." Now why had she blurted that out?

He stared at her hands, looking for a ring, she supposed. She pulled free. "Should have worn gloves. Come on, let's walk."

As they walked, he told her what he had been doing the last eighteen months; he was a resident at Saint Thomas' now, hoped to earn a fellowship within a year or two, if he passed the final examinations. He was still living in South Kensington.

"And how's that little housemaid of yours?"

"She had to go back to France. I have a lady that calls on me now five days a week; it's much cheaper, and it's stopped the neighbors talking."

"Don't tell me you're still rattling around in that big old house on your own," she said, and prayed that he was.

"Yes, I am. And what about you, Kitty? You look prosperous. I dare say even a great writer like yourself can't afford to live in this kind of style." His fingers brushed the cashmere scarf at her neck.

"I don't write anymore," she said. She wondered how much she should tell him.

He waited.

"Sure and I've made a mess of things. One starfish at a time you said once. Well I'll tell you, this starfish is so far up the beach, I can't even see the sea anymore."

"I could throw you back if you wanted. Is that what you want, Kit?"

"Tom, what would you want with a girl like me? You need someone you can take to cocktail parties with all the other fancy doctors and not have someone saying, 'Oh wasn't she the famous Communist? Wasn't she the one who the British were going to shoot for subversion in Dublin?' You need someone who can give you babies."

"Is that what I want? Thanks for telling me."

"You know what I mean."

"No, I actually don't. Truth is, I don't give a damn what other people think and I don't go to many fancy parties seeing as how I'm a socialist myself and I didn't go to the right schools and they don't much like my Irish accent either. And as for children, there's enough orphans made in the world these last few years, I could just as well adopt them if I couldn't have them. It's not the end of the world, if you love someone."

"How can you still love me, Tom?"

"Well, that's what I was wondering. I will if you give me the chance but I don't know if that's what you're asking me to do. I'll not let you leave me standing in Piccadilly with a stupid look on my face again."

"I don't want to hurt you again like that."

"Well that's entirely up to you now, isn't it? I just want you to be honest with me. You won't shock me, Kitty. I know what you are and what you're not."

"Do you, Tom? Do you really?"

He pulled her down onto a bench. He took her hands in his. "I know there's a man here in New York. Well it stands to reason, doesn't it? I'm looking at your expensive hair and your expensive coat and I'm thinking, is that why she's here? Is that what she wanted all along?"

"You know it isn't. But he saved my life."

"Then you owe him something."

"No, I don't. He bought me and he'll throw me away again when he's done, when he sees some new shiny toy he likes better. I won't be breaking his heart if I leave him." She thought she could smell the sea at Sandymount. "Why me? You must have women falling over themselves."

"They don't know me like you do."

"You should give them a chance."

"Well maybe I will. But I wanted to see you first before I make up my mind to go looking for another woman."

"And now you've seen me?"

"And now I've seen you, and told you that I love you, and that it's you I want, well then I guess it's your time to decide, Kitty O'Kane. I know the worst of you—I've always known it, I suppose—and I know the best. I want you to marry me. Come back to London and be my wife, thick and thin."

She stared at him, numb.

"Now I'll not expect an answer now, right here. You can think about it. This afternoon Michael and I are taking the train to Boston for our uncle's birthday. I get back here on the twenty-second to catch the *Majestic* back to London. I'll be staying here at the Plaza the night before I sail. If you want to come back to London with me, then be here, and we'll get you a ticket. You can be Mrs. Doyle for your sins so the other passengers don't gossip. If you're not here, then I'll know that Kitty O'Kane was never for me after all and that will be that, I suppose."

She thought about the banshee at the bottom of the street, reading the cards. She had been right; she had seen all that death, but in the end, it had not been hers. Finally, the future was up to her, she had the power to choose.

"I'd better go," Kitty said.

"I'll walk you back," he said.

They stopped outside the station, and he kissed her on the lips. People were staring, even in New York you couldn't do that on the street.

"People are watching us, Tom."

"They're not watching us, Kitty, they're getting on with their own lives, as we should. Remember what I said to you."

"I will."

"Good-bye, Kitty. If I never see you again, remember I will always love you."

She turned away and walked into the station. She could feel him watching her, but she didn't look back.

The El rattled back to the Bronx, up Sixth and over the Harlem River between the bridges at Third and Willis. She had already made up her mind; she didn't need time to think about what Tom had said. She knew now what she wanted, what she had always wanted.

But she couldn't tell him because she didn't want to disappoint him again. Despite what she'd told Tom, getting away from Flash Jack Finnegan would not be easy, and she didn't want Tom to get involved in it, didn't want him to get hurt. If she ended up at the bottom of the East River, then let him think she just didn't love him, and then he could get on with his life.

But if her luck held, if she could be the unkillable Kitty O'Kane just one more time, then in ten days she would get on the *Majestic* as the future Mrs. Thomas Doyle.

CHAPTER 47

Jack was sitting at the breakfast table when she came down. Their maid had made him scrambled eggs and coffee, and he was finishing off the meal with a cigar. He was still in his silk dressing gown, and reading the *New York Times*. Kitty sat down. The maid asked her if she wanted breakfast but she said, "Just coffee, please."

"You have to eat in the mornings," Jack said. "Just drinking coffee is no good for you."

"But staying out till three in the morning and sleeping with show-girls is better for the complexion, is it Jack?"

"Don't ride me. I got you out of the gutter; I can throw you back anytime I like."

He threw the newspaper away. She looked down at the date on the front page. It was the twenty-first. Tom would be sailing for London tomorrow night.

"It's our anniversary," she said.

"What anniversary?"

"Two years since you got me out of the gutter. That should be worth a celebration."

"Are you being cute?" He drained his coffee cup.

I wonder why he still wants me around? Kitty thought. When he first brought her to New York, he had paraded around the Broadway restau-rants and speakeasies as if she was Lillian Gish, but the novelty had long faded, and he had stopped making drunken visits to her bedroom. Jack always got what he wanted, just like he said, but when he tired of it, he got rid of it just as fast, whether it was a car or a club.

She wondered which one of the girls at Finnegan's was about to take her place.

The maid brought Kitty's coffee, and she picked up the *Times*. There was a picture of the ugly Italian-looking fellow Jack had been having an argument with in the club a few months before. According to the article his name was Frankie Pax, real name Francesco Pasquale, and two nights before he had been eating at a restaurant on Fifty-Second Street when two men walked in and shot him three times, twice in the head and once in the neck.

"Congratulations," she said, and tossed the newspaper back across the table.

"For what?"

"Wasn't he the one who tried to kill you?"

He shrugged.

"It says he's a bootlegger."

"So?"

"I hear it's easier to hijack from other bootleggers than risk bringing liquor across the state line yourself. A couple of trucks and some men who are handy with guns, it can turn a nice profit. I've seen Albert Rothstein in the club a few times. Is he the one you're selling on to?"

For a moment he just stared at her. "What the hell are you talking about?"

"Am I right?"

"How do you know about this?"

"I used to be a journalist. You think I'm stupid, Jack? I know what your business is. I don't care how you make your money. What I don't like is you crossing other gangsters and getting me get caught in the crossfire afterward."

"You better watch your mouth. You don't talk about this stuff to nobody."

"Like I said Jack, it's no business of mine."

"And make sure you remember that." He stubbed out his cigar on the breakfast plate and pushed back his chair. He got as far as the door, then turned back. "You and your do-gooders, getting them to ban booze, it just made it easier for the Jack Finnegans of this world to make money."

"I didn't get them to ban alcohol."

"Temperance Union, fecking suffragettes. What's the difference? You can look down on me, Kit, but I'm just giving people what they want. I help them get their mind off their troubles."

"I know, Jack. I tell everyone, you're one of Nature's philanthropists."

He gave her a look. She smiled. It was the kind of word Lincoln would use, only Jack didn't know what it meant, and he was too proud to say so.

"You're too clever for your own good," he said.

"I wish I was."

"I mean it, Kit, if you do wrong by me, I swear I'll go to the chair for you. Cross Jack Finnegan, and it's the last thing you'll ever do."

He stormed out.

She stared at the newspaper, imagined herself on the front page in some grainy photograph, lying in a pool of her own blood, just like Frankie Pax. She had to get away from the bloody man, get on the boat before he knew what she had done.

—➤—

It rained all that day.

She sat by the window, watching the rain weep down the windows, thinking it through. If she did get away, would he come after them in London? Somehow she doubted it; when she was gone, he would tell everyone he had kicked her out. As long as he didn't lose face, he would just think good riddance and move on to the next girl.

And what to do about Thomas? She would have to tell him that she couldn't marry him straightaway. She would get herself a job in a magazine or with a newspaper first. After the piece in the *New Republic*, there were plenty of editors even in London who would put her on staff, she was sure of it.

She wanted to be courted, not kept. When she had said she couldn't be a doctor's wife, she had meant it. Tom would have to get used to the idea of an independent woman, if that was really what he wanted.

She gave their cook two dollars and asked her to take a letter for her to the Plaza Hotel, addressed to Dr. Tom Doyle. Inside was the money for her passage on the *Majestic* to Southampton and a short note: she would meet him in the foyer of the Plaza tomorrow night at seven o'clock.

The time until then would seem endless. She went over and over her plans in her head. Tomorrow night she would leave New York for good.

She heard the rumble of thunder over the city. Rainwater teemed along the streets, blocking drains, and drummed on the roof, deafening. The worst storm in years, one of the maids said. What if the *Majestic's* departure was delayed for rough seas?

She stared at the clock on the mantelpiece, willing tomorrow to come.

CHAPTER 48

Kitty sat in a leather wingback antique chair by the window, a glass of brandy in her hand, almost gone. Jesus God, she wanted another one, but she couldn't afford to drink too much. She would need her wits about her tonight.

There was a radio broadcast from Carnegie Hall. She listened to it with half an ear while she flicked listlessly through the pages of a fashion magazine. The kitchen staff were a long time going home; she could still hear them banging around in the kitchen. She looked out of the window. Manny was still in the car, parked by the sidewalk at the front stoop. She could see the glow of his cigarette.

She went into the kitchen. Betty was still standing at the sink. "Leave those, Betty."

"I haven't finished tidying up, ma'am."

"Go home and see your family."

"Mr. Finnegan gets awful mad if we leave a mess."

"I'll deal with Mr. Finnegan. Now go on home."

"If you think. Thank you, ma'am."

Betty wiped her hands on her apron and untied the strings at the back, hung it up on the larder cupboard door. As soon as she had left, Kitty ran up the stairs and started throwing things in a carpetbag. She had decided days ago what she would take, had it hanging at one end of the closet ready. It wouldn't be much, only as much as she could carry through the back streets of the Bronx on a rainy night.

She found the cash that Jack kept in a drawer in his desk, and folded that into her purse. Her hands were shaking. She went through all the drawers, looking for the passport he had taken from her the day they left Dublin. She found it and tossed that in her bag. The last thing was the jewelry box. It had been everywhere with her; she wasn't leaving that behind.

She headed for the landing. She had her escape planned. She would go out by the back door, like she had the day she met Tom at the Plaza, but this time she would find a cab by the El; half an hour to get downtown, she should be there just as he was leaving for the ship.

She took one last look over her shoulder to be certain she hadn't forgotten anything.

She heard the door slam downstairs. Now what in God's name was that?

She looked at the clock. It was not yet eight o'clock; it couldn't be Jack, he never got home from the club until after two in the morning. She hid her carpetbag under the bed, hung up her coat, and walked out onto the landing, tried to look casual, as if she was just about to run a bath.

He was coming up the stairs red in the face. *Oh God, no.* He was in a temper, worse than that, he looked murderous.

What had gone wrong?

"Jack, what are you doing here?"

He didn't speak. He went for her. She tried to dodge out of the way, but his fist caught her on the cheekbone and sent her crashing back through the bedroom door.

She lay on her back on the floor, stunned. He stood over her, his fists clenched.

"You fucking lied to me." He kicked her with his boot. "You fucking lied!"

The shock of the blow stunned her. For a moment she couldn't move her arms or her legs. She crawled away, back into the bedroom, felt the cold, hard slate of the hearth under her cheek.

It'd been a good hard punch, and she hadn't seen it coming. Already she couldn't see a thing out of her left eye. No point arguing with him when he was filthy drunk like this. She saw his lips moving, his face red and twisted like it got sometimes. She could smell him, smell the drink, a sour smell, and bitter like hate.

"So, I'm sitting there at the club, and this guy says to me, 'I was headed to the Plaza and I saw your girlfriend I did. She was standing outside the El, and then she got on her tiptoes, right there in the street, and kissed him, like.'"

She tried to wriggle into the corner. Couldn't move her arms much, but her legs worked well enough, and she reckoned if she could get into the corner, she'd make a smaller target for him.

She could hear things again now, the horn from an ocean steamer leaving the docks. Wouldn't she love to be away on that one right now.

Jack threw off his jacket and unbuttoned his cuffs. "I warned you what would happen, Kit. I warned you. So now you're going to get what's coming to you, and you're going to get it hard, and you're going to get it slow. No woman makes a fool out of Jack Finnegan."

She started crawling again, inched herself further into the corner, curled up like a bug tossed in a fire. Pretend it's not happening, pretend you're on that ship, the sea wind is in your hair, salt and cold, and you're headed out to the white waves and only the gulls are screaming.

She watched him over her shoulder, rolling up his sleeves. No belt for Jack Finnegan. He was going to use his boots and his fists, no mistake.

She forced herself up onto her knees in front of the fireplace. She saw him coming for her, his eyes out of focus; he was mad, stark fucking mad.

And then he was reeling back, clutching at his face where the poker had hit him and there were worms of blood leaking through his fingers and he screamed like a girl, like a little girl getting hit with a belt in the Liberties. Just like that.

"And I warned you, Jack Finnegan," she said. "I told you. No man is ever going to hit me again."

And she raised the poker a second time and brought it down on top of his skull and his knees gave way and he crumpled to the floor, arms and legs at odd angles. A pool of blood leaked out of his head onto the Turkish rug, his favorite, fecking Turkish rug.

Kitty dropped the poker, reached under the bed for her bag and her purse, and was down the stairs and out of the back door in an instant. She stopped only to grab her coat.

Had she killed him? She didn't know, and if she was honest, she didn't much care.

CHAPTER 49

Yellow-and-black Checker cabs were pulled up two or three deep in the forecourt of the Plaza Hotel. Kitty dashed past them and ran to the front desk. The clerk looked up in alarm as a pertly dressed woman in a fox fur coat headed straight toward him. She was clutching a carpetbag, her Marcel wave was ruined from the rain, her left eye nearly swollen shut. There was a mad look about her.

The junior clerks backed away and let him deal with her.

"Mr. Doyle, please."

"I'm afraid he's left for the dock, miss. About half an hour ago."

Kitty leaned against the desk. All the fight went out of her. "He can't have done."

"Are you Miss O'Kane?"

She nodded.

"He left you this." He reached into a pigeonhole under the desk and handed her an envelope with neat copperplate writing on the front. She tore it open.

> *Dearest Kitty,*
> *It seems that you changed your mind after all. I imagine*
> *you have your reasons, though I cannot begin to fathom*
> *them. You have always been in my heart and you always*
> *will be. I will keep our Dublin days with me forever.*

I'll never be near the sea and not hear the waves at Sandymount.
Tom

The ticket he had bought her for the *Majestic* was inside. It fell out and dropped onto the polished marble floor.

⊰⊱

Jack Finnegan staggered into his study, went through the drawers in his desk. The passport and the money were gone, as he knew they would be. He swayed on his feet, blood leaking down his face and dripping off his chin onto the mahogany. He fumbled in the bottom drawer, found the revolver he kept there, snapped it open, and made sure there were enough bullets in the chamber.

Six. One for her lover, five for her.

He snapped the chamber shut.

If she had her passport, then it must mean the docks. She thought she could get away from him that way, but she was wrong.

"Bitch," he murmured.

Manny was waiting in the Marmon outside. As Jack staggered down the stoop, Manny saw him and started to get out of the car to help him, but Jack shouted at him to get back in the car. "Just drive," he said. "Get me down to the docks fast as you fecking can."

Manny sped through the rain-dark streets; Jack sprawled in the back seat, the gun held loosely in his right hand, pointed at the floor. He touched his fingers gingerly to his head; they came away sticky with blood. He couldn't see out of one eye; blood kept leaking into it.

Well that didn't bother him. He didn't need two eyes to put a bullet through that bitch's heart.

⊰⊱

It was the pier where the *Carpathia* had docked after picking her and her fellow survivors out of the sea after the *Titanic* went down. The waterfront had been crowded with horse-drawn cabs that day; now, just eleven years later, there wasn't a single horse outside the customs sheds, just rank upon rank of shiny black automobiles and Checker cabs.

Kitty pressed her way through the crowds, looking for Tom. She saw him just at the gates, he had his suitcases loaded on a trolley, a porter trailing behind him.

"Tom!" she shouted.

He turned and saw her, and a look of relief and joy came to his face. He shouted her name and pushed his way back through the crowds toward her.

When he saw the bruises on her face, his joy changed to shock and concern. "Kitty, what happened?"

"You should see the other fella."

"Who did this?"

"Don't worry, Tom." She threw her arms around his neck. "Don't worry, it's over."

She held tightly on to him. Over his shoulder she could see a black Marmon furiously beeping its horn, trying to get through the traffic—someone was in an awful hurry to get through. *Jesus God, it must be Jack.*

⸺⸺

Two men sat in the front seat of a black Packard on the other side of Brook Avenue. They had been there all night, waiting. When Jack Finnegan had come back so early, storming back into the house like that, it had taken them by surprise. But by the time he came out again, they had already decided how they would improvise on their original plan.

When Finnegan reemerged half an hour later and jumped into the Marmon, they slipped into the traffic behind it. When Manny made the turn onto Third Avenue, they followed. At the first opportunity, they accelerated to pull alongside, and one of them reached under his seat; there was a Thompson submachine gun wrapped in newspaper, lying there ready. He wound down the window.

The first volley of gunfire punched holes in the Marmon's coachwork. Manny slumped over the wheel, and the car skewed off the road into some railings. The Thompson gunner got out and fired another salvo into the car. "Joey Pax says hello," he said and then jumped back into the Packard as it drove away.

She tried to pull Tom away, but he wouldn't go, kept looking back where she was looking. They were trapped by the crowd anyway.

Kitty saw the black Marmon force itself to the curb.

"Kitty," he said. "What is it?"

"It's Jack," she said.

"What?"

The driver's side door flew open. A chauffeur in a neatly pressed black uniform hurried to help a woman in a chiffon gown out of the back seat. "We're still in good time, ma'am," he said to her. "I'll fetch a porter, and you'll be on the boat and in your cabin in no time."

The woman got out, holding a Pekingese in her arms. Kitty smiled. Some rich man's woman, clutching a lapdog. The world had turned a full circle.

"What's wrong?" Tom said.

"Nothing," Kitty said. "Everything's just fine."

CHAPTER 50

The RMS Majestic

Tom and Kitty sat together in the second-class lounge, all potted plants and oak paneling. Kitty had ordered a pot of tea. Tom laughed and shook his head when she offered him a cup, said he would wait until the sun was over the yardarm and have a proper drink. "I didn't get to sit down on the *Titanic* and have people bring me cups of tea, so to me it's a luxury."

"Luxury or not, drinking tea is an English affectation, Kitty, and I'll have nothing to do with it."

"Well my first stop when we get to London is Lyons teahouse in the Strand. I have one friend at least who won't stick her nose up."

"Elsie."

"I've drunk French champagne in a speakeasy and water out of a horse trough in Poland, and the thing that matters is not what I'm drinking but who I'm drinking with."

Tom laughed. "I'll not drink out of a horse trough, Kitty. Not even if I'm with you."

There was a couple playing dominoes at the next table. The woman had turned suddenly quite pale, and the man put his arm around her.

"Is the lady feeling all right?" Tom said.

The man smiled. "She's feeling a little faint. She was already nervous about sailing—this is her first time—and she heard you mention the *Titanic*."

"Oh, but there's nothing to worry about. You're sharing the boat with the unkillable Kitty O'Kane. Nothing bad can ever happen while she's on board. She has a charmed life. Don't you, Kitty?"

Kitty sipped her tea and smiled. "I do indeed," she said.

AFTERWORD

Anyone familiar with the lives of John Reed and Louise Bryant will see similarities between the adventures of those two intrepid journalists and those of Lincoln Randolph and Kitty O'Kane, particularly between 1915 and 1917. I drew on their writings for historical detail, particularly in the events of the Russian Revolution as described in Louise Bryant's *Six Red Months in Russia* and John Reed's *The War in Eastern Europe* and his seminal work, *Ten Days That Shook the World*. However, my two fictional characters in this book are not intended to represent their characters or relationship in any way.

The cameo appearance of Charlotte Reddings is based on another pioneering female writer and feminist, Charlotte Perkins Gilman. She, however, never sailed on the *Lusitania*; she died in California in 1935.

I have tried to faithfully portray the events around the October Revolution in Petrograd. The incident in which Trotsky is not allowed into Bolshevik headquarters because he has forgotten his identity papers is true, as attested by John Reed.

The idea of a woman surviving two shipwrecks comes from the life of Violet Jessop, who survived the sinking of both the *Titanic* and the *Britannia* and was on board the *Olympic* when it collided with the British warship *HMS Hawke*. She was known as "Miss Unsinkable." There, however, the resemblance ends. Violet worked her whole life on cruise ships and died of natural causes at the age of eighty-three.

I did consult her book *Titanic Survivor* for details on the working life of a *Titanic* stewardess and her memories of the shipwreck. However, the events of that night have been compressed, for the sake of the narrative. I referred to *A City in Civil War* by Padraig Yates and *The News from Ireland* by Maurice Walsh for certain details about the Irish Civil War and *Dublin Tenement Life* by Kevin Kearns for background on life growing up in the Dublin slums. On a personal note, my mother and grandmother were both Cockneys and grew up in the poorer parts of East London; their stories were poignantly similar to those described in Kearns's book, and some of their anecdotes found their way into this novel as well. Geography changes, but the lives of the poor don't, not that much.

The attack on the Beggars Bush barracks is fictional. The account of the assault on the Four Courts, as all Dubliners will know, is not.

As for the small section on Southend-on-Sea, I confess I grew up there. I can testify that the walk to the very end of the pier is a long one and that kids still venture a long way out to go fossicking in the mud underneath it. There was still a fortune-teller plying her trade out there, the last time I went, though not the same one, of course. I ventured into the tent when I was nineteen, and she told me I'd write a book one day.

She was wrong, of course; I've written dozens of them. Never trust a fortune-teller.

ACKNOWLEDGMENTS

My thanks to Danielle Marshall and all at Lake Union for helping bring the unkillable Kitty to life. My especial thanks to my amazing editor Jodi Warshaw, who hatched the idea with me on the phone and then nurtured it all along the way. I am indebted, Jodi. And a million thanks, too, to David Downing, who did such a wonderful job on the manuscript, looking for the angel in the stone, and doing it with such self-deprecating humor. It was such a huge pleasure working with you. And finally, to Lise, who did so much to make the first draft presentable enough to leave the house. No one will ever know how much work you did, but I will. Thanks, sweetheart.

If you enjoyed this book, I share the plaudits with them because it was so much better for their efforts; if you didn't, then the blame is all mine.

Feel free to find me at www.colinfalconer.org or connect with me on The Falconer Club Facebook group.

ABOUT THE AUTHOR

Photo © 2017 by Lisa Davies

Colin Falconer is an internationally bestselling author. Born in London, he was a freelance journalist and advertising copywriter for many years. His passion for writing novels led him to publish his first book, *Venom*, based on his own experiences in Southeast Asia.

He has published more than fifty books that have been translated into twenty-three languages. He travels widely for research, which has led to his chasing tornadoes in Texas, diving with sharks in South Africa, and running with the bulls in Spain.